THE GIANT BOOK OF
Celtic Myths and Legends

and

Tales of Old Ireland

PARRAGON

This edition published and distributed by Parragon, 1998

Parragon
Unit 13–17, Avonbridge Trading Estate
Atlantic Road, Avonmouth
Bristol BS11 9QD

Produced by Magpie Books,
an imprint of Robinson Publishing Ltd, London

ISBN 0-75252-402-X

A copy of the British Library Cataloguing-in-Publication Data
is available from the British Library.

Printed and bound by Firmin-Didot (France),
Group Herissey. N° d'impression : 40941.

CONTENTS

CONTENTS

INTRODUCTION

The two books featured in this volume – *Celtic Myths and Legends* and *Tales of Old Ireland* – gather together traditional tales from the Celtic lands of Scotland, Wales and Ireland and then concentrate solely on the Irish tradition of storytelling, evoking an Ireland that has all but vanished: Ireland before the industrialisation of this modern age when it was a country of rebellious peasants, tormented priests, eccentric country gentry and over-bearing English landlords.

The Celtic strongholds of Scotland, Wales and Ireland are rich in ancient customs; from these lands come tales of gods and giants, feasting and wooing, hunting and hurling, lust for battle, blood, bravery and deaths with honour. These stories were faithfully recited yet enriched with detail with each telling around the peat fires in great halls and village hovels, and have thus survived virtually unchanged down through the centuries.

The stories in this collection examine the very origins of the Celtic people and then tell the tales of their fabled beasts and magic folk – the fate of the Children of Turenn (Irish), the love between Pwyll and Rhiannon (Welsh), the legend of the Brown Bear of the Green Glen (Scottish), and many, many more.

The companion volume to *Celtic Myths and Legends, Tales of Old Ireland*, is a collection of famous names and great works, including James Joyce's *The Dead*, W. B. Yeats's *The*

INTRODUCTION

Twisting of the Rope, Somerville and Ross's *The Holy Island*, plus 15 other short stories which celebrate the spirit of nineteenth-century Ireland. This unique anthology must be read by anyone interested in the great tradition of Irish literature, evoking as it does a portrait of Ireland past with all the associated beauties and horrors that formed the daily lives of its people, from sophisticated townie to bog-dwelling peasant.

When read together, these two books will give a greater understanding of the genesis of Celtic tradition and how the recurring themes in these ancient tales survived and became incorporated into some of nineteenth-century Ireland's most famous and evocative writing.

CELTIC MYTHS AND LEGENDS

Michael Foss

CONTENTS

1

WHO
ARE WE?

A blessing westward from me to Ireland,
Westward to the melodious waterfalls.
She is the mother who nursed us,
She is not uncomely to look on.
A blessing from me to Ireland,
An ancient land is this Land of Promise.

WHO
ARE WE?

The first name given to the land was Island of the Woods, and this name was given by a warrior of the people of Nin, son of Bel. Three times indeed was the island all one woodland, as the poet says: 'Three times Eire put coverings on her, and three times bareness off her.'

The second name was Land at the Limit of the World, and the third name was Noble Island. In the time of the Firbolg it had this name on it.

The fourth name was Eire, and this is from the name of a queen of the Tuatha De Danann who was in the land at the coming of the people of Mile into it. And the fifth and the sixth names were also from queens of the Tuatha De Danann, that is to say Fodhla and Banbha.

The next name was Inis Fail, the Island of Stone, which is the stone of destiny that the Tuatha De Danann brought with them. It is a tabu-stone, for it used to roar under the person fit to be king when the assembly of the men of the island met at Tara. But it has not roared from the time of Conchobor forward, for the false idols of the world were silenced when Christ was born.

The next name was Isle of Mists, and the next was Scotia, and then Hibernia, and after that Irlanda. This means the Land of Ir, who was the son of Mile, and he was the first man of that clan to be buried on the island.

It is said that the Greeks called the land Ogygia, which is to say 'the most ancient land', and this is suitable, for it is a long, long time since it was first inhabited.

> Green and flourishing is the grass of the island,
> Thick are her nut-sweet woods,
> Plentiful the fruit upon the smooth hills.
> To depart from her is a cause of misery,
> To leave her is ground for weakness.
> Sweet is the sound of her gentle wind –
> Green Banbha enclosed by woods –
> And sweet is the voice of her rivers.
> The speech of her birds is sleep-music enough,
> In that land abounding in salmon:
> Hail to the land of bright fountains!

It is the three daughters of the wicked Cain who inhabited Ireland at first:

> Three virgin daughters of Cain,
> With Seth, son of Adam,
> They first saw Banbha.
> I remember their adventure.

Then three times fifty women came there, and three men. Forty years they were in the island, till a plague fell on them and they all died in a week. After that, Ireland was empty desert for two hundred years until the Flood came.

But others say that it is Ceasair, daughter of Bioth, son of Noah, who came to Ireland before the Flood. Noah would not give a place on his ark to Bioth, Ceasair and Fintan. So they consulted one with the other.

'Will you follow my advice?' says Ceasair.

'We shall do that.'

'Well then,' says she, 'take to you an idol, and adore him, and forsake the god of Noah.'

So they got them an idol, and the idol told them to make a ship and put to sea – for the Flood surely would come, though none knew when. They made ready a ship and went to sea, and seven and a quarter were the years for them on the sea till they landed at Dunnamark, in the district of Corkaguiney, on the fifteenth day of the moon. And that was forty days before the Flood began.

Then about one hundred and forty years after the Flood, there came a youth of the family of Nin, son of Bel, to spy out the island. But the stay he made in it was not long. He went in the woods and returned to his people with plucked grass held in the full of his fist. But he made no stay in the island, which was not occupied till three hundred years after the Flood.

At the end of this time Partholon, son of Seara, son of Sru, of the family of Magog and of Japheth, came to occupy Ireland. And this was twenty-two years before Abraham was born, when the age of the world was one thousand, nine hundred and seventy-eight years.

On the fourteenth day of May, Partholon landed at Kenmare in the western part. And he had with him his wife and their three sons, and the wives of those sons, and a host of a thousand along with them. When they had gone through the island they settled on a little bit of land in the middle of the Erne, which was named Saimher after a lapdog or whelp that Partholon killed out of jealousy of his wife. She did misconduct with her own attendant, Todhga, and made no apology for it but blamed the ill deed on Partholon and not on herself.

'O Partholon,' says she, 'is it possible for a woman to be

near honey, or a child next to new milk, or a cat smell fresh meat, or a workman see sharp tools, or a man and woman be close in private, without meddling the one with the other?'

In anger Partholon struck the little hound and killed it, as the old poet says:

> The king strikes the hound of the woman
> With his hand – is it not sad that it was so?
> The hound was dead.
> That was the first jealousy of Ireland.

But the cause that sent Partholon fleeing into Ireland was the slaying of his own father and mother, and for this reason God sent a plague on his race, even into Ireland. It did not go well for him and his people, for at last his followers were dead, nine thousand of them in one week at Ben Edar, afterwards called Howth.

After the destruction of the people of Partholon, Ireland was waste thirty years till Nemed, son of Agnoman, of the progeny of Magog, came to settle in the land. For every invasion of Ireland after the Flood was by some of the descendants of Magog. In the time of Sru, Partholon and the children of Nemed separated from each other, though well-related. And in the time of Seara, the Firbolg, the Tuatha De Danann and the children of Mile separated. But every tribe of these had the Gaelic tongue in their mouths, talking the one with the other.

Nemed journeyed from Scythia, between Europe and Asia. He gave his right hand to the mountains of Ural, till he came to the ocean of the north. Then he gave his left hand towards · Europe, till he came to Ireland with thirty-four ships, and thirty persons in every ship of them.

Now, at this time sailors of the race of Cham, named the Fomorians, fared from Africa, fleeing to the islands of the west to make a settlement for themselves. Nemed won three battles over them and repulsed them. Then Nemed died of sickness, and the Fomorians revenged themselves with great oppression and slavery on his people. Conaing, for whom is named the Tower of Conaing, had many ships at

Tory Island in the north. He forced great tribute on the children of Nemed, to the extent that two-thirds of the children, and of the corn, and of the milch-cows of the men of Ireland were taken by the Fomorians every year in November, on the eve of the feast of Samhain.

Then the Fomorians put still more tyranny on the people of Nemed, that is to say they demanded of every household three full measures of the cream of the milk, of the flour of the wheat, and of butter, to be brought to Conaing's Tower on Tory Island. Liagh, the female steward of the Fomorians, enforced this tax throughout the land.

Rage seized on the men of Ireland, by reason of the heaviness of this tribute. Three good warriors among them, children of Nemed, raised an army and took Conaing's Tower, and they killed Conaing. But Morc, the Fomorian, brought ships from Africa to Tory Island and struck at the children of Nemed so that they resolved to fare away from Ireland, to escape the tyranny of the Fomorians. Most fled and left the rest in servitude to the Fomorians until the coming of the Firbolg, which was two hundred and seventeen years after Nemed arrived into Ireland.

After a long time, when the fleeing children of Nemed had withdrawn into Greece, the Greeks also put bondage upon them, forcing them to raise earth in sacks of leather, to place on the stony crags so that they might become fruitful soil. In this weary labour great sadness seized upon the people, and they resolved to make boats of their leather sacks and return into the west isles. So the people descended from Simeon Breac, son of Starn, of the family of Nemed, sailed back to Ireland after two hundred and seventeen years.

Towards noble Ireland set out the five sons of Dela – Slainge of the spears, Rudraige, Gann, Genann and Sengann. They made off at daybreak and Slainge, the elder, who was judge among his brothers, spoke as follows:

'Now is the time for effort, care and watchfulness.
Fierce and grey with foam is the sea.

Each fair ship sets forth from unendurable wrong.
The tyranny of the Greek is unaccustomed.
Let us strive to win the plains of salmon-bearing Ireland.'

Onward they sailed before a southwest wind, until they saw Ireland in the distance. Then the wind rose high and strong, and the waves drove against the walls of the ships, and the fleet was torn into three parts: the Firbolg, the Fir Domnann, and the Gaileon. The men of the Firbolg were named for the leather sacks they had used to carry the earth of Greece. The men of the Fir Domnann were named for the pits that were left when the earth was dug out. And the men of the Gaileon were named indeed for the darts or spears that were their weapons.

But all in one week they came into Ireland, and it is one conquest that they made, beginning on Saturday, the first day of August. When all the parties were landed, anxiously each sent out messengers, to gather all together at one place, at the stronghold of the kings at Tara. They all assembled and said to each other, 'We give thanks to the gods for our return to you, O Ireland. Let the country be divided equally between us.'

Thus it was that five portions were made, one for each of the sons of Dela, though all the people in all the parts were commonly called Firbolg, which is to say 'men of the leather sacks'. Thirty-six years was the length of the dominion of the Firbolg over Ireland. Their leader had the title of high-king, and none had that title before the Firbolg.

Now, there was another band of men descended from Iobath, third chief of the people of Nemed, who had departed from Ireland after the fall of Conaing's Tower. And these people were called the Tuatha De Danann. Some say they settled in Greek territory, around the city of Athens. There they learned their magic and their arts till they became skilled in every trick of sorcery.

On a certain time, the army of Syria made war on the

8

Athenians, and each day, however many Athenians were slain, it was those same slain soldiers who would rise up on the morrow and fight again. And this necromancy was done through the art and the magic of the Tuatha De Danann, who put demons into the Athenian bodies to restore them. So the Syrians took counsel with their own priests, who set a watch on the battlefield, and at the end of the fighting towards nightfall they thrust stakes of ash-wood through the bodies of all the dead enemies. On the morn, when the battle renewed, the dead bodies did not rise up but the demons fled out of them in the form of worms. Then the Syrians fell on the rest of the Athenians and slaughtered them.

As for the Tuatha De Danann, they departed in fear out of that land, and they did not stop until they came to the country of Lochlann, which is to say Norway. They got them four cities – Failias, Gorias, Findias and Murias – and placed four sages in those cities to teach the youth magic and arts. And their chief at this time was Nuada, son of Echtach.

After some time in those cities the Tuatha De Danann went to the north of Scotland, where they remained seven years. They had four noble treasures, which they brought from Norway. The first was the stone of destiny from Failias, the stone that used to roar under each king of Ireland at Tara. The second treasure was the sword that Lugh of the Long Hand used, and it was brought from Gorias. The third was the spear of that same Lugh, and from Findias it was brought. And the fourth was the cauldron of the great god Dagda, which none left unsatisfied, and from Murias it came.

Seven years the Tuatha De Danann spent in Scotland, then they came to Ireland. They landed in the country of Ulster on Monday in the first weeks of May, on the eve of the spring festival of Bealtaine. They burnt their boats, and the chance of retreat went away with the smoke and vapour of the burning ships. Then they put a magic mist about them for the space of three days, so the Firbolg who were in the land would not see them till they came to the Iron Mountain in Leitrim. Then they sent an embassy to the chiefs of the

Firbolg saying, 'Give up the kingdom of Ireland, or do battle for it.'

So they fought, one with another, at the two battles of Moytura, the first in Mayo and the second in Sligo. The Firbolg were overwhelmed and a hundred thousand of them slain.

As to the Tuatha De Danann, they are called 'the tribe of the gods who are the children of Danann', though some explain it otherwise. Certainly, they ruled over Ireland after the defeat of the Firbolg for one hundred and ninety-seven years, till the coming of the sons of Mile, who were of the family of Gaedhal and thus also of the progeny of Magog.

So all the invaders of Ireland were related one to another, and though they were enemies fighting for the land they all spoke the Gaelic tongue. And what was true to each was common to all, and so the great things of the people continued from the beginning to the end of time in Ireland.

THE PEOPLE OF
THE GODS ARRIVE

Eochaid, High-king of Ireland, saw a vision in a dream. He thought on it with wonder and perplexity.

'I saw a flock of black birds,' he told his wizard Cesard, 'coming out of the ocean. They swarmed all over us, and fought the people of Ireland. They confused us and destroyed us. But one of us struck the noblest of the birds and cut off a wing. Tell me, O skilful Cesard, what is the meaning of this vision?'

'Bad tidings for you,' answered the wizard. 'Warriors come from the sea, a thousand heroes covering the ocean. The speckled ships will swoop upon us. All kinds of death they announce, a people skilled in magic arts. Evil spirits will deceive you and hurt you, and they shall have victory over you.'

From their landing place in the north, at wide Tracht

11

Mugha in Ulster, the Tuatha De Danann marched through Ireland to the Red Hills of Rain, in the east of Connacht, and camped there. Their hearts were content at last, for they had reached the land of their forefathers.

When the Firbolg of Ireland heard of this arrival and went to find the invaders, they spied on the camp and saw the most handsome of mankind, well and fiercely armed, skilful in music and playing, the most gifted that ever came across the sea. Then the Firbolg were afraid, for the Tuatha De Danann – the tribe of gods of the family of Danann – excelled all the other peoples of the world in every art.

'It will be an advantage to have some report of those lads,' said the Firbolg. 'Who are they, and what are they up to? Where do they mean to settle? Let Sreng visit them, for he is bold to ask questions. He is big and fierce and uncouth and terrifying to behold.'

So Sreng rose up and went. He took his red-brown shield and two thick spears, his deadly sword and four-cornered helmet and iron club, and he went on his way to the Hill of Rain. And when the Tuatha De Danann saw such a huge fearsome man approaching, they sent large Bres, son of Elatha, to speak with him. The two men drew near, looking keenly but saying no word. Each was astonished by the grim size and the weapons of the other. So they crouched behind their shields and at last gave cautious greetings, for the same language, the sweet Gaelic, was in each man's mouth.

After they had talked, Sreng said: 'When you speak of your ancestor Nemed, your cheerful words gladden my flesh and my tongue. Your people and mine are brothers, both descendants from Simeon Breac. So bear this in mind. Humble your pride, let our hearts draw together. Remember our brotherhood, and save your own men from destruction. If we clash, many will be crushed most cruelly. 'Tis not an entertainment that will amuse.'

'Remove your shield and reveal yourself,' replied Bres, 'so I can tell the Tuatha De Danann about the look of you.'

'I'll do that,' said Sreng, and he raised his shield.

'Those weapons have a strange and venomous look,' said Bres.

'What do you see?' asked Sreng.

'Huge weapons, broad-pointed, heavy, keen-edged. Woe to him they should strike. Death is in their mighty blows, wounds in their hard plying, overwhelming is the horror of them. What do you call them?'

'Battle javelins are these,' replied Sreng.

'Good weapons,' said Bres. 'Bruised bodies they mean, gushing gore, broken bones and shattered shields, scars and ill-health. Death and eternal blemish they deal. Those who would use them have a fratricidal fury in their heart. It is better that we make a covenant.'

So they came together and talked.

'Where were you last night?' said Bres.

'At the holy heart of Ireland, in the hill-fort of the kings at Tara, with Eochaid, the High-king of Ireland, and the chiefs of the Firbolg. And where were you?'

'On the hill, in the crowded camp yonder on the mountainside, with the Tuatha De Danann and Nuada, our king, who come from the north of the world in a cloud of mist and a magic shower.' So Bres said, but he did not believe it.

'I'll go now,' said Sreng, 'it is a long journey that awaits me.'

'This is our message,' replied Bres. 'Tell the Firbolg to give battle, or to give up half of Ireland.'

'On my word,' said Sreng, 'I had rather give up half Ireland than feel the edge of your weapons.' So they parted in peace and fellowship.

When Sreng returned to Tara, the Firbolg asked him, 'What tidings?'

'Stout are their soldiers,' he replied, 'manly their men, bloody and battle-sure. Great and strong are their shields, keenly sharp their blades. Hard it will be to fight with them. 'Tis better to give them half Ireland, as they desire.'

'No,' cried the Firbolg, 'we shall not grant that, indeed. If we do so, they will take all the land in time.'

At about the same hour Bres reached his camp and told of his meeting with Sreng.

'A big, powerful, fierce, ugly lump of a man,' he said, 'with large and wonderful weapons. He is warlike and hard, without awe or fear of any.'

So the Tuatha De Danann set out to look for some strong place. They travelled westward over plains and rivers till they came to the back-end of the Black Hill, which is called Slieve Belgadain.

"Tis a good place,' they said, 'rough and strong and impregnable. From here we shall wage our war.'

And from this summit, as the poets sang, the Tuatha De Danann laid hold of Ireland.

Then Badb and Macha and Morrigan, battle-crows and sorceresses of the Tuatha De Danann, went to the Hill of the Hostages, and the Hill of the Gathering Host, at Tara. And they sent forth magic showers of sorcery and compact clouds of mist and a furious rain of fire, with a downpour of red blood on the heads of the warriors. They gave the Firbolg neither safety nor rest for three days and nights.

So the Firbolg gathered their armies in a place of meeting. From all over Ireland the warriors came, and they numbered eleven large companies. When they were ready they marched to the Plain of Nia where the Tuatha De Danann, with seven companies, had taken their position at the western end. Once again envoys met, for the discussion of their troubles. But they could not agree.

'Then,' said the envoys, 'must it be war?'

'Hold hard now,' cried the nobles of the Firbolg. 'Some delay is called for. We must prepare, for tattered is our mail, dented our helmets, and dull the edges of our swords.' So an armistice was arranged to make all ready for battle.

Now, while they waited, Ruad, with twenty-seven of the sons of brave Mil, sped westward to the end of the plain, to offer a hurling match to the Tuatha De Danann. An equal number came out to meet them, and then there was a mighty clash of arms and legs, till flesh was bruised and bones were broken, and some stretched out a silent length on the turf, and so the match ended. They raised a cairn on the field, and buried the bodies at Glen Carne Aillem.

When the preparations were done, Eochaid, the High-king, said to his poet Fathach, 'Go to the west and ask the Tuatha De Danann how the battle is to be fought. Is it for one day, or for many?'

'What we propose,' answered Nuada and the Dagda and Bres, 'is a long steady fight between equal numbers on both sides. Let us go on till you or we are under the earth.'

This was sad news for the Firbolg, as they had the greater army. So they sent for wise Fintan and took counsel. They put a trench around a great fort. Later, this was called the Fort of the Packs, from the packs of dogs that ate the bodies of the battle-dead, or the Fort of the Blood Pools, from the red gore in which the wounded lay. Nearby, they dug a Well of Healing, sprinkled with herbs, for the cure of the wounded. And the Tuatha De Danann also made a fort, called the Fort of the Onsets, and dug their own Well of Healing.

Six weeks of summer were gone when the day of battle came. The armies rose that day at dawn, and the early sun glimmered on bare blades. In close-packed companies, swept forward by stern-voiced commands, the armies advanced across the Plain of Nia. And it was Fathach, the poet of the Firbolg, who went between them, to sing of their fury and spread the report of it. He raised up in the middle of the plain a pillar of stone, and rested against it, looking east and west. Fathach's Pillar it is called now. From there, in anguish, the poet wept melancholy tears, and cried: 'What show, what glory, in the advance! On the Plain of Nia most terribly they clash. 'Tis the Tuatha De from the frozen north on that side, the Firbolg of the blood-etched blades on this side. Badb, drinker of the red gore, will thank them for bodies. Many will not return from their visit to Moytura. They will lie gashed, with heads cut off.'

Then the Dagda began the attack, hacking from the west through Firbolg ranks, cutting a wide path. When he saw this, Cirb raised his arm against the Tuatha De, hurling death, clearing his own large space. All day the battle went on, in combats and deadly duels. The seams of the shields were torn apart, swords wrenched from their hilts, rivets popped from the heads of the spears. A great many bold fellows stretched out on the turf for the never-ending sleep.

By the fall of the light the Tuatha De Danann were driven back and they retreated to their camp. The Firbolg did not pursue them but went cheerfully to their fort. Each warrior brought with him to the king a stone and a head, which they built into a great cairn. Then the magicians and the wizards on both sides brought crushed, healing herbs to scatter on the well-water. Thick and green was the healing water, and the wounded men rose whole out of it.

In the morning, strong armies well-refreshed came at each other again. Big blows were dealt, bosses of the shields were shattered, and spears twisted out of the hand. Swords broke on splintered bones, and agony-screams covered the battle-cries. When night fell the Firbolg were driven across the battlefield, though each still carried a head and a stone to Eochaid their king.

'Is it you who were beaten today?' said the king.

'It is,' said Cirb, 'but it will not profit them.'

Next day, as they set out, the Tuatha De Danann looked at each other, saying, 'Who shall lead us?'

'It is I who shall do it,' said the Dagda, 'for in me you have an excellent god.' And he went forth with his sons and brothers towards the ranks of the Firbolg, drawn up by their pillars and wooden props in the plain. And for this reason the field of battle was called Moytura, or the Plain of Props.

The Dagda started breaking men apart at this end, and Cirb the Firbolg was slaughtering brave warriors at that end, and each heard the battering blows of the other. Then they came together with furious slashes of their good swords, till at twilight Cirb fell. Then the Firbolg were thrashed to their fort, and the Tuatha De went homeward with a stone pillar and a head each, and they took the head of Cirb also.

In that same sad night came Fintan the wise, with his sons, to join the Firbolg. Thirteen bleak and hardy men, the sons

16

of Fintan came to Eochaid, the High-king, and they formed a guard of battle-scarred warriors, the world's trustiest troops.

A flaming mass was the fight on the next day, lurid in colour, gory of hand. Fierce it was and pitiless and terrible, hard-packed and close-knit, furious, ebbing and flowing with many adventures. The wizards and wise men stood on the pillars in high places, making magic, while the poets took account of great deeds and turned them into song. As for Nuada of the Tuatha De Danann, he was at the centre of things. And as for Sreng of the Firbolg, he was likewise in the middle. Death and blood pooled at their feet. All this Fathach saw from his pillar, as he stared east and west.

"Tis sure the Firbolg will lose many brothers,' he cried. 'Many will be the rolling heads and headless bodies on the plain. They fall by their shields. I'll trust no more to the strength of them while I stay in stormy Ireland. I am Fathach, the poet. Strongly has sorrow conquered me. Now that the Firbolg are falling, I surrender to the swift advance of disaster.'

Furies and monsters and hags of doom cried aloud, and their voices were heard in the rocks and waterfalls and in the hollows of the earth. It was like the agony of the last day, when all men will depart from this world. Some heroes still bestrode the battlefield, hacking with stout arms, like woodsmen. At the sight of them the armies stopped and wavered, falling away like water boiling over a kettle. A place was cleared around the great chiefs, and to them was left the battle.

Their feet churned the firm turf. Thirty bows were given and taken, till Sreng slashed at Nuada. His sword-thrust cleaved the rim of Nuada's shield and cut off the right arm at the shoulder. The king's arm lay in the dust, but the Dagda came quickly and stood over Nuada. Then the chiefs of the Tuatha De Danann caught up their king and carried him from the field, while the blood of the severed arm trickled on their bent backs.

The bad day was done and night's black shadow covered all. Then Nuada, the stricken king, spoke from a place of rest.

'Tell me, great Dagda,' he said wearily, 'how does the battle stand?'

'I will tell you, noble Nuada,' replied the Dagda, 'how stands the fight. Its calamities and disasters I will also tell. Our nobles fell before the violence of the Firbolg. Our losses are great, we can hardly count them. But Bres on our side, a warrior like a tower, made glorious carnage among the Firbolg, to the number of one hundred and fifty.

'Then huge Sreng was angered. He rained nine blows on your shield. It looked as if you could withstand him, O impetuous Nuada, but he hacked off your right arm! Then we were disheartened and many died, good men, warriors reeking blood-red wounds.

'Eochaid, High-king of the Firbolg, and his son Slainge the Fair, also did powerful deeds against us. But the High-king grew thirsty with blood-work and went wandering for a drink to the Strand of Eothail. There, three sons of Nemed surprised him on the silent sands. They fought, and all fell. Lugaid, your son, was killed, and Slainge the Fair, son of Eochaid, is likewise dead.

'After that 'twas Sreng that ruled the fight – many changed colour when they knew it – but still back and forth went the footsteps of the warriors, staggering, heart-hurt, though none turned and fled. Weary were we now on either side, so we stopped slaughter and went aside to pause and think.'

Sad, wounded and full of heavy reproaches were the Firbolg that night. Each one buried his kin and friends. They raised mounds over the brave men, and gravestones over the warriors, and tombs on soldiers, and hills over heroes. After that they took counsel, whether they should leave Ireland, or give battle again, or share the land with the Tuatha De Danann. They resolved to make one more fierce onslaught, though it hurt them sorely to think on it, as Sreng lamented:

> Resistance is destruction for men.
> We resolutely gave battle;
> There was clashing of hard swords,
> The strong plying of spears by noble warriors,

The breaking of buckler on shield.
Full of trouble are the plains of Ireland.
Disaster met us in the woods,
With the loss of many good men.

In the morning they made one more keen, murderous charge, a band of wild fiery men, their spears as close as bristles, cutting their way in a flame of fury against all opposition. When the Tuatha De Danann saw this, they drew back aghast and begged a time to talk.

'Let Sreng have the province of his choice,' they said. 'Let us stop this slaughter.'

All were agreed, and so they made peace. Sreng chose the province of Connacht, and the Firbolg took possession there. The Tuatha De Danann spread themselves in the other parts of Ireland and made Bres their king. Indeed he was High-king for seven years. But he died, after drinking unwisely in the heat of hunting at Slieve Gam. Then Nuada ruled again, for his stricken arm was magically replaced by the sorcery of his wise men, and he became the High-king.

THE
CONQUEST

The Tuatha De Danann were in the northern islands of the world, studying magic and sorcery, black skills, witchcraft and the arts of the druids, till in these things they surpassed all the wise men of the heathens. Then the Tuatha De made an alliance with the Fomorians. Balor, the grandson of Net, gave his daughter Ethne to Cian, the son of Diancecht. And she gave birth to Lugh, most glorious of sons.

The Tuatha De Danann came with a great fleet to Ireland to take it by force from the Firbolg. The Firbolg were defeated, their king Eochaid was killed, and a hundred thousand of his people also, as has been told.

But the hand of Nuada, king of the Tuatha De Danann, was cut off in the battle – it was Sreng, son of Sengann, that did it – so the physician Diancecht, with the help of Credne the metal-worker, put on him a silver hand that moved as well as any other.

Those of the Firbolg who had escaped from the battle fled to the places of the Fomorians and settled in Arran and in Islay and in Man and in Rathlin.

Now, there was a contention between the men and women of the Tuatha De Danann regarding the kingship, for no man who was not whole-made might be king. It was more fitting that the king should be Bres, son of Elatha, though he was not completely of the Tuatha De Danann. He would draw them toward the Fomorians, the people of his father Elatha.

The making of Bres came about in this way. One day, Eriu of the Tuatha De Danann was looking from the house and she saw that the sea was as flat as a plank. Then a vessel of silver appeared to her, its size somewhat great but its shape unclear, and the drift of the tide brought it to land. In it was the fairest man, with golden hair to his shoulders, and a shirt and a cloak trimmed with gold. A brooch of gold was on his breast, five golden circlets about his neck, a sword with inlays at his belt, and a brace of shining spears in the grip of his hand.

'A fine time for love-making,' said the man.

'I've made no tryst with you,' she replied.

'What need for a tryst?' said he.

So they stretched themselves down together. When the man rose, the woman wept.

'Why the tears?' he asked.

'Two things,' she said, 'I lament. One, that you possess me now, though the youth of the Tuatha De have entreated me in vain. Two, that you are leaving now.'

He drew a gold ring from his middle finger and put it into her hand, saying, 'Part not with it either by sale or gift, except to one whose finger it will fit.'

'Another sorrow I have,' said she. 'I know not who has come to me.'

'No reason for ignorance there,' he replied. 'Elatha, king of the Fomorians, has lain with you. You will bear a son and let his name be Eochu Bres, that is to say Eochu the Beautiful. Every lovely thing to be seen in Ireland – field or fortress, ale or candle, woman or man or horse – will be judged by that boy, so people will say of it, "It is a Bres."'

In her time she gave birth to a boy and he was named as Elatha had said. In seven days he had made two weeks' growth, and in seven years he had the growth of fourteen summers. And when the contention arose among the Tuatha De Danann as to the kingship, Bres was made king. His mother Eriu gave him land, and the fort of Dun Brese was on that land, and it was the Dagda who built that fort.

But after Bres was king, three Fomorian kings put Ireland under tribute so that there was not smoke from a roof in Ireland that was not under this tribute. Even the champions of Ireland were pressed into service. Ogma carried firewood and the Dagda built ramparts and trenches, and he was the maker of Bres's fort.

Soon the Dagda was not happy with his work. He used to meet in the house an idle blind fellow called Cridenbel, whose mouth grew out of his chest. This Cridenbel thought his own ration was small and the Dagda's large. So he said, 'O Dagda, on your honour give me the three best bits of your meal!' And the Dagda, for the sake of honour, did so every night. But large indeed were the bits given to the satirist Cridenbel. Each piece was the size of a good pig, making in all a third of the Dagda's food. And the appearance of the Dagda was the worse for that.

One day the Dagda was working in the trench when he saw the Mac Oc coming to him.

'Very good, O Dagda,' said the Mac Oc.

'Even so,' said the Dagda.

'But you have a bad look about you.'

'I have good cause,' replied the Dagda. 'Cridenbel, that satirist, takes every night the three best bits of my meal.'

'It will not last,' said the Mac Oc. 'Soon you will finish your work, but seek no payment till the cattle of Ireland are

22

brought to you. Then choose the dark, black-maned, lively heifer.'

When the work was finished and Bres offered a payment, the Dagda asked for the heifer, which seemed a foolish choice to the king. He thought the Dagda would have chosen something more.

All this time that Bres held the kingship, there was murmuring against him among the Tuatha De Danann, for their knives were not greased by him, and however often they visited him their breaths did not smell of ale. And there was no entertainment in the household from either poet or bard or satirist or harper or piper or hornblower or juggler or jester. They saw no races, no sporting contest, and only Ogma was there to prove his skill before the king. Yet his poor duty was only this: to bring firewood to the fort. Each day he carried a bundle from the islands of Clew Bay, but the sea snatched two-thirds of his load, because he was weak for lack of food.

On a certain day Corpre, poet of the Tuatha De Danann, came in his travels to the house of Bres. He entered a narrow, black, dark little house, with neither fire nor chair nor bed in it. Three small cakes he was given, and they were dry. On the morrow he arose, and he was not thankful. As he crossed the threshhold he made this chant:

'Without food quickly on a dish,
Without cow's milk for a calf to grow on,
Without a man's abode under the dark of night,
Without pay for a company of storytellers –
Let that be Bres's condition.

'There's no prosperity in Bres,' he added, and that was true. There was blight on him from that hour. And this is the first satire made in Ireland.

After this the Tuatha De met together to talk with their foster son Bres. It was agreed that he might remain king for seven years, so long as he gave proper sureties. As he was not willing to give up the kingship, Bres made this delay so that he might gather the *shee*, the magical warriors of the Fomorians, and seize the Tuatha De by force.

Then he went to his mother and asked where his family was. 'I am certain about that,' said she, and she gave him the ring that Elatha had left her. He put it on his middle finger and it fitted him.

Together they went forward to the lands of the Fomorians. The people there, as was the custom, put them to the test, making races and fighting in sword-play. When the dogs raced, the hounds of Bres were faster, and his horses too were faster than those of the men of the Fomorians. Then they came to sword-play. But as Bres lifted his arm to strike, Elatha recognized the ring on his finger and asked who he was, and Eriu told the whole story of his birth.

His father was sad for him and asked him, 'What need brings you from the land you ruled?'

'Nothing,' said Bres, 'but my own injustice and pride. I took their jewels and their land and their food. Until this time, none had taken from them tribute or payments.'

'That is bad for the telling,' said his father. 'Better their prosperity than your kingship. Better their prayers than curses. Why have you come here?'

'To ask for soldiers, since I mean to keep the land by force.'

'Gain it by justice only.'

'Well, then, here's a question: what advice do you give me?' asked Bres.

But Elatha would not help him and sent him instead to Balor, king of the Hebrides, and to Indech, one of the other kings of the Fomorians. And these kings gathered all the forces from Lochlann westward to Ireland, to impose tribute and rule by force, and they made a single bridge of ships from the Hebrides to Ireland. No host ever came to Ireland that was more terrifying than these warriors.

After Bres had departed towards the Fomorians, Nuada was once more in the kingship of the Tuatha De, for the physician Diancecht had put a silver hand on him that was as good as any other hand, and he was once more a whole man. So, in celebration, Nuada held a great feast at Tara for the Tuatha De

Danann. And there came before the doorkeepers of Tara a warrior and a company of strangers, led by a handsome, sturdy young fellow with a king's diadem on him.

'Who is there?' the doorkeepers asked the leader.

'Lugh Lonnansclech is here, son of Cian, son of Diancecht and of Ethne, daughter of Balor.'

'And you,' they asked the warrior, 'what is your art? No one without skill enters Tara.'

'Question me,' said the warrior, who was named Samildanach.

'Well?' replied the doorkeepers. 'Speak on.'

'I am a builder, I am a smith, I am a champion, I am a harper, I am a soldier, I am a poet, I am a sorcerer.'

'All those skills we have and need no more,' said the door-keepers. 'As for sorcerers, our druids and magicians and witches are as many as the sands of the beach.'

'I will speak further,' went on Samildanach. 'I am a physician, I am a cupbearer, I am a metal-worker. Ho, door-man, ask the king if he has anyone with as many arts and skills as I have. If he has, I will not enter Tara.'

One of the doorkeepers went to Nuada and said, 'The warrior Samildanach has come to court. He practises all the arts and is the master of every skill.'

Then the courtiers brought out the chess-boards of Tara, and Samildanach won every game. When all this was told to the king, he said, 'Let him enter, for never before has a man like him come into our fort.' And Samildanach went into the hall and sat in the seat of the wise man, because he was wise in every art. And in the evening he played on the harp, playing the music of sleep and lulling the king and the court into sleep from that hour till the same time next day.

When he saw this man's many powers, Nuada wondered if he might save them from the Fomorians. So the Tuatha De held a council, and the next day Nuada spoke with Ogma and the Dagda on Girley Hill, and the king summoned also his two kinsmen Diancecht and Goibniu. A full year they spent in close discussion, and then the druids of Ireland were called together, with their doctors and charioteers and smiths and landowners and lawgivers. They all spoke together secretly.

'What is your power?' the king asked Mathgen, the sorcerer. And Mathgen answered that he would shake the mountains of Ireland under the Fomorians till their summits fell to the ground. Then it would seem as if the twelve chief mountains of Ireland were fighting for the Tuatha De Danann.

'And three showers of fire,' added the druid Figol, 'I will rain on the faces of the Fomorians. I will take out of them two-thirds of their courage and skill and strength, and I will block up the bladders in their bodies and in the bodies of their horses. And the courage of the men of Ireland will increase with every breath. Even if they fight for seven years, they will not be weary.'

Then the Dagda said, 'That power that you boast, I'll wield it all by myself.'

'You are the Dagda, the Great God,' shouted the Tuatha De Danann. And the name Dagda stuck to him from then on.

So they prepared for battle. Lugh and the Dagda and Ogma went to the three gods of Danu, and they gave Lugh his weapons, which they had been making ready for seven years. At last, everything was in place and the Tuatha De heard the cry of Morrigan.

'Awake,' cried the taster of blood. 'Go forward to the remorseless fight!'

And the druids answered straight out, 'Yes, we will wage war!'

Now the Dagda had a house in Glen Edin to the north, where he had arranged to meet a woman. The river Unshin of Connacht roars to the south. He saw a woman by the Unshin in Corann, washing, with one foot in Aghanagh south of the water, and the other at Lisconny to the north. Nine loosened tresses hung about her head. The Dagda called to her and they lay together. Morrigan was the name of the woman, and the place where they lay was 'the Bed of the Couple'.

Morrigan told the Dagda that the Fomorians would land at Magh Scene, and that he should summon the Irish champions to meet her at the Ford of the Unshin. She would destroy Indech, king of the Fomorians, and take from him the blood of his heart and his manly testicles. Later, she gave two handfuls of that blood to the crowd waiting at the Ford of the Unshin. And its name evermore was the Ford of Destruction, because of the killing of the king.

When the Fomorians were landed, Lugh sent the Dagda to spy on them, and to try to delay them until the men of Ireland were ready. The Dagda went to their camp and asked for a truce. This was granted. But to mock him, the Fomorians made him a porridge, because his great love of porridge was well-known. They filled for him the king's cauldron, and poured into it four-score gallons of new milk, and the same amount of meat and fat. They put goats and sheep and pigs into it, and boiled everything together. Then they poured it all into a hole in the ground, and the king said the Dagda would be killed unless he ate it all. Never might it be said that the Fomorians were without hospitality!

So the Dagda took his ladle, big enough for a man and a woman to lie in it.

'If the taste of the broth equals the smell,' he said, ''tis good food.' Then he put the full-charged ladle to his mouth, saying further, 'It's a wise man that says "the poor bits don't spoil it".'

He ate and ate, and at the end of his hunger scraped a bent finger in the bottom of the hole amid the mould and the gravel. Then he fell asleep with a belly as big as a house, and all the Fomorians laughing at him.

When the Dagda awoke and saw the derision, he went away from them to the beach of Eaba. It was not easy for him to move owing to the size and tightness of his belly. The look of him was not pleasant to behold: a cape to the hollow of his elbows; a dun tunic around him as far as the swelling of his rump; a ragged hole in the tunic; two brogues on him of horse-hide, with the hair turned outside and his private parts in the air. Behind him he pulled a wheeled fork that was the work of eight men to move, leaving a track deep enough for the boundary ditch of a province, and this became known as the Track of Dagda's Club.

As he walked he saw a girl in front of him, fine-looking and of a good shape, with tresses of beautiful hair on her head. The Dagda lusted for her, but he was impotent because of his belly. The girl began to mock him, and to tussle with him. She hurled him so hard that he sank to his rump in the ground.

'Woman,' he said angrily, 'what business do you have, throwing me from my proper path?'

'My business,' she replied, 'is this: to make you carry me on your back to my father's house.'

'Who is your father?'

'It is Indech, a king of the Fomorians.'

Then she fell upon him again and knocked him here and there till the pit about his belly filled with the excrement of his body. And she mocked him with satires three times so that he would carry her.

Weary of this, he emptied the contents of his belly and climbed out of the hole, and the girl was waiting for him and mounted on his back. Then stones fell from his belt, or it may have been his testicles. Howsoever it was, she jumped on him and smacked him a smart blow across his rump, and as she did so her curly private hairs were revealed. So one thing followed another, and she gained a lover. They lay together and rubbed themselves together.

Then the girl said, 'You shall not go to the battle by any means.'

'Certainly I shall go,' said the Dagda.

'You will not, because I will be a stone at the mouth of every ford you cross.'

'That will be true,' he replied, 'but you will not keep me from it. I will tread heavily on every stone, and the trace of my heel will remain on every stone forever.'

'But still you will not go past me until I summon the Fomorians who are the sons of Tethra from the fairy-hills, because I will be a giant oak in every ford and in every pass that you must cross.'

'Indeed I will go past, and the mark of my axe will remain on every oak forever.'

Then the girl, the daughter of Indech, relented and said, 'Gather the men of Ireland all in one place and allow the Fomorians to enter the land. I shall hinder the Fomorians, and sing spells against them, and practise the deadly art of the wand against them. And I alone will take on a ninth part of their host.'

The Fomorians advanced to Scetne. The men of Ireland were in Magh Aurfolaig. The two armies were threatening battle.

'Those Irish have a determined look,' said Bres, 'I expect they mean to fight.'

'We'll give them the same medicine,' said the Fomorian king, 'so their bones will be crushed small if they do not pay tribute.'

The men of Ireland had agreed to keep Lugh from the battle. They feared his early death, which would extinguish the great number of his arts. Nine foster fathers were set to guard him. When the guards and the chiefs of the Tuatha De Danann were around him, Lugh said to his smith Goibniu, 'What is the extent of your power?'

'Not hard to say,' replied Goibniu. 'Though the fight be for seven years, every splintered spear, every broken sword shall be mended by me. My forged spearpoints will not miss their mark. The skins they pierce will not taste life afterwards. Dolb, the Fomorian smith, cannot do as much. I am prepared for this second battle at Moytura.'

'And you, physician Diancecht,' Lugh went on, 'what is your power?'

'Not hard to say,' said he. 'Any of our wounded, unless his head be off, or his brain struck open, I will make him perfectly whole by the next day.'

'And you, Ogma, champion warrior,' said Lugh, 'what is your power?'

'Not hard to say,' said he. 'Neither the king nor twenty-seven of his friends will be a match for me, I will win a third of the battle for the men of Ireland.'

'And you, Morrigan, battle-hag, what is your power?'

'Not hard to say,' said she. 'I stand fast. I shall pursue whatever I watch. I shall destroy those I have my eye on.'

'And you, sorcerers, what power?'

'Not hard to say,' said they. 'Those overthrown by our craft will show the white soles of their feet. We will take two-thirds of their strength, and prevent them from pissing.'

'And you, druids, what power?'

'Not hard to say,' said the druids. 'We will bring showers of fire on the faces of the Fomorians and sear their sight, so our warriors can kill them easily.'

'And you, Corpre the poet, what can you do in battle?'

'Not hard to say,' said Corpre. 'I will make a metrical male-diction against them. I will name them and shame them, so by my spell they will offer no fight.'

'And you, Be Chuille and Dianann, my witches, what can you do?'

'Not hard to say,' said the witches. 'We will bewitch the trees and the stones and the sods of the earth so that they will appear like an army against them. And they will scatter in flight, terrified and trembling.'

'And you, the Dagda,' said Lugh. 'What power can you use against the army of the Fomorians?'

'Not hard to say,' said the Dagda. 'I will lay waste with heavy smiting and destruction and wizardry. Their bones under my club will be like hailstones under the hooves of horses.'

Thus the battle-ranks were drawn up, between fierce and proud men.

Then the Fomorians marched out of their camp in strong, indestructible battalions. There was not a soldier among them without armour against his skin, a helmet on his head, a broad spear in his hand, a sharp sword on his belt, a heavy shield on his shoulder. To attack them that day was like striking a head against a cliff, or putting a hand in a nest of snakes, or thrusting a face into the fire.

Balor and Bres led the Fomorians. On the other side, Lugh gave his guards the slip and took the forefront of the battle. In his chariot he led the Tuatha De Danann. He called to the men of Ireland to free themselves from the bondage of the Fomorians, for it was better to die for Ireland than to live and pay tribute. And to give them heart Lugh went around the warriors of Ireland on one foot and with one eye closed, and he chanted this spell: *Arotroi cath comartan. Fo, fo. Fe, fe. Cle. Amainsi!*

There was a great shout. The armies rushed together and started to hack at the one and the other. Many beautiful men fell in the stall of death. Great killing and grave-lying was seen there. Pride and shame were side by side, anger and indignation. Thick was the stream of blood over white skin. Harsh the tumult over the field: shouts and clashes and swishing and rattling and humming and whirring, and everywhere the clanging strokes of hard blows.

They attacked each other till their fingertips and toes almost met. Blood under their feet, and they slipping and falling down. A heavy, gory, hurt-inflicting, sharp, bloody battle, with shafts and blades red in the hands of foes.

Nuada Silver Hand fell before the blows of Balor. Then Lugh and eye-piercing Balor met in battle. An evil eye had Balor. That eye was never open save on the battlefield. Then four men would raise the eye-lid by a polished ring. Whoever looked in that eye, though they were thousands in number, were helpless. It had that poisonous power for this reason: once, when his father's druids were brewing magic, he looked in the window, and the fumes of the brew settled in his eye and gave it this dangerous power. Lugh and Balor came together, and Balor heard the challenge from Lugh.

'Now lads,' said Balor, 'lift up my eye-lid so that I can see this talkative fellow.'

The lid was raised from Balor's eye. Then Lugh hurled a stone from a sling-shot at him, which drove the eye through the back of his head, and it was Balor's own army that was looking at it. Balor fell on top of his own soldiers so that twenty-seven of them died under him, and the crown of his head struck the chest of his king so that a gush of blood spouted from his lips.

Then Morrigan came into the ranks with grim words, stiffening the hearts of the Tuatha De Danann to fight fiercely and resolutely. In a short time the armies broke apart, and the Fomorians were driven to the sea. Many called for mercy, and among them was Loch Half Green, the poet of the enemy. To him, Lugh replied, 'Grant me my requests.'

'That I will do,' said Loch. 'I will remove from Ireland forever all invasion and plundering by the Fomorians. And in all hard cases the judgement of your tongue shall resolve the matter until the end of life.'

So Loch the poet was spared, and he chanted to the Gaels 'The Decree of Fastening'.

After the battle, the Tuatha De Danann wished to kill Bres. But he stopped their hands, saying, 'It is better to spare me than to kill me.'

'What follows from that?' said Lugh.

'If I am spared,' replied Bres, 'the cows of Ireland will always be in milk.'

'Let us see what the wise men say,' said Lugh.

So Lugh went to wise Maeltne, who answered, 'He shall not be spared. Milk he might control, but what can he do about their age or their calving?'

'O Maeltne,' said Bres, 'a bitter alarm you give me.'

Then Lugh asked again, 'What else shall save you, Bres?'

'A harvest every quarter shall be yours, if you spare me.'

'No mercy for that,' replied Maeltne. 'It is not the proper way for us. What is suitable is this: spring for ploughing and sowing, summer for the growing of the grain, autumn for ripeness and reaping, winter for eating.'

'That does not save you,' said Lugh. And Bres cried out again, 'O Maeltne, another bitter alarm.'

But Lugh said, 'Less will rescue you.'

'What?' asked Bres.

'Answer me this: how shall the men of Ireland plough? How shall they sow? How shall they reap? Make known these things.'

'Say to them,' replied Bres, 'Tuesday for their ploughing, Tuesday their sowing, Tuesday their reaping.'

Thus Bres was spared and released.

Now, in the battle the champion Ogma found the sword of Tethra, one of the kings of the Fomorians. Ogma unsheathed the sword and cleaned it. Then the sword told him what it had done, because at that time it was the habit of swords to recount their deeds when laid bare. Therefore swords are entitled to the tribute of cleaning. By this means, many spells have been kept in swords from that time on, for demons used to speak from swords because men used to worship weapons, which were a safeguard of the people. And Loch Half Green, as was the custom, made a chant about that sword.

When the Fomorians fled, Lugh and the Dagda and Ogma went after them because they had carried off the Dagda's harper. After hard running they reached the hall where Bres and Elatha sat. There was the harp on the wall. It was the harp in which the Dagda had bound the melodies, so that it would not sound until he called forth the music.

Then the harp sprang from the wall, and it killed nine men altogether, and it came to the hand of the Dagda. Quickly he played for the Fomorians the three great musics: the sleep-music, the joy-music, and the music of sorrow. At the sorrowful music, the women wept. At the joyful music, the boys laughed. And at the music of dreams, the warriors slept. So the three were able to creep away unharmed, though the Fomorians had wished to kill them.

As they went away, the Dagda gathered up the cattle that the Fomorians had plundered. First he called to his dark, black-maned heifer, the one given him by Bres as his wages for fort-building. Then she mooed for her calf, and all the cattle of Ireland followed after her.

After the breaking of the battle and the cleansing of the slaughter, Morrigan, queen of war, proclaimed the triumph and the great victory to the royal hills of Ireland, to its spirit-army, to its water and rivers and estuaries. And the great deeds are still spoken of. 'What news?' the people call out. The reply comes, even from fierce Badb, the sister of Morrigan:

Peace up to heaven, heaven down to earth.
Earth beneath heaven, strength in each.
A cup very full, full of honey.
Mead in abundance, summer in winter.
Peace up to heaven.

That is the one side of the coin. But on the other side, she was also prophesying the end of the world, foretelling the evil of it, and every disease and every vengeance, and this is what she sang:

I shall not see a world that will be dear to me.
Summer without flowers, cows without milk,
Women without modesty, men not brave,
Conquests without a king.
Woods without mast, fishless seas,
Bad judgements by old men,
False precedents of the lawgivers.
Every man a betrayer, each son a robber.
The son will enter his father's bed,
The father also in the bed of the son,
A brother becomes his own brother-in-law!
None will look for a woman outside his own house.
O evil time, deception, deception.

2

THIS WORLD, THE OTHERWORLD, AND THE FATE OF MANKIND

O you that plant the tree,
Who shall live to pluck its apples?
When the bright shoot is grown,
Are you the one to see it?
Death has made even this doubtful.

THE FATE OF THE
CHILDREN OF TURENN

In the time when Nuada of the Silver Hand ruled over the
Tuatha De Danann, the Fomorians from Lochlann in
the north oppressed the people of Ireland and took a
heavy tribute: namely, a tax on their bread-troughs, and on
their millstones, and on their baking-pans, and on top of this
was an ounce of gold from each man besides. This tribute
was paid each year, on the Hill of Usnech, and those who
would not or could not pay had their noses cut off them.

Before the paying of the tribute, a great assembly met on
the Hill of Usnech, to the west side of Tara, and it was not
long before they saw an armed band from the east, with a
young man in command, and the brightness of his face was
like the setting sun, which was hard to look on. Then they
knew him for Lugh Lamfada – Lugh of the Long Hand – and

with him were the warriors of the *shee* from the Land of Promise, and his own foster-brothers, the sons of Manannan Mac Lir, the god of the sea.

And this is the way Lugh was: under him was Manannan's horse, Enbarr of the Flowing Mane, that was as swift as the naked cold wind of spring, and the sea and land were all one to her, and no rider was ever killed off her back. He had on him Manannan's breastplate, that kept the wearer from wounds, and the jewels of his helmet flashed like the sun on a summer day. At his side was Manannan's sword, the Answerer, that let none escape it in battle, and against it a man had no more strength than a new-born babe.

Nuada and the Tuatha De Danann welcomed these warriors, and it was not long before they saw another troop advancing. It was nine times nine surly, slovenly messengers from the Fomorians come to take the tribute from the men of Ireland.

'Why do you salute that surly band,' Lugh asked Nuada, 'when you did not rise up for us?'

'It is needful to do so,' replied the king, 'for even a child sitting before them would be a cause for killing.'

'Truly,' said Lugh, 'there is a strong desire upon me to kill these fellows myself.'

'That is a thing would harm us greatly,' said Nuada, 'for we would bring our own death and destruction on us.'

But Lugh shouted, 'Too long has this oppression lasted!'

With that, he attacked the Fomorians, dealing red slaughter to eight nines of them. But he let the last nine go, saying, 'I would kill you also, but it is safer that you take a message to tell your own country what you have seen.'

So that nine went back to Lochlann and told their story, which made the Fomorians wonder.

'Who is this young man?' said Balor of the Evil Eye.

'I know him well,' said Ceithlenn, his wife. 'He is Lugh of the Long Hand, son of your daughter and mine. It was foretold that he would bring to an end our power in Ireland.'

Then the chief men of the Fomorians took counsel, with their nine poets, and Lobais the Druid, and Balor himself, and his twelve white-mouthed sons, and Ceithlenn of the Crooked Teeth. At this time also came Bres, son of Elatha, to ask help from the Fomorians.

'Give me seven battalions,' he said, 'and I myself will go to Ireland and fight this Ildanach, this Master of All Arts, this Lugh. I will strike off his head and bring it to you here.'

Without delay all was made ready to set out for Ireland, with men and grim weapons sent on their road by Balor's high words.

'Give battle to Lugh,' he cried, 'and strike off his head. Tie that land called Ireland to the back of your ships, and let the indifferent waters rest in its place. Put it on the north side of bitter-cold Lochlann, far removed from the Tuatha De Danann till the end of life and time.'

Then the Fomorians set their painted sails towards the untilled acres of the wide-lying sea and held course for Eas Dara. Then the Fomorians went westward into Connacht, destroying it through and through. The king of Connacht at that time was Bodb Derg, son of the Dagda.

But Nuada of the Silver Hand was not minded to avenge the wrong done to Bodb Derg, and Lugh became angry with him. So Lugh himself rode westward out of Tara. He had not gone far when he saw his own father Cian coming with his uncles Cu and Ceithen. These three were the sons of Cainte.

'This is early rising, Lugh,' they called. And he replied, 'Good cause for it. The Fomorians are here and have robbed Bodb Derg. Go gather the warriors of the *shee* from every hidden place where they live.'

Away they went, south and north. Cian had reached the plain of Murthemne when he saw the three sons of Turenn, the son of Ogma. Between the sons of Turenn and the sons of Cainte there was hatred and bitterness, and if they were to meet, fighting would surely break out.

'If only my brothers were with me, it is a brave fight we would make,' said Cian to himself. 'But now it is best for me to draw back.'

He saw a herd of pigs nearby, so he touched himself with

a druid's wand. He changed himself into the shape of a pig and rooted in the ground with the rest.

But Brian, the eldest of the sons of Turenn, saw what had happened. Fearing that this might be the magic of an enemy, he touched his two brothers with his own druid's wand, turning them into thin, fast hounds that yelped in the track of the enchanted pig. They chased that pig into the edge of a wood where Brian threw a spear right through the pig's body.

'Evil is this thing you have done to me,' cried the pig, 'since you knew it was me.'

'It seems to me,' said Brian, 'you have the talk of a man.'

'Certainly,' replied the pig. 'I am Cian, son of Cainte. So give me your protection.'

'I swear by the gods of the air,' said Brian, 'if you had seven lives I would take every one.'

'Is that the way of it? But grant me this: let me go into my own shape again.'

'That we grant. It is easier to kill a man than a pig.'

Then Cian took his own shape and said, 'Though you give me no mercy, I shall have the best of you. The blood-money for a hog is nothing much. But kill me as a man and you shall pay the heaviest penalty ever put on a person. The very arms you kill me with shall tell the tale to my son Lugh.'

'No weapons shall kill you,' said Brian, 'but the stones on the ground shall do it.' With that, Brian and his brothers smote him so fiercely with great rough rocks that they made him a poor bloody pulp and buried him a man's height down in the field. But the earth would not take him and cast him up. Six times the sons of Turenn buried Cian, and six times the earth spat him out. But on the seventh time the earth closed over him and received him. Then a voice sang from below the ground:

> The blood you have spilled,
> The hero you have killed,
> Shall follow your steps
> Till your doom be fulfilled.

Now, when Lugh of the Long Hand had brought help to Bodb Derg in Connacht, and they had won the battle against the Fomorians, Lugh looked for his father Cian. 'If he were alive,' thought Lugh, 'surely he would have been at the battle. Neither food nor drink will I take till I know his fate.'

With the warriors of the *shee*, Lugh went about the country till they came to a place where the earth spoke and said, 'Lugh, here your father was in great danger, as he saw the sons of Turenn before him. Into the shape of a pig he went, but they killed him in his own shape.'

So Lugh and his men dug in that spot, to know what manner of death had been put on Cian. They raised the body tenderly from the grave, and it looked all one bed of wounds.

'O sons of Turenn,' Lugh groaned, 'you gave my dear father an enemy's death.' He kissed his father three times, and then he began to lament.

'I myself am a poor thing after this death,' he cried, 'for my eyes do not see, and my ears do not hear, and the pulse of my heart is stopped. O gods, why was I not here when this thing was done? The Tuatha De Danann have done treachery one on another. Loss and weakness will hound them now. East and west, all Ireland will not be free from trouble.'

Then they put Cian under the earth again, and spilt tears above the grave, and a stone was raised with his name on it in Ogham.

'The sons of Turenn did this thing,' said Lugh, 'and grief and anguish will fall on them from it, and on their children. It is no lying story I tell you. Have pity for the way I am, for the heart is broken in me since Cian, the dear man, is no longer living.'

Then Lugh returned to Tara and sat in the king's high seat. Before him he saw the three sons of Turenn. They were beyond all others for beauty and skill, for a bold hand in battle, and an honourable name. Lugh looked down and shook the chain of silence, and all listened.

'I have a question to ask,' he said. 'What vengeance would you take on a man who killed your father?'

There was great wonder in the crowd. They looked from one to another till a certain chief said, 'Is it your own father you speak of?'

'Indeed it is,' said Lugh, 'and I see here the men who killed him. No simple death in a day would I give his murderer, if I had him, but I would cut off his limbs day by day till I made an end of him.'

'We would do the same,' cried the chief men, and the sons of Turenn were among them.

'If I myself had killed your father,' said Nuada the king, 'I would be well content to pay the blood-fine.'

At this, the sons of Turenn muttered together, 'Let us tell of the killing.'

So said Iuchar and Iucharba. But Brian, the eldest, answered, 'I am in dread that he will not agree to a fine, if we acknowledge the deed.'

'Nay,' said his brothers, 'speak out. Tell of the killing.'

Then Brian spoke out, and Lugh agreed to impose a fine.

'This is it,' said Lugh, 'though it may be too much for your burden: three apples, and the skin of a pig, and a spear, and two horses with a chariot, and seven pigs, and a whelp-hound, and a cooking-spit, and three shouts on a hill. All that is the fine I am asking.'

'It is not too much,' said Brian, 'not by a hundred times. And we are thinking, because of its smallness, that you have some treachery behind it.'

'Not so,' said Lugh, 'I will ask no other thing. So let us pledge.'

Then the sons of Turenn bound themselves by the king, and by the son of the Dagda, and by all the chiefs of the Tuatha De Danann, to pay that blood-fine to Lugh.

'Now, for your better understanding of the fine,' said Lugh, 'this is the way it is: the three apples are from the Garden in the East of the World, the most beautiful and most virtuous of all apples. They are the colour of burnt gold, and the size of the head of a child, and the taste of them is like honey, and they take away the pain of wounds and sickness. Then the skin I ask is the pig-skin of Tuis, King of Greece, that overcomes all danger and turns running water into wine. I am thinking that it will not be easy to get it without leave.

'As for the spear you will seek, it is the very deadly spear of Pezar, King of Persia. The Slaughterer it is called. Its fiery head is kept in a cauldron of water, to save the palace from burning. And the other things I ask, would you know about them? The two horses and the chariot belong to King Dobar of Sicily. And the seven pigs, which will never know death, are those of King Easal of the Golden Pillars. And the whelp called Fail-Inis belongs to the King of the Cold Country, and this little hound is as beautiful as the sun so all wild beasts fall down at the sight of her. And the cooking-spit is that of the wild women of Fincara, where each woman is a match for three good warriors. And the three shouts you must give will be on the Hill of Midkena, in the north of Lochlann, where the people are under the holy injunction of a *geasa* never to shout. My father Cian got his learning with these folk, and even if I would forgive you his death, they would not. That altogether is the fine I set upon you.'

These were magical things, and among them were the things that Lugh needed for the final defeat of the Fomorians.

When they heard all this, there was silence and darkness on the sons of Turenn. In their doubt, they went to ask their father what to do. He told them that they needed the help of Lugh himself, or failing that at least the loan of Manannan's powerful possessions.

'You shall not have Enbarr, the horse of the flowing mane,' Lugh replied to their asking, 'but I'll grant you the loan of Manannan's boat, the *Wave-Sweeper*.'

Then the sons of Turenn went sadly away, with their sister Ethne, to Brugh of the Boyne where the boat was.

'O dear brother,' said Ethne to Brian, 'it was an evil thing you did, to kill the father of Lugh. Whatever harm may come to you, it is but just.'

'Sister, do not say that. We are in good heart and will

do great deeds. Better to be killed a hundred times over than to meet the death of a coward.'

'Grief and sorrow overwhelm me,' said she, 'to see you driven from your own fair land.'

The three sons of Turenn launched their boat from the sweet shores of Ireland. The *Wave-Sweeper* did not neglect their orders but sailed forward over the green-shaded waters and the deep places.

'Let us make straight to the things we need and attack them,' said Iuchar and Iucharba, 'and bring them away or fall ourselves, since we cannot escape the dangers before us.'

'Better that our story of bravery and skill be told after us than for folly and cowardice to hang on our names,' Brian agreed. 'Let us go in the shape of swift hawks into the Garden of the East, and snatch the apples in our claws, and make a quick flight away.'

With the touch of their druid's wand they became hawks. Boldly they swooped on the apples and bore them out, though the daughters of the Garden turned into sea-eagles and scorched the hawks with lightning before the sons of Turenn reached the safety of their boat.

Then they swept over the pathless seas to Greece. 'We shall arrive here,' said Brian, 'as poets of Ireland. In that way the lords of Greece will hold us in honour.'

'It will not be easy for us,' said his brothers, 'without a poem, and little enough we know how to make one.' But they resolved to try. They tied their hair in the fashion of poets, and went to the door of the court.

So in went the sons of Turenn, having the look of poets, and they fell to drinking and pleasure without delay. They had never had such a grand time, nor seen a better household. But after a while the king asked them for a poem.

'We have no poem,' they said to each other. 'The only poetry we know is to take what we want by the strength of our hands.'

'We must do better than that,' said Brian. So he rose up and spoke in this way:

> 'O Tuis of Greece, we do not hide your fame.
> We praise you as an oak among kings.
> The bounty I ask as a reward,
> It is but the skin of a pig.'

''Tis a good poem,' said the king, 'a grand poem. But I know not a word of the meaning.'

Then Brian explained the hardness of the poem, which was to say that he would have the pig-skin of the king or there would be trouble between them.

'Indeed the hard meaning is now clear,' said the king, 'but you talk too much of my pig-skin, O poet of Ireland. I would not give it up for all the poets of the world. But as the price of your poem I will give you as much gold as will cover the pig-skin three times.'

The skin was brought into the court. But as the gold was being measured out, Brian snatched the skin with his left hand and struck the keeper with a slash of his sword, making two halves of him. Then Brian threw the skin about him and the three brothers ran from the court, cutting down all who opposed them. They sprang to their boat and left the blue streams of Greece behind and sailed to the border of Persia.

The trick of the poetry had been a good trick in Greece, so they tried it again with King Pezar in Persia. But when the king learnt the inwardness of the poem, that Brian wanted the fiery spear, Pezar was angry.

'You have little sense to ask me that,' he said. 'Only respect for poetry stops my soldiers from killing you on the spot.'

When he heard this, Brian threw one of the apples from the Garden of the East, as round and heavy as a large stone, straight at the king and dashed his brains out at the back of his head. In the wink of an eye, the sons of Turenn had the spear in their hands and their heels were flying on the path to their boat.

Now the luck of the adventure was running with the sons of Turenn. They had little trouble taking the chariot and the two horses of the King of Sicily, and they drove away like the cold spring wind over both land and sea. King Easal, for fear of the three brothers, quickly gave up the seven pigs and sent them on their way in the company of friendly ships. But the whelp-hound, Fail-Inis, was not won without swords, and they left that Cold Country with blood on their hands.

At this time it was told to Lugh of the Long Hand that the sons of Turenn had already won all the things needful for the final battle against the Fomorians. So he sent a druid's spell after them, to make them forget for the time being the rest of the blood-fine. The spell settled on them and they had a great longing to see Ireland again, so they turned home with their whole task undone.

Lugh awaited them at Tara, and the smooth armour of Manannan was on him, and the enchanted cloak of the daughters of Flidas was over his shoulder. Then Lugh stepped out on the green grass and Nuada gave him the things of the fine collected by the sons of Turenn.

Lugh took the things he wanted. Then he said further, 'All this is good payment for a death. But there is something wanting yet. Where is the cooking-spit? And when did you give the three shouts on the hill?'

The sons of Turenn were sad when they heard this. Clouds of weakness covered them, and they were again in grief and darkness. On the morrow, their sister Ethne took them once more to the sea-banks, and again she was lamenting.

'Brian of my life,' she cried, 'where is the pity for you, where is the pity for the sons of Turenn? O salmon of the Boyne, O salmon of the Liffey, since I cannot keep my brother here I am loath to part from him. O Rider of the Wave, your enemy intends that you should not return. But your going is cause for pity. This heavy morn my eyes are filled with tears.'

Once more the sons of Turenn cast off onto the waves of the unforgiving sea. In a quarter year they had gone far from men, and then Brian put on his water-clothes and walked in the sea, looking for Fincara, the Island of Fair-Haired Women. He found it and went to the court, but all he saw was a band of women sewing and embroidering. In their midst was a bright cooking-spit lying on the table.

As he snatched up the spit the women began laughing and called out to him, 'That's a brave deed for your hand. The least of our women could make you hop most painfully, you and your brothers also. But for all that, we like the look of your daring, so take the spit along with you, and good luck to you.'

Brian bade them farewell and returned to his brothers just as their hearts were beginning to fail at his absence. Then away they sailed to the north of the world to look for the Hill of Midkena. After they landed, and the guardian of the hill saw them coming, he set on Brian, and the two of them fought like champions till the guardian fell dead. Then the three sons of Midkena fought the three sons of Turenn, and you might come from the Eastern End of the World without seeing a better fight for greatness of blows and courageous spirit. The men of Midkena drove their spears into the sons of Turenn, but that hardly stopped them at all, and they lodged their own spears fast in the bodies of the enemy so that the men of Midkena fell into the swoon and faintness of death.

But the sons of Turenn were sorely hurt. 'Dear brothers,' said Brian, 'how is it now with you?'

'Certainly, we are near death,' said they.

'Rise up then,' replied Brian, 'and give three shouts on the hill, for I feel the mist of death descending.'

Brian raised up his brothers, all of them leaking blood like storm-driven ships on the rocks, till three painful shouts rang on the hill. When that was done, they crawled to their boat, and they were travelling the sea for a long time with faintness and heartache upon them.

At last, Brian called out, 'I see Ben Edar, and the Hill of Howth, and our father's fort, and Tara of the kings.'

'Ah, we should have our fill of health,' said his brothers, 'if only we saw that. Raise up our heads, dear brother, till we see Ireland again. Then life or death will be the same to us.'

In the evening they came to Ben Edar and were carried to their father's house. Brian gave the cooking-spit to his father and told him to take it to Lugh. And he begged his father to bring back the pig-skin of Greece that had the healing of bodies in it.

'Ask for it,' said Brian, 'for the sake of friendship, for we are of one blood. Let him not return hardness for hardness. And dear father, be quick on the journey, or you will find us gone before you.'

But Lugh of the Long Hand denied them the pig-skin. He would not give it up even when the father returned to Tara carrying on his back the pitiful figure of Brian.

'You shall not have the skin that heals,' said Lugh. 'If you offered me as much gold as would span the world, I would not take it from you. It pleases me that death shall come to the sons of Turenn, in payment for the deadly deed they have done.'

When Brian heard this, there was no remedy but to go to the place where his two brothers lay. He rested between them, and the life went out of all three of them at the same time.

THE FATE OF
THE CHILDREN OF LIR

After the battle of Tailltin, when the Tuatha De Danann chose a king for the five provinces of Ireland, Lir heard that it was given to Bodb Derg, son of the Dagda. Lir went away with his mouth closed, for he thought he had a right to be king. The others were wishing to attack him, and burn his house, but Bodb Derg stopped them.

'That man,' he said, 'knows how to defend himself. Besides, I am still king, despite him.'

And so it rested. After a while Lir's wife died from him. That came very hard on Lir, and there was heaviness on his mind. There was great talk of the death in all Ireland, and the news came to the house of Bodb.

'If Lir minded it now,' said he, 'I could do him good friendship. I have here with me the three girls of the best shape, and the best appearance, and the best name in all Ireland:

that is to say my own dear foster-children Eve, Eva and Alva, the daughters of Ailill of Aran.'

The Tuatha De Danann said these were good words, and a message was sent to the house of Lir to say, 'If you have a mind to put yourself under the rule of the son of the Dagda, he will give you one of his foster-children for a wife.'

The offer pleased Lir. He set out next day with fifty chariots from Shee Finnaha, and he went every short way till he came quickly to Bodb's house on Loch Derg. There was a fine welcome for him and merry attendance that night.

The three daughters of Ailill were sitting in the hall, as quiet as you please, and Bodb said to Lir, 'Take your choice among them there, my three pretty nurslings.'

Lir saw them all and then looked aside. 'I cannot say which is my choice,' he replied. 'But she who is the oldest is the noblest and the best for me.'

That night, he chose Eve, the eldest, for his wife, and at the end of two weeks took her away to his own house for the wedding-feast.

In good time Eve gave birth to two children, a daughter and a son, whose names were Finnola and Aed. Then she was brought to bed again with two sons, Fichra and Conn. But she herself died in this childbirth, to the grief of Lir. Only that his mind was tender for his four children he would have gone near to death for sadness.

There was wailing among the people for her death, and Bodb Derg also lamented.

'We grieve this death,' he said, 'for our daughter's sake, and for the sake of the good man whom she bound to us. But I will stay ever close to him and give him now for wife my foster-child Eva.'

Lir came for the girl, and married her. And Eva held her sister's children in honour and affection. Certainly, no one at all could see those four mites without giving them the heart's love.

Bodb Derg came often to Lir's house for the sake of those children, and he took them often to his own estate. About this time the Tuatha De Danann came to celebrate the Feast of Age on the Hill of Shee Finnaha, where Lir was, and the beauty of those four children was a joy to everyone. Lir was glad in the sight of his children, and rose up at daybreak with them, and lay down among them at night.

Soon a fire of jealousy was lit in Eva, and she formed a hatred for her sister's children. She let on to have a strange sickness that lasted nigh a year, and all the time she was planning a cruel treachery against the children of Lir. She put the children in her chariot, as if to go to the house of Bodb Derg. On the journey, she took aside the guards and soldiers.

'Kill now the children of Lir, who have displaced my love in their father's breast,' she said. 'Then choose your reward from the good things of the world.'

'This is a bad deed you thought of,' they replied, 'and harm will come to you from it.'

So she took a sword herself, to kill the children. But being a woman with no good courage and no strength in mind she could not do it.

They continued their journey westward to the Lake of the Oaks, in Westmeath, and stopped there to rest. It was a hot day, so Eva told the children to swim in the lake, and they did so willingly. As soon as Eva saw them in the clear water she touched them with a druid's wand and put them into the shape of four white swans.

'Off with you,' she cried, 'on the water's wave, your luck is gone forever. Let your friends be sorrowful, but your laments will be lost in the clamour of the birds.'

'Witch,' Finnola called out, 'it is a bad thing you have done, and an evil friendship, to destroy us without cause. But vengeance for it will come upon you from those who love us. Tell us at least the bounds of this enchantment. When will it stop?'

'It will be the worse for you that you asked me,' said Eva. 'But I will tell you: three hundred years here on smooth Lake Darvra, and three hundred years on the Sea of Moyle between Ireland and Scotland, and three hundred years in the west, between Erris and the Isle of Glora – all these are to be your journeys. And your time of enchantment shall not end till the prince of the North weds the woman of the South.'

Then Eva repented a little, before these faces so sorrowful.

'There is no other help,' she said, 'to give you now, except you may keep your own Irish tongue. You will still be singing the sweet music of the magic *shee*, to lull men to sleep, and there will be no music in the world equal to it. You will keep also your sense and your reason, to lighten the load of your animal shape.

'Now go your way from my sight, you children of Lir, with your faces so pale and your Irish murmuring. Nine hundred years will you be on the waters, and a long time of pain it is indeed. The heart of Lir, that man of many victories, is now no more than a husk of death. His groaning will be a sickness to me, though it is I who have done this treacherous act.'

Then she whipped up the horses of the chariot and rode on to the house of Bodb Derg where there was a welcome for her.

'But where are the children of Lir?' said the son of the Dagda.

'I will tell you that,' said she. 'Lir has no liking for you. He will not trust them with you, for fear you might keep them altogether.'

'That is a wonder indeed, for those children are dearer to me than my own.'

He thought it was the deceit of the woman that had caused this, so he sent messengers to Shee Finnaha.

'Your children are not come to the house of Bodb Derg,' they said to Lir, 'and Eva says it is yourself who withholds them.'

Lir was in great sorrow when he heard this news, for then he understood well that his wife was trying to make an end of the four children. On the morrow he followed the road they had taken. As he went by the shores of Loch Darvra, his children saw his chariot and horses.

'A welcome to those horses,' said Finnola. 'By the sadness of them I think it is us they are following. Surely it is none other than Lir.'

At the edge of the lake, Lir heard swans calling to him in the voices of people.

'O Lir,' cried the swans, 'we are your own four children, destroyed out of jealousy by your wife, our mother's sister. There is no way to help us. No one in the world can change back our shape till the end of nine hundred years.'

When Lir and his people heard this, they gave three heavy groans of grief and sorrow and lament. That night, as they camped by the lake, the swans made them the sweet Irish music of the *shee*, and their hearts were eased a little. At dawn, Lir rose up to leave, and he laid this complaint on the quiet waters.

'O Finnola and handsome Conn,' he cried, 'O Aed and Fichra of the beautiful arms, I must leave though I am not ready. I lie down at night but I cannot sleep. To be parted from you torments my heart. I threw a cruel net about you, when I took Eva into my house. But how could I know what it would bring upon me?'

Then Lir went quickly to the house of Bodb Derg and told him what he knew. It was clear to the son of the Dagda that Lir spoke only the truth. Bodb sent for Eva and gave her hard words.

'This treachery of yours,' he said with anger, 'will be the worse for yourself in the end. What is the shape you hate the most?'

'The worst of it would be,' she said, 'to become a demon of the air.'

'And so you shall be,' said Bodb. Then touching her with his druid's wand he turned her immediately into a demon of the air. In that shape she rode way on the wind. She is in it yet, and will stay so till the end of life and time.

All the peoples of Ireland, the Tuatha De Danann and the Sons of Mile, used to be coming to the lake to hear the music of the swans. For there was never anything heard in Ireland to compare with that music. The men of Ireland gathered there every day, to be telling stories and talking with teachers and friends. And every night they listened to the sweet music of the *shee*. All who heard that music slept sound, free from the trouble and sickness that rest on mankind.

For three hundred years these meetings went on. Then on a certain day Finnola said to her brothers, 'Do you know our time here is almost spent? There is but one night left.'

And there was sorrow on the children of Lir, for they thought it better to be talking sweet Irish by the fair lake than to be swimming at Moyle on the cold north sea.

On the morrow they made ready to fly away.

'Farewell friends and kinsfolk,' called Finnola to the people. 'O farewell Bodb Derg, wisest of kings, and farewell our dear father, Lir of the White Field Hill. O most pleasant company, my grief it is not to see you again. We are banished to Moyle, of the tormented sea, for three hundred years, far from the dance of music and the talk of kin. It is a most sorrowful parting.'

Then airily they took flight to the Sea of Moyle, and those left behind in sadness, the people of Ireland, from this moment forbade for all time the killing of swans.

When the children of Lir came to their new home, they saw a wide coast filled with cold and storm. It was a bad dwelling-place for them. Often wind and gale drove them apart, and they struggled to meet again by the Rock of the Seals. Great storms, and the flash of lightning, and high-stepping waves scattered them to the ends of the ocean. Finnola, on the Rock of the Seals, waited often in fear for the calm day and rising sun to bring her dear brothers into safety, back under the feathers of her breast.

'O my brothers,' she would sigh, 'it was a foul night for us, and many others like this one are before us still.'

They lived there long, in the misery of the Moyle, till a night came such as they had never known before for frost and snow and wind and cold. They were on the Rock of the Seals and the water froze about them, and their feet and their feathers froze to the rock. They could not move at all. With great stirring, at last they tore themselves away, but they left feathers and the tips of the their wings and the skin of their feet stuck to the rock.

'Now our state is bad indeed,' said Finnola, 'for we cannot bear the salt water to touch our wounds. It will be the death of us. One daughter and three sons, surely it is a pity the way we are, torn from the ragged rocks, our only feast the salt water of the blue tide.'

Their feather grew again, and for a long time they went here and there, drifting on the mournful waters of the Sea of Moyle. Then one day, by chance, they came to the mouth of the Bann, in the north part of Ireland. On the shore-side, they saw bright-coloured horsemen, with white horses under them, riding the road from the southwest.

'What men are those?' they wondered. 'Surely they are from the Tuatha De Danann, or from the Sons of Mile. They have the look of our own people.'

The children of Lir swam close to the shore and called out in the voice of humans, and they mixed their talk with the troop of the horsemen. The chief men in this troop were two of the sons of Bodb Derg, that is to say Aed of the Quick Wits and Fergus the Chess Player, and they had riding with them a third of the warriors of the *shee*.

'What news,' said the children of Lir, 'of our people, of our father Lir, of the noble king?'

'They are well,' came the reply, 'in one place together, in your father's house at Shee Finnaha. There is no unhappiness on them, except for the lack of you yourselves, and not knowing what came of you after you left the Lake of the Oaks.'

Then Finnola answered with a heavy heart, 'That is not the way with us, for we have ageless misery on the tides of the sea. There is pleasure tonight in the house of Lir, with ale and wine for good company, but only a cold dwelling-place for his four poor children. Once we dressed in purple and drank the laughter-giving mead. Now the rock is our bed and feathers our bedclothes, and bitter water our only drink. The king's court used to ride after us to the Hill of Bodb. I remember the teaching of Manannan, the talk of the king on the pleasant ridge, the voice and sweet kisses of Angus. Now I waste my strength, to and fro without end, on the angry current of the Moyle.'

'There is no help for it,' cried the men of the Tuatha De Danann. 'We have no power to change you. But all will become well in the end of time.'

Then for the children of Lir their years were finished on the Sea of Moyle, and a new time of trial began on the western ocean, stark cold and gale-tossed between Erris and the Isle of Glora. Another three hundred years they had of it there. Then Finnola called her brothers gladly for the flight home.

Lightly they flew to Shee Finnaha. But the place was empty before their eyes, nothing in it but green hillocks and thickets of nettles, without house, without hearthstone, without fire.

'This is a wonder to me,' Finnola lamented, 'a broken house, without a chief, without women, without hounds for hunting. It was not thus in our father's day – no horns, no cups, no drinking. The stables are empty, the riders gone. Grass and bushes cover the ruins. The person is not living who would know us. Strange would we be to any visitor.'

The children of Lir stopped that night in the place of their father and their grandfather, and they sang the sweet sad music of the *shee*. In the morn, they rose up early and flew to the Isle of Glora, and all the birds of the land gathered around them at the Lake of the Birds. Each day, they went to feed to Iniskea and to Achill, to the western isles of Connacht and to the place where Donn, son of Mile, was drowned and buried. Then each night they returned to sleep on the Isle of Glora.

Now, there came a time when blessed Patrick and the faith of Christ arrived in Ireland, and Saint Kemoc went into the Isle of Glora. The first night he was there the children of Lir heard the voice of his bell ringing near them. They started up, and the brothers said, 'What is that weak, unpleasing voice we hear?'

''Tis the bell of Kemoc,' said Finnola, 'and through that bell we shall be free of our pain and misery.'

They listened to the bell till the matins were done, and then they began to sing the sweet sad music of the *shee*.

Kemoc heard their singing and went down to the lake. But he saw only four swans on the water.

'Is it you,' he said, 'that are the children of Lir?'

'Indeed we are,' they replied.

'Then I give thanks to God,' said he, 'since I came to this island for your sakes. Let you come to land now, and give me your trust, that you may do good deeds and depart from your sins.'

So they came to land and trusted Kemoc. He brought them to his own little place, and then he asked a good smith to make chains of bright silver. One he fixed between Aed and Finnola, and the other between Conn and Fichra. And the four of them gladdened his heart and his mind. The swans were content to rest in peace and had their troubles on the wide sea put behind them.

At that time, the king of Connacht was Largnen, son of Colman, and his wife was Decca, daughter of Finnin. And the joining of this pair was the coming together that Eva had spoken of long ago, when a prince of the North should marry a woman of the South. Now, the woman Decca heard talk of the wonderful swans, with their sadness and their music, and she had a great desire to have them. Her husband sent messengers to Kemoc to ask for the birds, but he would not give them up.

In anger Largnen himself went to the place of Kemoc. He grabbed hold of the swans, two birds in each hand, and pulled them from the little altar, to bring them to Decca. But no sooner had he touched them than their skins fell off, and what was in their place but three withered men and a wrinkled old woman with scant flesh or blood?

Then the king jumped with fright and instantly left that place. When he was gone, Finnola said to Kemoc, 'Come, holy man, baptize us now, for the time of our death is near, though it will be a sorrow for us all to part from each other. Make our grave here and lay Conn at my right side and Fichra at my left, and put Aed before my face in the compass of my arms.'

The children of Lir were baptized, and they died. They

were buried as Finnola had said, with Conn at her right side and Fichra at her left and Aed before her face. A stone was put over them, and their names were written in Ogham. That night, there was a wailing at their going, but their souls were already on the road into heaven.

MANAWYDAN, SON OF LLYR

There was a time when Manawydan looked about him, and on his companions, and he heaved a great sigh and felt much grief and longing within him.

'Alas, unhappy that I am,' he said to Pryderi, 'there is none save me without a place of my own.'

'Lord, be not so sad,' said Pryderi. 'You have never coveted land nor office. Not without reason are you called one of the Three Ungrasping Chieftains. But hear now what I have to say. Seven estates of Dyfed were left to me, and Rhiannon my mother is there. Her and the land both I will bestow on you. Had you no other land except those seven estates, yet would you be well pleased with yourself. And as for Rhiannon, who is more pleasant than she? In her youth there was none more beautiful, and even now her looks will still make you glad.'

Together they went to Arberth in Dyfed, and Rhiannon and Pryderi's wife Cigfa prepared a feast for their coming. Then Manawydan and Rhiannon began to sit together and talk. As they talked, his head and heart grew tender towards her.

'Pryderi,' he called out, 'I will keep to your offer.'

'What offer was that?' said Rhiannon.

'Lady,' replied Pryderi, 'I have bestowed you as wife upon Manawydan, son of Llyr.'

'I will abide by that,' said Rhiannon.

'And gladly will I too,' said Manawydan.

Before the feast ended he slept with her, and a great celebration began. After a time, as they were sitting in the midst of company, there was a mighty peal of thunder and a fall of mist so that none could see the other. After the mist every place was filled with light. But when they looked up, where before they had seen flocks and herds and houses, now they could see no manner of thing. Neither house nor beast nor smoke nor fire nor man nor dwelling was there. The court was empty, desolate, uninhabited. All their company was lost and gone save the four of them only, Manawydan and Pryderi and their wives.

'Alas, where is our court and company?' said Manawydan in wonder. So they looked in the hall and the bower and the sleeping-chamber, and not a soul was there. They looked in the cellar and the scullery and the kitchen, and all was desolation.

There was no help for it but to eat and hunt and take their pleasure. They wandered, each one, here and there in the land, but no person or house could they see, only wild beasts. They lived on the meat of the hunt and on fish and on the gifts of nature. They passed a year, and a second, and at last they grew weary.

'By our faith,' said Manawydan, 'we cannot live like this.' But they kindled fire and hunted and went on for another year.

One morning, Pryderi and Manawydan made ready their dogs for hunting. Soon the dogs drove a wild boar out of a thicket, and they bayed after it. They followed it close, pursuing it into a large fort, newly built, in a place where neither stonework nor building had been seen before. From the top of a mound the men looked and listened for the dogs, but they neither saw nor heard them.

'We never saw this fort here,' said Pryderi. 'Let us be warned not to go inside. Surely he who has put this spell on the land has also made this fort. But faith, I'll not lose my dogs.' And at once he ran into the fort.

In the middle of the floor he saw a marble fountain, with a golden bowl at its edge fastened to four chains that went up into the air without any ends in sight. Wondering at the beauty of the gold and the exceeding fine work of the bowl, Pryderi took hold of it. But his hands stuck to the bowl, and his feet to the marble slab below it. The power of speech was driven from his mouth, and thus he stood all dumb.

Manawydan waited outside till the close of day. He was afraid to enter, so he went away and told Rhiannon what had happened.

'You are a bad friend,' she said, 'but a good comrade have you lost.'

Then she went quickly to the fort, and finding the gate open she went in at once. When she saw Pryderi with his hands fast on the bowl, she laid hold to help him, and then she herself was stuck fast and unable to utter a word. In this way, they were rooted till nightfall, when once again there was a peel of thunder and a fall of mist, and the fort vanished and they too.

When Cigfa saw that her husband was gone and there was no one left to her but Manawydan, she cried that she might as well be dead. But Manawydan rebuked her.

'Have no fear of me,' he said. 'I give you my word that you will find no truer friend. Were I in the very flush of youth, still I would keep faith with Pryderi, and for your sake too I will keep it.' Then she was content and thanked him.

'But we cannot stay here,' he went on. 'We have lost our dogs and cannot hunt for food. Let us try some other place.'

As they made their way through Dyfed towards Arberth, Manawydan found that he had in the folds of his clothes some ears of wheat. He set up his dwelling in Arberth, in the place that had pleased him most when Rhiannon and Pryderi were with him. He fished and snared wild animals, and afterwards he began to till the ground and sow three fields of wheat. The wheat sprang up, the best in the world, and his crop thrived. No mortal had seen finer wheat.

In time the harvest was ripe and he thought, 'I'll reap it in the morning.' In the grey dawn he came with his sickle, but he found all the stalks naked, with the ears of the wheat broken off and carried away. And on the next morn, so it was with the second field.

'Who is doing this thing that ruins me,' said Manawydan, 'and ruins the country also?' That night he decided to keep watch over his third field.

Towards midnight he heard the greatest commotion in the world. He looked and saw a mighty host of mice, so many they seemed numberless. Mice were running up all the stalks of the wheat, biting off the ears and leaving the stalks naked. There was not a single stalk that had not a mouse on it.

In anger he rushed amid the mice. But it was like attacking a swarm of gnats or a flight of starlings. The mice divided and flowed and eddied about him like water. One, at least, he could see was heavy and dull with no fleetness of foot. So he caught that mouse and put it in his glove and tied up the mouth with string. When he returned home, he greeted Cigfa and stirred the evening fire and hung the glove by its string from a peg.

'What is there, my lord?' said she.

'A thief,' he replied, 'whom I caught red-handed.'

'But what kind of thief,' she asked, 'could you put in your glove?'

Then he told her the tale, how his crops had been laid waste by the mice. 'One only was I able to catch, and I will hang that mouse tomorrow.'

'My lord, you are right to be angry,' she said. 'Yet consider, is it seemly for a man of rank and dignity to hang such a little creature? Do not meddle with such nothingness. Let it go.'

'If I could have caught them,' said Manawydan, 'I would have hanged them all, else I would be shamed. But this one I will hang.'

'Do what you will,' she said. 'I only speak to keep you from discredit.'

On the morrow he took the mouse to Gorsedd Arberth. On the highest point he planted two sticks. While he was doing this he saw a reverend clerk coming towards him, dressed in old, poor, threadbare clothes. Now it was seven years since Manawydan had last set eyes on any human other than his three companions – and two of those were now gone from him.

'What kind of work are you doing here?' asked the man.

'Hanging a thief.'

'What kind of thief? I see a creature in your hand very like a mouse. Let it go. It ill becomes a man of your rank to touch such a thing.'

'I will not let it go,' said Manawydan. 'I caught it thieving, and I will execute on it the law of thieves.'

'My lord, lest a man of your rank should be seen in such work, I will give you a pound that I have taken in alms, if you will let the creature go.' But Manawydan refused, and away went the clerk.

Manawydan began to fix a crossbeam to the forks, and then he saw a priest on a horse approaching.

'A blessing on you,' called the priest. 'What work are you doing there?'

'Hanging a thief,' he answered.

'What thief is that, my lord?'

'A creature in the shape of a mouse. It has stolen from me, and the doom of a thief will I give it.'

'My lord, lest you be seen handling that lowly thing, I will redeem it for three pounds. Let it go.'

'Between me and God,' said Manawydan, 'I want no price for it, save what is its due. And that is to hang.' So away went the priest.

Then Manawydan put a noose of string around the neck of the mouse. But as he was drawing it up he saw a bishop with his followers and his loads and his baggage making towards him.

'My lord,' cried the bishop, 'is not that a mouse I see in your hand, that you are about to hang?'

'It is a mouse, and a thief also.'

'Why, man, let the silly thing go. I will redeem it for seven pounds, lest a man of such rank should be seen destroying a worthless creature.'

'By God, I will not let it go.'

'Yea, you shall let it go, and I will give you four and twenty pounds of ready money.'

'I will not, not for as much again.'

'Then I will give you all the horses you see on this plain, and also my own seven horses and the seven loads of baggage that go with them.'

'By heaven, I still say no.'

'Well,' said the bishop, 'name your price for that worthless mouse.'

'It is that Rhiannon and Pryderi be set free.'

'You shall have it.'

'Still the mouse dies.'

'What more then?'

'Let the charms and enchantments be removed from the seven estates of Dyfed. Also, I would know who this mouse is.'

'She is my wife,' said the bishop, 'and were it not so I would take no trouble to free her. I am Llwyd, son of Cil Coed. It was I who cast the enchantments over the seven estates of Dyfed, to avenge the trick that Pryderi played on Gwawl, son of Clud. Hearing that you dwelt in this land, my soldiers asked me to change them into mice that they might destroy your corn. That happened on the first and second nights. On the third night my wife and the ladies of her court also asked to become mice, and I did that too. But she was great with child, and heavy and slow, or else you would not have caught her. Now I will give you Pryderi and Rhiannon and remove the enchantment, if you will let her go.'

But Manawydan answered, 'I will not let her go.'

'Well, what more then?' said Llwyd.

'Never again put any spell on the seven estates of Dyfed.'

'Easily agreed.'

'Yet still your wife shall not be free.'

'What now?'

'Promise further that no more vengeance shall fall on Pryderi and Rhiannon, nor upon me.'

'Faith, that was a shrewd stroke, but you shall have it. But for that condition no end of harm would have lighted on your head. Now set her free.'

'One last thing. I shall not let her go till I see Pryderi and Rhiannon safe and well.'

'See,' said Llwyd, 'here they are coming.'

Then Manawydan rose up to greet his dear friends. He welcomed them in joy and they sat down to talk.

'Ah, my good lord,' cried Llwyd, 'do not play false with me. You have received what you asked. Now set my wife free.'

Manawydan took the noose from the neck of the mouse, and Llwyd touched her with his wand and changed her into the fairest young woman that any had seen.

'Look now on this wide land,' said Llwyd. 'See the houses and the courts and the people, they are now as fair as they ever were.'

So they all rose up and looked about. And they saw all the land inhabited and complete again, with all its herds and flocks and people and dwellings.

Then Manawydan said to Llwyd, 'What pains and servitude did you put on Pryderi and Rhiannon?'

'Pryderi,' he replied, 'had the weights of the gates of my court hung about his neck, and Rhiannon had about her neck the collars of the asses after they had carried the hay. That was the extent of their pain and imprisonment. But that story is ended now.'

THE DREAM OF
RHONABWY

There was a time when Rhonabwy was on a quest in Powys, and he arrived for lodgings at the house of Heilyn Goch. As he and his companions came towards the house they could see a black old hall with a straight gable-end, all smoke-grimed. Inside was a floor full of holes and bumps, so a man might hardly stand, and the floor was slippery with the stale and dung of cattle, mixed in with half-chewed branches of holly. Above the floor was a dusty platform of bare boards, and an old crone feeding a fire. Against the cold she threw on a lapful of husks, so that it was not easy for any man alive to endure the smoke in his nose. At the far end of the platform was a yellow ox skin, and good luck to the one of them who would get that to sleep on.

The crone greeted them rudely and they waited awhile for

66

the people of the house to return. Then there entered a wizened, bald old man with a little fuzz of red hair, and a skinny, blotched-faced woman with a bundle under her arm. And they too had no more than a cold welcome for the guests. The woman lit a meagre fire of sticks. For food, she brought them cheese and barley-bread and watered milk.

After they had eaten, a storm of wind and rain settled on the house, so that a man might hardly go out, even to relieve himself. The travellers were exceedingly weary from their journey. They drowsed and nodded, dozing without comfort in the smoke.

The resting place was covered with flea-ridden straw and the thick ends of the branches eaten by the oxen. A greyish, threadbare, flea-hopping blanket was spread on the straw, and over it was a coarse sheet in tatters, and a filthy pillow as hard as a stone. Here, sleep came heavily to Rhonabwy's two companions after the fleas and the lumps and the cold had gnawed at them. But Rhonabwy tossed about. He thought it would be less of a torture to rest on the yellow ox-skin of the platform. And there at last he slept.

As he slept, he was granted a vision. He and his companions were crossing the plain of Argyngroeg towards Rhyd-y-Groes on the Severn. Ahead of him he heard a commotion the like of which he had never heard before.

He saw a youth with yellow curly hair and a new-trimmed beard, riding a yellow horse, and his legs all in green. The tunic of the horseman was yellow brocade silk sewn with green thread, and on his thigh was a sword with a golden hilt in a scabbard of new leather with a clasp of gold and a deerskin thong. He had a mantle of yellow silk, and the fringes of this were green. And all these green colours were as green as the fronds of the fir-tree, and the yellow of it was as yellow as the flowers of the broom.

Rhonabwy and his companions fled from this large awesome figure, and the rider galloped after them. When the horse breathed out, the men fleeing grew distant from the rider, and when it breathed in they were drawn right up to the horse's chest. Then Rhonabwy and his friends asked for mercy.

'Gladly,' said the rider, 'let there be no fear upon you.'

'My good lord,' they replied, 'tell us who you are.'

'I will tell that. I am Iddawg, the Embroiler of Britain. And I will tell you the reason for that name. I was an envoy at the battle of Camlan, between Arthur and Medrawd his nephew. A bold young man was I then! I loved battle and I stirred up strife. When I was an envoy I changed fair words into ugly threats, so that Arthur and Medrawd would fight. Out of that was woven the battle of Camlan, and thus I was named Iddawg, the Embroiler of Britain. Even so, three nights before the end of the battle I was ashamed and I fled to do penance at Y Llech Las. Seven years I did penance, and then I was pardoned.'

After speaking together they all went on across the great plain as far as Rhyd-y-Groes on the Severn. A mile from the ford, on both sides of the road, they could see the tents and pavilions of a great host. From the bank of the river they saw Arthur seated on a flat island below. With Arthur were Bedwin the bishop and Gwarthegydd the counselor and a big auburn-haired youth. This young man had his sword in his hand, and about him was a tunic of pure black silk. His face was as white as ivory and his eyebrows were as black as jet. His wrist between his glove and his sleeve was whiter than the water-lily and thicker than the calf of a warrior's leg.

As they came up to Arthur, the king greeted them. 'God prosper you,' he said, 'but Iddawg, where did you find those little fellows?'

'I found them, lord,' said Iddawg, 'way up on the road.'

Arthur smiled, and Iddawg asked him, 'My lord, why do you laugh?'

'Nay, I am not laughing,' replied the king, 'but I feel it sad that men as mean as these now keep this Island, after men as fine as those that kept it before.'

While the king was talking, Iddawg said quietly into Rhonabwy's ear, 'Do you see the bright stone in the ring on the king's hand? It is a virtue of the ring that you shall remember all you see here tonight. Otherwise, not a whit of this would you recall.'

Then Rhonabwy looked about him and saw a troop of men coming to the ford. Every one of that troop, man and horse, was as red as blood. Each was like a pillar of fire mounting into the sky. And at the same time, another troop was coming to the ford, and their upper parts were as white as lilies and their lower parts as black as jet. The foremost rider spurred into the ford and made the water splash over Arthur, wetting him as wet as a man in the sea. Then swords were drawn and rebukes given and taken.

There was much riding to and fro, and soon many men at arms were gathered. Then a proud, handsome man came forward and said it was a marvel how a host so big was contained in a place so small. But he thought it a greater marvel that he should find here, at this very hour, those who had promissd to be in Baddon by midday, to fight against Osla Big Knife.

'Now you speak the truth,' said Arthur calmly. 'Come, let us go together.'

'Iddawg,' said Rhonabwy, 'who is he that dares to speak to Arthur in that way?'

'It is Caradawg Stout Arm, Arthur's counsellor and cousin, a man who may speak as bluntly as he wishes.'

Then Iddawg took Rhonabwy up behind him on the saddle and they set out with a great host towards Cefyn Digoll. As they passed over the river, Rhonabwy saw coming in one direction the warriors of Scandinavia, in white silk bordered with black, and in the other direction the men of Denmark, in black silk bordered with white.

Below Caer Faddon, as Iddawg and Rhonabwy joined the swelling ranks of this army of the Mighty, there was turmoil and disorder in the host. Then the call went out for Cadwr, Earl of Cornwall. He arose and took Arthur's sword in his hand, and the sword had the image of two serpents on it chased in gold. When the sword flashed, two flames of fire were seen in the mouths of the serpents, and the sight of it was dreadful and not easy to look upon. Men cast down their eyes and the tumult ceased.

Then Eiryn, Arthur's servant, advanced. He was a large,

rough-headed, ugly fellow, with a red moustache, and red hair standing up like pig's bristles. In front of Arthur he dismounted from his big red horse, which wore a parted mane, and took from his pack a golden chair and a cloak of ribbed silk. The cloak was spread on the ground, weighted by a golden apple at each corner, and the chair, big enough for three warriors, was placed on the cloak. Gwen was the name of that cloak. It was a magic cloak that made the wearer invisible.

Arthur sat on the chair in the middle of the cloak. Then he turned to Owen, son of Urien, who was standing beside him.

'Owen,' said Arthur, 'will you play at chess?'

'I will, my lord,' said Owen.

The red-headed servant set up the chessboard, gold pieces on a silver board. And they began to play.

As they bent over the game, a youth came from a white and red pavilion with a black serpent pictured on the top. Red, venomous eyes were in the serpent's head, and its tongue glowed like a flame. The blue-eyed youth had curly fair hair and a beard just sprouting. He wore a tunic of yellow silk, and greenish-yellow hose. His shoes were of speckled leather, with buckles of gold across the instep. A heavy triple-grooved sword with a gold hilt hung at his side in a scabbard of black leather.

This squire advanced and greeted Owen.

'My lord,' he said, 'is it with your leave that the king's young knights are harassing and molesting your ravens? If not, have the king call them off.'

'O king,' Owen said to Arthur, 'you hear what this squire says? If it please you, call them off my little ravens.'

'Play the game,' said Arthur. And the squire returned to his pavilion.

They finished that game and started another. In the middle of that game a ruddy, keen-eyed, well-built lad, with his beard shaved, came from a bright yellow pavilion with a red lion on top. He was dressed in yellow sown with red silk. His stockings were white buckram, and his shoes were of black leather. He pulled a huge sword from a sheath of red deer-skin, and he came to the place where they were playing chess. He saluted Owen.

'Is it your will,' he said, 'that the king's young knights should be wounding your ravens? Beseech the king to call them off.'

'My lord king,' said Owen, 'call them off.'

'Play the game,' said the king, and the squire went away.

That game was ended and another begun. Just as they were starting, they saw a spotted yellow pavilion, the largest ever seen, with the emblem of a golden eagle on it. A fair and graceful youth advanced from the pavilion, with a pale face and great hawk-like eyes. He held a standard flying from the end of a thick speckled spear, with the bright point newly sharpened. He rode in rage and passion at a quick canter to the place where the chess was being played.

'The best of the ravens are slain,' he shouted to Owen, 'and the others so wounded and hurt that not one of them can rise up on wings six feet from the ground.'

'My lord,' said Owen, 'call off your men.'

'Play the game,' said the king, 'if you will.'

Then Owen turned to the squire and said, 'Away with you. Where the battle is thickest raise high the standard, and let it be as God wills.'

So the squire raised the standard in the thickest part of the battle. As the standard was raised, so too the ravens rose into the air in rage and courage. They threw off their fear as they felt the wind in their wings. They recovered their magic power and strength, and they swooped down to earth on the men who had given them injury and loss. They struck the heads off some, and from others they plucked eyes or ears or arms. There was a thrashing and clamour in the air, and anguish and agony on the ground from wounded and dying men. In amazement at the great noise, Arthur and Owen looked up from the chess.

They saw coming towards them a rider in strange barbaric colours, vermilion and yellow and green and dapple-grey, and each part of him was in a colour different to another part. He wore the armour of a distant land, and his helmet was crested with the emblem of a yellow-red leopard. Which was the worse to look on, the leopard of the helm or the man's fierce face? This horseman held a long spear and on its point were the blood and guts of the ravens.

'O king,' said this grim knight, 'the ravens are slaying your young men.'

Arthur looked at Owen and said, 'Call off your ravens.'

'My lord,' said Owen, 'play the game.'

They played on. Around them they could hear the howls of the men and the shrieks of the ravens as they dashed and tore at their enemy and let them fall in pieces to the ground.

Then out of this tumult rode a horseman in heavy green armour on a white horse. The coverings and trappings of the horse were pure black with fringes of yellow. On the rider's head was a helm with the crest of a golden lion, and a tongue of flame a foot-length came from the mouth of the lion. In his hand he had a blood-stained lance of ash-wood.

'My good lord,' he cried to Arthur, 'your young knights have been slain, those noble sons of the Island of Britain. Now who will defend the Island from this day forth?'

'Owen,' said Arthur, 'call off your ravens.'

'My lord,' he replied, 'play this game.'

That game ended and another began. As they played towards the end-game of the chess, out of the blood and turmoil came a large stern knight on a handsome black horse. His cloak was purple and his helmet was crested with a griffin. In a rage he galloped all hot and bloody to within a foot of Arthur.

'My lord,' he shouted, 'my warriors are dead and my army destroyed. It is the work of the ravens.'

Then Arthur took the golden pieces of the chessboard and crushed them till they were dust.

'Owen,' he said, 'tell your standard-bearer, Gwres, son of Rheged, to lower his banner.'

Therewith the standard was lowered and all was peace.

When the fighting was over, Osla Big Knife sent four and

twenty knights to King Arthur, to ask for a truce for a month and a fortnight.

Arthur summoned his council of chief men, and with him were Bedwin the bishop, and Gwarthegydd, son of Caw, and March, and Caradawg Stout Arm, and many other bold men. And while they talked bards came with the songs of their poems. All they sang was in praise of Arthur, but never a man could understand such rich and wonderful words except he be Cadyrieith the bard himself.

After this, twenty-four asses arrived with their loads of gold and silver, bringing tribute to Arthur from the Isles of Greece. The truce was granted to Osla Big Knife for a month and a fortnight, and the treasure brought by the asses was given to the bards, in reward for their songs.

Then Cei arose and said to the whole company, 'Whoever will follow Arthur, let him be with us tonight in Cornwall. As for the others, let them meet with Arthur at the end of the truce.'

At once, there was a swirl of men and horses, and a stamping and a shouting, and in the midst of this noise Rhonabwy awoke. He was stiff and cold on the yellow ox-skin, and he had slept for three nights and three days.

3

FABLES
AND
TALKING BEASTS

'Here's meat and music!' said the fox
as he ate the bagpipe.

FABLES

A fox caught a fine fat goose asleep by the side of a loch. As the goose was cackling and hissing, the fox taunted her.

'Weel now, cackle away,' said Rory, 'but if you had me in your mouth, as I have you, what would you be doing?'

'Why,' said the goose, 'that's an easy question. I'd fold my hands, shut my eyes, say a grace, and eat you.'

'Exactly,' said Rory.

He folded his hands, put on a solemn face, shut his eyes, and said grace. As he did so, the goose spread her wings and was off, halfway over the loch.

'I'll make a rule of this,' muttered Rory as he licked his dry lips, 'never in my life to say grace till after I feel the warm meat in my belly.'

A fox and a cock were talking one day.

'How many tricks can you do?' said the fox.

'I can do three,' said the cock. 'How about yourself?'

'At least three score and thirteen,' said the fox scornfully.

'Surely that's a great number. Tell me one.'

'Well, my grandfather taught me to shut one eye and give a great shout.'

''Tis nothing,' said the cock. 'I could do that myself.'

And the cock closed an eye and crowed fit to burst. But the eye he shut was the one next to the fox, so the fox grabbed him by the neck and was away with him.

But the good housewife saw her cock being carried away and cried out, 'Let go of that bird. He's mine.'

At this, the cock whispered to the fox, 'Tell her that this cock now belongs to you.'

The fox opened his mouth to speak and out dropped the cock. In a moment he had flown up to the roof of the house, with one eye shut, and crowing to beat the band.

A magpie had a nest in the holly-bush, but the fox robbed it and ate the young ones. So the magpie had no love for the fox.

One day when the fox had nothing to eat, he met the magpie.

'Fine day,' said she.

'Fine day,' said the fox, 'but I'm fasting.'

'No need for that,' said the magpie, 'you'll eat soon enough.'

Two girls were going to the turf bog with baskets on their heads. One had bread and butter in her basket, and the other had a load of curds. The magpie flew softly on top of one basket and threw down bread and butter, then she flew onto the other and threw down the curd. The fox gobbled it all up, as much as he could, and soon he had to lie down to ease his belly.

'Now I'm fit to burst,' groaned the fox, 'what will I do?'

'Rest you quietly there,' said the magpie. 'I'll steal some medicine from the doctor and give you a purge.'

But the magpie flew fast to the man who kept hounds.

'In such and such a place,' she said, 'you'll find a fox who has eaten too much and can't move. Fetch your hounds and kill him.'

The magpie flew back to the fox and said, 'The doctor himself is coming. He's got the medicine for you.'

It wasn't long before one of the hounds bayed, and the fox cocked an ear.

'Is it the hounds?' he cried.

'Just a small one chasing the sheep,' said she.

But the hounds came with a rush, snarling and snapping. As the fox shook himself in terror, the magpie called out, 'Here's your purge. Try it now.'

The fox shook and stretched and tried to run but it was no use. The hounds caught him and tore him to pieces. That's the purge he got.

The eagle and the wren were seeing who could fly the highest. The winner was to be king of the birds. The wren flew away first, straight up. But the eagle came by, soaring easily in great circles. The wren was tired, so as the eagle passed he settled himself softly on the eagle's broad back.

At last, the eagle was growing weary.

'Where are you, wren?' he cried.

'I'm here,' answered the wren, 'just a little above you.'

And so the wren won that match.

The old crow was teaching the young one and she said to him: 'If you see one coming, and a thin stick in his oxter with a broad end to it, flee. That will be a gun, and he'll mean to kill you. If you see one bending down to lift a pebble, flee. That will be a stone he means to throw at you. But if you see one coming fair, straight ahead, without stopping or stooping, with nothing in his oxter, don't stir. That one will not touch you.'

'But what,' said the young one, 'if the stone is in his pocket?'

'Oh no,' said the old crow, 'be off with you. I see you need no more instruction.'

There was a woman before now, and she bore a hen in the rocks by the shore.

When the hen grew big, she used to be going to the king's house every day to get something to give to her mother. One day the king saw her.

'Nasty little creature,' he said, 'what are you doing standing upon my door?'

'Well,' said the hen, 'I may be little, and even nasty, but I can do a thing your fine big queen cannot.'

'What is that?' said the king.

'I can spring from rafter to rafter, with the tongs and the pot-hook trailing after me.'

So the hen did it, and the queen tried it. The queen took a spring out of herself, and she cut the edge of her two shanks, and she fell and the brain went out of her.

The king had four queens but the hen put them all out with this trick.

'It would be better for you now,' said the hen, 'to marry my mother. She is a fine woman.'

'Away with you,' cried the king. 'You have caused me enough loss already, you nasty creature.'

'It is best for you to marry her,' the hen said again.

So the king sent down for the hen's mother and had a good look at her. And the mother had a good look at him. That was satisfactory, so she herself and the king were married.

It was a bitter cold evening and the Old Crow of Achill didn't know how he would last out the night. He flew here and there till he saw, at the top of the tallest tree, a big nest. It would be a grand place to spend the night.

In the nest he found a fledgling eagle whose mother was away looking for food. The Old Crow took hold of the fledgling, and carried it off, and killed it in the wood. Then he flew back and settled in the nest.

It wasn't long before the mother eagle returned with a lump of meat. Night had fallen. She heard a stirring in the nest and dropped the meat to what she thought was her fledgling. The Old Crow ate it up quickly. Then the eagle settled down on top of him. It was a cold night, a most bitter night, and the eagle rose up and jumped about to keep warm. Never, she complained, had there been a colder night.

The Old Crow of Achill was in a sweat the whole night, warm under the breast-feathers, but he feared that the eagle would see him at dawn and kill him. So as the eagle was hopping up and down, moaning about the cold, the Old Crow piped up.

'This last night was nothing much,' he said. 'Certainly there's been a colder one.'

'How do you know that,' said the eagle, 'and you barely a month out of the shell?'

'Old May Night,' said the Crow, 'that was certainly a colder night. If you don't believe me, see the old Blackbird of the Forge. She'll tell you.'

The eagle still didn't believe it, but she flew off to the forge and found the Blackbird standing on an iron rod.

'Last night,' said the eagle, 'was the coldest I've ever known. I spent it rising up and down to try to keep warm. But my chick, not a month out of the shell, told me at dawn that there had once been a colder night, and that you would know it.'

'Certainly,' said the Blackbird, 'last night was the coldest I've ever felt. I've been here since I was young. The iron rod I'm standing on was long and thick at the time. Once every seven years I rub my beak on it, and if I rub it once more it will break. I've been here that long, and I can tell you last night was the coldest yet. But why don't you ask the Bull in the Field, he will know.'

The eagle flew off and she never stopped till she came to the Bull. She told her story and asked the Bull if there had ever been a colder night.

'I've been here for thousands of years,' said the Bull. 'Each year my two horns fall off and go to make the fence around this great field. Now, only two are wanting to complete the fence, that's how long I've been here. And last night was the coldest night I've known. But the Blind Salmon of Assaroe is older than I. Maybe he can help you.'

So the eagle flew far away and she didn't stop till she saw the Blind Salmon swimming in his usual river.

'Are you the Blind Salmon of Assaroe?' said the eagle.

'That I am,' said he.

'Did you feel the cold last night?'

'That I did.'

'Tell me, was there ever a colder night?'

'Certainly,' said the Blind Salmon, 'there was a night colder than last night. It was on Old May Night long ago. I was here in this river. It was so cold I was jumping up and down in the water. It was freezing so hard that, one time when I jumped, the water froze while I was in the air and I froze on top of the ice. I was as stiff as a log and helpless. Soon after daybreak who should be passing but the Old Crow of Achill? When he saw me stuck in the ice, down he flew and started to peck. He made a hole in the ice and pecked out my eye and ate it. Ever since I've been called the Blind Salmon of Assaroe. But look you here,' the Blind Salmon went on, 'don't you think it was the Old Crow of Achill, and not your fledgling, in your nest last night?'

'Ah, surely not,' cried the eagle.

'It was,' said the Blind Salmon. 'Only he would know about the Old May Night.'

The mother eagle sped home in a panic. But both her chick and the Old Crow were gone. Just as well for the Old Crow. If the eagle had caught him, it would have been the end of his old, old days.

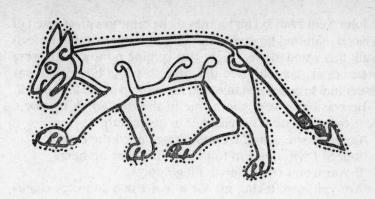

THE BROWN BEAR OF
THE GREEN GLEN

There was once a king in Ireland who had a leash of sons. John was the youngest one, and it was said that he was not wise in the head. Then his father, this good worldly king, lost the sight of his eyes and the strength of his feet.

The two eldest brothers said they would seek three bottles of water from the Green Isles, which were somewhere in the heaps of the deep. So away went these two brothers. Then the young fool said to himself that he would go also.

The first big town he reached, there he sees those blackguards, his two brothers.

'Ho, my boys,' says the young one, 'is it thus you are?'

'With swiftness of foot,' said they, 'take yourself home, or we will have your life.'

'Rest easy, lads. It is no wish of mine to stay with you.'

John went away on his journey till he came to a great desert of a wood. 'Oh ho,' he says to himself, 'it is not canny for me to walk this wood alone.' Night was coming now, and growing pretty thick. So John tied the crippled white horse that was under him to a root of a tree, and he went up in the top himself.

He was but a very short time in the tree when he saw a bear coming with a fiery cinder in his mouth.

'Come down, son of Ireland's king,' cried the bear.

'Indeed I will not. I'm thinking I am safer up here.'

'If you won't come down, I'll go up.'

'Are you, too, taking me for a fool?' said John. 'A shambling shaggy creature like you climbing a tree!' But the bear fell at once to climb the tree.

'Lord, you can do it?' said John. 'Whoa there, keep back from the trunk and I'll go down to talk to you.'

John climbed down, and they came to chatting. Then the bear asked him if he was hungry.

'Weel, by your leave,' said John, 'I am a little at this very same time.'

The bear made a wonderful watchful turnabout and caught a roebuck.

'Now, son of Ireland's king,' said he, 'is it boiled or raw that you like your share of the meat?'

'The sort of meat I'm used to,' replied John, 'would be kind of boiled.'

John got his share and when they had eaten the bear said, 'Lie down between my paws and you'll have no cause to fear till morning.'

Early next morning the bear roused John.

'It is time,' said the bear, 'to be on the soles of your feet. 'Tis a long journey, the best part of two hundred miles. But tell me, John, are you a good horseman?'

'There are worse than me,' said he.

'Then you had best get on top of me.'

He did that. But at the bear's very first leap John was flat on the earth again.

'Fie, fie,' cried John. But he struggled back on top and got a grim grip with his teeth and his nails. He was fastened to the bear in this way till they went the two hundred miles and reached a giant's house.

'Now John,' said the bear, 'you shall pass the night in this giant's house. You'll find him mighty grumpy, but say that it was the brown bear of the green glen that set you here for the night, and don't you be afraid that you'll not get a share of food and comfort.'

John went into the house, and the giant gave him a greeting.

'Son of Ireland's king,' he said, 'your coming was in the prophecy. If I didn't get your father, I have got the son. Shall I put you in the earth with my feet, or in the sky with my breath?'

'You'll do neither,' replied John, 'for it is the brown bear of the green glen that sent me.'

So that changed the tune of the giant. 'Come in,' said he, 'come in, and you shall be well taken to this night.'

And that was true, for John got meat and drink without stint, and good rest.

In the morning John and the bear went on, day after day, till they came to a second, and then a third giant.

'Now,' said the brown bear of the third one, 'I've little acquaintance with this fellow, but you'll not be long in his house before you must wrestle with him. If he is too hard on your back, you must say, "If I had the brown bear of the green glen here, that would be your master."'

Almost as soon as John went in that house, he and the giant got to grips. As they wrestled, they made a boggy bog of the rocky rock. In the hardest places they would sink to their knees, and in the softest up to their thighs, and they brought gushes of spring water from the face of the rock.

The giant gave John many a sore wrench so that at last he cried out, 'Fie, fie, if I had the brown bear of the green glen here, your leap would not be so hearty.'

No sooner had he spoken the words than the worthy bear was at his side.

'Ah, yes,' said the giant, 'now I know your business better than you do yourself, O son of Ireland's king.'

Then the giant ordered his shepherd to kill and bring home the best wether on the hill, and to throw the carcass before the great door.

'Now, John,' said the giant, 'an eagle will come to settle on this carcass. There is a wart on the ear of this eagle which you must cut off. But not a drop of blood must you spill.'

The eagle swooped down, and she was not long eating when John gave her such a close stroke of the sword that the wart was cut off without the least drop of blood. The eagle lifted her head from the carcass and put her sharp eye on John.

'Ride on the root of my wings,' said she, 'for I know your business better than you do yourself.'

Away they went on swift wings over land and sea, till they delved into the heaps of the deep where the Green Isles were.

'Quick John,' said the eagle, 'the black dogs are away. Fill your three bottles with water.'

As John was filling the bottles from the well, he saw a pretty little house, and he thought he would go in and take a look. In the first chamber he saw a full bottle. He filled a glass and drank, and it tasted good. But the bottle was still as full as before.

'I'll take this along with me,' he thought, and he added the strange bottle to his three bottles of water.

He went into another chamber and saw a loaf. He cut a slice, but the loaf was as whole as before. 'A man would be a fool to leave that,' said John, and he tucked it under his arm. In the next chamber, the same thing happened with a great round of cheese. In the last chamber he saw a young woman lying in the bed, and she was the prettiest little jewel of a girl you could ever find.

'It would be a great pity not to kiss your sweet lips, my love,' said John. And so he did.

John left the house and returned to the eagle. He jumped up between her wings and they flew over the sea back to the house of the big giant. There were some visitors in the house and the giant was giving them a great feast of meat and drink.

'Weel, John,' the giant welcomed him, 'was there ever such fine drink as this in your father's house?'

'Foo, my bold fellow,' said John, 'that's nothing. I have a drink here that is more rare than your drink and than my father's drink as well.'

Then he gave the giant a dram from his bottle, which stayed as full as before.

'Grand stuff indeed,' said the giant. 'For that, I'll give you myself two hundred notes, a bridle and a saddle, and all for that little bottle.'

'It's a bargain,' said John, 'but on this condition: you must give the bottle to the first sweetheart I had, if ever she comes this way.'

So it was agreed. And to make a long story short, John went and left the loaf and the cheese with the other two giants, under the same condition, that his first sweetheart should get them if she came that way.

At the end of these travels John went home to his father's big town in Ireland, and he saw his brothers – those black-guards! – as he had left them.

'You'd best come with me, lads,' says he, 'for I've got a dress of cloth and a bridle and a saddle for each of you.'

They went with him gladly, but as they approached their father's house they thought they had better kill him. So they set about him to do it. They left him for dead and threw the body behind a dike. Then they took his three bottles of water and home they went.

After some hours John came slowly to his wits, for he was not quite killed. He heard a cart coming down the road, clanking a load of rusty iron, and he called out, 'Whatever Christian man is there, O let him help me.'

His father's smith was the driver of the cart. He came to help John, not knowing who he was, so he picked him up and threw him among the old iron, to take him to town. As the cart jogged and jigged on the bumps, the rust went into John's every wound till he was scarred and blotched and rough-skinned and bald.

Meanwhile, at the pretty little house in the Green Isles,

the little jewel of a girl that John had left grew pale and heavy. In three quarters of a year, she gave birth to a fine baby lad.

'Lord help me,' says she, 'but how did I find this?'

'Fie, fie,' said the hen-wife, 'don't be worrying about that. Here's a bird for you. As soon as he sees the father of your son, the bird will hop on top of his head.'

Then the folk of the Green Isles were gathered from end to end, and all the people were put in the back door and out at the front. But the bird never stirred, and the father was not found. So the pretty little jewel said she would wander through the world altogether, till she found the father of her babe.

In a while of travelling she came to the house of the big giant and saw the bottle taken from her own home. 'Ah well,' she cried, 'who gave you this bottle?'

'Young John it was,' replied the giant, 'son of Ireland's king, that left it.'

'The bottle is mine,' she said, and she took it away.

In like manner she came to the houses of the other two giants, and she found and took away the loaf and the cheese. Then she journeyed some more and came at last to the house of the king of Ireland.

For her sake, five-fifths of the folk of Ireland were gathered, and the nobles of the land also. One by one, they were put in at the back door and out at the front, yet the bird did not stir.

'Is there any one other,' she asked, 'or any at all in Ireland who has not been here?'

They thought and they thought, and then the smith remembered.

'There is a bald, rough-skinned, ugly lump of a servant in my smithy,' he said, 'but surely he cannot be . . . '

'Rough or not rough,' she replied, 'bide no time but send him here.'

The servant was summoned, and no sooner did the bird see the head of this uncouth fellow than he took to flight and landed on the bald top. So it was made known that this lad was John and the father of her babe, and then she caught the dear man and kissed him.

'But John,' said the great king of Ireland, 'was it really you that fetched the three bottles of water that cured me?'

'Indeed, 'twas I.'

'Weel, then, what's to be done with your two brothers?'

'The very same thing,' said John, 'that they tried to do to me.'

In a moment, that same was done. And that was the end of those blackguards.

Then John married the pretty little jewel, who was the daughter of the king of the Green Isles. They made a great rich wedding that lasted seven years and seven days. And for all that time you could see the gold crushed from the soles of their feet to the tips of their fingers – yes, for the length of seven years and seven days.

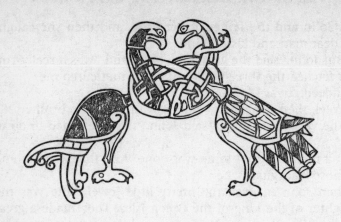

THE BATTLE
OF THE BIRDS

On this day of all the days, the creatures and the birds were gathering for battle. The son of the king of Tethertown wanted to see how the battle went. But it was over before he arrived, except for one fight between a great black raven and a snake. The victory seemed to be going to the snake, so the king's son lent a hand to the raven, and at last the raven took the head off the snake with one mighty blow.

The raven puffed out his cheeks and had a look at the dead snake. Then he said to the youth, 'For your kindness to me this day, I will give you a sight. Come up now on the root of my two wings.'

So the king's son mounted upon the raven who flew away with him over seven bens, and seven glens, and seven mountain moors.

'Now,' said the raven, 'do you see that house yonder? It is a sister of mine who makes her dwelling in it, and I'll go bail that you are welcome there. If she asks you, Were you at the battle of the birds? say that you were. And if she asks, Did you see my likeness? say that you saw it. But be sure that you meet me here in this place tomorrow morning.'

Indeed, the king's son got good and right good treatment this night, with meat of each meat, drink of each drink, warm water to his feet, and a soft bed for his limbs.

Next day, they again flew over seven bens, and seven glens, and seven mountain moors, and the king's son had the grandest entertainment as before. But on the third morning, instead of the raven to meet him, what should he find but the handsomest lad he ever saw, with a bundle in his hand.

'Ho, laddie,' said the king's son, 'has a big black raven been seen hereabouts?'

'Never again,' said the young man, 'will you see that raven, for I am that bird. I was put under spells, and it was you and our meeting that loosed me. For that you are getting this bundle. Now, turn back on the self-same steps you took before, and you will lie a night in each of the houses you saw on your way out. But do not let open the bundle till you are in the place your heart would like most for dwelling.'

The king's son turned about and put his face towards his father's house. On his way, he got lodgings from the raven's sisters, just as before. As he came near to his father's house, going through a close wood, it seemed to him that the bundle was growing heavy. He thought he would see what was in it.

He loosed the bundle and sprang back, and he was not without astonishment himself. In a twinkling he saw the very finest place that ever was. A great castle, and an orchard about the castle, in which was every kind of fruit and herb.

Then he was in wonder and regret, for it was not in his power to put it all back in his bundle. Yet he would rather have it that this grand estate would be in the pretty green hollow by his father's house. While he was thinking this, at a glance he saw a big giant coming towards him.

'Bad is this place where you've built your house, king's son,' said the giant.

'Truly, it is not here that I would wish it,' said he, 'but here it is by mishap.'

'What reward would you give if I put it all back in the bundle?'

'What would you ask?'

'Give me your first-born son,' said the giant, 'when he is seven years old.'

'If I have a son,' replied the king's son, 'you shall have him.'

In a twinkling all was returned to the bundle, the fruit and the herbs and the orchard and the castle, as they had been before.

'Now,' said the giant, 'take your own road and I will take mine. But mind your promise. And though you forget, I will remember.'

In a few more days the king's son reached the place he liked best. He loosed the bundle, and at once the castle and the gardens were planted there, as grand as ever before. The king's son opened the castle door and in front of him was the most beautiful maiden he had ever seen.

'Advance, king's son,' said the pretty maid, 'all is in order for you. Will you marry me, this very night?'

'I am the man that is willing,' said he. And that same night they married.

In seven years and a day, who is seen coming to the castle door but the big giant. Then the king's son minded his promise, but till that moment he had told nothing to his wife.

'Turn out your son,' roared the giant, 'mind your promise.'

'You shall have him,' said the king's son, 'but first let his mother put him in order for the journey.'

Quickly the wife was told of the matter, so that she might dress the cook's son as her own and take him by the hand to the giant. Away they went, but the giant had not gone far when he put a rod in the hand of the little laddie and said, 'If your daddie had that rod, what would he do with it?'

'Why, he'd beat the dogs and the cats, if they would be going near the king's meat.'

'You're the cook's son,' cried the giant, and he grabbed the little fellow by the ankles and dashed his brains against a rock.

Then the giant returned to the castle in a rage.

'Turn out your son,' he roared, 'or the highest stone of this castle will be the lowest.'

'Try the trick yet once more,' pleaded the wife. 'The butler's son is of an age with our little laddie.'

So she dressed the butler's son and gave him by the hand to the giant. They had not gone far when the giant put a rod in the wee lad's hand and said, 'What would your daddie do with this?'

'Why, he'd beat the dogs and cats that came among the bottles and the glasses.'

'You're the butler's son,' said the giant, and he dashed him on the rocks too.

Now the giant returned to the castle in a very great rage, and the earth shook under the soles of his feet, and the tops of the towers trembled.

'Out with your son,' he roared, 'or in a twinkling the topmost stone will be the lowest.'

Then it needs must be that they give the right lad to the giant.

The giant took him home and reared him as his son. After a time, on a day when the lad was grown and the giant was away from home, the little fellow heard the sweetest music coming from a wee room at the top of the house. He glanced in and saw the prettiest face ever seen. She beckoned him and told him to be sure to be at the same place about the dead of midnight.

It was the giant's daughter to whom he made this promise, and sure enough at midnight she was at his side.

'Tomorrow,' said the girl, 'you will have the choice of my

own two sisters to marry. Choose neither, but take me. I am promised to the son of the king of the Green City, but he does not please me.'

On the morrow, the giant gathered his family together and said, 'Now, prince of Tethertown,' – for by this time, the lad's father had himself become king – 'you will not lose by living with me. Choose between my two eldest daughters for wife, and she shall go home with you after the wedding.'

'It's a good choice,' replied the youth, 'but better for me is this pretty little one. Give me her and I will take you at your word.'

Then the giant was angry and said, 'These three things you must do before you get that one: first, which I'll tell you now, there is the dung of my hundred cattle in the byre, that has not been cleansed for seven years. I am going from home this day. If by tonight the byre is not so clean that a golden apple will run undirtied from end to end, 'tis not my daughter you'll get, but it is a drink of your own blood that you'll give me for my thirst.'

The lad began cleaning the byre but he might as well have tried to bale the great ocean. At midday, when the sweat of effort was blinding him, the youngest daughter came to him.

'You are being punished, prince of Tethertown,' said she.

'Aye, that I am,' he replied.

'Come over, and lay down your weariness.'

'For that, death is waiting.'

But he was so tired he sat down beside her and fell asleep at once. When he awoke, the girl was not to be seen, but the byre was scrubbed so clean that a golden apple might run unsullied end to end. Then in came the giant at the end of the day.

'Have you cleaned the byre, king's son?' he said.

'It is clean,' he replied.

'Then someone else did it,' cried the giant in anger. 'But if you think you are so sprightly, this is what I have for you tomorrow. By this same time of day you must have thatched this byre with the feathers of birds so that no two feathers are of one colour.'

Next day, the lad was up before the sun, and he was out with bow and quiver in his hand. He wandered the moors but the birds were not easy to catch. Round and about he went till the sweat was blinding him. Then at midday, who should arrive but the giant's youngest daughter.

'You are wearying yourself, king's son,' said she.

'That I am,' he replied, 'but so far only two blackbirds have I caught, and both are of one colour.'

'Come over and lay your weary head on this pretty hillock.'

'I am right willing,' said he. He sat beside her, for he thought she might help him again, and very soon he was asleep.

When he awoke, the girl was gone and the byre was thatched in a multitude of coloured feathers. The giant saw it, and again he did not believe that the young lad had done it.

'Now,' said the giant, 'another task is this: down below is a fir-tree beside the loch, with a magpie's nest at the very top. Five eggs are in the nest. I must have them for my breakfast, and not one burst or broken.'

At first light, the young man went to look for the tree, and it was not hard to find. From root to first branch was five hundred feet. And the trunk was so stout he could get no grip on it. As he was going round and round, again the girl arrived.

'You are losing the skin of your hands and feet,' said she.

'Aye, that I am,' he said. 'I'm no sooner up than I'm down again.'

'No time to stop now,' she said. Then she thrust finger after finger into the tree till she had made a ladder for him to go up to the nest.

'Make haste now,' she called as he reached for the eggs, 'for my father's breath is burning my back.'

He slithered down, but in their hurry to be away, she left one little finger in the top of the tree.

'Haste you home with the eggs as quick as you can,' she cried, 'for your tasks are done. Tonight you will choose between us again, but I and my sisters will look exactly alike in the same kind of dresses. So when my father says, "Go to your bride," look for the hand without a little finger.'

Then all went well. The lad gave the eggs to the giant, and he picked out the pretty girl with the missing finger, and so the giant agreed that there should be a wedding.

And it *was* a wedding! Giants and gentlemen and the son of the king of the Green City were there, and the dancing began, and that *was* a dance. The giant's house was shaking from top to bottom. At the end of the feast, the giant said, 'Go to rest, king's son, and take your wife with you. You have aimed well to find her. But there's no knowing, we may meet you yet another way.'

As they went to the chamber at the top of the stairs, the bride said to her husband, 'Sleep not, or else you die. Quick, quick, we must fly away before my father kills you.'

Out they went, as secret as moles, and untied the blue-grey filly in the stables. As they got ready to mount, the girl stopped for a moment.

'Wait a little,' she said, 'I've a trick to put in the path of the old fellow.'

So back she stole and cut an apple in nine pieces. Two shares she put at the head of the bed, two at the foot, two at the kitchen door, two at the big front door, and one outside the house.

After a while the giant awoke and called out, 'Are you a-bed and asleep, my pretty young ones?'

'Not yet,' answered the apple at the head of the bed.

Again and again he called, one time after another, and the apples answered in turn to the big front door.

'You are going far from me now,' cried the giant.

'Not so,' replied the apple outside.

'Yes, you're flying away,' said the giant. He jumped to his feet and ran to the bridal bed, but it was cold, cold, and empty.

'I am tripped by my own daughter's tricks,' he muttered. 'But here's off and after them!'

Wife and husband fled all night, but in the mouth of the day the girl felt her father's breath burning her back.

'Put your hand quick,' she told her husband, 'in the ear of our filly. Whatever you find, throw it behind us.'

He found a twig of sloe-tree and threw it. In the twinkle of an eye there rose up twenty miles of blackthorn wood, so thick that scarce a weasel might go through. The giant rushed into it headlong, and the thorns fleeced all his head and his neck.

'Here as before,' he grumbled, 'my own daughter's tricks. But if I had my big axe and wood-knife, I'd make short work of the way through.'

Home he went for his axe and his knife. He was not long on his journey, and he was a bonny lad to put some weight behind the big axe. Very soon he had cleared a path through the thorns. Then on he went at a mighty brisk clip till in the heat of the day his daughter once more felt her father's breath burning her back.

'Reach again in the filly's ear,' she said, 'and throw behind whatever you find.'

He found a speck of grey stone and tossed it behind, and in a twinkling there rose up, broad and high, twenty miles of grim grey rock. The giant came full pelt, but past the rock he could not go.

'The tricks of my daughter,' he groaned, 'are the hardest things that ever I met. But with my crowbar and pickaxe I'll not be long cleaving that rock.'

There was no help but that he must get them. And when he did, he was the bonny lad to split those stones. Then on he raced, and at the closing of the day, again his daughter felt his breath burning her back.

This time, the young king's son plucked a bladder of water from the filly's ear and threw it behind. At once, there grew a freshwater loch, twenty miles in length and twenty in breadth. The giant rushed on with all speed, and before he could stop he was halfway over the water. Then his legs thrashed the water and down he went, and he rode no more.

Next day, the bride and the husband came in sight of his father's house.

'Go you in,' said she, 'and tell them that you have the like

97

of me. But remember this: let neither man nor creature kiss you. If you do, your eyes will forget that they ever saw me.'

As he went in everyone he met gave him welcome and luck, but he charged them, and his father and mother also, not to kiss him. But as mishap would have it, an old greyhound had such joy to see him that she sprang up and licked his face. After that he forgot entirely the giant's daughter.

He had left her sitting by a well in the wood, but he did not return to her again. In the mouth of the night she climbed into an oak for fear of the wild and lay in the fork of the tree. In the morn, a shoemaker that lived near the well sent his wife for a pitcher of water. As the wife looked in the well, she saw the reflection of the girl above in the tree. The woman was so surprised – she took the shadow on the water for her own and never had she looked so beautiful – that she dropped and broke the pitcher and went home.

'Wife, where's the water?' said the shoemaker.

But his wife had turned mighty proud and she answered, 'Shambling old fool, get it yourself. Too long have I been your slave for wood and water.'

'Woman, have you gone mad?' he cried. 'Well then, daughter, go quickly and get me a drink.'

His daughter went to the well, and it happened to her as it had to the mother. Never before had she looked so pretty and loveable, so she took herself home.

'Up with the drink,' said her father.

'Leather-stinking, homespun oaf,' she replied, 'do you think I'm nothing but your slave?'

'These women have taken a turn in the head,' the shoemaker thought, and away he went to the well himself. But when he saw the reflection in the water he had the wit to know what had happened. He looked up in the tree and saw the prettiest lass ever seen.

'Your perch is shaky,' he called to her, 'but your face is fair. Come down and I'll take you into my own house. I've only a little hut, but you'll get a decent share of all that goes.'

She went with him to the house, and at the end of a day or two there came a leash of young gentlemen lads to the shoemaker. The king's son had come home, and he was going to marry, and they needed new shoes for the wedding. Then the gentlemen lads saw the new girl in the house, and if they gave her one look they gave her two more, so pretty was she.

'Certainly, it is you that has the pretty daughter,' they said to the shoemaker.

'Aye, pretty she is,' said the shoemaker, 'but she's no daughter of mine.'

'By St Nail,' said one lad, 'I'd give a hundred pound to marry her!' And the other lads said the very same.

'Tell her this night what we have said,' they told the shoemaker, 'and send us word on the morrow.'

The girl had heard the sound of the talk, and after the lads had gone the shoemaker told her the drift of it.

'Go after them,' she said, 'I'll marry the one with the best purse.'

So the richest lad was called back and gave the shoemaker a hundred pound. After this, the girl and the lad went to rest. As the girl lay down she sent the lad for a tumbler of water. He took the tumbler from the board, but out of that grip he could not come, and he stood the long night with the glass in his hand.

'Ho, laddie,' she called, 'why will you not lie down?' But he stood like a stone till break of day.

Next morn, she asked the shoemaker to take away this lubberly boy. So this wooer went in a froth of puzzlement, and he did not tell his two companions how it had fared with him.

Then the second chap came and tried his luck with the pretty lady. They too went to rest, and she said to him, 'Look to the latch, if it's fastened on the door.' Well, the latch caught hold of his hand, and there he was till the break of day.

He was sent away in shame and disgrace, and it was the turn of the third lad. This time, the youth was rooted to the floor. In the morn he took his soles out of that house, and he was not seen looking behind him.

'Take the purses of gold that the foolish lads left,' said the girl to the shoemaker, 'for I have no need of them. They will better you, and I am no worse for your kindness.'

After a day and a day the shoemaker had the new shoes ready, and that was the very day of the marriage. As he made up his bundle to go to the court, the girl said to him wistfully, 'Such a day! How I would like to see this king's son before he marries.'

'Come with me,' said the shoemaker. 'The servants of the king know me well, and you shall get a sight of the king's son and all the company.'

When the gentlefolk saw a new pretty girl suddenly among them, they took her to the wedding-chamber and filled for her a glass of wine. She made as if to drink, and then a flame rose from the glass, and a golden pigeon and a silver pigeon flew out.

Then three grains of barley fell on the floor. The silver pigeon swooped down and ate them.

'If you had kept in mind,' said the golden pigeon, 'that I cleared the giant's byre, you would not eat that without giving me my share.'

Three more grains of barley fell, and the silver pigeon again ate them.

'If you had kept in mind,' said the golden bird, 'that I thatched the byre, you would not eat those without giving me my share.'

Another three grains fell, and the silver pigeon had them also.

'If you had kept in mind,' said the golden bird, 'the magpie's nest, you would give me my share. I lost my little finger then, and I lack it still.'

Then the pretty girl held out towards the king's son her hand without a finger, and he remembered at once who she was.

He sprang to where she was, and kissed her from hand to mouth. They called for the priest and they were married a second time, to make the matter sure. And that is where we leave them.

4

THE HERO-DEEDS OF CUCHULAIN

Here am I – no easy task –
Holding Ireland's men at bay.
My foot never turned in flight
From single man or ranks of foe.

Pillow-Talk

Once, when the royal bed was spread out at the fort of Cruachan in Connacht, Ailill and Maeve spoke together with their heads upon the pillow.

'True is the saying,' said Ailill, 'that it is well for a woman to be a rich man's wife.'

'True indeed,' said his wife, 'but what's in your mind?'

'It comes to my thought,' said Ailill, 'that you are better off today than when I married you.'

'I had wealth enough before you,' said she.

'Not so much, but only women's things, and enemies about you running off with spoil and booty.'

'Not at all,' said Maeve. 'My father, Eochaid the Steadfast, the High-king of Ireland, had six daughters and I was the best of them. I was great-hearted and generous and bold in battle. Fifteen hundred soldiers were in my pay, all mercenaries, and the same number of freeborn Irish followed me. I was my own woman, Maeve of Cruachan, ruler of this province given me by my father. Towards me the great men came wooing, from Leinster and from Tara. From Ulster also messengers came, from Conchobor and from Little Eochaid, and I would not go with them. For I asked a strange bride-gift, never before asked of a man of Ireland, namely, a husband without meanness, without jealousy, without fear.

'I am great in largesse and gift-giving, and if my husband were mean it would not be fitting to be together. I am strong in battle and victorious, and my courage would be reproached by a timid man, who should at least be of equal spirit. A jealous man would be wrong too, for I had lovers enough waiting in one another's shadow. So I found the man I wanted. It was yourself, Ailill, Rus Ruad's son from Leinster, not mean, not jealous, and no sluggard. I brought you gifts worthy of a noble bride: clothing for a dozen men, a chariot worth thrice seven bondmaids, the breadth of your face in red gold, the weight of your left arm in white bronze. Whoever brings shame and confusion upon you, the compensation is mine, for you are a kept man.'

'Not so,' said Ailill, 'for though my brothers are elder, and I let them govern, they are no better than I. I never heard of a province ruled by a woman except this one. So I came to the kingship here, following after my mother, Magach's daughter. And who better for my queen than yourself, daughter of the High-king of Ireland?'

'It may be so,' said Maeve, 'but my fortune is greater than yours.'

'I marvel at that,' he replied, 'for I know very well that none has more property or riches than I have.'

Then the poorest of their things were brought out to them, to judge who was the richer: their pails and cans and tubs and iron pots, their jugs and basins and eared pitchers. Then the gold treasure was brought out, bracelets and neck-laces and rings for fingers and thumbs, and after that their garments and cloth, purple and blue and black and green and yellow, vari-coloured also, and grey, dun, mottled, brindled.

Their flocks were taken from the fields to be counted and

reckoned, and they were found to be equal. And Maeve's ram was no better than the ram of Ailill. Then from pasture and paddock came herds of horses, and Maeve had a match for Ailill's stallion. Great droves of pigs were gathered from the woods and glens and waste places, and one boar was as fine as another. The cattle were measured and compared, and the herds were the same in number and size.

But the great bull Finnbennach, the White-horned, had moved from the queen's herd to Ailill's, refusing to belong to a woman. Without a great bull, Maeve felt the heart go out of her, as if she owned not a pennyworth.

She sent for her messenger and said, 'Answer truly, Mac Roth, is there a match for this bull in any province of Ireland?'

'That there is,' said Mac Roth, 'a great and better one, at Cooley in Ulster, at the house of Daire, son of Fiachna. The Brown Bull of Cooley it is called.'

'Go, Mac Roth,' said Maeve, 'ask of Daire a year's loan of the Brown Bull. Let the payment be fifty heifers. And say further, Mac Roth, if the folk of the border object to the lending of their brown jewel, let Daire himself bring the bull and he shall have these gifts: a piece of the Plain of Ai equal to his own land, a chariot worth thrice seven bondmaids, and my own friendly body in bed.'

Away went Mac Roth to Ulster with this message. And Daire was so pleased with the offer that he burst the seams of his mattress for joy.

'On my heart and mind, to the devil with the wishes of Ulstermen!' he cried. 'My Brown Bull, my sweetheart, my treasure, shall go to Maeve and Ailill in the land of Connacht.'

Then there was good eating and drinking for all among the rushes and the straw, and soon the wits went awry with the drink.

''Tis true what I say,' said one of the men from Connacht, 'a good fellow we have here, this man of the house.'

'Certainly, a good man,' said another.

'None better in Ulster.'

'Nay, not so. The king Conchobor is a better man, and it's no shame to be his follower. Yet is it not a grand thing that Daire will give us the Brown Bull of Cooley? It would take the four provinces of Ireland to carry off that bull from Ulster.'

'What are you saying?' cried another. 'May your mouth gush blood! We would take the bull anyway, with or without permission.'

When he heard this, Daire's servant dashed down the dishes without grace or good word and went straight to his master.

'Was it you,' he said, 'that gave our treasure, the Brown Bull, to the messengers from Connacht?'

'Certainly, I did that,' said Daire.

'Was that a noble thing to do? It is true, then, what they say: they would have taken the bull by force, by your leave or not.'

'By all the gods, not so,' said Daire. 'I'll make the choice, fair or foul.'

So they went tumbling to bed, and in the morning the messenger of Connacht came to Daire's house.

'Tell us, noble sir,' said they, 'where the Brown Bull is.'

'I will not,' replied Daire. 'It is not in me to murder messengers or travellers, otherwise not one of you would leave here alive.'

'How so?' said Mac Roth.

'I have good cause for it. I hear say that I must give up the bull, or else the army of Ailill and Maeve, and the cunning of Fergus, will force me to it.'

'That speech,' said Mac Roth, ''twas the drink doing the talking. Count it not against Maeve and Ailill.'

'Nonetheless, Mac Roth, I'll not give up the Brown Bull, at this time.'

So Mac Roth returned to the court of Connacht and told Maeve how the matter had fallen out.

'No need to smooth the knots and polish the knobs,' said she. 'It was well known that if the Brown Bull of Cooley came not freely, it would come by force. And taken it shall be!'

The Rising of the Men of Connacht

A call went out to the men of Connacht and to the provinces of Ireland. Ailill's brothers, six sons of Magach, sent their followers to the number of three thousand. And three thousand more came with the exiles from Ulster, Cormac, son of Conchobor, and Fergus Mac Roig. To Cruachan Ai they all gathered.

The first band of these men had shorn heads, green cloaks about them with silver brooches, and next their skin they wore shirts of gold thread. They carried broad swords with handles of silver.

There was a second, and then a third band. These last men had long hair, yellow-golden and streaming. They wore purple cloaks with gold embroidery, and their long silken shirts reached to their heels. Each man had a shield and a long stabbing spear. Altogether, they lifted their feet and set them down in order.

'Now,' said Maeve gladly, 'Cormac is come, for I see him yonder.'

They pitched camp, and that night they lay under the dense smoke of camp-fires, between the four fords of the rivers. For two weeks they stayed there, drinking and feasting, so that their future journey would be the lighter for them. Then Maeve took her chariot to go and speak with her druid. From him, she would discover the signs and the auguries.

'All who part today from friend or family,' said Maeve, 'and do not return will curse me, for this army is mine.'

'Whoever else falls or fails,' said the druid, 'you yourself will return.'

As they departed, the charioteer wheeled his chariot by the right, to get the power of a good omen, and Maeve saw a thing that surprised her. A young woman with a bright face and thin red lips stood by the pole of the chariot. Her teeth were shining like pearls. As white as night-fallen snow was the lustre of her skin, and her voice was as sweet as the strings of the harp.

'What woman are you,' said Maeve, 'and what is your task?'

'Not hard to tell,' she answered. 'I am Fedelm, the poetess of our Connacht, from the magic *shee* of Cruachan. The learning from Scotland I have, which is the Light of Foreknowledge.'

'Well Fedelm, prophetess, how do you see our army?'

'I see red on them, I see crimson.'

'But my messengers return from Emain Macha,' said Maeve, 'where Conchobor suffers his pains. He cannot stir. Therefore we do not fear the Ulstermen. Speak truly, Fedelm, how do you see our army?'

'Still I see red on them, I see crimson.'

'Red is no matter between armies. Wounds will weep when great forces meet. But Fedelm, prophetess, tell me again, how do you see it?'

'Once more,' said she, 'I see red, I see crimson.'

Then Fedelm began to prophesy, and she foretold Cuchulain to the host of the four provinces of Ireland:

> I see a man, strong in battle,
> Wounds in his fair flesh.
> The hero's light is on his brow,
> The wreath of victory about his head.
>
> A radiant face, amazing to women,
> Cuchulain of Murthemne, man of fame.
> Is it he? I cannot tell.
> But his foe is stained with blood.
>
> He moves through the battle.
> Stop him or die!
> He will lay waste your army.
> I am Fedelm, I conceal nothing.

On a Monday at summer's end, the four provinces of Ireland set out, going southeast through many places into the land of Ulster. Maeve was the last into camp, making a circuit of the army, to see who was ready and who was loath. Foremost and most eager among the troops were the men of Galian from Leinster.

'Why do you praise them above others?' said Ailill.

'Good soldiers,' said Maeve. 'While others are clearing the ground, they have already pitched their tents. While others are setting tents, they are cooking. While others eat, they are ready for the music of harpers. When the others have eaten, they are asleep.'

'They are welcome then,' said Ailill, 'for it is with us they march and fight.'

'Not so. They do it for themselves.'

'Let them remain here then.'

'How can that be?' said Maeve. 'They will take our lands while we are away.'

'Then what shall we do?'

'Kill them,' said Maeve.

'Fie, 'tis a woman's trick,' said Ailill. 'Shame on you.'

Then Fergus, the exile from Ulster, said, 'They are friends. Kill them over my dead body.'

'Fergus, that too is possible,' said Maeve. 'We have enough men to kill you all.'

'Not wise,' replied Fergus. 'Seven chiefs of Munster are my allies, and the bold soldiers of Galian are tied to me by oath. But I shall scatter the troops of Galian among the whole army, so that not five of them shall be together in one place.'

This was done and the host moved on, though in the fetching of food and the hunting of deer it was always one of the Galian men that brought down the prey. Fergus led the army, for he knew the country. Seven years had he been king in Ulster, before exile drove him out. But it was not long before old affection called to him, and he began to lead the army astray, wandering north and south. And he sent a secret warning to Ulster, till Maeve saw what he did.

'Friend Fergus, what wandering path is this?' she said. 'We are straying north and south. Ailill and the army fear treachery. Would you betray us, O Fergus Roig? You have gained much wealth among us, here in your exile.'

'No treachery, Maeve, rest easy,' said Fergus. 'This is my land of Ulster. If I turn and twist, it is to avoid Cuchulain, that mighty warrior.'

A sharp anxiety came to Fergus that Cuchulain could be near, and he warned the men of Ireland to be on their guard. It was a slashing lion they were up against, the doom of enemies, the slaughterer of hosts, the flaming torch: that is to say, Cuchulain, son of Sualtam.

That same day, as the army of invaders went eastward over the moors, Cuchulain and his father came to the pillar-stone at Ard Cuillenn. His father's horses cropped the grass to the bare soil, but Cuchulain's horses bit down to the bedrock.

Then Cuchulain made a hoop of an oak sapling, and cut a message in Ogham on it. He forced the hoop over the pillar-stone, as a warning and challenge to the men of Ireland. And when the army came to that place, Fergus saw the hoop and knew its meaning.

'If you of the four provinces of Ireland ignore this hoop,' he said, 'and do not rest here till one of you has made a similar hoop, standing on one foot and using one hand and one eye as he did, the royal hero who made it will slay you before the dawn hour.'

So the host turned aside and camped in a great wood. Heavy snow fell in the night. It lay up to the shoulders of the men and the flanks of the horses, and all Ireland was a level white plain. Tents could not be set and no food was prepared for lack of fires. All huddled together, white men. Who was friend, who was enemy? Certainly, it was a night of hardship.

As for Cuchulain, he was away that night, being after a woman. But he rose early and scrubbed himself, and yoked his chariot, to find that track of the enemy.

'Alas, Laeg,' he said to his charioteer, 'we were wrong last night to be after a woman. We betrayed our trust. The army of the four provinces has slipped by us. Track the enemy, Laeg, and reckon their number.'

Laeg went after the track but could not read it. Then Cuchulain read the signs and numbered the enemy.

'You are confused in your reckoning, little Cu,' said Laeg.

'Not so,' replied Cuchulain. 'Eighteen divisions have gone by. But the last, that of the men of Galian, is dispersed among the rest.' Cuchulain knew this because of his many powers of insight and knowledge, which were beyond the gifts of other men.

'Friend Laeg,' he said, 'put the whip to the horses, for on my life my weapon must taste some blood before this night.'

So they sped to Ath Gabla where, with a single stroke, Cuchulain cut a forked pole with four prongs, which he set firmly in the ford of the river. As he was doing this, Err and Innel, two stripling sons of Nera, surprised him and vied together to be the first to attack him. But Cuchulain took the heads from the bodies of the warriors and their charioteers, and stuck a head on each prong of the pole.

It was not honourable to take bodies or horses or trappings, so Cuchulain sent the horses homewards to the men of Ireland, with the reins loose over the ears, and the headless trunks dripping red into the chariots. When these came in sight, the van of the army stopped and the rear piled forward, and all were thrown into a great fear.

Maeve was travelling as usual in the midst of her nine chariots, so that the filth and splatter thrown up by the army would not reach and darken her golden diadem. When she saw the bloody remains in the chariots, she thought it was the work of many men, and she sent Cormac, the exiled son of Ulster's king, to spy out the land. At the ford of the river he saw only a forked pole with four heads dripping, and the track of a single chariot drawn by two horses. The nobles of Ireland, following after Cormac, stood amazed at the sight.

'Pitch tents,' said Ailill, 'prepare food and drink, make music and then go to rest, for last night was a terrible night indeed. And Fergus, tell me this: who has come so swiftly and suddenly and killed these four at the ford?'

'Not hard to say,' replied Fergus. 'Who would it be but the little lad Cuchulain, the foster-son of Conchobor the king.'

'I've heard speak of him,' said Ailill. 'What age would this boy be, this little Hound of Culann of Ulster?'

'It is not his age that is most troublesome,' said Fergus, 'for this boy did the deeds of a man long before now. There is no wolf more blood-thirsty, no hero more fierce, no man equal to even a fourth part of Cuchulain's warlike deeds. He is a sledgehammer for smiting, a raven for flesh-tearing, a lion for ferocity. None can measure up to his roar, his speed, his fury, his quick and certain triumphs.'

'No need to scare ourselves,' said Maeve. 'He has only one body. He can be wounded or captured. How can a beardless boy hold out against seasoned, resolute warriors?'

'He may do so,' said Fergus. 'Already, this little fellow is the author of mighty deeds.'

The Youthful Deeds of Cuchulain

'He was reared,' said Fergus, 'in the oak house of his parents on the Plain of Murthemne, hearing day by day the stories of the young lads of Emain Macha. For it was there that King Conchobor of Ulster spent his time. One third of the day the king watched the boys at play and hurling, one third at the chessboard, and one third feasting and drinking till he fell asleep. There is no greater lord and warrior in Ireland than Conchobor. I, Fergus, say it, though he himself banished me into exile.

'Cuchulain longed to join those lads in Emain, but his mother said he was too young and would not let him go. So he set out himself, with his hurley-stick and his silver ball and his sharp little spear which he tossed before him till he came to the field of Emain. Thrice fifty youths and the king's son, Follamain, were playing their games. The little lad went into their midst and caught the ball and kept it close from them and carried it away over the goal.

'"Attack that fellow," cried Follamain. "Let him meet his death. Does he not know that no son of Ulster may join our game unless he has our protection?"

'Then they all attacked him with thrice fifty hurley-sticks and thrice fifty balls. He beat down the sticks and warded off the balls, and struck those boys to the ground, chasing some of them even to the chessboard on the mound where Conchobor was playing. As Cuchulain came leaping over the board, the king caught and held him. '"Now, little fellow," said Conchobor, "you are rough indeed with these boys."

'"Good reason for that," replied Cuchulain. "It is a strange way they have to honour a guest from a distant place."

'"Who are you?" said the king.

'"I am Setanta, son of Sualtam and of your own sister Dechtire."

'Then the king welcomed his sister's son, and told him how it was in Emain, and took him under protection. This little boy who overthrew the sons of warriors and champions was but five years old.'

Thus spoke Fergus, and in a while Cormac, son of Conchobor, took up the story.

'In the next year,' he said, 'that little lad did a second deed. Culann the Smith of Ulster was preparing a feast for Conchobor. Only a few were asked, for Culann was not rich. He had only his hammer and his anvil, his tongs and his fists, to work with.

'As Conchobor was leaving Emain Macha, he went by the field to say farewell to the boys. He saw a wonderful sight. Thrice fifty boys guarded the goal at one end of the field, and at the other end stood a little lad alone. And in the hurling and the throwing the little lad put the ball past the thrice fifty youths, but none of them could go past the lad. Then it came to fighting and wrestling, and the lad stripped them all naked though they could not even pluck the brooch from his cloak.

'The king was astonished and asked the lad to go with him to the feast. But he replied, "Not yet indeed. I shall not leave these fellows till we have had our fill of playing. But I shall follow you." The king took no account of these words. He went on to the house of Culann, and when he was within the smith let loose the guard-dog, a ferocious large bloodhound. It was a wild, savage, surly dog, as strong as a hundred. It lay growling beyond the door, with its shaggy head on its paws.

'In a short time the little boy came following, throwing his hurley ball from hand to hand. When he came to the green before the house, the dog began to bay. It was minded to make a feast of the boy and swallow him entire up to the middle of his breast. As the dog came roaring at him, the little lad cast the ball with all his might into the gaping mouth, and the ball carried the dog's guts out through the back way. Then the boy gripped the dog by the hind legs and dashed it against a large stone so that its limbs jumped from their sockets.

'When the household heard the roars and the commotion, they ran out, fearing that the boy was devoured. They saw that he was safe and welcomed him. Culann also greeted him, but not gladly.

'"I fear now," he said, "my livelihood is wasted, for you have taken my guardian from me."

'"Be not angry," said the boy. "I will rear you a new pup from the best breed in Ireland. And till that pup grows to strength, I myself will be your hound, the keeper of your household, your flocks and your herds."

'Then Cathbad the druid said, "Let him be called Cu-Chulain, the Hound of Culann, because of this, and that name will forever be on the lips of the men of Ireland and Scotland."

'Thus it was that Cuchulain gained his name, and he was but six years old.'

After that, there was a silence, and then Fiachu Mac Firaba spoke out.

'There was another deed that Cuchulain did,' said he, 'when Cathbad the druid was teaching the law and cunning of druids to eight eager pupils, as was always his way. "Master," asked one, "what is the omen for this day?" Cathbad replied that the boy who took up arms on that day would be famous on the tongues of all men, but his days would be short-lived and fleeting.

'When Cuchulain heard this, he threw away his playthings and went to Conchobor to ask for weapons. The king gave him spears and a shield and a sword, but Cuchulain shook them and shattered them. And he did the same with fourteen more sets of arms till Conchobor had no more at

Emain and gave the lad his own weapons. Cuchulain shook these arms and they held, and then Cuchulain saluted the king. When Cathbad saw this, again he warned of the omen, that the life of the boy would be short.

'"Though there would be to me but one day and one night in this world," said Cuchulain, "I would be content so long as my fame and my deeds live after me."

'Then Cathbad said, "Come, little lad, mount this chariot, for it holds the same omen for you."

'Cuchulain mounted the chariot, and it broke under him, and a second and a third also up to the number of seventeen, till Ibar, the king's charioteer, yoked the king's own chariot to the king's horses, and that chariot held. Then Ibar drove Cuchulain around all of Emain Macha and the youths on the playing-field stood and saluted their young companion.

'"Now, little lad," said the charioteer, "let the horses go to the pasture."

'"Not yet," said Cuchulain, "I shall go as far as the road goes."

'So they rode onward to Sliab Fuait, to the border of Ulster. Conall Cernach was the man who guarded the border that day, to welcome poets and to ward off enemies. As he stood, Ulster's champion, at the ford of the river, he heard a little fellow in a chariot say, "Go home now, master Conall, and let me keep watch for the province."

"Nay, little boy," said Conall, "you are too young for war."

"Then I shall go south to the banks of Loch Echtrann, to redden my hands today in the blood of an enemy."

'But Conall would not let him go alone. For a while they travelled in company, then suddenly Cuchulain loosed a stone from his sling and smashed the yoke of Conall's chariot, so Conall could not go on.

"Good aim!" cried Cuchulain. "See, O Conall, I shoot straight. Is that the making of a good warrior?"

'With that, he left Conall and went on to the south. He found no enemy, but at the White Cairn, on the summit of

Sliab Moduirn, the charioteer Ibar showed him the whole extent of the renowned province of Ulster, from mountains to plains, from the rivers to the sea. Below them was the fort of the sons of Nechta Scene, rogues who boasted that they had killed as many Ulstermen as the number still alive. Ibar was afraid to challenge these fierce sons, but Cuchulain laughed at him and went boldly to the fort.

'Where bog and river met they turned loose the horses. At the green before the fort Cuchulain took a hoop of wood with the challenge on it and placed it over the pillar-stone.

'"Now Ibar," said Cuchulain, "take the skins and coverings from the chariot that I may sleep on the grass for a while."

'As he slept, Foill the Deceitful, son of Nechta Scene, came and woke the boy. Angry words passed between them till Foill reached for his arms.

'"Go softly, little lad," said Ibar, "neither points nor sharp edges can hurt that man."

'But Cuchulain sent a ball of tempered metal hurling through Foill's shield onto the flat of his forehead so that his brains went out at the back of his head, and the light of the air was visible as if through a hole in a sieve.

'At once, Tuachall the Cunning, the second son, came running, and he was so fast and nimble hardly any weapon could touch him. But Cuchulain took in hand the great poisoned spear of Conchobor and pierced Tuachall through shield and breast and rib and heart, and struck off his head before the body hit the ground.

'That was the signal for the last of them, Fannall the Swallow, to try his luck.

'"Watch out for this one," said Ibar. "He can travel over water like a swallow. No one can cope with him near water."

'But Cuchulain, who had swum like a salmon in the pools of Emain, clasped his arms around Fannall at the ford, bashed off his head, and let the current run away with the body.

'Then Cuchulain went into the fort and pillaged it and burnt the buildings to the level of the walls. He took the three heads of the sons of Nechta and went away to Sliab Fuait.

'"Let the horses exert themselves," Cuchulain said to Ibar, "because of the storm and pursuit that is after us." And the chariot flew over the Plain of Breg faster even than the wind and the birds.

'Towards Sliab Fuait, they saw a herd of wild deer and it seemed a worthy thing to catch some alive for the men of Ulster. So Cuchulain caught and harnessed two great stags. Then they saw a flock of swans and it seemed a wonderful thing to bring those alive also. With small stones Cuchulain knocked some out of the air, but Ibar was afraid to jump from the racing chariot to fetch them. With one look Cuchulain quelled the fierce bucking and tossing of the galloping stags. Their sharp antlers were stilled, and Ibar went safely past them to get the swans.

'So in this manner they rode back to Emain Macha – wild deer about the chariot, a swan-flock above, and three heads in the hand.

'As they came to Emain, a cry went up, "Some terror is here. A warrior with blood-stained heads under pure white birds. Let us meet and please him, or he may do damage to the men of Emain."

'They sent out to please him the women of Emain, thrice fifty women, all naked, to expose their shame to him. But when he saw all those young women flaunt their naked bodies before him, he hid his face. Then they seized him and plunged him in a vat of cold water, to cool his ardour. The first vat they tried burst its staves, the second vat seethed with bubbles of heat, but the third went from hot to cold as the wrath and the ardour abated.

'He rose from the vat, blushing crimson from head to foot. They dressed him in a tunic with a thread of gold and a green mantle held by a silver pin. He came and stood by Conchobor's knee, and the king stroked his fair yellow hair.

'At seven years old, this little lad did those deeds,' said Fiachu Mac Firaba. 'It is no marvel that we have reason to fear him, now that he has reached seventeen.'

Alarms and Deadly Excursions

As the four provinces of Ireland went eastwards, over the mountain of Cruinn, Cuchulain followed them and came upon a broken chariot. It was the chariot of Orlam, son of Ailill and Maeve. The charioteer stood apart, cutting wood from a holly-tree.

'What is your task?' said Cuchulain.

'Cutting a new chariot-pole. Ours broke chasing that wild deer Cuchulain. Here, friend, lend me a hand, either cutting or trimming.'

Cuchulain began to strip a pole, rubbing it so smooth and polished in his fist that not even a fly might keep a footing on it. When he saw this, the charioteer was surprised.

'Friend, who are you?' he said. 'This work seems beneath a man of your looks.'

'I am that wild Cuchulain you spoke of just now.'

'Alas,' cried the charioteer, 'now I am a dead man!'

'Rest easy,' replied Cuchulain, 'I do not kill servants. But where is your master?'

The charioteer pointed to Orlam, who was resting on a hillock. Then Cuchulain took Orlam by the hair and cut off his head.

'Tie this head to your back,' Cuchulain told the charioteer, 'and do not stop till you reach the middle of your camp. I shall be watching you. There is a stone in my sling, ready to break your head.'

When Ailill and Maeve saw the remains of Orlam, it was a misery and a warning to them. 'This is another thing entirely from catching birds,' said the queen.

Then Cuchulain went about death's business, striking the enemy wherever he found them and taking their heads from them. The men of Ireland were afraid of sudden attack, and they looked on all strangers with cold eyes. Even the tuneful harpers of Cainbile, who had come out of friendship to please the army with music, were taken for Ulster spies and chased mercilessly from the camp. Scattered to the north, amid the stones of Lia Mor, these harpers in their fright turned themselves into deer, for they were both men of music and men of magic.

And Cuchulain went on with his slaughter, one man after another. He had a look on him for Maeve. He swore that if he saw her a stone from his sling would not go far from the side of her head. The first shot he tried killed the pet bird on her shoulder, and the second shot killed a little squirrel on the other shoulder. All the while the list of the slain grew longer.

'I'll make two halves of any man who scoffs at this Cuchulain,' said Ailill. 'Let us hurry to Cooley. If we don't reach there soon, this young fellow will have destroyed two thirds of our host.'

The four provinces of Ireland went on quickly across the plains of Breg and Murthemne, with the warning of Fergus in their ears.

'In truth,' he said, 'though you do not find Cuchulain, he will come to you.'

At the same time, the Brown Bull of Cooley was in the country of Mairgin, pawing the earth and casting up turf and earthworks with his heels. Morrigan, daughter of Ernmas, came from the magic *shee* in the form of a bird. She settled on a pillar-stone and spoke to the bull.

'Be on your guard, you Brown Bull of Cooley, you pitiful one,' she said. 'The men of Ireland aim to carry you off, just like any old ox in a raid.'

So the Brown Bull went, with his fifty heifers, to Sliab Culinn in the north, though the strongest man would be hard put to catch him. These were the virtues of the Brown Bull. He serviced fifty heifers a day, and those that did not calve by the next day burst from the hardness of the begetting. He was so large that fifty youths played hand-ball against his backside, and a hundred warriors took shelter in his shadow from heat and cold. In his bold presence all ghosts and spirits hurriedly departed. In the evening, when he came to his byre, he made a musical lowing that had enough melody and delight in it for any man. That was the power of the Brown Bull of Cooley.

Cuchulain was still shadowing the army, killing the unlucky ones, with his eye open for Maeve. But she remained in the very midst of her host, covered by a canopy of shields, lest Cuchulain should spy her from the hills and strike her with a sling-shot. Daily, she called for bold men to go and do combat with Cuchulain.

'Not I,' said one.

'Certainly not,' said another.

'Nothing is due from me,' said a third. 'Besides, who is strong enough to oppose him?'

Then Maeve sent for Fiachu, one of the exiled Ulstermen, to parley with Cuchulain.

'Trust my welcome,' said Cuchulain, 'and tell me your terms.'

'We offer compensation for damage done to Ulstermen,' replied Fiachu. 'Then entertainment for yourself in Cruachan, with the best wine and mead. And for you also, service with Ailill and Maeve, who will be better for you than that petty lord you now serve.'

'All that is nothing for me,' said Cuchulain. 'I would not change my mother's brother for another king.'

'Well, Maeve and Fergus would speak with you further.'

On the morrow, when Maeve and Fergus went to meet Cuchulain, he seemed to Maeve to be nothing but a boy.

'Speak to him, Fergus,' said Maeve.

'It's yourself should speak,' replied Fergus. 'You're close enough to him, in the narrowness of this glen.'

Then Cuchulain himself spoke up and said to Maeve, 'In virtue of my power, and in the name of those I have slain, I will accept no less than every woman and every milch cow of the men of Ireland.'

But there was no agreement and they parted from each other in anger.

The host of the four provinces camped on the Bird's Ridge for three days and nights, but they had neither food nor music nor rest. Every night, before the bright hour of dawn, Cuchulain killed a hundred warriors.

'This cannot last,' said Maeve. 'We are being destroyed

entirely. Let us offer him the milch cows, and the base-born captive women, so that he may stop his night-work and at least let us sleep. Let Mac Roth, the messenger, take these terms.'

Heavy snow had fallen and the land was white. Cuchulain had cast off the twenty-seven waxed shirts that were bound to his skin with cords, to keep him safe in the fit of his fury. For thirty feet around the snow melted, from the ardour and heat of his body. Such was his condition when Mac Roth approached.

'A single warrior is coming, little Cu,' said Laeg the charioteer.

'What warrior is that?'

'A dark-haired, broad-faced fellow, with a fine cloak about him. A stout tunic next the skin, and two shoes between his feet and the ground. A staff of white hazel in one hand, and a single-edged sword in the other.'

'Those are tokens of a messenger,' said Cuchulain. 'Let us hear him.'

Then Mac Roth came near shouting, 'Where is this famous Cuchulain?'

'What would you say to him,' replied Cuchulain, 'that you would not say to me?' And then Mac Roth offered his terms.

'He whom you seek would not accept those proposals,' said Cuchulain. 'When we feast a guest, let us say a poet or a satirist, the men of Ulster need their cows. As for base-born women, why, our men take them to bed and make more children. Your terms are useless.'

Mac Roth returned to Maeve and said, 'I found a surly, fearsome, fierce fellow between Fochain and the sea. I do not know if he is the famous Cuchulain.'

'Did he accept the terms?' asked the queen.

'Indeed he did not,' replied Mac Roth. And he told them what the man had said.

'Certainly, that was Cuchulain,' said Fergus.

Again, Mac Roth was sent, to ask if Cuchulain would accept any terms.

'If there is one person among you,' replied Cuchulain, 'who knows what I have in mind, I will accept what he says.'

When the message was given to Maeve she looked at the wise and cunning Fergus and he answered at once, 'What he has in mind bodes you no good. He demands that one of us should fight him in single combat every day. When that man has been killed, our army may march on till the next fight is due. If no man comes, then the army shall go no further. And also, while these fights last, Cuchulain is to be fed and clothed by you.'

'Go to him, Fergus,' said Maeve. 'Tell him his terms are good, for it is better to lose one warrior every day than a hundred each night.'

As Fergus was setting out, a young man called Etarcumul wished to go with him, to discover the size and the look of this famous Cuchulain. But Fergus warned him, 'With your pride and arrogance, and his strength and savagery, no good will come of your meeting.'

Still, Etarcumul insisted on going. Fergus and Cuchulain made their agreement, with civil and friendly words, and then Fergus went on his way. But Etarcumul stayed to stare at the Ulster hero.

'What do you gape at?' said Cuchulain.

'You,' he replied.

'Make your eye red with staring, but know that the little creature you are looking at, namely, me, is angry. How do you find me?'

'O fine enough maybe, splendid and handsome. But as for reckoning you among the heroes – the great heroes – we don't count you at all.'

'That is enough speech,' said Cuchulain. 'You came under the protection of Fergus, otherwise only your shattered bones would return to the men of Ireland.'

In great wrath, they agreed to fight in the morning. But Etarcumul could not wait and swung his chariot round a hill and back towards Cuchulain.

'That fighter we just saw, little Cu,' said Laeg, 'he's coming back, and his left chariot-board is turned towards us.'

'A pity to disappoint him,' said Cuchulain. 'Hurry to the ford, Laeg, for I'm the man to give him a fight.'

Then they met at the water's edge, and Cuchulain, out of respect for Fergus, merely cut the sod from under Etarcumul's feet, so that he went tumbling.

'Begone now,' said Cuchulain. 'But for Fergus, I'd have chopped you in pieces, but I won't be washing my hands in your blood today.'

Again, the young man would not leave, and then Cuchulain had patience with him no more. He split him apart from his head to his navel and cut him cross-wise in two. After Etarcumul was dead, Fergus saw the rash fellow's chariot running free, empty of its master, so Fergus wheeled about and reviled Cuchulain.

'Devil,' he cried, 'little demon, what of the pledge you gave me? Do you think my club is too short to strike you?'

'Friend Fergus,' replied Cuchulain, 'do not be angry. Was it better that I should punish that vain fool, or that he should conquer me? The fault was his, as his charioteer will tell you.'

Then Fergus was content. The ankles of Etarcumul were tied to his chariot and he was dragged to the camp. His lungs and his liver knocked on every rough stone till his body was dumped at the tent of Ailill and Maeve.

'What brutality is this?' cried Maeve. 'Where is the guarantee that this monster gave to Fergus? This is how a coward honours his word!'

'Woman, are you mad?' Fergus answered her. 'If it is wise, a common cur does not snap at a bloodhound. Why, even I myself would hardly dare to raise a hand against Cuchulain.'

Then there was nothing else to do but to bury the poor fool Etarcumul.

The Finding of the Bull

Each day, Cuchulain fought in single combat, and in a very short time there was no competition among the four provinces of Ireland to meet him. Anxious to find the bull and stop the slaughter, Maeve went away with a third of her force. But Cuchulain followed closely to guard his territory, for his own land was dearer to him than any other.

Then from the direction of Sliab Culinn came twenty-four cloaked figures, driving the Brown Bull with fifty of his heifers. Buide, son of Ban, was the man in charge. Cuchulain saw the cattle and approached the party.

'From where are these animals?' he asked.

'From off that mountain.'

'And who are you to take them?'

'Buide, son of Ban,' he replied, 'one that neither loves you nor fears you.'

'For you, Buide,' said Cuchulain, 'I have the special gift of a little spear.'

And Cuchulain threw a spear which shattered Buide's ribs and ran into his heart.

While they argued and fought, with shouting and banging of shields the Brown Bull was driven towards the encampment where the men of Ireland were expected that night. The herdsman, who had been captured with the bull, did his best to prevent this. At a narrow gap, he stood in the path of the herd, to turn the cattle aside. But the tumult drove the cattle on, and they trampled the herdsman thirty feet into the ground and made a mincemeat of his body. Now nothing prevented the Brown Bull from falling into the hands of his enemies.

A part of the cattle raid on Cooley was complete, but Maeve had no satisfaction to see that Cuchulain was still close upon her.

'The best man to deal with him,' said the men of Ireland, 'is Cur Mac Dalath, a man unpleasant to be with, a danger to friend and foe. It would be no loss to us if he fell, though better indeed if he were to kill Cuchulain.'

Now Mac Dalath held the little boy of Ulster in contempt, but he went out to meet him with a cartload of weapons. He found Cuchulain practising his warlike moves and his passes at arms. He was practising the Apple feat, and the Edge feat, and the Level Shield feat, and the Little Dart feat, and the Rope feat, and the Feat of Cat, and the Hero's Salmon Leap, and the Pole-cast, and the Breaking of the Sword, and the Champion's Cry. He was doing his running and jumping and dodging and sideway leaping, with many cat-like twists and turns, roaring the while with many fierce shouts and howls. It was hard work indeed to get near him.

For a third of the day Mac Dalath stayed behind the boss of his shield, trying to get a blow in. Cuchulain took no notice. At last, Laeg the charioteer said, 'Little Cu, have the goodness to take a look at this fellow trying to kill you.'

Then Cuchulain suddenly looked up and flung an apple over the shield-rim and knocked a piece of brain the size of a ball out the back of Mac Dalath's head. That was the end of Cur Mac Dalath. After this, many of the men of Ireland cowered in their tents, while a few were sent out unhappily to do combat against Cuchulain. Loth and Srub Daire and Morc and Mac Teora and several others suffered and died. It is tedious to relate so many unlucky names.

There was no help for it but that Maeve must bribe with certain gifts those who had so little desire to meet Cuchulain in battle.

'Who is it,' said Cuchulain to Laeg, 'that will come next to meet me? Go to their camp with greetings to my foster-brother Lugaid. He shall know.'

'It is Ferbaeth,' Lugaid said to Laeg, 'Cuchulain's own kinsman, and mine too. Ferbaeth has gone to the tent of Finnabair, the royal daughter of Maeve and Ailill. It is she who pours the wine for him, and kisses him at every drink. Not for everyone is that liquor, for there's fifty loads of it and no more.'

Now, Cuchulain much disliked it to fight his own foster-brother, a man trained in his own school of weapons. But he made short work of it and removed Ferbaeth forever from the arms of Finnabair.

Next into the tent of Finnabair, to drink and kiss and burst the flock mattress with joy, was Larine. He was brother to Lugaid, a silly proud lad, but a strong-armed fighter. Even in the arms of Finnabair, Larine longed for day, to prove his mettle against Cuchulain. Out he went at first light, with arms of every kind. But the four provinces of Ireland yawned in their tents and turned over, and the women scoffed at his folly.

Cuchulain met him unarmed and took away his weapons, like taking toys from a child. Then he grabbed hold of Larine and crushed him, and squeezed all the excrement out of him till a poisonous gas arose around them. From that time, Larine never woke without complaint and never ate without pain. He had trouble in the gut, and a tightness in the chest, and cramps, and a running at the bowel. But he was the only man to survive single combat with Cuchulain, though he died later from his hurts and weakness.

About this time, Morrigan came to Cuchulain, in the guise of a pretty girl, dressed in many colours.

'I am the daughter of Buan, the Eternal King,' she said. 'Out of love for your fame I have brought you my treasure and my cattle.'

'No good,' replied Cuchulain. 'We are far gone here, famished rather than full. What use is a woman in such a struggle?'

'Women give a kind of help.'

'Do you think I make war for a woman's soft thighs?'

Then Morrigan turned on him and said, 'If not my help, then take my hindrance. When you fight, in the shape of an eel I'll entangle your feet. In the shape of a grey wolf I'll drive the cattle over you. In the shape of a red heifer I'll lead the herd that tramples you into the mud.'

Soon, when Loch, son of Mofemis, came to do battle at the ford, Cuchulain found a slippery eel tripping his feet, and a grey wolf howling the cattle into fright, and a red heifer leading the thunder of the stampede. Cuchulain squashed the eel in the fork of his toes, and took an eye out of the wolf with his sling-shot, and smashed the legs of the heifer from under it. But all the time Loch was hacking at him and drawing the life-blood from his body. In high anger, when he was free to turn on Loch, Cuchulain pierced the heart in his breast with a barbed spear and his spirit fled away.

'Give me a favour,' cried the dying man. 'Step back a pace, so I may fall to the east and not the west.'

'A warrior's request,' said Cuchulain, 'and I shall grant it.'

So Loch died for all men to see that his face was still toward the enemy.

Then Cuchulain was weary and wounded, and he called aloud in his sore distress:

Go forth, friend Laeg, and rouse the men of Emain.
Tell them I am sore wounded, blood drips from my
    weapon.
Tell Conchobor I stand alone at many fords.
I cannot hold the enemy, with only Laeg for friend.

Loch has mangled my hips, the she-wolf has bitten
    me,
The eel tripped me and Loch punished my liver.
Ulstermen, give battle to Maeve and Ailill,
While I'm here in sorrow, blood-flecked and
    wounded.

While he was calling in this despair, hag Morrigan came again from the magic hill of the *shee* in the shape of a one-eyed crone, milking a cow with three teats. She knew that only Cuchulain himself could cure her from the wounds he had given her. In his weakness and thirst, Cuchulain begged for a drink, and she gave him the milk of one teat. But his thirst still raged and she gave him the milk of the other two teats.

'A blessing on you, woman,' said he. 'May she who gives be quickly healed.'

And at once she was cured of the three blows Cuchulain had given her, when she was in the form of an eel and a wolf and a heifer.

The Great Sixfold Slaughter

The four provinces of Ireland pitched their camp in the Plain of Murthemne. Cuchulain kept watch on them, close by the fire that Laeg kindled against the night cold. Far off, Cuchulain saw the fiery glitter of the bright gold weapons in the setting sun. Rage filled him once more at the multitude of his enemy. He shook his arms and uttered a hero's roar. All the demons of the air gave answer, and Nemain, the war-goddess, brought confusion on the men of Ireland. They clashed their weapons to raise their courage, but a hundred fell before the night was done. The agreement was broken. No more was there single combat only. Carnage and blood-lust held the field.

In the morning, Laeg saw a solitary man coming from the enemy camp.

'What man is that?' asked Cuchulain.

'Soon told,' said Laeg. 'A tall, broad, fair man, close-cropped. A royal cloak about him, and a hard black shield in his hand. Wonderful is his work with spear and forked javelin. But no one is heeding him. Is it that they cannot see him?'

'True for you, friend Laeg,' said Cuchulain. 'It is a good spirit from the *shee* come to help me in my sore distress, as I stand alone against the four provinces of Ireland.'

'I am Lug, son of Ethlenn,' said the strange warrior, 'your spirit-father from the magic world of the *shee*. Sleep, little Cu, for your wounds are heavy upon you. I will hold the line against the men of Ireland.'

For three days and nights Cuchulain slept at Ferta, and the depth of his sleep matched the extent of his weariness. From the Monday of summer's end to the Wednesday of the beginning of spring he had not slept but only dozed a little, leaning on his spear, with his head resting on his fist. All the rest of the time he was striking and cutting and slay-ing and hacking the warriors of the four great provinces of Ireland.

Then Lug took plants from the *shee*, and healing herbs and curing charms, and he cleaned and bathed all the wounds and gashes of Cuchulain's body. Thus, in his sleep, Cuchulain was quietly healed.

At the end of three days Cuchulain awoke. He was revived

128

and ruddy with health. He was ready for a march or a feast or a battle or love-making. But he cried out, 'Alas, that I was not in my full mind and strength, for the youths that fell in the days of my sleep would not have done so.'

'Good words, little Cu,' said Lug. 'But be content. There is no stain on your honour, and your courage is no less.'

'Then stay, O warrior from the *shee*, and we will avenge the dead youths together.'

'Indeed I will not stay,' replied Lug. 'No man can match your bravery, or outdo your fame. Go on alone. At this time, none has power over your life.'

Then Cuchulain said to Laeg, 'Yoke the scythed chariot.'

Laeg got ready the chariot and then dressed himself in the manner of a hero. Carefully he looked at every point of his arms and armour, and he did not forget to cast a protective spell on both his horses and his companions. Today he prayed for the three gifts of the driver of horses – the leaping of the gap, the unerring driving, and the handling of the whip.

When the chariot was ready, Cuchulain put on his battle-array. First came the twenty-seven stiff, waxed shirts bound to his skin with cord. Over these he strapped on a jerkin of hard leather, made from seven yearling ox-hides. From this jerkin, spears or arrows fell back as if from stone. Then he put on a coat of smooth, fine silk bordered with gold, and he covered that with a surcoat of soft, black pliable leather. When he was dressed, he took up his arms: his ivory-hilted sword, his five-pronged spear, his javelin, his darts, his sling-shot, his curved shield with a rim so sharp it could shave hairs.

Lastly, he put on his great crested war-helmet, from which his howling battle-cry echoed and re-echoed like the roars and shouts of a hundred warriors. And from the helmet there came also the screams of devils and demons ringing in the air all about him, foretelling the bloodshed of many warriors. He wrapped about him his cloak of concealment, brought as a gift from the Land of Promise by the sea-god Manannan Mac Lir. Then he was ready.

The rage-fit was upon him. He shook like a bulrush in the stream. His sinews stretched and bunched, and every huge, immeasurable, vast ball of them was as big as the head of a month-old child. His face as a red bowl, fearsomely distorted, one eye sucked in so far that the beak of a wild crane could scarcely reach it, and the other eye bulged out of his cheek. Teeth and jawbone strained through peeled-back lips. Lungs and liver pulsed in his throat. Flecks of fire streamed from his mouth. The booming of his heart was like the deep baying of bloodhounds, or the growl of lions attacking bears.

In virulent clouds, sparks blazed, lit by the torches of the war-goddess Badb. The sky was slashed as a mark of his fury. His hair stood about his head like the twisted branches of red hawthorn. A stream of dark blood, as tall as the mast of a ship, rose out of the top of his head, then dispersed into dark mist, like the smoke of winter fires.

Then the hero sprang into his scythed chariot, with its bright blades and points of iron. The horses were lithe, fast-leaping, high-prancing, great-hooved. Cuchulain drove at his enemy, the warriors of the four provinces of Ireland, and performed his thunder-feat. He killed a hundred, two hundred, even five hundred. He did not think it too much, for he was now in full battle with the army of invaders. He remembered the wrongs done to Ulster.

He attacked with hatred in his heart, circling the enemy, throwing up great ramparts of corpses. Round and round he went, three times, leaving six layers of bodies lying foot to foot and neck to headless neck. Who can tell the full number of the slain? But not one in three of the men of Ireland escaped without the loss of an eye, or a broken thighbone, or a trench in the side of the head. Six score and ten kings did Cuchulain slaughter on the Plain of Murthemne, and a countless number of hounds, horses, women and children besides.

This was the Sixfold Slaughter of the Cattle Raid of Cooley. It was one of the three greatest slaughters ever seen.

The Encounter with Ferdiad

How could the four provinces of Ireland stand against Cuchulain? Now only Ferdiad, son of Daman, seemed man enough to protect them, a warrior with a skin of horn, and Cuchulain's own foster-brother.

But Ferdiad refused. He would not fight the friend of his youth, his foster-brother, his little Cu. Maeve sent druids and satirists to lampoon him and spite him and raise on his face the three blisters of shame, blemish and disgrace. Then for the sake of his honour Ferdiad went with Maeve's messengers, for he thought it better to die by the stroke of the sword than by the shafts of satire and reproach. In the camp of the men of Ireland, Ferdiad was greeted with respect. Strong liquor was pressed on him till he was merry and drunk. Fair Finnabair sat next to him, knee to knee, and gave him three kisses with every drink, and sweet apples plucked from the bosom of her dress.

Then Maeve spoke softly to him and said, 'Listen, O Ferdiad, to the rewards I offer you: a chariot worth four times seven bondmaids, clothes for a dozen men, a piece of the Plain of Ai, and freedom from tribute for you and yours for ever. This brooch I wear you shall also have, and my daughter Finnabair as your wedded wife. Is that not enough? Then take your pleasure as well from my own firm thighs.'

''Tis much,' said Ferdiad, 'but still I would rather not fight.'

'Then it is true,' replied Maeve with her usual cunning, 'what Cuchulain says, that it would be no great feat of arms for him to kill you.'

'He should not have said that,' Ferdiad answered. At once he gave his promise and prepared for the fight.

Now, when this became known to Fergus, he feared for his foster-son Cuchulain, for Ferdiad was a mighty warrior, and kinsmen had no business fighting each other. Fergus yoked his chariot and went to warn Cuchulain.

'Your own foster-brother Ferdiad, son of Daman, is coming against you,' he told Cuchulain.

'Bad news,' said Cuchulain. 'Out of love and affection I wish to avoid him. But if he comes armed to the ford, I swear the point of my sword will make his body sway and fall like reeds in the spring flood.'

That night, Ferdiad slept heavily but woke with the dawn, no longer drunk and merry, but starting up in full anxiety. He ordered the horses to be harnessed, but when the chariot was ready, he turned aside.

'Heavy I am with care and anxiety,' he said to the charioteer. 'Spread the skins and the coverings and I shall sleep some more.'

But Cuchulain was up by now. He mounted and advanced to the ford amid noise and uproar, the ringing of breastplates, the creek of harness and chariots, the drumming of hooves.

'Up, up, sir,' cried Ferdiad's charioteer. 'A large man comes, rising high out of his chariot. It is Cu the Hound, bright and deadly as steel.'

'Enough, man, praise him no more,' said Ferdiad. 'Make ready my weapons. I'll meet him at the ford.'

So they advanced, one from each side of the stream.

'In the matter of greetings,' Cuchulain called out, 'it is more fitting that I welcome you. For it is you that have invaded my country and province.'

'Little Cu,' Ferdiad replied, 'why do you mean to fight me? When we were youths, you were the helper who tended my spear and prepared my bed.'

'True indeed. But then I was young and small. That is not the way I am today.'

With many bitter reproaches they broke their friendship, and they threw at each other insults and strong words and taunts and threats.

'The malice and meddling of Ailill and Maeve have sent you here,' said Cuchulain, 'but things go badly for all who face me. And all for the sake of Finnabair! You will never wed her. She has deceived many men and will destroy you too.'

'Enough speech,' said Ferdiad. 'Now let us fight. Remember, little Cu, the feats of arms we practised with the masters of our youth? Let us put them to use.'

First, they threw darts and javelins so thick and fast that

they hummed in the air like the bees of summer. Then from midday to nightfall they hurled smooth-polished spears, evading the shields, making each other a red mess of gore and blood. 'Let us cease now,' they cried to the setting sun, and they handed their weapons to the charioteers.

Then they threw out their arms and kissed each other, and they went to rest on beds of fresh rushes and soft pillows. Their horses grazed together and their charioteers settled around the same fire. Of the herbs and charms brought for Cuchulain's wounds, he sent a portion across the stream for the healing of Ferdiad. And of the food and strong drink brought for Ferdiad's hunger, he sent a portion across the stream to raise the strength in Cuchulain.

So they went out on the second day. They fought again from dawn to night, till they went to their beds all bloodied and sore. But next morning, as they approached, Cuchulain said, 'Your look is not good today. Your hair is dark and dull, your eyes overcast, your figure drooping.'

"Tis not from fear of you,' said Ferdiad. 'There's no man in Ireland who can defeat me.'

But Cuchulain pitied him. 'Ferdiad, is it truly you?' he said. 'Sure it is that you are utterly doomed. Why do you fight your foster-brother for the sake of that woman?'

'O Cuchulain, noble warrior,' Ferdiad replied, 'all men must make the journey to the cold sod of the grave. Our darts and spears have settled nothing. Let us resolve the matter with our hard-smiting swords.'

They hacked and hewed and cut lumps from each other as big as fists, but no result came of this sword-play. Next day, Ferdiad came early to the ford. He felt the time of victory or defeat was on him, and he began to practise the brilliance of his war-feats.

'Laeg, look yonder,' said Cuchulain in admiration, 'those are the bold tricks and passes aimed at me.'

'Beware,' said Laeg, 'lest he will chastise you as a mother corrects her child. He will hammer you as flax is beaten in a pond. He will grind you as a mill grinds malt. He will pierce you as an axe splits oak.'

This day, they came together like charging bulls. Once more, the rage-fit was on Cuchulain. He grew huge, like an inflated bladder, and towered high over Ferdiad. In the closeness of the encounter, their heads and hands and feet knocked together and meddled with each other. The fury of their footwork thrashed the water out of the river-bed. Ferdiad caught Cuchulain below his guard and brought a torrent of blood from his wounded breast.

Then Cuchulain called for his barbed spear, which pierced and could not be withdrawn unless the flesh was cut away. Ferdiad saw it and took shelter, crouched low behind his shield. But too late. The spear drove through his thick apron of iron and entered Ferdiad at his backside, and filled every cranny of him with its barbs.

'Now I fall,' cried Ferdiad. 'My ribs are broken, my heart is gore. O why did I fight? Cu, little Hound, I am finished.'

When Cuchulain saw the end of Ferdiad, he ran forward and lifted him bodily.

'Madness and grief constrict me,' he lamented, 'after this deed. Alas, Ferdiad, I am sad that you did not follow the advice of Fergus. Sad indeed that you were deceived by the promises of the false woman of Connacht, fair-haired Maeve. No hero's hand hacked warrior's flesh so well as yours, O Ferdiad, companion of my youth.'

'Tug the guts over the stream,' said Laeg to Cuchulain, 'so the spoils will belong to us.'

But Cuchulain only looked at the body for a long time. Then he said, 'Strip him, friend Laeg, that I may see the brooch of Maeve for which noble Ferdiad did this battle.'

The clothes were stripped and the brooch removed, and then Cuchulain spoke again. 'Cut open the body, friend Laeg, and take out my barbed spear, for I cannot fight without that weapon.'

Laeg did so, and the blood and offal poured on the ground. Again, Cuchulain cried out, 'My weapon is crimson, your blood is drained, O Ferdiad, companion of my youth. Sad what befalls us, my foster-brother, one battle for both of us. But at the end of it there stands your death and my life.'

'Well, little Cu,' said Laeg, 'leave this ford now. We have been here too long.'

'Truly, it is time to leave,' said Cuchulain. 'But every battle I ever had now seems but play and sport after this fight with Ferdiad.'

The Men of Ulster Awake from their Pains

While these things were happening, Sualtam, the father of Cuchulain, heard of the distress of his son, fighting against so many.

'Is it the sky that cracks,' cried Sualtam, 'or the sea bursting, or the splitting of the earth? Or is it the howl of my son, alone in the face of the multitude?'

Hurriedly he came to help his son, but Cuchulain was wary of his help, for his father was only a middling fighter.

'Go rather to Emain Macha and to the men of Ulster,' Cuchulain said to him, 'and rouse them from the sloth of their pains. I can no longer protect them. I have been fighting from summer's end to the beginning of spring, and there is no point of my body, from hair to foot, where a needle might touch without blood on its tip.'

So Sualtam went and cried out to the men of Emain, 'Listen, O Ulstermen, men are being murdered, women raped, cattle plundered!'

Again and again he shouted this message. But he raised no answer, for none could speak before the king, and Conchobor never spoke before his druids. At long last, Cathbad the druid spoke out.

'Who is this,' he asked, 'that murders, rapes, and plunders?'

'It is Ailill and Maeve of Connacht,' replied Sualtam, 'who ravage your land, kill your folk, steal your cattle. Cuchulain alone holds in check the four provinces of Ireland. He is ragged and sore and his joints are bursting. A hazel twig secures his cloak, wisps of straw staunch his wounds.

Then said Conchobor the king, 'A little too loud is your cry, O Sualtam. The sky still holds, the earth is firm, the sea is calm. As for those warriors from the four provinces of

Ireland, I shall bring back from them every woman of Ulster to her home, and every cow to its byre. Let Finnchad of the Horned Helmet muster our army. Now the men of Ulster are awake from their pains.'

It was an easy task for Finnchad. All the princes and chieftains of Ulster had been waiting for Conchobor to recover and speak.

'We will not wait for the laggards,' said the king. 'We will catch the men of Ireland before they know that I have risen from my pains.'

Large hosts gathered on each side. Three thousand chariots were with Conchobor and Celtchar. The Connachtmen were ranged against them. Then Celtchar called out to his king, 'A hundred druids lead us, good men are at your back, O Conchobor. Let the warriors prepare for battle at Garech and Ilgarech!'

That same night, in the tents of the four provinces of Ireland, Dubthach of the Black Tongue cried out in his sleep:

> Fearful morning, monstrous time,
> Armies ravaged, kings undone
> Necks broken, blood on the sun.
> Host of Ulster – Conchobor's men –
> From that quarter red death comes.

Warriors burst into wakefulness, startled by prophecies and doomsaying. Nemain, goddess of war, muddled their wits. They clanged their weapons and struck about them wildly so that a hundred were killed.

'We have taken their women and their cattle,' Ailill shouted, 'we have levelled their hills. Why wait for their army any longer? Let us spy out a battle-ground on the broad plain of Meath.'

Mac Roth, the messenger, went forward, but soon he heard a thunder of tumult. The earth seemed to be in motion. Wild beasts poured over the plain like winter floods. But wise Fergus knew the cause of this. 'The din and uproar,' he said, 'is the work of Ulstermen attacking the woods. Champions and warriors are clearing the trees from the path of their chariots. It is this that has driven the animals over the land.'

Again Mac Roth went to spy the country. He saw a grey mist between sky and earth, and in the gaps there seemed to be caverns or islands in a lake. A pure white curtain like sifted snow hung before his eyes. In it he saw points of light that might have been shimmering birds, or the stars of a frosty night, or the sparks of a great fire. A strong wind tried to tear the hair from his head.

When all this was told to Fergus, again he knew the cause.

'Not hard to tell,' he said. 'It is the Ulster heroes on the march. The grey mist is the heavy breath of horses and men. The heads of the warriors, standing tall in the chariots, are the islands, and the caverns are the gaping mouths of angry horses from which drop the froth and spittle that makes the pure white curtain. The points of light are the fierce eyes of the warriors sparkling from the beauty of their rich helmets.'

'All this is of no account,' said Maeve, 'we have good soldiers to oppose them.'

'It may not be so,' Fergus warned. 'You will not find in Ireland or Scotland any warriors to match the Ulstermen when the rage-fit is upon them.'

The two armies advanced in sight of each other and halted in Slemain Mide. Then Maeve spoke to her chief counsellors.

'Let us make a good swift plan,' said she. 'Yonder huge, vehement fellow who would attack us is Conchobor, king of Ulster and son of the High-king of Ireland. Draw up our host in open array, face to face with the enemy. Take prisoners rather than kill, for those who oppose us are just the number of prisoners we need.'

While she was speaking, the Ulstermen began to muster on the hill, and they kept coming from dawn to twilight. By the hour of night they were all settled, each chieftain with the full number of his war-band ranged around the king.

'Well now, Mac Roth,' said Ailill, 'relate for us the number and the look of the enemy.'

Cuscraid the Stammerer was there, Conchobor's son, with the silver bands of victory on his spear. Next to him was handsome Sencha, he of the eloquent tongue. Tall Eogan, from the north, brandished his long sword, which was ornamented with ivory from walrus tusks. Near him was grizzled Loegaire, yellow-eyed, gaunt, merciless in close combat. At the head of a large troop was a scarred red face beneath a bush of black hair. It was thick-necked Muremur, son of Gerrcend. Connud Mac Morna curled his pretty hair. A salmon-brooch of bright metal held his long cloak. But he was a lion in heart and hard in battle.

Spreading over the hill, at the head of strong battalions, were many other bold and mighty men – stiff-necked champions, flaming torches of war, heroes, ridge-poles of the army, dragons, thunderbolts, destroyers, boars and breech-makers, the god-blessed and the battle-mad. Tight-knit, they closed their ranks around Conchobor the king.

'But who is he?' said Ailill to Fergus. 'I mean that wrathful, big-nosed, large-eared, coarse-haired, thick-lipped, great-bellied, ill-favoured one.'

'He is half of the battle,' replied Fergus, 'the head of the strife. He is the storm-wave that drowns, the sea that floods over. It is mighty Celtchar, from Lethglas in the north.'

Then Mac Roth said, 'I am tired of all this describing, but there is one more thing to say. I heard one last outcry spreading both east and west.'

'Indeed we know it,' replied Fergus. 'It is Cuchulain struggling off his sick-bed, trying to rise for battle despite his wounds and gashes. The men of Ulster hold him back, for he is unfit to fight after his combat with Ferdiad. They have tied him to his sick-bed with hoops and bands and ropes.'

The Final Battle

In the night Morrigan sowed strife and despondency between the camps. In darkness she sang:

The beak of the raven in the neck of men,
Blood will gush, flesh will be hacked.
Madness of battle, the warrior's storm,
Ruin descends on Cruachan's men,
Grief to Ireland, but to Ulster, all hail!

This woe whispered in Connachtmen's ears. In the same night, the voices of Nemain and Badb, sisters of war, summoned the men of the four provinces of Ireland to meet their fate on the fields of Garech and Ilgarech. When they heard this, many died wholly of fright. Surely it was a bad night for them.

Next morning, all the men of Ulster rose together at the call of their king. They rose stark naked but for the weapons in their hands. In their haste they trampled their tents to make a short way towards the enemy. This news reached Cuchulain, as he lay nearby at Fedan Collna.

But King Conchobor said to Sencha, 'Hold the men back. Look to the omens first. Let no man dare move before the rising sun.'

As they watched they saw the sun rise up golden, without blemish, radiating into the valley and filling all the wide glen.

'Now rouse the men of Ulster, bold Sencha,' said the king, 'for the time of battle has arrived.'

Then both armies took their weapons in hand and began to strike and hew and cut and slay and slaughter each other for a long time. This tumult was loud music to Cuchulain on his sick-bed, and he called out, 'How goes the fighting now, friend Laeg?'

'Bravely, most bravely,' replied he. 'My chariot could ride their backs from end to end, so thick are they on the battle-field.'

'Alas,' cried Cuchulain, 'that I have not the strength to be there.'

'Rest easy, little Cu. It is no disgrace for you. Your task is done.'

Then the armies on both sides re-doubled their efforts to strike and hew and cut and slay and slaughter each other for a long time.

In the midst of this battle Maeve saw that the hands of Fergus were idle.

'It is fitting, O Fergus,' she said, 'that you add your strength to our fight. When you were banished from your own country, we gave you help and land and kindness.'

'Had I but my sword today,' replied Fergus, 'I would cut the trunks of men and pile them high, and the limbs of Ulstermen scattered by me would be as numerous as the stones of a hailstorm.'

So Ailill sent a servant quickly for his own sword and gave it to Fergus. When he had it, Fergus struck so fiercely and mercilessly against the men of Ulster that Conchobor himself hurried forward to stem this rout. He raised his shield in front of Fergus, who gave it three strong brutal blows. The shield strained and groaned, and all the shields of Ulster groaned with it. But it held.

'Who holds this shield against me at Garech and Ilgarech?' cried Fergus.

'One younger and mightier than you,' replied Conchobor, 'one nobler also, who banished you from your territory and estate to live with deer and foxes. Make no attempt now to measure the length of your stride in your own land, you who are dependent on the charity of a woman, you who are already guilty of the death of the sons of Usnech. I, Conchobor, king of Ulster, repulse you and drive you back to the four provinces of Ireland.'

Fergus grasped the sword in both hands and swung it back till the point touched the ground. His intent was to strike three terrible blows, to make the Ulster dead outnumber the living. But Cormac, the exiled son of Conchobor, threw two arms about him.

'Angry and ungentle is this, O Fergus,' he cried. 'Remember that the days of your life began in Ulster.'

'Away from me, fellow,' shouted Fergus. 'I'll not live this day unless I give three mighty blows against Ulster.'

'Then turn your aim elsewhere,' said Cormac. 'Cut the tops from the hills above the battle-field, if that will appease your anger.'

Now the sword Fergus held was a sword from the magic mounds of the *shee*. When it struck it grew as big as the rainbow. So Fergus turned his hand level and cut off the tops of the three hills. They fell into the marsh below, leaving above the three Bald Heads of Meath.

On his sick-bed, Cuchulain heard the clang of sword on shield and said to Laeg, 'who dares to strike the shield of Conchobor while I am alive?'

'It is the hero Fergus,' Laeg told him. 'His sword grows as big as the rainbow. Slaughter slips from it like dross.'

Cuchulain struggled with his bonds while two false poetesses mocked his sickness with satire and feigned tears.

'Quick, friend Laeg,' he cried, 'cut me free of hoops and cords.'

In a twinkling this was done and he sprang from his bed. His first effort was to catch the poetesses and clash their heads like eggshells till their skulls oozed red blood and grey brains, even though his own wounds pulled apart and burst out the dressing of straw and moss that staunched them. His chariot was unyoked, his weapons not ready. But his eagerness was such that he took the body of his chariot up on his back and ran towards the battle.

'Ho, you there, Fergus,' he roared, 'turn and face me. I will scour you like washing in a tub. I will stoop like a hawk on a lark. I will abase you as if under a cat's tail. I'll grind your bones.'

'Who in Ireland dares to speak to me like that?' said Fergus.

'I, Cuchulain, your own foster-son. Your lot falls due. Now give way before me.'

Then Fergus turned and ran with mighty strides, and the men of Ireland went with him, routed towards the west. It was midday when Cuchulain joined the battle. At sunset the last band of Connachtmen fled over the hill. Nothing was left of Cuchulain's chariot but a fistful of spokes and a broken shaft.

The Battle of the Bulls

Under the shelter of shields, Maeve covered the retreat of the four provinces of Ireland. Quickly, she sent the Brown Bull of Cooley into Connacht by a safe route, with fifty heifers and eight guards, so that the Bull, if no one else, would arrive at Cruachan as she had sworn.

Then Maeve felt the monthly issue of her blood.

'Cover the retreat of the men of Ireland,' she said to Fergus, 'till I relieve myself.'

'By all the gods,' cried Fergus, 'this is ill-timed!'

'No help for it,' she replied, 'I must do it or die.'

So Fergus guarded the retreat while Maeve relieved herself. Three trenches she filled, each big enough for a household, in the field called the Foul Place of Maeve. Cuchulain, chasing the retreat, found her there. But he held his hand, for he would not strike her from behind.

'Grant me a favour today,' she said when she saw Cuchulain.

'Well?'

'Safeguard this army in retreat, at least till the men of Ireland have one westward past Ath Mor.'

Cuchulain granted this, and the host slowly marched westward while Fergus watched.

'A fitting end,' he said to the queen, 'to a shambles led by a woman.'

But Maeve replied with spirit, 'It was a band of foals led by a mare into unknown country. We perished for lack of good counsel.' And so the broken remnant of the four provinces of Ireland limped back to Cruachan.

As for the Brown Bull of Cooley, when he saw the beautiful strange land of Connacht he bellowed three times. Finnbennach, the White-horned heard him and advanced to the challenge. But who would judge this contest? Bricriu, son of Carbad, was the most just of men, for he favoured his friend no more than his enemy. He was the best man to judge, and he went to the gap where the bulls would fight.

Then the bulls pawed the ground and threw up fountains of earth. Their cheeks swelled like bellows in a forge. They rushed together, goring and thrusting with their horns. In the midst of their chasing and thundering, Bricriu could not avoid their trampling and was crushed to death. Such was the sad death of Bricriu.

The White-horned gored the side of the Brown Bull and stirred his inward guts. When Cormac saw this happen, he took a spear and gave the Brown Bull three jabs from head to tail.

'O wonderful treasure is this brute to us,' said Cormac, 'that cannot defend himself against a calf. Rouse yourself, bull of Cooley, men on both sides have died for you.'

The Brown Bull heard this, for he had human understanding. He roused himself. In his rage he whirled in a circle and smashed the leg of the white-horned. Still they fought on till the sun set, and even throughout the night the men of Ireland could hear bellows and uproar echoing throughout the bounds of the whole land. And in the morning, when they awoke in Connacht, they saw the Brown Bull coming from the west to Cruachan with the mangled mass of Finnbennach hanging from his horns.

Fergus saw them coming and said, 'Well now, men, let them be. White-horned or Brown Bull, great things have been witnessed here.'

And the men of Connacht meddled no more with the Brown Bull of Cooley. The bull went forward, fiercely shaking the remains of the White-horned all over Ireland. The liver of Finnbennach he left at Cruachan. The loin came to rest at Ath Mor. The thigh was thrown as far as Port Large. The rib-cage landed at Ath Cliath, later called Dublin.

At last, in his rampage across the land, the Brown Bull turned north and saw the summit of Sliab Breg, and he knew that he had come to the land of Cooley. Still in his rage, he turned on the women and children who had gathered to wonder at him, and he did great killing among them. But when he saw what he had done, he turned his back on the hill and his heart broke like a nut in his breast.

Ailill and Maeve made peace with Cuchulain and the men of Ulster. The men of Connacht were in their own land, and the men of Ulster returned to Emain Macha with their great triumph. And for seven years there was no more killing among all the provinces of Ireland.

5

UNDER THE SPELL OF LOVE

My body is out from my control,
It has fallen to her share.
I am in two pieces,
Now my bright gentle one is gone.

She was one of my feet, one of my sides –
Her face like the white-thorn –
I was hers more than mine,
She was half my eyes, half my hands.

She was the half of my body,
The fresh torch.
I am faint as I tell it –
She was the very half of my soul.

PWYLL
AND
RHIANNON

Once, when Pwyll was in Arberth with a great host of his men, he wished to stretch his body after the feast and he walked towards a low hill.

'Lord,' said one of the court, 'it is the virtue of this hill that whoever sits upon it will not go from it without wounds or blows, or the sight of a wonder.'

'Wounds or blows I do not fear,' said Pwyll, 'and as to the wonder, I would gladly see it.'

So they sat on that mound, and soon there came along the way a lady in shining brocaded silk on a big, fine, pale white horse. The horse ambled at an even pace. But when Pwyll sent a rider after the lady, no matter how much he put his spurs to his horse, he could not catch up with her.

The same happened on the next day, and the next. However fast the pursuer went, he could not reach the lady. The more he spurred on his horse, all the further was she from him. At last, Pwyll himself took his horse and drove it to its utmost speed. But when he saw it was idle to chase after her, he called out, 'Maiden, in the name of love, stay for me.'

'Gladly,' she answered, 'and it had been better for the horse if you had asked this long since.'

The lady waited for him, and then she drew her veil from her face and they began to talk. He looked on her and thought that the face of every woman he had ever seen was unlovely compared with her.

'Lady,' said he, 'tell me your errand.'

'My errand,' she replied, 'it was to see you. I am Rhiannon, the daughter of Hefeydd the Old, and I am promised to a husband against my will. Out of love for you, I will have no other man, unless you reject me. It is to hear your answer that I am come.'

'Between me and God,' said Pwyll, 'if I had choice of all the ladies in the world, 'tis you I would choose.'

So they were pleasing to each other, and they made a tryst to meet in a year, when a great feast for his coming would be ready in her father's court.

'Lord,' then said Rhiannon, 'if I am not to go to another man, keep you your promise.'

In a year they met again and seated themselves for a feast in the court of Hefeydd. As they were eating they saw enter a tall, auburn-haired, regal youth who came boldly before the company.

'A welcome to you, friend,' said Pwyll, 'take a place among us.'

'I will not,' said he. 'I am a suitor, and I come to ask a boon of you.'

'Whatever you ask,' said Pwyll, 'so far as I can get it, it shall be yours.'

'Alas,' cried Rhiannon, 'why do you give such an answer?'

'Lady, he has given it in the presence of nobles,' said the stranger. 'Now, my lord, this is my request. The lady I love best is to sleep with you this night. I have come to ask for her, and for this feast I see before me.'

Then Pwyll was silent till Rhiannon upbraided him. 'Be dumb as long as you will,' said·she, 'for never has a man made more feeble use of his wits. That is the person I was promised to against my will. It is Gwawl, son of Clud, a rich and powerful man. Now you have given your word, bestow me on him lest you dishonour yourself.'

'Lady, what answer is that?' said Pwyll. 'How can I do what you say?'

Then Rhiannon took Pwyll to the end of the hall and said, 'Bestow me upon him, and I shall ensure that he never has me. I shall make a tryst with him for a year from tonight, to sleep with me. And I will offer then a feast for him and his men. Let you be standing by, up yonder in the orchard, in shabby clothes, with a little bag I shall give you, and a hundred horsemen with you. When he is in mirth at the feast, enter with this bag in your hand and ask for nothing but the bag full of food. I will bring it about that not even the produce of seven counties would fill that bag.

'And he shall say, "Will this bag ever be full?"

'"It will not," you shall say, "unless a great man of power shall press it down with both his feet."

'So he shall tread down the food in the bag. Then quickly gather the bag over his head and knot the thong in the mouth. When he is tied, blow a blast on the hunting-horn about your neck, as a signal for your horsemen to fall upon the court.'

While thus they spoke privately, Gwawl grew impatient. 'Give me your answer,' he demanded in anger. So Pwyll granted his request, and he promised a tryst and a feast for Gwawl at the end of a year.

At the appointed time, Gwawl came eagerly to the court of Hefeydd and a welcome was given him. Beyond, in the orchard, Pwyll hid with his hundred men, and he was coarsely dressed with rags on his feet. When he heard laughter within, Pwyll entered with humble looks and asked a boon.

'Ask within reason,' said Gwawl, 'and you shall surely have it.'

'It is only for hunger. The boon I ask is this little bag full of food.'

Then servants arose and began to fill the bag. But for all that went into it, it was no fuller than before.

'Friend, will your bag ever be full?' said Gwawl.

'It will not,' replied Pwyll, 'unless a great man of power shall press it down with both his feet.'

'Brave sir,' cried Rhiannon to Gwawl, 'rise up and do it.'

At her call, Gwawl rose and put his two feet in the bag and stamped. And then Pwyll pulled up the neck of the bag and slipped the knot tight. He gave a full blast on his horn and his hundred warriors fell on the feast and tied fast the followers of Gwawl. When Pwyll had thrown off his rags and tatters, he ordered each of his men to strike a blow against the bag.

'What have we here?' each cried. 'A badger, a badger,' the others answered. Thus they played with the bag, kicking it and poking it with a staff. 'What is this game?' said one. 'Why, it is the game of Badger in the Bag,' replied the rest.

But Gwawl in his misery cried out, 'My lord, if you can hear me. This is no death for me, to be slain in a bag!'

'True what he says,' added Hefeydd the Old. ''Tis but a mean end, to be slain in a bag.'

'He has had punishment enough,' agreed Rhiannon. 'My lord Pwyll, take a pledge from him that he will never lay claim to me, nor seek vengeance for this.'

'Gladly, gladly I will give it,' came the voice from the bag.

Then Pwyll released Gwawl from the bag, and terms were drawn up and sureties given, as Rhiannon advised.

'Now I am content,' said Pwyll.

'Aye, but I am sore wounded and bruised,' said Gwawl, 'and I have need of a bath. Let me go on my way.'

Then Gwawl departed and the hall was made ready for Pwyll, as it had been the year before. They ate and made merry, and when the time came to sleep Pwyll took Rhiannon to their chamber, and the night was hardly long enough for the pleasure they had of it.

At last, in the new young day, Rhiannon said tenderly, 'Arise, lord, and reward the poets and minstrels. Refuse no one a gift today.'

Each suitor and minstrel was contented, according to the wish of each. And none was denied while the feast lasted. And when the end was reached, Pwyll said to Hefeydd the Old, 'With your permission, I will set out for Dyfed tomorrow.'

'God speed to you,' said Hefeydd. 'Appoint an hour when Rhiannon may follow you.'

'Between me and God,' replied Pwyll, 'we shall go hence together.'

So they travelled in the morn to the court of Arberth, and more gladness and feasting awaited them there. The foremost lords and ladies of the land came to them, and none left Rhiannon without a mark of goodwill – a gift of a brooch, or a ring, or a precious stone. And Pwyll and Rhiannon governed the land well and prosperously, that year and for many a year.

THE STRUGGLE WITHIN
THE HOUSE OF MATH

Math, son of Mathonwy, was lord over Gwynedd, and Pryderi, son of Pwyll, was lord over one-and-twenty counties in the south. And at that time Math might not live except he had his two feet in the fold of a maiden's lap. Now the maiden who was with him was Goewin, daughter of Pebin, and she was the fairest maiden of her time.

Math had two nephews, Gilfaethwy and Gwydion, the sons of Don, and these two lads lusted after Goewin. To get to her chamber, they devised a quarrel between Pryderi and Math. They stole from Pryderi the hogs that came from the underworld of Annwn, and when Math went to claim those hogs the sons of Don found Goewin alone. At Caer Dathyl, Gilfaethwy and the maiden Goewin were put in the bed of Math, and that night she was lain with against her will.

Then there was war between Pryderi and the sons of Don, over the theft of the hogs. In the course of the campaign, Gwydion and Pryderi agreed to meet in single combat, body to body, and by strength and magic Gwydion slew Pryderi. In the land above Y Felenrhyd, Pryderi was buried, and his grave is there.

When Math returned to Caer Dathyl, he sent for his maiden that he might put his feet in the fold of her lap. Goewin came but she said, 'Lord, seek another maiden to be under your feet. I am a woman now.'

'How is that?' he asked.

'An open assault was made upon me, lord, by your sister's sons. They did rape upon me and dishonour on you, and this was in your own chamber and bed.'

'As for them, my nephews,' said Math, 'I will have redress for you and revenge for me. As for you, I will make you my wife, and my realm I will give into your hands.'

Then a ban was made against the sons of Don, that none should give them meat or drink, and at last this forced them to come to Math.

'Lord,' said they, 'we are here at your will.'

'My dishonour you cannot make good to me,' said Math, 'let alone the death of Pryderi. But I will begin a punishment on you.'

Then Math struck them both with his magic wand, so that one became a stag and the other a hind.

'Go together and be coupled,' he said. 'Act like beasts and give birth as they do. And in a year from today return to me.'

A year went past, and on the appointed day there was an uproar of dogs beneath the wall. Then three beasts appeared – a stag, a hind, and a fawn. Math took his wand again and touched two of the beasts, turning the stag into a boar and the hind into a sow. But the fawn he changed into a boy whom he kept and fostered.

And so it happened, in the next two years, that Gwydion and Gilfaethwy, first in the form of hogs and then of wolves, brought forth two more sons whom Math kept and cherished. Then Math thought that the sons of Don had been punished enough, and he changed them with his wand back into their own flesh.

'Make them ready a bath,' said Math, 'and have their heads washed. And now, my nephews, you have had great shame, that you have coupled like beasts and brought forth young. Soon I shall offer you peace and friendship, but tell me first, what maiden shall I now seek?'

'It is easy to answer,' replied Gwydion. 'Aranrhod, daughter of Don, your sister's daughter, is the maiden for you.'

When the girl was fetched, Math summoned her and ordered her to step over his wand, to see if she were truly maiden. But as she did so, there was a loud infant squall and she dropped a fine boy-child with rich yellow hair. After the loud cry she rushed for the door, but some other small thing dropped from her. In a moment, Gwydion snatched it up and wrapped it in a sheet of silk and hid it in a chest at the foot of his bed.

Math was left with the yellow-haired boy whom he baptized and gave the name of Dylan. At once, Dylan made for the sea and went into it and received the sea's nature. He swam as well as any fish, and for this reason he was called Dylan, Son of the Wave.

Some time after, when Gwydion was in his bed, he heard a small weak cry from the chest at the foot of the bed. He opened it and saw little arms thrusting from the silk sheet. When he saw it was a baby boy, Gwydion gave him to be nursed to a woman who had milk, and at once the boy grew wonderfully. In one year he was as big as a two-year-old. The child stayed in the house of Gwydion and came to love him, and he became a sturdy lad always twice as big as another of his own age.

One day, when the two of them were walking, they came by Caer Aranrhod. When the lady had come out to greet them and they had talked, she asked Gwydion, 'What is the boy that goes with you?'

'This boy is your son,' said Gwydion.

'Alas, man,' said she, 'why do you pursue my shame and remind me of it? But what is the boy's name?'

'Faith, there is as yet no name on him.'

'Nor shall he have one,' said Aranrhod, 'till he get it from me. And I will swear on him a destiny.'

'Wicked woman,' cried Gwydion, 'you are angry with him because he made a question of your maidenhood. But never again shall you be called maiden"

The two went away and Gwydion plotted how to get the better of Aranrhod. He made a magic and put it upon himself and the boy. They appeared as shoemakers and sailed in a ship into the lee of the wall at Caer Aranrhod. Aranrhod was pleased to have new shoes. The boy began to measure her foot but then he saw a wren alight in the rigging. He took an aim and hit the little bird between the sinew and the bone of the leg.

'Faith,' laughed Aranrhod, 'the fair youth has hit it with a deft hand.'

'Now he has a name,' cried Gwydion at once, 'and a good one too. Let him be called Lleu Llaw Gyffes, that is to say Fair Deft Hand.'

Then the ship vanished away into the seaweed from which it had been formed, and Aranrhod saw again Gwydion and her son.

'He is named,' she said, 'but he shall never bear arms till I myself equip him.'

Gwydion reared the boy till he could ride any horse and was perfect in all exercises of the body. But he could see that the youth pined for arms. Once more they went to Caer Aranrhod, but this time in the guise of bards from Morgannwg.

'God's welcome to bards, now and always' cried Aranrhod.

In they went, and in the hall there was great joy at their coming and good meat and story-telling, for Gwydion was a great teller of tales.

That night, in the closeness of their chamber, Gwydion devised more magic. At dawn, he made it happen that there was a clamour of trumpets and a tumult of armies around the fort. Soon Aranrhod came bursting into their chamber, crying, 'Good sirs, we are in a bad place. I cannot see the colour of the deep for all the ships that swarm upon us. What shall we do?'

'Lady,' said Gwydion, 'there is no other counsel but to close the fort upon us, and to defend as best we can.'

With that, Aranrhod went to collect arms and armour, and when she returned Gwydion told her to assist in the arming of the youth, which she gladly did.

'Is the arming of that youth completed?' he asked.

'It is,' she said.

'Then we may now doff our arms, for we have no need of them. That fleet was raised by magic, to break your destiny concerning your son and to get him arms. And now he has them.'

'Wicked man,' she said, 'many a good youth might have lost his life in this mustering. So I will swear another destiny on this son. He will get no wife of the race that is now on the earth.'

When he heard this, Gwydion went to Math and made the most sustained complaint in the world against Aranrhod.

'Well,' replied Math, 'let us seek, you and I, by our enchantment and magic to conjure a wife for him out of flowers.'

Now, by this time Lleu Llaw Gyffes had become big in stature, as large as any man, and the handsomest youth ever seen. So Math and Gwydion took the flowers of the oak and the broom and the meadowsweet, and they conjured forth the fairest of maidens with the best of figures. And they called this maiden Blodeuedd, or Flower. Then the two young folk were brought together, and each was pleasing to the eye of the other. They talked and feasted and slept together. For their support, Math gave them good land and territory. They settled there and governed it, and all the people were content with their rule.

One time, when they were visiting Caer Dathyl, the chieftain Gronw Bebyr rode by hunting the stag. He chased long and hard, but as the night fell he was far from home and he went to the fort for lodging. That day, her husband Lleu had departed, but Blodeuedd out of charity came herself with a welcome for Gronw. The chieftain washed and changed and combed well his hair and went to sit with the lady. She looked upon him, and at that moment there was no part of her that was not filled with love. He gazed on her, and his heart was struck to the same degree, and they could not conceal it. Then their talk was all of joy and love, and before the night was old they had embraced. In the dark, they fled to a chamber and slept together.

Then they secretly took counsel how to remain together.

'There is no other way,' said Gronw, 'than this: you must learn from him how his death may be brought about. But do it underhand, in pretence of loving care for him.'

When Gronw departed and her husband returned, Blodeuedd greeted him most gladly, but when they went to bed she put a black look on her face.

'What has befallen you?' he asked. 'Are you not well?'

'I am troubled by the thought of your death,' said she, 'if you should die sooner than I.'

'God repay your loving care,' he said, 'but it is not easy to slay me.'

'Then for God's sake tell me the way. For my memory is a surer safeguard than yours, that we might scheme to avoid this death.'

'I will tell you gladly. The spear that kills me must be a year in the making, working only when folk are at Mass on Sunday. And I shall be slain neither within nor without a house, nor on horseback nor on foot.

'How, then,' she asked, 'may it come about?'

'In this way. Make a bath for me on the river bank, tightly vaulted over by a thatched frame. Bring a he-goat and set it beside the bath. Then if I shall be caught standing with one foot on the goat and one on the edge of the bath, whoever smites me will kill me.'

'I thank God for that,' said Blodeuedd, 'for all of this is most easily avoided.'

At once, she took this news to Gronw, and he laboured for a year in the making of the spear and in getting all things ready on the banks of the Cynfael river. Bath and thatched frame were prepared and a he-goat tethered nearby. Then Blodeuedd begged Lleu Llaw Gyffes to show her, for their greater security, just how the act might be done.

So in an evil hour he went into the bath, and when he was cleansed he stepped from it with a foot on the rim and a foot on the goat, and then Gronw loosed the spear with deadly aim. The shaft stood out from his side but the head of the spear stayed in him. With a loud scream Lleu flew up in the form of an eagle and vanished. Then the lovers were free for each other, and they subdued the land and ruled it.

Math, son of Mathonwy, heard this news with grief, and the sorrow of Gwydion was even greater. Very soon, Gwydion set out to seek that eagle. He travelled the length and breadth of the land till he came by chance to a house in Arfon where a swineherd was relating the strange journeys of his sow.

'Every day,' said the man, 'when the sty is open, out she goes, so fast that no one can keep in touch with her. It is as if she disappears into the earth.'

'For my sake,' said Gwydion, 'do this. Do not open the sty till I am prepared and ready to follow her.'

It was easily done, and then when the sow leapt forth Gwydion was after her. She went fast up the valley, but after a while she stopped and began to feed, and Gwydion could see that she fed on rotten flesh and maggots. He looked into the top of a tree and saw an eagle shaking maggots and flesh onto the ground. Gwydion thought that this eagle might be Lleu Llaw Gyffes, so he sang three verses of a powerful song and enticed the eagle down from the tree.

The eagle hopped down painfully and alighted on Gwydion's knee. Then Gwydion touched it with his wand and the bird took on human form again. Yet no one had ever seen anything as pitiful as this man. It was Lleu Llaw Gyffes and he was nothing but thin skin and out-sticking bones.

He was brought to Caer Dathyl and good doctors tended him, and before a year was out he was whole again. Then he lusted for revenge. He mustered a band of warriors, and they set out grimly after Gronw and Blodeuedd. When Blodeuedd heard them coming, she fled away with her maidens into the mountains. But as they ran, in their fear they looked ever backwards, and thus they stumbled into a lake where all were drowned except Blodeuedd.

While she was recovering on the bank, Gwydion and his men galloped to her, and Gwydion's face was like the thundercloud.

'I will not slay you,' he cried, 'but I will do worse. You shall be changed into the form of a bird. But for fear of other birds you will not dare to show your face to the light, and there will be enmity between you and all other birds. They will mob you and molest you wherever they see you. No longer shall you be Blodeuedd the Flower, but you shall be Blodeuwedd the Owl.'

As his lady had been taken and humbled, Gronw sued for peace. He offered reparation for injury, either land or gold or silver.

'By my faith, I will not accept any of that,' said Lleu. 'But I shall aim a spear at you in the manner that you aimed at me, and that is the best I shall offer you.'

'Well, let it be thus,' said Gronw sadly. But then he suddenly cried out, 'My men and foster-brothers, is there none of you that will take the blow for me?'

'Faith, there is none,' they all cried. And so Gronw could not avoid the blow.

They came to the bank of the Cynfael river and all was prepared as before. Gronw got up in the place between the bath and the goat and then said to Lleu, 'Lord, since a woman's wiles deceived me, I beg you let me set a stone between me and the blow.'

This request was granted. Gronw took a large stone from the bank and held it in front of his breast. But the spear of Lleu pierced right through the stone and the man. His back was cut asunder and Gronw was slain. And the stone is still there, on the bank of the river, with a hole through it.

Then Lleu Llaw Gyffes regained his Land, and he ruled prosperously over all of Gwynedd.

CULHWCH
AND OLWEN

When Cilydd took to himself a wife, the country prayed that the couple might have offspring. Through these prayers, the wife grew big with child, but she went mad and wandered far from house and home. So when her time was upon her, she was in a wild place where a swineherd was keeping pigs. Through terror of these pigs the queen was delivered. The swineherd took the boy and named him Culhwch, because he was found in a pig-run. But this child was of good and gentle birth, being first cousin to Arthur.

After the birth, the mother of the child continued to fail, and she said to her husband, 'My death is near, and then you shall wish for another wife. Wives bring many gifts. But do not despoil your son. For my sake, take no wife till you see a two-headed briar on my grave.'

The king promised this, and then the queen died. After a time, the king sent each morning to the grave, to see what was growing there. But before she died the queen had secretly ordered a servant to keep the grave stripped of growth. And the grave was bare for seven years till this man neglected his duty. One day, when the king was out hunting, he saw a briar on the grave, and then he wished for a wife. He asked his counsellors what woman would suit him. They answered that the wife of King Doged would be best for him. So Cilydd attacked Doged, slew him, took his wife and daughter, and possessed his land.

Culhwch grew up away from the court and it was a long time before the new queen learnt of her step-son. Then she chided her husband and had him bring her step-son to court. She saw that he was a bold brave youth.

'It were well for you to take a wife,' she said to Culhwch, 'and I have a daughter worthy of any nobleman.'

'But I am not yet of age to take a wife,' said Culhwch.

'Then I will swear a destiny upon you,' replied the queen. 'Your body will never lie against woman till you win Olwen, the daughter of Ysbaddaden, Chief Giant.'

The youth flushed red, and love of that maiden entered into every bit of his body, though he had never seen her. At once, he went to his father.

'My step-mother has sworn on me,' he said, 'that I needs must win Olwen, daughter of Ysbaddaden, Chief Giant.'

'It is not difficult,' replied the king. 'Arthur is your first cousin. Go to Arthur to trim your hair, and ask a gift of him.'

Off went Culhwch on a grey horse, and not the tip of his sleeve fluttered, so lightly did the horse step. The boy had a sword at his side and a battle-axe in his hand, sharp enough to cut the wind.

'Is there a porter here?' Culhwch called at Arthur's gate.

'There is, and the head lies uneasy on those who ask. I am porter each first day of January, and then there are others. One goes on his head to spare his feet, like a rolling stone on a hard floor.'

'Open the gate,' cried Culhwch.

'That I will not. There is a throng in the hall, knife has gone into meat, and drink into horn. Now, save for a crafts-man or the son of a king, none may enter. But in the hospice you may have food enough for fifty men. Meat for your dogs, corn for your horse, hot peppered chops for yourself. Also wine brimming over, and delectable songs, and a woman for your bed. And tomorrow, when the gate is open, you shall sit where you like in Arthur's hall, high or low.'

'I will do nothing of that,' replied Culhwch. 'If you do not open, I will give three shouts at the entrance, no less audible in Cornwall than in the depths of the north or in Ireland. And every woman bearing child will miscarry, and those not with child shall have a stone in the womb.'

'Shout as much as you like,' said the porter, 'but wait here till I have a word with Arthur.'

The porter went into Arthur and said, 'I have seen at the gate many fair kingly men, but never one so comely as the one now there.'

'Well,' replied Arthur, 'you have entered walking but go out running. It is a shameful thing to leave one such as that in the wind and rain.'

'Nay, sir,' said Cei, who was listening, 'the laws of this court should not be broken.'

'Not so, fair Cei,' said Arthur. 'We are noble men only so long as our folk call to us. The greater our bounty, the greater our nobility and fame and glory.'

Then Culhwch was brought in, and he saluted the king and the company.

'O king,' he said, 'I come here not to beg meat and drink. If I ask a boon, I will repay it, and I will praise it. I will carry your renown to the four corners of the world.'

'Fair youth,' replied Arthur, 'you shall have your boon as far as the wind drives, the rain wets, the sun runs, and the sea stretches.'

'God's truth thereon?'

'Gladly. Name your request.'

'I will,' said Culhwch. 'I would have my hair trimmed.'

Then Arthur took silver shears and a golden comb and trimmed him.

'Tell me your name and ask what you wish,' said Arthur, 'for my heart grows tender towards you.'

'I am Culhwch, son of Cilydd, and I wish that you would get me Olwen, daughter of Ysbaddaden, Chief Giant. I invoke her in the name of your warriors.'

But Arthur had never heard of this maiden, nor could his messengers find her.

After a time, when they had looked far and wide, Culhwch said, 'Everyone has obtained his boon, yet I am still lacking. I will go away and take your honour with me.'

'Be not so hasty,' said Cei, 'and come with us. If she exists in this world, we will not part from you till we find her.'

Arthur called on his best men to go with Cei. First was one-handed Bedwyr, who could still spill blood in the battle better than any three warriors. Then there was Cynddylig the Guide, and after him came Gwrhyr, Interpreter of Tongues, and Gwalchmei the Walker and Menw the Caster of Spells.

Away they went, travelling far across a wide open plain till they saw a fort in the distance. They could also see a great flock of sheep without limit or end. And a shepherd in skins was attending them, with a shaggy mastiff bigger than a nine-year-old stallion. Never a lamb had this shepherd lost, much less a grown beast. No man could pass the shepherd without deadly hurt, and his breath seared black the dead trees and bushes.

'Interpreter of Tongues,' said Cei, 'approach yonder fellow and have words with him.'

'It is safer to go all together,' said Menw. 'And have no fear, for I will put a spell on the dog.'

So they went forward to speak to the shepherd.

'The world goes well with you, shepherd?' said they.

'As well with me as with you,' he replied. 'There is no affliction to do me harm save my wife.'

'Whose sheep are these, and whose fort?'

'Are you fools? All the world knows that this is the fort of Ysbaddaden, Chief Giant.'

'And you, who are you?'

'I am Custennin the Shepherd, and because of my wife the Chief Giant has wrought my ruin. But who are you?'

'We are messengers from Arthur, come to seek Olwen.'

'Ho, men, God protect you! Never a man has asked that and gone away with his life.'

Then Culhwch gave Custennin a gold ring, so that he might be a friend to them. And when the shepherd's wife saw this ring, she knew that the Culhwch, son of Cilydd, who had arrived was her own sister's son. And she was sad because his quest for Olwen made his life in danger.

The travellers were taken to the shepherd's house, and then the wife opened a coffer in which was hidden a little lad with curly yellow hair.

''Tis a pity to hide a lad like that,' said Gwrhyr.

'He is the only one left,' said she. 'Three and twenty of my sons have been killed by Ysbaddaden, Chief Giant, and I have no more hope for this one than the others. But God protect you, how will you win your way to Olwen?'

'Is there a place where we may see her privately?'

'Every Saturday, she comes here to wash her head,' replied the wife, 'and all her rings she leaves in the bowl. But I will not betray one who trusts me. Only if you pledge her no harm will I send for her.'

That promise was given, and Olwen came, with a robe of flame-red silk about her. Her hair was more yellow than the flower of broom, and her flesh whiter than the foam of water. Her eye was brighter than the eye of a falcon, and her breast fairer than that of the white swan. Whoever beheld her was filled with love for her. White trefoils grew in her path, and for that reason she was called Olwen.

When she came and sat in the shepherd's house, Culhwch knew her at once. His heart went out to her and he said, 'Ah maiden, 'tis you I have loved. Now come with me.'

'It would be my sin if I did so,' said Olwen. 'I cannot go without my father's consent, for his life will end when I get a husband. But go and ask my father. However much he demands from you, promise to give it, and then you shall have me too.'

She took them to her father's fort where the gates were down and the men on guard. Nine men were killed at the gates without a sound, and nine mastiffs without one squealing. Then the messengers of Arthur went to the hall.

'In the name of God and men,' they cried, 'greetings unto you, Chief Giant! We have come to seek Olwen, your daughter, for Culhwch son of Cilydd.'

'Where are my rascally servants?' roared the giant. 'Raise up the forks under my two eyelids that I may see my future son-in-law.'

That was done and he had a good look. Then he said, 'Come again tomorrow and I'll give you some kind of answer.'

But as they rose to leave, Ysbaddaden, Chief Giant, snatched up a poisoned spear and hurled it after them. Bedwyr caught it, hurled it back, and pierced the giant through the ball of the knee.

'Cursed savage son-in-law,' he cried. 'Now I shall walk the worse up a slope. The poisoned iron has pained me like the sting of a gadfly.'

Next day, they came again with pomp and brave combs in their hair to demand the daughter of the giant. He asked for more time to take counsel, but again as they were leaving he threw a second spear. Menw hurled it back, and it pierced the giant through and through, coming out at the small of his back.

'Cursed savage son-in-law,' he roared again. 'The hard iron has pained me like the bite of a big-headed leech. When I go uphill I shall have tightness of chest, and belly-ache, and a frequent loathing of meat.'

On the third day they begged the giant to throw no more spears. But still he grabbed one and threw it. Culhwch hurled it back, and it pierced the giant through the ball of the eye and came out of the nape of the neck.

'Cursed savage son-in-law,' he roared again. 'The iron has wounded me like the bite of a mad dog. So long as I am alive, my sight will be the worse. My eyes will water against the wind, and I shall have headache and giddiness each new moon.'

But on the next day the messengers said roughly, 'Shoot no more. Seek not deadly hurt and martyrdom, or you may get worse. Give us your daughter.'

'Who seeks her?' asked the giant.

''Tis I, Culhwch, son of Cilydd.'

'Give me what I shall name to you, then you shall have my daughter.'

'Then name what you wish.'

Ysbaddaden, Chief Giant, began to name the many hard things that he wanted for the celebration of a wedding and a feast, and a myriad of things were these indeed.

'See that great thicket yonder?' the giant began. 'All in one day it must be uprooted and burnt and ploughed and manured and sown, so that the crop will be ripe in the morning against the drying of the dew, in order that the feast may be cooked for my daughter and my guests.'

'That is easy for me,' replied Culhwch, 'though you think it not easy.'

'There is more,' went on the giant. 'Fetch the man to till the land. He will not come of his own will, nor can you force him.'

'That is easy for me,' said Culhwch, 'though you think it not easy.'

'There is more. Bring the man to the headland, to form and make the iron plough. He will not willingly work, nor can you compel him.'

'That is easy for me, though you think it not easy.'

'There is more. Yoke two oxen together to plough the rough ground, and one ox is on this side and the other is in Scotland. And though all this you might get, there are things you will not get.'

'That is easy for me,' said Culhwch again, 'though you think it not easy.'

'But there is more, and many things more,' said the Chief Giant. 'For the proper conduct of the feast I must have nine measures of flax seed sown. I must have honey sweeter than that of a virgin swarm. The drinking-cup of Llwyr. The food-hamper of Gwyddneu. The serving-horn of Gwlgwad. The harp of Teirtu. And the birds of Rhiannon that wake the dead and lull the living to sleep.'

'That is easy for me, though you think it not easy.'

'But listen further. I must have the Irishman's cauldron to wash my head, and the tusk of the Chief Boar to shave me, and the blood of the Black Witch to dress my beard, and the vessel of the Dwarf to keep the blood in.'

Thus on and on went the Chief Giant, piling difficult thing on more difficult thing. Yet to everything Culhwch only replied, 'That is easy for me, though you think it not easy.'

'No sleep at night and wakefulness,' said Ysbaddaden, Chief Giant, 'shall you have in seeking all those things. And still you will not get them, nor will you get my daughter.'

'I have horses and horsemen,' replied Culhwch, 'and my lord and kinsman Arthur will get me all those things. I shall win your daughter, and you shall lose your life.'

With that, the messengers left the fort of the Chief Giant and returned to the court of Arthur and told him how it had gone with them. Arthur offered his own help, but after the first task had been done, the men said to him, 'Lord, get you home. It is not worthy of you to seek things as petty as these.'

So Arthur went no more but sent his men on the quest with many kind words.

The men took counsel together and decided to begin their quest with the search for the huntsman, Mabon, son of Modron. When three nights old, he was taken from his mother and no one knew where he was, or whether he was alive or dead.

After long searching, Mabon was found and rescued from his prison. Thus the quest was well begun. As they went on over the Three Realms of Britain, and even into Ireland, one by one they accomplished what Ysbaddaden, Chief Giant, had imposed on them, and at last they returned to Arthur's court.

'What marvel is still to be done?' he asked.

'There is one,' they replied. 'We have yet to fetch the blood of the Black Witch from the Valley of Grief in the uplands of Hell.'

Now this was a task worthy of Arthur, so this time he set out with them. They found the hag and attacked her in her cave. But she caught the servants of the king by the hair of the head and threw them down and disarmed them. Then she drove them out squealing. Arthur was angry to see his servants well-nigh killed. He wanted to grapple the hag with his own hands, but his men stopped him.

'It is not seemly or pleasant,' said they, 'to see you scuffling with an old hag. Let your servants deal with her.'

More servants entered the cave but they fared as badly as the others. And God knows, not one of them would have left that place whole had not each one been loaded on Llamrei, Arthur's own mare. Then Arthur himself entered the cave and threw his great knife at the hag. It struck her across the middle and separated her in two, as if she were two tubs. At once, Cadw of Prydein caught up the witch's blood, and they all fled away from that dire place.

When all the marvels had been collected together, Culhwch took them to the court of the Chief Giant. With him were the son of Custennin and all those others who had reason to hate Ysbaddaden, Chief Giant. The giant demanded the performance of all the promises made to him. One of the tasks was to shave the giant with the tusk of the Chief Boar. Cadw was the man to do the shaving, and as he did so he cut flesh and skin to the bone and took off the giant's two ears outright.

'Is that shave enough for you, man?' asked Culhwch.

'It is,' said the giant.

'Is your daughter now mine?'

'Yours indeed,' said Ysbaddaden, Chief Giant. 'Do not thank me for her. It is Arthur who has secured her for you. You would never have gained her alone. And now it is the time to take away my life.'

So the son of Custennin, the little lad who had been

hidden in the chest, took the giant by the hair and dragged him to the mound of the fort. Then he cut off the head and set it on a stake on the battlements, and the son of the shepherd took possession of the fort and the lands of the Chief Giant.

That night, Culhwch and Olwen slept together, and she was his only wife for as long as he lived.

MIDIR AND ETAIN

Midir was from the hill of the *shee* in Bri Leith and he had a wife called Fuamnach. But his heart went towards Etain and he married her also, to the great jealousy of his first wife. Fuamnach asked the help of the druid Bresal, and he put a spell on Etain and drove her out of her own house.

The wind caught her up and whirled her away to Angus Og, the son of the Dagda, and he kept Etain and nourished her. He made a bright house for her, with clear windows, and filled it with the scent of flowers, and she could see out but none could see in. After a time, Fuamnach heard that Etain was safe and well, and this made her hatred grow stronger. She went to the bright glass house when Angus was away. Then with more druid spells she turned Etain into a butterfly, and she raised such a blast of wind that Etain was thrown high and far across the sky.

For seven years the wind buffeted Etain about till she was blown into a house in Ulster where the men of Inver Cichmany were feasting. From a beam of the roof she fell into a gold cup that was beside the wife of Etar. The woman drank her down with the wine, and at the end of nine months Etain was re-born from the womb of Etar.

Then this new child grew up in the house of Etar with fifty maidens about her, and she was well fed and well clothed. On a certain day, when all the girls were bathing in the bay of Cichmany, they saw a rider with very high looks coming towards the water. He was on a big bay horse with a curly mane and a flowing tail. A green cloak was about him, and his shirt was embroidered with red-gold thread. A shield of silver rested on his back, and his spear had rings of gold from shaft to head. Fair yellow hair he had, drawn back from his forehead with a braid of gold.

'Etain is here,' he called, 'by the Hill of Fair Women. among the children at play. O Etain, for your sake Eochaid of Meath will fight many battles. War will come to the *shee*, and thousands will suffer.'

After he had spoken he vanished, and no one knew where he went.

Now, while Etain was growing to womanhood, Eochaid was High-king of Ireland. At this time, he ordered a feast at Tara and invited the men of Ireland there to make their tribute.

'We will not come,' they answered, 'during such time, long or short, that the king of Ireland remains without a worthy wife. For among our noble men there can be none who is wifeless, and no king without a queen. Nor does any man go to the feast without his lady.'

So Eochaid sent messengers to search all the land for a maiden girl worthy to be queen. Soon they returned and told the king of the girl at Inver Cichmany, beautiful beyond all others.

The king set out to see her, and as he rode over the green at Bri Leith he saw a fair woman letting down her hair to wash it, with a golden basin by her side. Her arms coming out of her smock were as white as the new night snow, and her cheeks were as rosy as the foxglove. Her eyes were blue as hyacinth, her lips crimson, and her teeth like pearls. The brightness of the moon was in her face, high pride on her forehead, and the light of wooing in her eyes.

The desire of her seized upon the king and he said, 'Maiden, who are you?'

'Easy to tell,' she replied. 'I am Etain, daughter of the king of Echrad. Twenty years have I grown by the magic mounds of the *shee*, and their kings from below have been wooing me. But never one of them has slept with me. 'Tis for you I have come here. I have heard such high tales of your looks and splendour that I have come to love you. I will be yours. Pay whatever bride-price befits me, and after that let my desire for you be fulfilled.'

Eochaid paid her bride-price and took her to Tara where a fair and hearty welcome was made for her.

It was the feast of Samhain, at summer's end, and for a fortnight there was good eating and drinking. Ailill, brother to Eochaid, was at the court for the festival. He was also called Anglonach, for he had Only One Fault. When Ailill saw Etain, his brother's fair wife, he could not look away.

'What far thing are you gazing at?' said his wife. 'Such long looks are a sign of love.'

At this, Ailill turned colour in his face and looked no more. But he could not forget what he had seen and he became sick with desire and envy.

For a year, Ailill grew pale and thin, then his brother Eochaid came to him and put his hand on his breast.

'Brother, how fares it with you?' he said.

'I am not any easier,' said Ailill, 'but worse day and night. I cannot say what ails me.'

So the king sent Fachtna, his own doctor, who came and listened to Ailill's heart.

'This sickness will not kill you,' said Fachtna, 'for I know it well. It comes from the pangs of envy, or the pangs of love, and you have not found a way out of it.'

When he heard this, Ailill was shamed and would not confess himself to the doctor, so Fachtna left him.

Soon after this time, Eochaid went on a visit of all the provinces of his realm. As he was still worried about the health of his brother, he said to Etain, 'Fair lady, while I am away care for Ailill gently so long as he lives, and make a grave in the sod for him if he dies. Raise a stone over the grave and write his name on it in Ogham.'

Then Eochaid left for the space of a year. And Etain dealt tenderly with Ailill. Often they talked together, and when she saw that he got no better she sang for him and then said, 'Fair youth, whose step was once so strong, what ails you? You are wasting in bed, yet the sun still shines.'

'There is good reason for it,' he replied. 'My joy is gone, my harp no longer pleases, my lips turn away from food.'

'Tell me, you poor man, of your trouble. I am wise and may help you.'

'My words would choke me. Woman-secrets are best hidden.'

'If there is one among the fair faces of Ireland who torments you so, I myself will woo her to come to your side.'

'Woman,' replied Ailill, 'you yourself can put this sickness from me. A love, as long as a year, holds closer to me than my skin, and its strength is stronger than wrath. It shakes my world into four pieces.'

Then Etain stood rooted, for she saw now what his sickness was, and it was a heavy trouble to her. But she still tended to him, and brought him food, and poured water over his hands, for it was a grief to her that he should pine away for her sake. And on a certain day she came to him early and said, 'Rise-up, Ailill, son of a king.'

Then she threw arms about him and kissed him and said further, 'I will heal you. Come at the break of day to the house outside the fort, and I shall give you all you desire.'

That night, Ailill struggled with sleep, but close by the dawn he slept soundly at last, well into the day. Etain went to the place of meeting, and at the right hour she saw a weary sick man coming slowly towards her. But when he came close she saw it was not Ailill. Then the man went away and she returned to the fort.

Ailill woke at mid-morning, and when he knew he had missed his meeting he would rather have had death than life. But Etain soothed him with words, and they made another tryst for the next morning.

The same thing happened on the second, and on the third day. But on that day Etain spoke to the strange man.

'It is not you I come to meet,' she said. 'Why are you here? The man I would meet, I come to him not from desire or fear but to cure him from the sickness he has caught from the love of me.'

'It is more fitting for you to meet me,' said the stranger, 'than any other man. Long ago, I was your husband and your first man.'

'What thing are you saying?' she cried. 'And what name have you in this land?'

'That is easy to tell. I am Midir of Bri Leith.'

'And what made you part from me, if it was as you say?'

'It was the jealousy of Fuamnach and the sorcery of Bresal the druid that drove us apart. And now, Etain, will you come with me?'

'I will not,' she said. 'What sense is it to give up the high-king of Ireland for a man unknown to me and of unknown kindred?'

'It was I myself,' said Midir, 'who filled the mind of Ailill with love for you. And it was I who stopped him from meeting you, to keep your honour whole.'

Then Etain returned to the house of Ailill and told him all that had happened. When he heard this, Ailill was cured of both his sickness and his desire.

'It has fallen well for both of us,' said he, 'for I am cured in body and mind, and you are unhurt in your honour.'

'Thanks be to all our gods,' she replied, 'for this blessing upon us.'

Soon after, Eochaid came back from his journey. He saw that his brother was cured, and he praised Etain for the good deeds she had done for Ailill's health.

Now, in the summer of that year Eochaid the king was at Tara. He was looking over the Plain of Breg, a place beautiful in its colour, and excellent as to blossom, with all manner of growing things. Then he saw a strange young warrior approaching, and this was the very same high handsome rider that appeared before, when the girls of Inver Cichmany were swimming in the bay.

'I give you welcome,' said Eochaid, 'though to me you are as yet unknown. Declare yourself.'

'A good greeting,' replied the stranger, 'but in truth I know you well. My own name is nothing very great. I am Midir of Bri Leith. I have come to play a game of chess with you.'

'Truly, I am skilful at chess-play,' said the king. 'But the chessboard is in the house, and Etain is asleep there at this time.'

But Midir produced his own silver board set with precious stones, and his own chessmen of gold. He set out the pieces and said, 'What stake shall rest on the game?'

The first game was played for fifty grey horses. Midir held back his hand, so the king won and Midir paid the stake. They played again and the king won, and this time he gave Midir a hard task. He was to clear rocks and stones from the plains of Meath, and reeds from the lands of Tethba, and trees from the forest of Breg, and lastly to build a causeway across the bog of Lamrach.

Midir summoned his people of the *shee* from Bri Leith, and even though they had the powers of magic there were still hard days enough for them in the doing of all these things. Eochaid was out at the daybreak watching them, and he saw that the folk of the *shee* yoked their oxen at the shoulder and not by a strap over the forehead, as used to be done. Then the king taught this way to his own farmers, and for this he gained the title of Eochaid Airem, that is to say Eochaid of the Plough.

Thin and weak was Midir after all this work, but he came to Eochaid to play a third game of chess. They played, and this time Midir did not hold back his hand.

'The stake this time,' said he, 'it is Etain your wife.'

'That shall not be,' said the king.

'Then let me put my arms about her and kiss her but once,'

said Midir. This was agreed, and a time was set for the end of the month.

On the appointed day Midir came back to Tara and stood in the hall as handsome a man as ever was seen. The champions of Ireland, ring upon ring, stood guard around the fort, and the king and the queen were in the midst of their house, with the outer courtyard shut and locked. It would be a hard fight to break in or out.

'I have come to be paid,' said Midir. 'Etain is the price due to me.'

When Etain heard this she changed colour and was ashamed. But Midir said to her, 'Let there be no shame on you, Etain, for I have sought your love through the length of a year. You have refused my riches and my treasure and my body till such time as your husband would give you leave.'

'That is spoken truly,' said Etain. 'Now what says my husband?'

'You shall not go,' said Eochaid. 'He shall have only as much as I promised, that is to say one kiss with his arms around you.'

Midir took his sword in his left hand and the woman beneath his right shoulder, and he kissed her. The warriors of the king closed in on them and made a rush for them, but Midir lifted Etain as lightly as a spider's web and they flew up through the skylight of the house and out into the air. The champions of Ireland gazed up but could not follow. What they saw was a pair of swans steadily beating the air with great wings, joined by a slender gold chain.

In his anger, Eochaid searched for them throughout all Ireland. But nothing was heard of them, for they were safe under the hills, in the dwellings of the *shee*.

THE SONS OF
USNECH

Fedlimid, son of Dall, was harper and bard to
Conchobor the king, and the men of Ulster listened to
his tales. On a certain day Fedlimid was speaking, and
the men were in their cups, and the wife of the bard stood
by the board to serve them. She was big with child. At
the end of the feast, when the men went fuddled to
bed, the wife of Fedlimid wished also to sleep. But as she
went through the silent house her child cried in the womb,
and the cry went to every chamber so that men sprang up
in alarm. The woman was brought before the company and
Fedlimid spoke to her.

'What is that cry,' he said, 'torn from the womb by terror
and hurt? My heart is full of foreboding.'

The woman turned away, having no words to say, and went
to the druid Cathbad for the help of his secret knowledge.

'O druid,' she said, 'I know nothing of that cry from within me. The understanding of woman enters not into the womb.'

Cathbad laid his hand on the body of the woman and felt the baby stir within.

'It is indeed a girl-child who is there,' he said. 'Deirdre shall be her name, and sorrow shall be upon her. Blood shall be shed for her, and the light of many bright heroes of Ireland shall be snuffed out.'

And when the child was born, Cathbad held the baby in his arms and told of her fate.

'O Deirdre,' he sang, 'flame of beauty, fair of face, men shall weep and women wail for the trouble you bring. Pity Ulster, have pity for the angry deeds that shall be done in Emain. In your face I see the shadow of banishment and death. Poor fair child, you shall be a giver of wounds, a cause of blood-letting.'

Then the young men of Ulster cried out. 'Let the babe be slain!'

But Conchobor the king would not have it so.

'This child,' he said, 'shall be reared apart, according to my will. In time, she shall be my wife and the companion of my years.'

Who could stand against the wish of the king? The nurse, Levarcham, took the babe to a place far from eyes and ears. On the wild mountainside a little house was made, by a green hillock, with apple-trees beside it and a wall all around. A roof of green sods covered the house, and none entered there except by the command of Levarcham.

Deirdre grew up without the friendship and meetings of people, wandering alone in the lonely hills. She was as fine a girl as you might see, none prettier, as slim and tall as a rush, as graceful as a swan. She was a friend to all birds and beasts, but the folk of the world she did not know.

On a certain day in winter, when Deirdre was well-grown, she and her woman were walking the hills when they chanced on a hunter, who was skinning an animal. Blood lay on the white snow and a raven poked about for a bit to eat.

'Levarcham,' said Deirdre, 'I see here signs that tell of the only man I shall ever love. He shall have hair as black as a raven, cheeks as red as blood, and a body as white as snow.'

'Good fortune to you, woman,' said the hunter when he heard this. 'There are people beyond the hill who are such as you desire. And the best of these are Naoise and his brothers, the three sons of Usnech.'

'However that may be,' cried Levarcham, 'I'll not thank you for telling it. Get you away on the other road.'

But Deirdre had heard him well, and she said to Levarcham, 'I shall never be in health again till I shall see this Naoise or his brothers.'

Now some time later Naoise, son of Usnech, found himself in the wild, near to the little house where Deirdre lived. Like all of Ulster, Naoise had heard the prophecy of Cathbad, and he knew the intent of the king to marry this girl, so he was ready to pass by on the other side. But Deirdre came from the house and skipped past him as light and quick as a fawn.

'Fair is the young heifer that springs past me,' he called.

'Indeed, young heifers are frisky,' she replied, 'in a place where none may find a bull.'

'Your bull,' he said, 'is the bull of the whole province of Ulster, even Conchobor the king.'

'If I would choose, I would take for myself a younger bull, such a one as you are.'

'Not that, for I fear the prophecy of Cathbad.'

'Say you so?' said Deirdre. 'Do you mean to refuse me?'

'Yes indeed,' said he.

Then she leapt upon him and seized him by his ears and cried, 'Two ears of shame and mockery shall you have unless you take me for your wife.'

'O my wife, release me!" cried Naoise. And she did.

Naoise returned to his two brothers and told them what had happened. When they heard this, the other sons of Usnech hurried to hold back their brother.

'What have you done?' they said. 'Do not stir up war between us and the men of Ulster.'

But Naoise would not undo what had been done.

'Evil will fall upon you,' lamented his brothers, 'and you

shall lie under the reproach of shame for as long as you live. But we will stand by you. Let us flee with her into another place, for there are kings in Ireland who will welcome us still.'

They departed that same night, with three times fifty warriors and their women and dogs and servants. And Deirdre went with them. For a long time they wandered from one court to another, from Ballyshannon in the west to the mountain of Howth in the east. Often Conchobor sent men to kill them, by ambush or by treachery, and the warriors of Ulster chased after the sons of Usnech. In time, their enemies drove them over the sea to Scotland where they lived among the beasts of the wilderness.

Then there came hard times, when hunting failed, and the sons of Usnech raided the cattle of the country, and the men of Scotland met together to destroy them. So the sons of Usnech begged mercy of the king of Scotland. And since they were likely men and good warriors he took them into his following and they fought for him. They built for themselves houses in the meadow a little way distant from the king's court. These houses were set apart for Deirdre's sake. They wished to hide her away, lest men might see her, and kill them for her.

One day the steward of the king was going by the house of Naoise early in the morning. He peeped in the window and saw two heads on one pillow, and he thought the face of the woman in the bed was the fairest ever seen. The steward hurried back to the king and woke him.

'Until this day,' he said, 'we have never found a wife worthy of your fame and dignity. But Naoise, son of Usnech, in his house by the meadow, has a woman sufficient for the emperor of the western world. Let us kill Naoise, and let his woman share your bed.'

'It would be to our shame to kill him,' replied the king. 'But rather go yourself each day to her house and secretly woo her for me.'

Then the steward went with whispers and gifts, but all that he said was repeated by Deirdre to Naoise. When the king saw that he was gaining nothing by this wooing, he sent the sons of Usnech to war, into the most dangerous battles, hoping that they might be killed. But they were too strong and brave to be easily slain. Then the men of Scotland met again to plot their destruction. But this also was told to Deirdre.

'Flee from this place,' she said to Naoise. 'If you are not gone this very night, in the morning you shall be killed.'

So they fled away that night to an island in the sea. And after some time the news of their escape was brought to the land of Ulster.

''Tis pity, O Conchobor,' said the men of Ulster to the king, 'that the sons of Usnech should die for the sake of that woman in the lands of an enemy. If die they must, let it be here in their own sweet country. It is a sorry thing to die among foes.'

Then Conchobor sent messengers and sureties to the sons of Usnech, inviting them to come home.

'Indeed we will come,' they replied. 'It is welcome news. But let the sureties for our well-being be Fergus and Black Dubhtach and Cormac, son of Conchobor.'

Now the sons of Usnech hurried home, for they swore to eat no more meat till they sat at the tables of Ireland. But the sureties were feasting across the sea before they left for home, and this was by the contrivance of Conchobor, who was planning some treachery against the sons of Usnech.

At that same time, Eoghan, son of Durthacht, had come to Emain Macha to make his peace with Conchobor, for the two of them had been enemies for many years. Then the king said to Eoghan, 'The price of peace for you is the death of the sons of Usnech.'

On their journey home, Naoise and his brothers had come to the flat of the meadow that lay before Emain, and the women sat on the battlements ready to welcome them. Fiacha, the son of the surety Fergus, stood with Naoise. Suddenly, Eoghan and his warriors rushed from the gates and bore down on the sons of Usnech. Eoghan himself greeted Naoise with a mighty thrust of his spear through the side. The spear passed through Naoise and broke his back in sunder. At once, Fiacha threw his arms around Naoise and carried him to the ground to try to protect him. But Naoise was utterly slain, even through the body of the son of Fergus.

A general murder followed in all parts of the meadow. The warriors of Eoghan, by the points of their spears and the edges of their swords, did not allow any to escape, except for Deirdre. She was captured and bound tight and taken to Conchobor to be in his power.

When the carnage was over and the green of the field was red with blood, the sureties arrived from their feasting beyond the sea. And when they saw what had been done, in despite of their own honour, they were angry beyond measure. Fergus and Dubhtach and Cormac ran forward to attack the men of Eoghan, and in their wrath they did great deeds. Many of the best in Emain were killed. Even Conchobor could not contain the fire and the heat of the foe. In blind rage Dubhtach slew the women of Ulster, and before the rising of the dawn Fergus had put a blaze to Emain itself.

After this destruction the sureties, even Fergus and Dubhtach and Cormac, son of Conchobor, went into exile, into the land of Connacht to find shelter with Ailill and Maeve. Three thousand men went with them, and these exiles showed no more love to their homeland of Ulster. For sixteen years their raids and forays made men quake, and the cries of lamentation among the people of Ulster did not cease.

When the battle was over, Conchobor took Deirdre into his house and kept her. For a year she made no smile and gave no laugh. She could hardly eat or sleep, and she wept with her head on her knee. By the grave of Naoise she used to lie down, and here she made a lament.

'For half the night I sleep not,' she cried. 'My mind wanders amid clouds of thoughts, I eat not, nor smile. The man under heaven who was fairest to me – so dear a man – has been torn from me. Great was the crime. I shall not see him till I die.

'O Naoise, your absence is the cause of grief to me. I see the shadow of this son of Usnech showing through the dark sod that covers now his white body, a body that I desired above most other things. If King Conchobor and all his warriors stood on this plain, I would give up all of them without a struggle for one more moment in the sweet company of Naoise.'

Conchobor heard this lament, and he went to her and tried to comfort her. But she gave him only sad and bitter words.

'And Conchobor the king, what of you?' she said. 'You have given me only tears and sorrow. Such will be my remaining life, for your love will not last me. O King, soon I shall reach my early grave. Stronger than the sea is my grief – do you not know it, Conchobor?'

Then the king turned away from her and said, 'Who is the worst of those you see and hate?'

'It is yourself,' she answered, 'and with you Eoghan, son of Durthacht.'

'Then I give you to him,' said the king, 'and you shall live with him for a year.'

In the morning Deirdre was placed in a chariot, and she saw that the two men with her were those she hated most upon the earth.

'Ha, Deirdre,' Conchobor mocked her, 'the look you share now between me and Eoghan is the same that the ewe gives between two rams.'

As the chariot ran across the plains of Macha, they came to a place of great bare stones. All at once Deirdre leapt from the speeding chariot and struck her head against a large rock. Then her head was shattered, and so Deirdre died.

THE PURSUIT
OF DIARMUID AND
GRAINNE

One fine morning, Finn Mac Cool rose early and went out on the dew of the grass. Oisin, his son, and Dering the druid saw him there in the dawn and went to speak to him.

'This is early rising, Finn,' said Oisin.

'Not without cause,' said Finn. 'Since my wife died from me, there is no quiet sleep for me.'

'There is remedy for that,' said Oisin. 'Throw your glance on the most or least girl in all green Ireland and we will bring her to you for your wife.'

'I myself know a worthy woman,' said Dering. 'It is Grainne, the daughter of King Cormac Mac Art. She is the woman of the best look and shape and speech in all Ireland.'

'There is strife between Cormac and myself,' said Finn. 'It might please him to refuse me in my person. But go the two of you and ask for his daughter, for he may speak better to you than to me.'

Then the two of them went to Tara to see the king, and they asked for his daughter Grainne in marriage for Finn Mac Cool, captain of the Fianna.

'There is not a champion in Ireland,' replied the king, 'who has not been refused by Grainne. But I will take you and you will find the answer from her own mouth.'

Cormac took the messengers to the women's house and sat in the seat beside his daughter.

'Here, Grainne,' he said, 'are two of the people of Finn, who would have you for Finn's wife. What say you?'

'If he is fit to be your son-in-law,' said she, 'then why should he not be my husband?'

They were satisfied with that answer, and a time was appointed in two weeks for Finn to come to Tara. Finn collected seven battalions of the Fianna from every part of Allen in Leinster, and they went bravely in bands and troops into Tara. The wedding feast was prepared in the great hall, and the people of Cormac and the people of Finn were seated in their places.

Then Finn spoke to Grainne and questioned her.

'What is hotter than fire?' he said.

'A woman's reasoning between two men,' she replied.

'What is swifter than the wind?'

'A woman's thought between two men.'

'What is sharper than a sword?'

'The reproach of a foe.'

'What is softer than down?'

'The palm on the cheek.'

'What is whiter than snow?'

'There is truth.'

'What is blacker than the raven?'

'There is death.'

Finn asked no more, for he was satisfied. But Grainne was not satisfied.

Now it chanced, as the feast went on, that Daire the poet was close to Grainne and they passed pleasant talk between them. After a while Grainne said, 'Why have this Finn and his Fianna come here? And what means his questioning of me?'

Daire was mighty surprised at this and replied, 'Do you not know that he comes to take you as wife?'

She was a long time silent. Then she said, 'If Finn wished me for his son Oisin or for his youthful grandson Oscar, it would be no wonder. But I marvel that he wants me for himself. He is older than my father, with many white hairs.'

Then she thought again, and she looked well around the table. 'This is good company,' she said, 'but I know not these men, apart from Oisin, son of Finn.'

So Daire named many heroes, and told her of their strength and boldness and high lineage, till she stopped him at a certain face.

'What is that youth of the sweet words,' she asked, 'with the fair, freckled cheeks and the raven-black curls?'

'That man is Diarmuid, grandson of Duibhne, and he is the best lover of a woman in the whole world.'

'That is good company indeed,' said Grainne.

She called her servant to bring a great golden cup, to fill it to the brim, and to pass it around the table. Finn drank, and Cormac drank, and so the cup went around till all had drunk except Diarmuid. Then Grainne stopped the cup, and soon all who had drunk were in a sleep like the sleep of death. Then Grainne rose softly and went down the hall to sit by Diarmuid.

'Receive my love, Diarmuid,' said she, 'and give me back your own.'

'I will not, and I dare not,' said he, 'meddle with a woman who is promised to Finn Mac Cool.'

'Then, O Diarmuid, I will put you under a *geasa*, a spell of danger and destruction, if you do not take me out from this house tonight, before Finn and the king awake.'

'Those are evil bonds, woman,' replied Diarmuid, 'and why have you chosen me above many great men at this feast? Not one of them is less worthy of love than myself.'

'Do not question me. My eye fell on you, and my love followed my look.'

'But it is a hard burden you place on me. And do you not know that when Finn sleeps at Tara, he himself keeps the keys of the house?'

'All the world knows,' she replied, 'that a good warrior of Ireland can leap the wall by the shafts of his spear. You shall do that, and I shall follow through a little hidden door.'

Then Diarmuid took counsel among his own people. Oisin and Oscar and other companions told him to go with Grainne, for it was a bad stroke indeed to break the bond of a *geasa*, and the maiden herself was worthy to be loved. But Dering the druid spoke a warning.

'In the footsteps of that woman death awaits you. But you must go with her, for the spell and the bond placed upon you shall not be broken.'

When he heard this, Diarmuid made one last appeal.

'My friends, is this your counsel?' he cried.

'Yea, it is so,' they said, one and all.

So Diarmuid armed himself, and he wept some tears for his friends. Then he stood before the wall and thrust down on his spears, and with a light airy leap he cleared the wall of the fort and the ditch beyond. On the green of the field Grainne was waiting, but still Diarmuid held back.

''Tis a bad journey we are starting on,' said he. 'Much better for you would be Finn Mac Cool. Who in all Ireland can hide us from his anger? Return now, before the sleepers awake.'

'I will not go back,' she replied, 'and I will not part from you till death carries me away.'

There was no more to say. Away they went before the dawn, westward into Connacht. They crossed the ford on the Shannon and came to Two-Hut-Wood in Clanrickard. Diarmuid cut branches and made a fence with seven wattle doors, and in the middle he made for Grainne a bed of soft rushes and the tops of the birch-trees.

When Finn saw that the lovers were gone, a burning jealousy seized him. At once, he sent trackers from the Clan

Navin after them, but they lost the scent at the Shannon. Finn was so angry, he was about to hang the sons of Navin without delay. But the trackers, having a good reason for greater effort, went hurriedly up the river-bank and picked up a trail that led to Two-Hut-Wood. Then Finn was sure that he had caught the lovers.

But the friends of Diarmuid wished to warn him of the danger, and Oscar went to one side to give orders to Finn's hound, Bran. Bran pricked his ears and understood well. He ran ahead into the wood and hunted out the hiding-place. Then he thrust his nose into the bosom of sleeping Diarmuid.

Diarmuid started from sleep and said, 'Here is Bran, Finn's hound. Surely this is a warning that Finn is near.'

'Take the warning,' said Grainne, 'and fly.'

'I will not,' replied Diarmuid, 'for Finn is hard to escape. It is best to face him here, where I am prepared.'

When nothing moved in the wood, Oisin feared that Bran had failed, and he looked for another warning. He sent for Fergor, whose shout might be heard in three distant counties, and Fergor sent three roars that Diarmuid could not miss.

'I hear the shouts of Fergor,' said Diarmuid, 'it is certain that Finn is upon us.'

'Take the warning and fly,' said Grainne, but still he would not. Then fear and great dread came on Grainne.

Now the trackers had entered the wood and they searched all about till they came to the strong fence that Diarmuid had made.

'This is the work of Diarmuid,' said Finn, raising his voice. 'Is it not so, O Diarmuid?'

'Your judgment does not err,' came the answer. 'Grainne and I are indeed here.'

Then he comforted Grainne openly with three kisses, which Finn saw, and it made him rage. He put a company of the Fianna to guard each wattle gate so none might escape.

Now, this meeting and challenge in the wood came to the ears of Angus Og in Brugh on the Boyne. He feared that his foster-son Diarmuid was in the greatest danger, so he set out on a clear cold wind and did not rest till he came secretly into Two-Hut-Wood.

'Let each of you come under the border of my cloak,' said he to the lovers, 'and I will fetch you from here without the knowledge of Finn and the Fianna.'

Grainne agreed but Diarmuid would not go. So Angus put her into the shadow of his cloak and away they fled to Two-Willow-Point at Limerick. But Diarmuid stood straight as a pillar and armed himself. He went to the first of the seven gates and called out, 'Who is there?'

'No enemy of yours,' was the answer, 'but only Oisin and Oscar. Come forth to us without harm.'

'I will not,' said Diarmuid, 'for I seek Finn.'

He went from gate to gate, finding friends only, till he came to the gate held by the sons of Navin.

'Come out,' they cried, 'and we will mark you with swords and spears.'

'No fear of you, you sour-faced sniffing dogs, keeps me within,' replied Diarmuid, 'but your blood would be a stink on my weapon.'

He went to the last gate and heard from beyond a loud voice that said, 'Finn Mac Cool and the men of the Fianna are here. No love awaits you. Come without and we will spill the marrow from your bones.'

But Diarmuid rose on the shaft of his spears and jumped high and lightly far over the heads of Finn's people. They did not see him, and in a moment he was on his way to Two-Willow-Point. And there he found Angus Og and Grainne in the snug of a hut, with a fire a-blaze and the half of a wild pig turning on the spit. And when Grainne saw him, the life all but went out of her for joy.

Early next morning Angus rose to leave, but before he went he had advice for his foster-son.

'O Diarmuid,' he said, 'in your flight from Finn go not into a tree with one trunk, nor into a cave with one opening, nor to an island with only one approach. Where you cook, eat not there. Where you eat, sleep not there. Where you rest tonight, sleep not tomorrow night. And so farewell.'

Many times, in the days that followed, the lives of Diarmuid and Grainne were in danger. Finn looked for them far and wide. Enemies from the sea and venomous hounds chased them till at last they left Two-Willow-Point and went into the forest of Dubhros, where there was a famous quicken-tree, or rowan. This rowan grew from a berry brought by the Tuatha De Danann from the Land of Promise. The Tuatha De Danann had dropped the berry by accident during a hurling-game against the Fianna, and from it grew a wonderful tree. The berries of this tree had the taste of honey, and those who ate them felt the liveliness of wine, and a person of a hundred had the youth again of one aged thirty.

The guardian of the tree was a Fomorian from Lochlann called Searbhan the Surly, and he was very big and black and ugly, with crooked teeth and a single eye in the middle of his forehead. He had a belt of iron and a club of iron, and he would not die except from three strokes of his own club. Fire could not burn him, nor water smother him, nor weapons kill him. He slept in the tree by night and watched it by day, and he made a wilderness around where none, not even the men of the Fianna, dared hunt or chase. If Diarmuid and Grainne could settle there, it would be a safe place for them.

Diarmuid went to this giant and made a bond with him to live there and hunt so long as he touched not the rowan or the berries. Diarmuid made a hut and he and Grainne lived safely in the wood of Dubhros, eating beasts from the wild and drinking water from the spring.

Now, Finn at this time had returned to Allen, and there came to him to sue for peace enemies from the past, men of the families that had slain Finn's own father at the battle of Knocka. The leaders on this journey were Angus, son of Art Mac Morna, and Aed, son of Andala.

'Peace you may have,' said Finn, 'but what fine will you pay in satisfaction for my father's death?'

'We have no gold or silver or cattle to give you,' said they.

'Then I shall ask from you one of two things only. The

head of a champion, or the full of my fist of the berries of a rowan tree.'

But Oisin warned the two chiefs and said, 'Take counsel, you children of Morna, for it is not an easy thing that Finn asks you. The head he is asking is that of Diarmuid O'Duibhne, and twenty times your number would hardly be enough for that task. As for the berries, they are the magic fruit of the rowan in the wood of Dubhros, which is guarded by Searbhan the Surly.'

'Since peace is our great desire,' replied the chiefs, 'let us pay the fine or die in the attempt.'

Then they went with many arms to the wood of Dubhros and called out for Diarmuid. He met them with weapons in his hands and heard their demands.

'It is a melancholy thing for you,' said Diarmuid, 'to be under bonds to that Finn. Did he not himself slay your own two fathers in revenge for the death of his father, and should not that be satisfaction enough for him?'

'That is not well said,' the chiefs answered. 'First you steal his wife, and then you speak ill of him. It is best if we fight.'

They agreed, for the better display of valour and honour, to fight without weapons, by the strength of their hands only. But the two chiefs were as infants in Diarmuid's grasp, and he threw them down and tied them fast.

Diarmuid and Grainne had a relief from this victory, and Grainne in her happiness found a great wanting for the magic berries of the rowan. She told Diarmuid that she must have them or die. To hear this was no pleasure for Diarmuid as he had made a pact with the surly giant. The two chiefs were listening to Grainne and they said, 'Untie us and we will help you in this task.' Diarmuid doubted this. But as their lives were already forfeit to him, he took them with him for whatever help they might give.

Searbhan the Surly was dozing at the foot of the rowan. Diarmuid gave him a thump with his foot, and the giant raised his baleful red eye.

'Have you a mind to break our peace, grandson of Duibhne?' said he.

'Not so,' said Diarmuid, 'but Grainne has a great desire for those berries, and I would have them for her.'

'Not even to save a child in her womb would I give her those berries.'

'Still, she must have them or die, and I shall fetch them whether you wish it or not.'

Then Diarmuid and the giant fought. Diarmuid cast aside his weapons and moved in close. He grappled the giant by his iron belt and heaved him from his feet. With a nimble skip he caught up the giant's own club and knocked out his brain with three mighty blows. Then, while Diarmuid rested, the two chiefs put the huge body under the sod and went to call Grainne. Diarmuid plucked berries for her, and the sons of Morna filled a fist from the top of the tree to take to Finn. The fruit from the top of the tree was sweetest of all, but the ones from below were bitter.

As the two chiefs returned to Finn they called out. 'We have killed the surly giant, and we bring you the berries of the rowan tree. Let that be for your satisfaction, and now let us go in peace.'

But when they handed the berries to Finn, he put them to his nose.

'These berries,' he said, 'have the smell of Diarmuid on them. He plucked them, not you. And sure I am that he killed the surly giant. I will go now and see for myself.'

Finn summoned the seven battalions of the Fianna and away they all marched to the wood of Dubhros. They saw that the rowan was unguarded and they filled themselves with the berries as much as they pleased. In the hot sun of noon they lay down to rest, while Diarmuid and Grainne were in the nest of the giant at the top of the tree.

In the quiet of this hour Finn set out his chessboard to pass the time, and he played a game against his son Oisin. After a while there was but one move to make to win the game, though Oisin could not see it. But Diarmuid was awake and watching from the top of the tree, and he threw a berry that hit the piece to be moved. Oisin did so, and the game was won. They played again, and so it happened twice more that

Diarmuid threw a berry for the winning move, and the Fianna gave a great shout that the games were won.

'It is a fine thing for you,' said Finn to his son, 'to have in these games the help and advice of Oscar and Dering. But the best of all teaching was that which Diarmuid O'Duibhne gave you.'

'Is it only your jealousy, Finn,' said Oisin, 'to think that Diarmuid would stay in this tree, and you within his reach?'

Then Finn called out in a loud voice, 'Who speaks the truth, myself or Oisin?'

'True for you, Finn,' Diarmuid replied. 'I myself and Grainne are above, in the bed of the surly giant.'

Grainne began to tremble and weep, but Diarmuid comforted her with three kisses, in the sight of Finn and all the Fianna. Then Finn was scorched with anger and jealousy.

'Your head shall be the price, Diarmuid,' he cried, 'for those three kisses.'

The men of the Fianna surrounded the rowan, standing hand in hand, and one after another nine warriors climbed into the tree to bring Diarmuid down. But with kicks and blows Diarmuid hurled each to the ground and killed every one.

While the Fianna were making this attack, Angus Og again heard that his foster-son was in deadly trouble. Quickly he flew through the pure cold air and threw his druid's cloak around Grainne and carried her away to Brugh on the Boyne. When Diarmuid saw her safely gone, he called out to Finn.

'I will come down now,' he cried, 'for I am certain you will give me no rest till you have killed me. Is there no friend or comrade who will welcome me in any part of the great world? Often I fought for the love of you, Finn, and for the sake of the Fianna. Then listen well. You will pay hard for me, and my death will be no free gift.'

When Oscar heard this he was troubled in his heart and he went to his grandfather Finn.

'It is a shame and a reproach on you,' he said to Finn, 'that you will not give peace to our warrior Diarmuid. But I give my word under the heaven that I will not let you or the Fianna of Ireland hurt him. I will shorten the bones of any man who attacks him. Then come you down, Diarmuid, and leave in peace. On my body and life no harm shall touch you today.'

Diarmuid felt joy at these words. From a high bough of the tree he pressed on the shafts of his spears and sailed lightly and airily over the heads of the surrounding Fianna. Oscar met him, and together they retreated, clearing their way with a flight of javelins that sounded like the rush of water in a rocky stream.

Then they were beyond reach, and the Fianna put up their weapons and marched with Finn back to Allen in Leinster.

Sixteen years went by, and then one morning early Angus Og went through the pure cold air to the house of Finn and asked him to make peace with Diarmuid O'Duibhne. Finn was weary of the enmity, with such time lost, and so many killed. He agreed to give up the hunt against Diarmuid and Grainne. King Cormac Mac Art and Diarmuid himself were also glad to make an end of the feud, and thus it was done on the condition that Diarmuid, for his suffering, was given certain good lands.

These lands were granted. Then Diarmuid and Grainne went far away and lived in the place called Rath Grainne in the district of Kesh Corran. Grainne bore five children, four sons and one daughter, and the folk of that country agreed that there was no man more content than Diarmuid, nor any richer in gold and jewels and sheep and cattle-herds.

After many years Grainne's heart began to yearn for her father, for she had had no sight of him from the day they left Tara. She also thought it a poor thing that, rich and settled as they were, they had never welcomed to their house Finn Mac Cool, for Cormac and Finn together were the two best men in all Ireland.

'What are you saying, Grainne?' replied Diarmuid. 'Would you give me to my enemies?'

'What is done is forgotten,' said she, 'and a good feast soothes memories and is a way to the heart.'

So for a full year they were preparing for the visit and the feasting. Then Cormac came, and Finn with the seven battalions of the Fianna, and they all stayed in Rath Grainne for another year of good fellowship.

On the last day of that year Diarmuid was in his sleep when he heard the voices of hounds go through his dreams. He started up, but lay down again in the sweet comfort of Grainne's arms. Three times this happened. Then he rose in the weak dawn light and went out after the baying of the dogs, with his small sword at his side, and his little spear in one hand, and the lead of his hound Mac an Chuill in the other.

Diarmuid went to the top of Ben Bulbin and found Finn there alone. Finn told him that some men of the Fianna had set out at midnight on the scent of a boar. But the trail was lost and it was pointless to continue.

'Many a time,' said Finn, 'we have hunted that boar to no end except danger and damage to us. This very night he has killed thirty of our men. And now let us leave with speed, for I hear him coming up the mountain.'

'I will not leave this hill,' said Diarmuid, 'for fear of a wild pig.'

'You had best do it, Diarmuid, for this is the earless and tailless boar that you are under a *geasa* not to hunt. Angus Og in your young days put you under this bond, for he knew the boar was likely to be the death of you.'

'I know nothing,' replied Diarmuid, 'of the incantations and prophecies of my childhood. But here I stay. Leave me your hound Bran to help my Mac an Chuill, and I will take my chances.'

But Finn and his hound were away down the mountain-side, and the boar was showing his fierce snout over the shoulder of the hill. Diarmuid unleashed Mac an Chuill, but the hound took one look and was gone with his tail tucked in behind. Diarmuid put his finger in the silken loop of his little spear and cast it full force into the face of the boar. But it made not so much as a scratch. So he drew his small sword and gave a smart heavy blow, which left the sword in two parts and the boar still unhurt.

'Alas,' cried he, 'Grainne told me this morning to take my large sword and great spear. To spurn the advice of a good woman, that is indeed a foolish thing.'

Then the boar made a charge that cut the sod from below Diarmuid's feet and felled him. The beast wheeled and made another rush, and with his tusk he opened Diarmuid's side from neck to thigh. As he took this wound, Diarmuid got a hold on the boar and drove the jagged broken blade of the sword through the eye-socket and into the brain. The brute fell dead on the spot.

It was not long before Finn and some men of the Fianna came back up the mountain and saw that the bowels of Diarmuid were hanging out of him and death was very close.

'Now it pleases me well,' said Finn to Diarmuid, 'to see you in this way. Only I wish that the women of Ireland might see you also, with your handsome looks befouled and your proud body in a broken heap.'

'Those are ignoble words,' said Diarmuid. 'And it lies within your power to heal me, if you wished.'

'How so?' said Finn.

'When you received the gift of foreknowledge at the Boyne, it was granted to you also that you could heal all those who drank from out of your hand.'

'You are not deserving of this healing power,' replied Finn. 'At Tara, secretly you stole Grainne from me, though you were then under orders to guard her.'

'Blame me not for that, Finn. Grainne put the heavy bonds of a *geasa* upon me, and this I could not break through on my life or all the world. But remember the goodness of all my past service to you and the Fianna. From the day I was first admitted among the Fianna, I did save you in many deadly straits. Always I put myself in the worst place of danger and wagered my body on behalf of your safety. Good men have died for you, and yet there is no end to death. I see a day coming for the overthrow and slaughter of the Fianna, and few of their seed will be left after them. Then you would cry for my help, O Finn. But I grieve not for you, old man. My sorrow is for my dear companions of the Fianna, and for Oscar, and for Oisin who shall be lamenting after the Fianna during many long years.'

Then Oscar turned on Finn in anger and said, 'My blood is nearer to you than to Diarmuid, but your unkindness warrants a strong reply. By the power of my hand, give him a drink without delay!'

Nine paces away there was a well of fresh water. Finn went with slow steps and took water in the full of his two hands. But then he thought of Grainne, and he let the water dribble between his fingers.

'How could you spill it?' groaned Diarmuid. 'O hasten, for my death is near.'

So Finn fetched water and spilt it again. And Diarmuid, when he saw it, gave a piteous wail of anguish.

'I swear,' cried Oscar in his rage, 'if you do not bring water, only one of us will leave this hill alive.'

Then Finn saw the black looks of his men, and he hurried to Diarmuid with water in his hands. But the life had fled from the body, and all the men of the Fianna gave three heavy shouts of sadness and despair.

And after a time Finn sad, 'Let us go softly now, lest Angus Og come upon us. We had no hand in Diarmuid's death, but would Angus believe it?'

Diarmuid's hound had crept back, to whine at the death. Finn took it by the lead and went down the hill. The friends of Diarmuid wrapped him in their cloaks and followed Finn.

As they came towards the fort, Grainne was on the wall, waiting for news. When she saw the hound led in without the master, her spirit fled from her and she pitched forward in a faint. And when she had recovered she sent five hundred of her people to bring Diarmuid from the mountain. The procession approached slowly, and she was keening for her dead lover.

'O Diarmuid,' she cried, 'my handsome man, Finn has given you a hard bed indeed, lying on stones in the wet of the rain. Your blue eyes are closed. You were my hawk and my hound, my secret love hunted with you. And you were the prop for the men of Ireland, the head in every battle. Now I hear your harp no more. I am sorrowful, without mirth, without light. I am grief, I am dying. O Diarmuid, you pitiful man!'

Then as she was crying, suddenly there was another by her side, for Angus Og had flown on the pure cold wind to claim the body of his foster-son.

'The boar of Ben Bulbin has cut you down,' Angus lamented, 'as the prophecy foretold, O my Diarmuid of the bright face. Did I abandon you to the treachery of Finn? Certainly I shall forever feel the bitter pangs of sorrow. Take up the body now and bring it to the Boyne. I cannot restore his life, but I shall breathe a spirit into him so that every day, for a little while, we may talk together as we used to do.'

They took the body and placed it on a golden bier, and over it were the upward-pointing spears of Diarmuid. Then they went on a long road till they came to Brugh on the Boyne.

Finn Mac Cool saw now that Oisin and Oscar and many bold men of the Fianna had abandoned him. He did not know how he could face the danger from them, and the danger from Diarmuid's sons, without the help and forgiveness of Grainne. So he went secretly to Rath Grainne and cunningly gave her sweet words. She reviled him with her keen sharp-pointed tongue. But he flooded her mind with gentle and loving speech till he brought her to his own will. Then he got from her the desire of his heart and soul.

Finn took Grainne by the hand and they went towards the Fianna of Ireland. When the warriors saw them coming together, with the look of a man and his wife, they raised a great shout of mockery and derision, and Grainne bowed her head in shame.

'Now we know, O Finn,' Oisin called out, 'that Grainne will be ever in the sight of your best eye from this time on.'

Some said that the changes in a woman's mind flow like running water, but others said that Finn had put a spell on Grainne. But certain it is that they stayed by one another till the day of death.

6

FINN MAC COOL
AND
THE FENIANS

Hear the words of Finn, and hide them not.
It grieves me to see the number of grey-faced
  foreigners,
Though I myself would be driving them out.
But soon I and the Fianna shall not exist.

Round Sligo a battle will be fought.
It is unlikely that I shall be present,
Much it grieves me, O woman.

First psalmist of the Irish am I,
The Son of God will carry me to heaven.
I dislike the nature of women, but I've had
  many of them.
I am Finn, son of the noble Cool.
I believe in the King of Heavens.
I am the best prophet under the sun,
Though I have done the will of women.

FINN'S BIRTH
AND YOUTH

At the time of the birth of Finn Mac Cool, his father, of the family of Baskin, was killed in the battle of Knocka by the sons of Morna. Then there was danger for the little lad, for the enemies of his family wished to kill him also. They took him from his mother and threw him from the window of the fort into a loch. But the babe rose again holding hard to the tail of a big salmon.

It happened that his grandmother was walking by the shore and saw him come up from the water.

'Is it not my grandson,' she cried, 'the true son of my own true child?' And she caught the babe from the water and vanished away with him to the deep forest.

In the heart of the forest she saw a woodman by a great oak tree, and she asked him to cut a chamber in the tree. He set to and made a nice snug room, big enough for her and the babe and the little whelp-hound she had brought with her. As the axe fell, the fine chippings flew, and the pup ate them up.

'Is it good eating?' the old woman laughed. 'Now you will be called Bran, or the Wood-chip, from this time out.'

Then the work was finished and she asked the woodman for the axe. He gave it into her hand, and in a minute she swept the head off him, saying, 'Your tongue will never tell of this place.'

All three together lived in the tree, and the woman did not take the lad out till he was five years old and still unable to walk. Then she took the boy to the top of a hill and gave him a good cut with a switch.

'Tumble down the hill,' said she, 'and I'll be after you with this switch. But on the way up I'll go ahead and you can strike at me.'

At first, the lad got all the blows. But very soon he was so nimble on his feet that his grandmother could not reach him. But he whipped her uphill with a stroke at every step.

When the youth was fifteen, a great runner and a strong hearty lad, the old woman took him to a hurling match where his enemies were taking part. The young fellow joined the play against his enemies. He took the ball in the air and carried it up and down and drove it through the goal so that he won every game. The old king was angry at the defeat of his people. He cried out against the young skilful runner with the very fair hair, wanting to know who was this youth with the *finn cumhal*, that is to say the 'white cap'.

'Aye, that is it,' said the old woman. 'Finn will be his name, and Finn Mac Cool he is.'

Then the old king knew it was his enemy, and he ordered Finn to be seized and killed on the spot. But the old woman took her grandson by the hand and away they went, a hill at a leap, a glen at a step, and thirty miles at a jump. The pursuers were after them, and they all ran a long while till Finn was tired. Then the grandmother took him on her back, putting his feet into two pockets of her dress, and ran on as swiftly as before.

Still the pursuers were after them, and the hot breath was on their backs.

'Look behind, young Finn,' said the grandmother, 'and tell me what you see.'

'A white horse,' said he, 'with a champion on his back.'

'Nothing to fear,' she replied, 'for a white horse has no endurance. He'll not catch us.'

On they went and the breath of pursuit on their backs was hotter yet.

'I see a warrior on a brown horse,' said Finn.

'Nothing to fear,' said she, 'for a brown horse is giddy and will not overtake us.'

But the next time Finn looked he saw a black warrior on a black horse following fast.

'Now we'll not escape,' said the old woman. 'There's no horse so tough and resolute as a black one. Since one of us must surely die, save yourself.'

Then Finn slipped off her back, and she went headlong into the deep bog and sank to her neck. The black rider galloped to the edge of the bog calling out, 'Where's Finn?'

'Here in the bog before me,' she replied. 'Can you not see I'm trying to find him?'

'One white head,' he said, 'may please the king as well as another.' With that, he cut off her head and rode away.

After this, Finn wandered the land with his hound, Bran. He learnt the two ways of poetry and the three ways of wisdom. He knew the songs for all the seasons, but the long tales of winter pleased him best.

'The ox is lowing in the stall,' he used to sing, 'high and cold is the wind, low the sun, the sea full of quarrelling cries, the summer is gone. The ferns grow red and their shape is hidden. The wild geese cry, cold has caught the wings of the bird. The ice-frost comes. I have another story to tell. Listen.'

When Finn was ready in himself, he went for the feast of Samhain to the court of the high-king at Tara. Now, it was the law of the feast that none should bring there any grudge or quarrel. The high-king was in his place, and with him were Caoilte, son of Ronan, and sharp-tongued Conan, and Goll son of Morna, the chief of the Fianna. The Fenian warriors of the Fianna were ranged all about, and into this company came the young Finn, though none knew who he was.

The high-king saw him and put the drinking-horn of meeting into his hand and asked who he was.

'I am Finn Mac Cool,' said he, 'son of the man who was both king of Ireland and chief over the Fianna. And I am come to get friendship and to give service.'

'Then indeed you are the son of a friend,' replied the high-king, 'and a well-trusted man.'

The high-king took Finn by the hand and between them they made a bond of loyalty and service, and then they all fell to good eating and good drinking.

Now, every year at Samhain-time there came out of the north a man of the Tuatha De Danann and he set fire to Tara. Aillen was his name. The way it was, he came with the music of the *shee* that turned all who heard it towards sleep. While they slept, he let a flame out of his mouth that burned all Tara. The coming of this man was a fear and sorrow for the king.

'He who could stop Aillen,' said he, 'I would give him whatever inheritance he wished, little or much.'

The men of Ireland were silent, for they knew the power of the sweet pitiful music of the *shee*. When it sounded, even wounded men and women in labour fell asleep. But Finn took the task upon himself and promised safety from the fire of Aillen.

It was a hard promise to make good. While Finn was thinking on the matter, there came to him Fiacha, son of Conga, his father's old friend.

'Well, boy,' said he, 'would I bring you a deadly spear that never made a false cast?'

'What would you be asking for it?' said Finn.

'A third of what your right hand wins and a third of your trust and friendship.'

'Willingly, you shall have it,' said Finn.

Fiacha brought him the spear in secret and said, 'When you hear the music of the *shee*, let you pull the cover from the head of the spear and hold it to your forehead. The power of the spear will keep sleep from your eyes.'

Finn rose with the spear and stood guard by the gate at Tara. Soon he heard the approach of the long sorrowful music. He stripped the cover from the head of the spear and put it to his forehead, and then he was awake before the face of Aillen. Fire was belching from the mouth of Aillen but Finn caught the flames in his crimson cloak, and wrapped the fire in his cloak, and buried it deep in the sod of the earth.

When Aillen saw that his spell was broken, he fled back to the north. But Finn chased him hard, and caught him at the very door of his house, and pierced him through and through with a cast of the spear. He cut off his head and took it back to Tara and fixed it on a crooked pole. In the rising dawn the high-king and his chief men and the Fenians saw the gory head of Aillen ringed with sunlight, and they knew that Tara was saved from fire.

Then the chief men of Ireland came together in council, and they agreed that Finn Mac Cool, son of a renowned father, should become leader of the Fianna of Ireland, and all the Fenian should swear loyalty to him.

'Well, Goll,' said the high-king to the son of Morna, 'is it your choice now to quit Ireland, or to give way and put your hand in the hand of Finn?'

'By my word, I will do that,' said Goll. And he was the first to give his hand so that the rest might easily follow.

Now Finn remained captain of the Fianna till the end, and the place where he lived was Allen in Leinster, in the great pale fort made by Nuada of the Tuatha De Danann out of the white lime of Ireland mixed with the white horns and bones of cattle.

As to Finn Mac Cool himself, he was a chief and a poet and a man of wisdom, and all he said was sweet-sounding to his people. And never was there a better fighting man, and whatever anyone said about him he was still three times better than that. Fair justice he gave, even between his enemy and his own son. Generous he was, and never denied any man who had a mouth to eat with, or legs to bring away what was given him. He left no woman without her bride-price, and no follower without pay. He promised at night only as much as he could do on the morrow, and he fulfilled at night what he had promised in the day. Never did he forsake his friend.

But if he was quiet in peace, he was angry in battle. And his son Oisin and his grandson Oscar were at one with him in the madness and raging heart they all showed in the red mist of the battle.

FINN IN THE HOUSE
OF CEANN SLIEVE

At the beginning of summer, Finn Mac Cool feasted the chief people of Ireland at Allen on the broad hill-slopes. And when the feast was done, it was time to start the chase through the wilderness of Ireland.

Now this was the way of it, how the Fenians spent their time. Each year, from May to November, they hunted with their dogs every day. But from November to May they lived in the friendship of the land, so that there was not a chief or a great lord in the whole country who had not nine of the Fenians lodged with him for a half of the year.

At this time, after the feast, Finn and his men went to hunt the stag on the mountain of Torc, by Loch Lein. They had started up the most nimble bucks, scared foxes astray, roused badgers from the clefts, driven birds to the wing. The fawns and young animals had shied away to the very summit.

Fenian hands were stained with blood and hounds were mangled with gore, for success was theirs that day.

But Finn had lagged behind and only Dering was with him at the end of the hunt.

'Well, Dering,' said Finn, 'do you take the watch while I sleep, for I rose early this day. And it is early rising when a man cannot see his five fingers against the sky, or tell a hazel from an oak.'

Then Finn fell into a pleasant slumber. At last, Dering had to wake him, for the night was close upon them and they had no safe place for the dark. So Finn rose and they went on till they saw a strong, well-lit fort on the edge of a sheltering wood. They knocked at the gate and told their names.

'May poison and crushing into pulp be your portion,' said the porter. 'Unfortunate is your visit, for the lord here is Conan of Ceann Slieve, and it was Finn Mac Cool that killed his father, mother and four brothers, and also the father and mother of his wife.'

The porter went away grumbling, to tell the master of the visitors.

'There is at our gate,' he told Conan, 'a tall, fair-haired, manly, powerful fellow, of the best shape. He leads a ferocious, small-headed hound, with the eye of a dragon, claws of a wolf and venom of a serpent, and a collar of bright gold about his neck. There's another fellow too, brown-haired, ruddy-faced, white-toothed.'

'By your description I know them,' said Conan. 'It is Finn of the family of Baskin, the Fenian prince, and his hound called Bran. The other man is Dering. Let them enter.'

So they went in, and their arms were received out of their hands, and a feast was made ready for them. By the one shoulder of Conan was his wife, and by the other was his daughter Finndealbh, a maiden like a pearl, with hair of burnished gold, eyes as blue as the cornflower, and lips more red than the berry of the rowan.

They all sat a while, and it was not easy between them. Then Finn spoke.

'O Conan,' he said, 'true it is that your malice towards me

is very great. But recall the time that I saved you and your wife from death, and then we put our hands together in a bond of friendship. At that time your wife was carrying a child, and you promised the child to me. If a boy, he would become a Fenian. If a girl, she would be raised up for me to marry, should that please me. I see now that she does please me, and I am come to claim her.'

'Cease, O Finn,' replied Conan, 'for she is promised to one as good as you. He is Fatha Mac Avric, son of the king of Easroe.'

'Let your glib tongue be ripped out,' cried Dering, 'and a portion of guilty death be doled out to you! Finn is a better man than all the warriors of the Tuatha De Danann rolled into one body.'

'Be silent, Dering,' said Finn. 'We have not come to commit murder but to get a wife, and we shall have her despite all of the Tuatha De Danann.'

'Let us not quarrel, Finn,' said Conan in a soothing voice. 'Let us talk and then I'll put you under the bond of a *geasa* to answer all my questions. Win victory and blessings, O Fenian chief, and tell me first of the character and quality of the Fenian men.'

'That I may do,' said Finn. 'I myself am the best man, and Deara Dubh is the worst, for he never yet spoke a word that was not reproach and provocation. Liagan is the swiftest, and Life the fire-raiser of Allen is the slowest. The longest journey he ever made, in the length of a summer day, took him from the fountain by the gate of Allen to his own bed. Daolgas is the tallest, and Mac Minne the dwarf is the smallest. Sour Conan Mael with the bald head has the worst temper and the meanest disposition, and Diarmuid is the most handsome. But enough of this for the moment, O Conan. If you have musicians let them come forward now, for it is not my habit to pass any one night without music.'

'What music delights you best?' Conan asked.

'I will tell you. Very sweet to me is the sound of the seven battalions of the Fianna gathering on our plain, with the blast of the dry cold wind whistling about them. And sweet to me is the clink of the cups drained to the last drop in the drinking-hall of Allen. Sweet too is the scream of the seagull and the cry of the heron, the roar of the waves at Tralee, the whistling and humming of Mac Lughaid, the voice of the cuckoo in the first month of summer, the grunting of hogs on the plain of Eitne, and the echo of loud laughter in Derry.'

'Not without interest to me is all that you say,' said Conan of Ceann Slieve. 'But tell me further, O Finn, who was the man that had only one leg, one arm, and one eye, yet escaped you by his great swiftness? And what is the meaning of the saying, "As Roc came to the house of Finn?"'

'No secret there,' replied Finn. And so he told Conan how it came about.

Once, when the Fenians were hunting at Tara, they got nothing but a fawn in the chase. Finn divided it and gave a piece to each hunter, and there remained to him only a haunch bone. He was looking at it without pleasure when he saw hop towards him a huge, black, detestable giant with one eye, one arm, and one leg.

'The talk of men is that you are liberal in gift-giving, O Finn,' said the giant. 'So I have come, by the agility of my arm and leg, to ask for wealth and valuable presents.'

'If I owned all the world,' replied Finn, 'I would give you neither little nor much.'

'Well, then,' said the giant, 'give me at least that haunch in your hand, and allow me the length of a hop to get clear from you, and I'll shake your unfriendly Fenian dust from my shoe.'

So the giant snatched the haunch and hopped over the high stockade of the fort, and he made use of the utmost swiftness of his one leg to outrun all the Fenians except Finn, who went with his minstrels to the top of the fort to watch.

When he saw that the giant was outstripping all others, Finn put on his clothes for running, and taking his sword Mac an Loin in hand he gave chase. He overtook the hindmost at Sliabh an Righ, the middle runners at Limerick, the Fenian chiefs at Athlone, and the swiftest pursuers on the right hand of Cruachan in Connacht, where the giant was less than a stone-shot in front.

The giant hopped the river at Ballyshannon, and Finn leaped after him. Then their course was towards Ben Edar, by a right-hand circuit of Ireland. At the estuary of Howth they both rose over the water, and their leaps were like the flight of birds over the sea. In that great jump, Finn caught the giant by the shirt in the small of his back and laid him to earth.

'You deal unjustly with me, O Finn,' cried the giant. 'My contest was with your Fenians, not you.'

'The Fenians are not perfect,' replied Finn, 'unless I myself am with them.'

Very soon, all the Fenians rushed up, led by Liagan the swift and Caoilte the slender, and they wished to slaughter the giant for his insulting ways but Finn prevented it. So they bound the giant strongly and took him to the house of Bran Beag, where a feast was ready for the Fenians. The giant was thrown to the middle of the hall, and then he spoke.

'Roc, son of Diocan, is my name,' said he, 'and I am foster-son to Angus the Lawgiver of Brugh on the Boyne. My wife poured a current of surprising affection and a deep torrent of love upon Sgiath Breac, who is your foster-son, O Finn. It hurt me hard to hear her boast of the power and swiftness of her lover, and of Fenians in general, and I resolved to challenge in a race all the Fenians of Ireland. But she sneered at me. So my beloved guardian Angus charged me thus, and gave me the swiftness of a druidical wind, as you have seen. That is my history, and you ought to be satisfied with the shame and injury put on me already.'

With this, the giant was set free, and no man knew where he hopped. But that was the cause of the saying, 'As Roc came to the house of Finn.'

'With clear memory and sweet words you relate these things,' said Conan of Ceann Slieve, 'but another thing I would know. What is the meaning of the saying, "The hospitality of Finn in the house of Cuanna?"'

'There is a true tale concerning that,' replied Finn.

On a time when the Fenians were hunting by the summit of Cairn Feargall, they saw a tall, rough, uncouth giant carrying a grunting hog in the prongs of a fork. A well-grown girl followed, driving the giant before her. The Fenians set out fast after the two of them, but a dark, gloomy, druidical mist came down between them.

When the mist cleared they saw a comfortable house at the edge of a ford. There was grass in front of the house, and two fountains. Beside one of these was an iron vessel and beside the other a bronze vessel. About the house were several people. A grey-haired man stood by the door jamb, and a beautiful maid sat before him. The rude, huge giant was cooking the hog on an open fire. Beyond the flames sat an old man with white in his hair and twelve eyes in his head, each beaming with discord. In the house was a ram with white belly, black head, green horns and green feet. And in the end of the house was a hag in a long ash-coloured garment.

'Let homage be done to Finn Mac Cool and his people,' called the man at the door-post. And all the company rose up respectfully.

Finn was thirsty from the hunt and the chase, and when the man saw this he reproached Caoilte, saying, 'To fetch a drink for Finn you have only to step beyond, to whichever fountain you please.'

Caoilte did so and handed Finn a drink. The water tasted like honey as he drank, but like bitter gall when he put the cup down. Darting pains and whispers of death seized him, and agonizing sweats from the poisonous draught. Then the man ordered Caoilte to fetch water from the other fountain. At the first sip of this, Finn never knew such misery, even in the hardship of battle. But when he had finished the drink, health and joy came back to him, to the great happiness of his people.

Then the grey-haired man ordered the giant to divide the hog that was cooking, and he did so evenly among the Fenians and among the folk of the house. But the ram complained that he had been forgotten entirely, and he snatched the quarter given to the Fenians. The ram backed into a corner of the house and began to devour the meat, and then the four Fenians attacked the ram instantly with their swords. But they might as well have laid blows on a rock.

'Upon my truth,' said the man with the twelve eyes, 'he is doomed for evil who has companions such as you four fellows, who allow a single sheep to take and eat your portion before your very faces.'

Then he rushed at the sheep, caught him by the feet, and gave him a violent heave out of the door. The ram was seen no more.

When she had eaten, the hag in the end of the house gave a loud belch of wind and suddenly threw her ashy-grey covering over the four Fenians, changing them into four withered, droop-headed old men. Finn himself was seized by fear, but the man by the door-post beckoned him, placed Finn's head on his bosom, and put a great sleep upon him. When Finn awoke, the covering was off his men and they were themselves again.

'O Finn,' said the man of the door-post, 'is it a surprise to you, the happening in this house?'

'Truly, I never saw the like,' said Finn.

'Then I shall tell you what it is. The giant with the hog on the prongs of his fork is he who is yonder, and his name is Sloth. The young woman who was forcing him along, who sits by me here, she is Energy, who whips Sloth to work. The man with many bright eyes is the World, who is more powerful than anyone, as he proved by throwing the ram. The ram is the Crimes of Man. And that hag there beyond, she is wizened Age, and she can afflict even your young Fenian men. The two wells from which you drank are Falsehood and Truth. For a lie is sweet first but bitter last, and the truth is the other way round.

'Cuanna of Innistuil is my own name. I have shown you these thing, O Finn, out of my love for you, and in admiration for your wisdom. Now let you and your men come together, and do you all sleep soft till five in the morning. This story you will not forget, and to the end of the world it shall be called "The hospitality of Cuanna's house to Finn."'

'Good for the telling, O Fenian chief,' said Conan of Ceann Slieve, 'but I have another cause of puzzlement. What reason was there for your greyness, for the blemish on your countenance, for the lifeless chill on your skin, for the weakness of death upon your frame? And how long were you in that state?'

'These thing are not hidden,' said Finn.

One day, when Finn was having pleasurable drinking in the hall of Allen of Leinster, and the other chief Fenians were with him, there came two women of the Tuatha De Danann to offer him their joint love. They were sisters, Milucra and Aine, daughters of Cooley.

Aine had boasted that her own husband should never grow grey, but Milucra summoned the men of the Tuatha De Danann and had them dig a druidical lake on the slope of Slieve Cullinn. Any man in the world who bathed in that lake would become grey and hoary.

Then Milucra took the shape of a fawn upon the plain of Allen when Finn was hunting alone with his hounds. He slipped the hounds after the fawn and pursued her to Slieve Cullinn in Ulster, in the district of Cooley. Hunter and hounds were close behind, but the fawn reached the mountain and doubled back and lost the dogs. Finn was exceedingly astonished that any deer could hold off his hounds in a chase of such length.

He was puzzling over this when he saw a fair, lovely girl sitting downcast by the edge of the lake.

'What is the cause of your sorrow, fair maid?' said Finn.

'A ring of red gold have I dropped while bathing,' said she, 'and I now put you under the bond of a *geasa*, O Finn, to bring it back to me.'

Swimming was not Finn's desire that day, but he would not suffer himself to be long under a *geasa*. So he dived into the lake, found the ring and brought it to the girl. With a nimble leap she sprang over his head into the lake, and then she was gone.

Finn had left his clothes only a short distance up the shore, but he had hard trouble to reach them. For he had dived into the lake of Milucra, and he was changed into a wizened, decrepit old man. His hounds sniffed at him, but they knew him not and ran from him. Finn felt so old and weary he could hardly move, so he sat on the edge of the shore till his Fenians arrived, drawn to that place as they followed the noise of the hunt.

'Inform us, old man,' said Caoilte, who was in the lead, 'if you have seen a fawn pursued by two hounds and a man of huge frame and bold, warlike appearance.'

'I have seen them,' replied Finn in a thin, cracked voice, 'and it is not long since they left me.'

He dared not tell the Fenians who he was for his condition was shameful. But he could not keep the secret for long and soon admitted it when all his men were around him. Then they gave three loud cries of surprise and alarm, and ever since that time the lake has been called Loch Doghra.

They made a little cart for Finn and carried him to the *shee* on the hillside that belonged to Cullinn of Cooley. Then the seven battalions of the Fianna spread around the *shee*-mound and dug it away for three nights and days. At the end of that time Cullinn of Cooley came out from the ground and handed Finn a drink in a golden cup. As soon as he drank Finn became himself again, and his strange appearance departed entirely, except for one half of his hair which kept a silvery grey colour. This hoary look in his hair pleased both Finn and the Fenians.

When Finn had drunk, the cup was passed to Mac Reith and then to Dering, and they too drank from it. But as Dering passed the cup, it fell from his hand into the loose earth of his digging. Though every Fenian hastened to save it, it sank before all eyes. This was a cause of affliction to Finn and his people, for had all of them drunk from that cup they would have possessed foreknowledge and true wisdom.

'And that, O Conan,' said Finn, 'is the manner in which I gained both my grey hairs and my true wisdom.'

FINN AND
THE GILLA DEACAIR

At this time, Finn and his men were hunting towards Knockainy in Munster. The hounds roused up some deer, and then the chase was on, from Ardpatrick to Fermoy, from Hy Conall Gavra across the shores of Loch Lein to the blue stream of Suir. And there was not a plain or a valley or a wood or a brake or a mount or a wilderness in the two provinces of Munster that they did not hunt over.

They reached the plain of Cliach, and here Finn pitched his tent, and he had with him his chief men. Oisin and Oscar, son and grandson, were there, and so was mighty Goll Mac Morna, and that slender man Caoilte Mac Ronan, and Diarmuid O'Duibhne of the bright face, and swift-footed Liagan, and Conan Mael, he of the bald head and the foul mouth.

When all were settled, the deep-voiced hounds were unleashed, and the cry of the dogs as they flushed deer from covers and badgers from dens, to the whoop and whistle of huntsmen and heroes over the broad plain, was sweet music to Finn's ear. Then, when the day's hunt was done, Finn and his men had the chessboard between them, while Mac Bresal stood guard, with a view to the four points of the sky.

He had not been watching long when he saw a Fomorian of vast size leading a horse from the east. It was a great, strong, ugly, clumsy, crooked, flat-footed fellow, with a thin neck, and thick lips, and broken teeth, and hair on his face like an unkempt bush. He was fully armed, but his weapons were old and rusty and dented. He dragged a great iron club that left a furrow as deep as a farmer's plough. The horse he led was as bad as the big lump of the master himself: a large, tangled, scraggy, sooty-black carcass of a beast, with ribs out of his side, and knotty legs, and a twisted neck, and a jaw as long as a jetty.

The great fellow hauled this ugly brute along by a halter, giving the lazy-bones severe blows from his club that sounded like the thunder of surf on the rocks. Mac Bresal was not an easy man to frighten, but now he took his heels from the ground and ran swiftly to Finn's camp. Then with wonder on their faces, all the Fenians watched the coming of this Fomorian.

Slow, heavy steps brought the woeful fellow to Finn, who received a respectful salute. And then Finn had many questions to ask him, as to his birth and lineage, and his craft and his calling, and as to the nature of that ugly brute that could hardly be called a horse.

'O great chief of the Fianna,' was the mournful reply, 'my parents, either noble or ignoble, I did not know. I am a Fomorian of Lochlann in the north. But I dwell nowhere, being a wandering man, looking always for service. You I have heard of, O king, and from you I would now take my wages, which I shall fix myself according to my custom. My name is the Gilla Deacair, or the Slothful Fellow, and for a good reason. There never was a lazier or worse servant than

I, or one that grumbles more. Certainly, I'm a hard fellow to deal with. However noble my master, or however kindly he treats me, he'll get nothing but bad words and foul reproaches from me.'

'It is a poor account indeed you give of yourself,' said Finn, 'and true it is that there's not much to praise in your looks. But I never refused any man service or wages, and I will not refuse you now.'

So they made a covenant and the Gilla Deacair was engaged for a year. Then the Gilla asked Conan Mael whether the foot-men or the horse-men had the better wages among the Fenians. And Conan told him that mounted men had twice as much as the others.

'Horse-service is the one for me,' said the Gilla Deacair, 'as I have a fine horse of my own. And as to this horse, I must attend him myself, for I see no one here worthy to put a hand on him.'

At this, all the Fenians could not help but laugh, for they had never seen such a worthless skeleton of a nag.

The Gilla took his sorry beast to the herd and set him to graze. At once, the horse began to make mischief among the Fenian herd, throwing his tail out as straight as a rod, and thrashing with wild hooves. Left and right, he kicked and butted so that hardly a horse escaped without a broken leg, or a rib fractured, or an eye gouged, or an ear bitten off. Conan roared out to take the monster away, or he himself would knock the brains from the vicious brute. So the Gilla Deacair handed the halter to Conan and told him to try what he would.

In a mighty rage Conan threw the halter over the head of the great bag-of-bones. But the horse stood rigid, as stiff as a log in a little breeze, and try as he might Conan could not shift him an inch. Conan was blue between effort and anger, but the rest of the Fenians were weeping tears of laughter.

'I never thought to see,' said Fergus the poet, 'Conan Mael do such low horse-service. Since you've made yourself a groom to this four-legged devil, would it not be better to get up on his back and revenge yourself for this trouble? A few fierce cuts would drive him up mountains and down valleys. Put him through stones and bogs and crooked places till you've broken the heart in that comical body.'

Stung by taunts and laughs, Conan climbed up on the back of the horse and beat mightily with heels and two heavy fists. But the horse never stirred.

'The reason he will not go,' said Fergus, 'it is that he is used to far more weight. The Gilla Deacair is a heavy lump indeed. Let your friends join you on that uncomfortable height.'

So Conan called for men to join him, and one by one they mounted above till there were, as well as Conan himself, fourteen of the men of Baskin and of the men of Morna on the horse's long back. They all began to thrash with might and main, but never a twitch or a jump did they get out of the beast. And soon they found that their seat was not at all easy, for the back was as sharp and bony as a thin mountain ridge.

When the Gilla Deacair saw the many blows fall on his horse, he was angry and turned against Finn.

'O king,' said he, 'is this true conduct among such famous warriors? Then my service is at an end, and I swear I'll not even wait till morning for my wages. Now I know what to think of Finn and his Fenians.'

With that, he stood straight as a pillar, faced southwest and walked slowly away, with his horse drooping along behind. It was a sight that raised a large hoot of laughter. When he heard this, the Gilla looked back. Then he tucked up his shirt and picked up his heels and ran with such a speed in his long legs that a swallow on a windy March day might hardly keep with him. And his horse, not to be left behind, galloped after him.

Now the men on the back were frightened by the mad bounding of the horse, and they wished to throw themselves off. But the pace was so fast, and the far-away ground looked very hard, and the hooves of the beast whirled most dangerously, so they clung on for their lives, and Finn and the rest of the Fenians ran after them.

From Cliach plain they flew to Hy Conall Gavra, from

there to Slieve Lougher, from there by Slieve Mish to the deep green sea at Cloghan. Finn and his men were just able to keep the horse in view, but only swift Liagan was fast enough to catch him. At the water's edge he caught hold of the tail with the two of his hands. But the horse still plunged straight into the waves. Liagan was streaming out behind like a banner and the other Fenian riders were clinging hard, their knees clamped fast to the bony ribs and their arms about each other's necks.

Into the wild sea went the horse as easily as upon the dry strand. And though the wave tumbled all around, neither horse nor riders felt a drop of brine or a dash of spray.

Finn and his men stopped at the beach, puzzled by the watery departure of the Gilla Deacair and his horse. Then they saw two young men approaching, in scarlet cloaks held by brooches of gold. It was the two princes, Feradach and Foltlebar, sons of the king of Innia, and they were looking for a chance to practise their arts.

'My art,' said Feradach, 'is the making of a ship without delay. Cover your heads close while I give three blows of my axe and three throws of my sling, and when you open your eyes you shall see a ship all ready.'

'And my art, O chief of the Fenians,' said Foltlebar, 'is the tracking of the wild duck over nine ridges and nine glens, even to the furthest nest. And I can track by sea as easily as by land.'

It was what Finn wished for most, and at once he bound the young men to him. Hardly a moment later there was a ship all prepared, with a guide in the bow. Then some that were steadiest and bravest stayed to guard the kingdom, and Oisin was to be their chief. And others who were bold and adventurous went with Finn in the ship.

Sad was the parting of Finn from his son as he set course towards unknown seas. Foltlebar was guide and navigator, and Feradach the helmsman. The ship was on the broad back of the sea, and soon the high black waves of a great storm came against them. But in the roar of the rain and the blinding spray, Foltlebar still found the track of the Gilla, and Feradach held the helm steady.

As the blackness of the storm cleared, they saw a little way off a towering cliff with its head lost in cloud. It looked as smooth as glass. Examining the four points of the sky, Foltlebar tracked the Gilla and the horse to the foot of the cliff and no further. It was upwards that they must have gone. Then the Fenians were puzzled what to do. They looked at the high smooth rock with vexation in their hearts.

Then the sons of Innia considered the way it was, and Foltlebar thought there might be a way at the backside of the cliff. The Gilla Deacair had taken pains to cover his track, but Foltlebar was the man to sniff it out.

From the backside of the cliff they were off again, by islands and bays and many shores till they reached the Land of Promise. And when they knew where they had come, they were glad of it, for in this land Diarmuid O'Duibhne had been raised by Manannan Mac Lir, the yellow-haired god of the sea.

Now, it was a man of the Tuatha De Danann, named Avarta, who was king here, and this very man had himself taken the form of the Gilla Deacair, to bring the Fenians on the back of the horse into bondage and so to test the power of Finn and the Fianna of Ireland. And when Finn knew that his companions were taken in this country, he planned a speedy onslaught with swords and spears, to make the people learn that none could do outrage to the men of the Fianna and go unpunished.

'It is wise, O Finn, to tread carefully,' said Diarmuid. 'The men here are masters of the druidical knowledge, and it is not safe to stir them up. Let us rather send a messenger to King Avarta, and if he does not free our friends only then will we waste the land with fire and sword.'

Then Foltlebar, the guide, took the messenger by the hand through dim and shadowy places, along paths made crooked by enchantment, till they came to the house of Avarta. The lost men of the Fenians were lying quietly in the sun, not without contentment, for any hard ground was soft enough after a ride on the back of the Gilla's horse.

Then there were tears and many greetings, when the

Fenians saw the messenger. And Avarta himself listened with respect to the message from Finn, for he saw now that Finn had the power and the courage to make good the capture of his men. In a little while Avarta went to meet Finn and he promised the release of the Fenians and a reward for the injury done to them. Then Finn and Avarta joined hands in friendship.

Out of joy to see his Fenian again, Finn wished to lay no fine or penalty on Avarta. But foul-mouthed Conan Mael was not so kind.

'Listen, O Finn,' he said, 'it is an easy matter for you. You have suffered nothing but a little bit of a chase. But we who have endured the sharp bones of the Gilla's horse, the pain of the mad gallop across seas and rocks and deserts and tangled woods, we need some reward for our suffering.'

Those who recalled the sight of the brave Fenian lads helpless on the monstrous horse could hardly keep from laughing. But Avarta did not smile.

'Name your price,' he said, 'and I will pay it all. For I know well your reputation, Conan. I dread the gibes and taunts and insults of your foul tongue.'

'Then let it be done,' replied Conan, 'to you and your people as it was done to us. Let fifteen of the best men of the Land of Promise ride on that long ruinous back, following the very course that we took through thorny forest and jagged rocks and dark glens and storm-bound seas. And Avarta, you yourself shall take hold of the tail of the horse, stuck fast, like a burr on the coat of a wild dog.'

Finn was content that Conan's evil temper had asked no more than like for like, and Avarta was content to make this pledge. Then Finn and his men took their leave, and slid over the broad green sea to Ireland.

They landed and went to their tents at Knockainy and waited for the coming of the Gilla's horse. And sure enough, from the beach at Cloghan the beast came bumping and bucking. Avarta had gone from the back end of the horse to the front. Once more he had taken on the form of the Gilla Deacair, and he was loping along as large and ugly and doleful as before, with the fifteen chiefs from the Land of Promise painfully bobbing behind, like seed-husks in a fast rocky stream.

When the Gilla Deacair and his horse came up to Finn, the Gilla made a wave of his hand towards the clouds and the green hills and the herds of the Fenians peacefully grazing. All the Fenians looked around the familiar land, and it seemed to them that it was good. But when they turned again to the Gilla Deacair, he and his horse and the fifteen chiefs from the Land of Promise had all disappeared, and they were never seen again from that time out.

FINN AND BRAN

One day, Finn was in the front of his house, with no one about him but his hound Bran, when he saw a boat coming to the shore. Three big men jumped from the boat, hauled it seven fathoms length on the green grass, and turned it over so none might launch it. Then they straightened their backs, and one of them looked down towards Finn.

'Well, little fellow,' said he, 'what news can we expect from such a small herd-boy and his wee doggie?'

'No news,' said Finn, 'unless I hear something from big men who have just come from the sea.'

'Our news is that we come to make war and combat with Finn Mac Cool, so go you nimbly and fetch him down.'

Finn went off muttering to himself that he would lay the big men under spells. And he swore by the power of druidical women and the magic of hornless calves to take their heads should he return and find the big men still there.

In anger he set sail for the Kingdom of the Big Men, taking only Bran with him. Wind and tide served him well and soon he landed. He looked about him and saw a very tall man going round a tree.

'A grand day,' said Finn.

'Certainly,' said the tall man, 'but what news has the dwarf with the lap-dog?'

'No news,' said Finn, 'but I expect to hear something from a big man going round a tree.'

'The thing I have to tell is this,' replied the tall man. 'Long since has the king of this land wanted a dwarf and a pretty little dog, and now I can bring them to him.'

Away he went, dragging the tree for firewood, and he took Finn and Bran with him. They had not gone far when they met another big man, and he too thought that the dwarf and the pretty dog would be a fine present for the king. So the big men began to fight, till they grew tired.

After a time one of them said, 'Hold your hand now. There's little sense in the work we are doing. Is it not better to lay our quarrel before the dwarf himself?'

'For better or worse,' said Finn, 'I will follow the big man who saw me first.' Then that man lifted Finn in one palm and Bran in the other and went to the house of the king.

The king was well pleased, and he accepted the gift for a year and a day. He gave Finn a chamber next to his own, and Finn was in and out as he wished, ever at the king's side. And he soon noticed that the king was missing every night but returned, cold and wet, just before the dawn. Finn asked the king why this was.

'Should I tell that to the like of you?' said the king.

'There would be no harm to tell it,' replied Finn.

'Not tonight,' said the king, 'so go you to sleep.'

After the next night, when the king was again absent, Finn spoke to him once more.

'A master should tell his mind,' said Finn. 'Let me know the reason for your night departure, or I will not stay with you.'

'What good can it do me,' replied the king, 'to tell such a small weak fellow?'

'Advice may be equally good, from a small man or a tall man.'

So the king said, 'I am seventeen years without sleep or rest, because of a huge monster that worries my kingdom every night.'

'Then sleep tonight,' said Finn, 'and I will meet it.'

'I have need of that sleep,' said the king. But he feared Finn would be destroyed, such a little man was he.

Finn took Bran to the shore. And soon there was a seething-white, rolling, loud-roaring swell out of the sea, and a sea-monster with one blubbery eye measured its great length on the beach.

'Ho,' it said, 'a little man and a smaller dog! What news?'

'The king is dead,' replied Finn. 'Stay away this night, till the nobles get another king to give you combat.'

'Would that be the truth?' said the monster.

'I have no wish to lie,' said Finn. So the monster departed.

When the king awoke from unusual sleep, he cried out in great fear, for he thought that his kingdom was gone together with his dwarf and his lap-dog. But Finn soothed and comforted him.

Next night, the king wished to go to the shore, but Finn and Bran went again in his place. The monster burst from the sea, as before. This time Finn told it that the queen was dead, and once more the kingdom was relieved. Still, the king was full of fear and asked Finn how the monster looked.

'It was not frightening to me,' said Finn.

The king sighed and said, 'You have done much good to give me this rest.'

That night, again the monster came roaring from the sea, shaking its whole blubbery length.

'What news tonight,' it said, 'from the little man and the smaller dog?'

'The news I have is this,' replied Finn. 'It is absurd for such a great brute as you to be listening night after night to lies from such a little fellow as I am.'

'Is that how it is?' the monster shouted. 'Then look to defend yourself.'

It leapt towards Finn and put him to such dodging and twisting that he was soon well-nigh worn out.

'O Bran,' he called to his hound, 'are you likely to remember me at all tonight?'

So Bran took a turn around them and sat where he was before. The wrestling was becoming the worse for Finn, and he called again to Bran, 'Are you like to forget me altogether?'

Bran took a second turn about them and sat down as before. The struggle was now going entirely against Finn, and he was growing faint.

'Bran,' he gasped, 'you need not rise anymore. I am gone. There is no help. What you have done for me, you will never do again.'

Then Bran jumped up and went behind the monster. He uncovered his venomous claw and slashed the monster, and in the blink of an eye the heart and the liver were out of it. Finn hacked off the head, and he rolled it and carried it the way to the king's house. He stuck it on a pole towards the house, with the big goggle eye staring at the king's window. Then he went softly to his place at the feet of the king.

About midnight, the king woke in fear and cried out, 'My kingdom is lost to me, my dwarf and lap-dog are gone.'

'Neither of them is wanting to you,' replied Finn. 'Look from your window and see for yourself.'

The king did so. And when he saw the head and the goggle eye of the monster his knees knocked and he fell beside the bed where Finn lay.

'It was foretold long since,' he said, 'that only Finn Mac Cool would give rest to me and my kingdom. Welcome to you, O Finn Mac Cool!'

'But are you deserving of forgiveness from me?' said Finn sternly. 'Did you not send three big men, without provocation, to combat me in my own kingdom?'

'These are three men,' replied the king, 'who are not under

the law. They are not friendly to me, and their witch-women have made them magic shirts. But when these shirts are taken off them, they will be as other men. I will give you a drink to make them sleep, and then you may strip the shirts from their backs.'

Finn took the drink with him and launched his boat at once, and Bran returned in the boat also. As they came to the shore of his own land, Finn threw out the bottles of the sleeping-draught towards the big men, who were still camped about the house waiting for Finn. The first big man knocked the top off the bottle and drank from it. His companions did likewise, and soon they were all asleep. Then Finn pulled off their shirts and shook them awake.

'Here you are,' said Finn.

'We are,' said they.

'And now you are but as other men, and I have power and chance to take your lives. I shall not release you till you come under a bond of law.'

So they submitted to be bound under covenant. And they swore on the cold sword to stand by Finn in right or wrong, for Finn saw that big men were good men in battle or war. In any danger of distress he had only to think on them and they would be with him wherever he was. Then he restored to them their shirts.

That was satisfactory, and Finn went home to an entertainment that was the fourth greatest ever held among the Fenians.

FINN IN THE HOUSE OF THE YELLOW-FIELD

This day, Finn and his men were on the hunting hill, and they had done a great deal of chasing before the end of the day, and they had killed a good number of deer.

While they were resting from the hunt, Finn had a look down the glen and saw the appearance of a strong warrior approaching.

'Looks like a stranger is among us,' said Finn.

'If he is coming without business,' said Conan of the foul tongue, 'he will not leave without it.'

After the greeting of the day, the stranger said he was a servant seeking a master, and then Finn was willing to engage him, as was his custom.

'It would not be my advice,' said Conan. 'We have enough of these wandering rogues already.'

'Be quiet, you rascal,' replied the strong lad. 'Your tongue puts your head in trouble, and if I am not deceived you shall indeed suffer some pains on account of the talk this day.'

But Finn smoothed over that talk and asked the lad what wage he wished at the end of a year and a day.

'It is this,' said the lad, 'that you and your men shall go with me to a feast and an entertainment when my time is out.'

All the Fenians took courage from this, that no evil thing should befall them all together. And so the agreement was made.

When his time was out, away went the lad, and it was a hard matter for the Fenians to keep up to him, even for Liagan the swift or slender Caoilte. The big lad set off bare-headed, bare-footed, with a spring from gap to height, from height to glen, through glen to broad valley. With flying foot he led the Fenians till he reached the Yellow-field. When the last breathless man of them had come up to him, he took his way over to a large house and asked them to go in.

Finn entered first, and his men followed. They all got seats by the wall except Conan, who was so far behind he had no choice but to drop down on the hearthstone. At first they were tired and glad for the rest. But soon they grew impatient for the promised feast. After a long time, some of the Fenians offered to go for the food. They tried to rise but they could not. Their haunches stuck to their seats, and the soles of their feet to the floor, and their backs to the walls.

'Did I not tell you in good time,' cried Conan from the hearthstone, 'what would happen with these wandering lads?'

Finn spake not a word, but he was in great anxiety lest this might be the death-strait for all of them. Then he remembered his tooth of knowledge, and he put his finger under it to learn what to do. And it became known to him that nothing would set them free but the blood of the three sons of the King of Inish Tilly, filtered through silver rings into golden cups.

Then he blew his wooden whistle, which he never sounded except in terror of a death-strait. Oscar and Leary had been absent from the company of the Fenians that day, but they heard the whistle. They would have heard it even in the Uttermost World, for the sound passed through the seven borders of the earth.

Three times the whistle sounded, and before the rising of the sun Oscar and Leary were outside the wall of the house in the Yellow-field.

'Are you there within, O Grandfather Finn?' cried Oscar.

'We are within,' Finn shouted back, 'and at our peril.' And then he told them of the blood needed to release them.

'But where shall we watch,' asked Oscar, 'to find the sons of the King of Inish Tilly?'

'Watch well the ford at the mouth of the river over yonder,' said Finn. 'But the day is young yet. See first if you can seek out food for us, for we are faint of hunger.'

Oscar and Leary set their faces towards another big house that was over against them. They found that the cooks were making ready the dinner. As Oscar peeped into the kitchen, he saw a fierce cook lifting a quarter of a deer from the cauldron. In a while the cook departed and Oscar and Leary crept in to steal the food. A buzzard was guarding the pot but Oscar pierced it with a dart, and they ran from the kitchen with every bit of food they could hold.

At the prison-house of the Fenians, Oscar and Leary made a hole in the wall and threw in enough food to satisfy each man, except Conan. He lay on his back, with hands and feet stuck fast to the hearth. Only food dropped from above could get to his mouth. A few pieces and crumbs thrown in the air landed about his face, and in this way he got a morsel or two.

'Now take your watch by the ford at the river mouth,' Finn called, 'for the host from Inish Tilly will be coming.'

'But how shall we know the sons of the king?' said Oscar.

'They will be walking apart on the right hand, and their dress will be all in green.'

Oscar and Leary went to the river mouth and waited at the ford. Soon a great host came in sight.

'Who are those two uncomely lubbers,' shouted the advance guard of the host, 'there at the ford at the beginning of night? It is a time for them to be getting afraid.'

'A third of the fear will be on yourselves,' replied Oscar, 'and only a small bit of it on us.'

'Then wait,' cried the men, 'and it will be to your hurt.'

So they went at each other. Oscar and Leary violently assailed under and over the enemy till not a man of them was left alive to tell the tale. But the sons of the king had not been there that night, and Finn heard this news with sorrow.

'It is needful to try again,' said he. 'But feed us first and watch the ford next. And do not forget to take your three-edged blade and your shield.'

Again the Fenians were fed, though Conan's portion was very small. But still, in the evening, the sons of the King of Inish Tilly did not come to the ford.

'No help but to feed us and prepare again,' said Finn. 'But, Oscar, be sure to carry your spear and shield. If your spear shall taste the blood of the Winged Dragon of Sheil, then the King of Inish Tilly will surely lose a son tonight.'

Now, when Oscar went to steal the food that day, he went armed, and it was well that he did so. The fierce Winged Dragon of Sheil was coiled about the cooking-pot to guard the food. Oscar lifted his shield and with one thrust of his spear he pierced the head of the dragon. As the blood flowed from the dragon the thrashing of its body grew weak, and then it disappeared.

'Did your spear taste blood?' Finn asked when Oscar brought the food.

'A cubit length,' said Oscar, 'and a handbreadth of it drank greedily.'

'Then let your rings for filtering and your cups for holding be with you this night.'

At the ford of the river mouth that evening they saw a host advance with three young men at the right hand in garments of green. Leary stood to face these sons of the king, while Oscar set himself against the rest of the host.

'Who are those lubberly fellows at the ford in the evening?' the enemy called out. 'It is time for them to be fleeing.'

'Three-thirds of the fear will be on you now,' replied Oscar, 'for none at all is on us.'

Then Oscar went among that host and cut them about till not one was left alive. And Leary had the three sons of the king on two knees, and they had Leary only on one knee. Leary needed no help, so Oscar put his mind to the blood that was flowing fast onto the ground. He began to filter it through rings of silver into cups of gold, but before the cups were full the bodies were stiff and bled no more.

'Have you the blood?' Finn called out when they returned. 'Then rub it into every bit of you that may touch the house, from the hair of your head to the soles of your feet. Then enter here and do the same for every man of us.'

As the blood was rubbed on each Fenian man, he came unstuck from seat and floor and wall. In this way all were released except Conan. They came to him last, spread out on the hearthstone, and by that time only a smear and stain were left in the cups. It was enough to free the most of him, but none was left for the back of his head. The hair and the skin of his head till stuck to the hearth.

When they were loose, Finn and his men set off rejoicing, and they had not gone very far when they heard the loud voice of Conan behind. As he came up they saw that the back of his head was stripped, without any tuft of hair and with a long bare patch of skin. In his effort to free himself, after the rest left him, he gave his head a great fierce pull and abandoned to the hearthstone his hair and his skin. From that day forth all men called him Conan Mael, or Bald Conan without Hair.

With glad hearts Finn and his men reached home. And then Finn gave word and oath that he would never again engage a wandering lad.

FINN AND THE
WISDOM OF THE WORLD

O n a fine day, Finn and his men were hunting in the
mountains of Donegal. All day they had chased a
deer high and low. But they lost her and they were
tired.

'Let us face for home, men,' said Finn, 'or the night will
catch us before we reach our beds.'

They were not far down the hillside when a black fog fell
on them. So they sat where they were, not knowing east
from west.

'A fog like this is a horror to us,' said Finn. 'I'm afraid, lad,
that we are astray for the night.'

But keen-eyed Diarmuid was peering about, and through
a chink in the fog he saw the weak gleam of a lime-white
house. Gladly, the Fenians hurried to it, but found there only
a little withered old man, and a sheep tied along by the wall.

The old man looked up from the edge of the hearth and gave Finn a weary welcome.

'Upon my soul,' said Diarmuid in a low voice, 'it is unlikely that we will get any ease in this hovel.'

The old man called to a woman below to bring food, and then there came in a fine handsome girl, as lovely as the day. And it did not take her long to spread a big table with all manner of food and drink. Finn sat at the head of the table and every man found meat before him. But hardly a bite was in their mouths when the sheep that was tethered along the wall broke the hemp rope, upended the table, and pitched every scrap of food onto the floor.

'Devil take you,' roared Conan. 'You've made a fine mess of the dinner, and we badly in need of it.'

'Rise up, Conan,' said Finn, 'and tie the sheep.'

Conan caught the sheep by the top of her head and tried to drag her to the wall. But he could not move her, though his heart might burst in the attempt.

'By heavens,' he said, 'here's this great warrior that I am, and I can't tie up a sheep. Let someone else move her.'

First Diarmuid tried, and then every one of them. But it was no use.

'Shame on you all,' said the old man. 'Great and brave as you are, there's not a one of you can tie a poor sheep with a bit of rope.'

Then he rose from the edge of the hearth and hobbled down the floor. Six pints of ashes fell from the backside of his trousers, from his long lying on the hearth. He took the sheep by the scruff, and tugged her easily to the wall, and tied the rope. When the men of the Fianna saw this, they felt fear and trembling, for he could do himself what brave warriors had failed to do. Quietly the old man returned to his place by the fire and called for the young woman to bring more food.

It was not long before there was more meat and drink on the table.

'Start eating, lads,' said the old man, 'you'll have no more trouble.'

When they were full, and resting their bellies in the glow of the fire, Finn saw the young woman sitting apart. He had a desire to talk to her and went down the room to her.

'Finn Mac Cool,' said she sternly, 'you had me once and you won't have me again.'

Finn turned back with a red face, and then Diarmuid went down to her. But he got the same answer, and so did every one of the Fenians. When Oisin was the last to try, she took him by the hand and led him in front of the company.

'Finn Mac Cool,' she said, 'you and the Fenians were ever famous for strength and courage, yet still each one of you failed to tie the sheep. 'Tis an unusual sheep. She is Strength. And the old man beyond the hearth is Death. As strong as the sheep is, the old man will overcome her. In the same way, Death will come upon you, strong as you all are. And I am Youth. Each of you had me once, but you never will again. Now I will give you any wish.'

Finn was the first to ask. He wished to lose the smell of clay, which had clung to him ever since he sinned with a woman now dead. Then Diarmuid wanted a love-spot on his body, to bewitch young women. Oscar asked for an unbreakable thong for his sling. And Conan wished to be invulnerable, and for the power to kill hundreds in battle.

'Alas,' cried Diarmuid when he heard this, 'that Conan should ever have the use of such a power! He is such a vicious, ill-tempered man, he may not leave a Fenian alive.'

So Conan was granted the power but he could not use it, except once at the Battle of Ventry, when he looked at his enemies through his fingers and killed every one of them.

When all the wishes had been granted, Finn turned to see what his men thought of their gifts. And when he looked again, he found himself and the Fenians standing on the mountainside, with nothing but sheep and goats grazing nearby.

FINN TOWARDS THE
END OF HIS AGE

Now, after Finn had been some long time in the
house of Conan of Ceann Slieve, he thought he had
been questioned more than enough. At last, he was
impatient and turned-aside.

'Prepare a bed for myself and Finndealbh,' said he, 'for you
have asked enough, O Conan, concerning the plight and
troubles of Finn and the Fenians. The back end of the night
is upon us, and it is time for more blissful things.'

Finally, Finn slept. But a bad vision infected his dream, and
he sprang thrice from his bed in fear.

'I saw the Tuatha De Danann,' he said to Finndealbh. 'They
were raising a quarrel against me and making a bloody
carnage of my Fenians.'

As for the Fenians themselves, they had no tidings of Finn
so they pitched camp where they were. Early next day, Bran

Beg and Bran Mor went to Mac an Reith to learn where Finn lay. Then the two Brans went quickly to the house of Conan of Ceann Slieve. And when they came in to Finn, they reproached him for going forward with his wedding-feast without the presence of the Fenians.

'We have a banquet prepared and ready at Allen in Leinster,' said Bran Mor. 'Let us go and partake of it.'

So they all went to the hall in Allen, and the Fenian men were intent on pleasure that night. But they had not been long there when they saw Cairbre, son of Cormac, son of Conn the Hundred Fighter, shape his way directly to where they were.

'No good thing is coming to us,' said Finn, 'since our *geasa* forbids us to break up our entertainment. Yet this son of the king of Ireland will expect us to make way for him at the head of the feast.'

'We will not do so,' said Oisin. 'But rather let us give up half the hall for him and keep half for us.'

This was willingly done, but certain of the Tuatha De Danann took it as an insult.

'Is this how Finn Mac Cool makes disrespect to us,' said one of them, 'while he himself possesses the woman who had been promised to Fatha Mac Avric, the third best man of all the Tuatha De Danann?'

These men departed in the dawn and went to Finbarr at Magh Feabhail, and they told him of the insults and wrongs offered by Finn to the people of the Tuatha De Danann.

Then Finbarr collected six powerful battalions, from all parts of Ireland, and they gathered at Loch Derg. This muster took place on the very day that Conan of Ceann Slieve himself gave a wedding-feast for his daughter and Finn.

Finn was coming to the feast with none but a few of the men of the family of Morna.

'Never, O Goll,' said Finn, 'have I had such fear and misgivings to attend a wedding-feast. My forces are few in number. I have a fore knowledge that evil broods over me. The Tuatha De Danann are ready to slaughter my people.'

Then Goll Mac Morna promised faithfully to defend him,

and they went forward to the wedding-feast in the house of Conan. In the hall, Finn sat by the door with Goll on his right and Finndealbh to his left.

At this time Finbarr and the warriors of the Tuatha De Danann were covering themselves with a magic mist and marching without delay, invisibly, steadily, powerfully, to a place on the plain next to the house of Conan. But they were not confident to fight that day.

'What use for us to be here,' they asked, 'since Goll Mac Morna himself defends Finn against us?'

'Goll shall not protect him,' replied Ethne the druidess, 'for I will beguile Finn from the house, whatever care is put over him.'

She went to the house and saw Finn just within the door.

'Who is that before my face?' she said.

'It is I myself,' replied Finn.

'I put you under a *geasa*, which you shall not break as you are a true hero,' said she, 'to come forth to me immediately.'

Finn would not break the bonds of a *geasa* and went outside, though none in the house but Caoilte saw him leave. Then the warriors of the Tuatha De Danann let fly a flock of dark birds with fiery beaks into the fort of Conan. These birds perched on the chests of those within and so scorched and tortured them that men, women and children fled in all directions. Canana, wife of Conan, ran with flaming clothes into the river and was drowned.

Then Ethne said to Finn, 'Run a race with me for your freedom.'

'What distance will that be?' asked Finn.

'From the forest of Two-Wild-Boars in the west, to the Great Ford in the east.'

Thus it was agreed. They ran and ran but Finn was leading toward the ford, and Caoilte, who had followed him out from the house, was chasing hard. Finn was urging him forward.

'Shame on your running, O Caoilte,' he called out, 'for your small amount of swiftness. A woman is leaving you behind.'

Then Caoilte sprang forward and made a most exemplary leap onto the druidess, and struck his shoulder against her chest. As she staggered, he turned about and made a slash of his sword to her waist, so that he cut her into two parts.

'Win victory and blessings, O Caoilte,' cried Finn. 'Many is the good blow you have struck in your time, but never a better one than that.'

They faced about and as quick as they could ran back to the green of Ceann Slieve. They found that the Tuatha De Danann had thrown off the cover of the magic mist and were drawn up in warlike ranks.

'We are fallen in the thick of enemies,' said Finn to Caoilte. Then back to back they stood against waves of attack till groans of hurt and faintness broke from them.

This noise of unequal combat came to Goll and wrung his heart. He called to his friends, and rallied the household of Conan and his sons, and they all rushed upon the green in a dense body, intent upon great feats of arms and carnage and murder.

Now Goll Mac Morna, the chief of champions, the body-mangler, the terrible thunderer, was enraged. Like a towering mountain under his grey shield was he in battle. He laid low the leaders, and crushed the bodies of their nobles, and burst through all enemy ranks. He shortened limbs and emptied skulls till he reached the pillar of the opposition, Finbarr himself. They fought like great lions, but Finbarr could not withstand the heavy, double-handed strokes of Goll, and he fell.

Chief slew chief, and good men went down before the blows from good men. Few were the battles in Ireland fought with such dreadful spite and force. None wished, or was so without honour, to yield or retreat a single step. For these were the two most hard-fighting bodies of men to be found in any of the four corners of the globe: that is to say, the manly, bloody, robust, unbowed Fenians of Finn Mac Cool, and the white-toothed, large-limbed, grim-armed warriors of the Tuatha De Danann. They were both well-nigh finished before the sun set on that battle.

At last, in the declining of the day, all the Fenians of Ireland who had missed the battle were seen approaching. When they saw this, the Tuatha De Danann wrapped themselves in the magic mist and melted away most suddenly. Finn himself was in fainting fits from the pain of his wounds. And Oisin despaired at the great number of the fallen. Of Finn's thousand heroes, all but one hundred were slain. And even these were maimed, weak and wounded.

As to Finn Mac Cool, he was carried to the house at Ceann Slieve where he remained under cure for a month and a fortnight. Then he and his few followers limped home to Allen in Leinster. And they stayed a long time quietly in Allen, with the memory of their hurts and their wounds still painfully upon them.

OISIN
AFTER THE FIANNA

Oisin, son of Finn, survived after the time of the Fenians. He lived in the house of his daughter. He was blind, deaf and limping, and there were nine oak skewers in his belly. He ate the tribute that holy Patrick had over Ireland. He was telling the old histories, and they were writing them.

They killed a grand stag, and stripped the shank, and brought him the bone.

'Did you ever see a shank thicker than that in the Fenians?' they asked.

'I saw a bone of the blackbird's chick in which that would be lost,' he replied after he had felt the bone.

But they said, 'There's nothing but lies in what you tell us.'

Then he caught hold of the books in a rage, and he set them in the fire. But his daughter rescued the books, and quenched them, and kept them.

Oisin was wailing and asking for company. 'Would that even the worst lad and dog in the Fianna,' he cried, 'might lay a hand on my chest.'

He felt a weight and said, 'What's this?'

''Tis the son of the Red One,' came the answer. There was another weight at his feet, and that was the son of the Little Yellow One.

In the morning they arose and Oisin asked one of the lads to take him to the glen. When they reached it, Oisin took a wooden whistle from his pocket and played on it.

'What goes past on yonder mountain?' asked blind Oisin.

'I see deer on it,' said the lad.

'What sort of deer?'

'I see some slender and grey.'

'Let them pass. Those are the seed of the swift elk. But what see you now?'

'I see some gaunt and grizzled.'

'Let them pass. Those are the seed of the fierce red deer. But what see you now?'

'I see some heavy and sleek.'

'Then unleash the dog.' And away went the dog after the deer.

'Little Yellow One,' said Oisin, 'when the hound has caught a dozen we shall check him.' And when that time came, Oisin played on his whistle and checked the hound.

'If the pup is sated with chase,' said he, 'he will come quietly. If not, he will come with his gape open.'

But the hound was coming with his gape open and his tongue out at his mouth, so Oisin said, 'Catch hold of my hand and try to put it in his gape, or he will have us.'

The lad put Oisin's hand in the mouth of the hound, and he shook the throat out of the dog. Then the lad dragged the dead deer to a rushy knoll, and when he had taken them all there were nine stags on it. That was enough for Oisin alone, so the lad's portion was lost. Oisin delved into the rushy knoll, and in it was the great cauldron of the Fenians. The lad put a fire under the cauldron and in a little time the stags were cooked.

'Touch not the meat,' said Oisin, 'till first I take my fill.'

Oisin began upon the animals, and as he ate each one he took one of the skewers out of his belly. Six were eaten, but Oisin found no more. The lad had taken three.

'Have you done this to me?' Oisin asked.

'I did it,' said the lad, 'for you took so many and I had need of a few.'

'Well, then,' said Oisin, 'now let us face for home.'

The lad caught him under the arm and away they went. As Oisin felt they were nearing the house, he said, 'Is the house close by?'

'It is,' said the lad.

'Would the shout of a man reach the house from where we are?'

'It would reach it.'

'Set my foot straight toward the door.' And the lad did this.

When he was sure that he was set toward the house, Oisin suddenly caught hold of the lad, put his hands to his throat, and killed him.

'Now,' said he, 'neither you nor another will ever tell tales of the son of Finn again.'

THE LAMENTATION
OF OISIN FOR
FINN MAC COOL

The battles of Gavra and Ollarba had been fought, and the Fianna were for the most part destroyed. Those who remained scattered in small bands throughout Ireland, till only two good warriors were left: Oisin, son of Finn, and Caoilte Mac Ronan.

Oisin lived on, even into the days of the blessed Patrick, the apostle to the Gaels. That religious man said benediction over the fort of Finn Mac Cool, and he sprinkled the holy water that drove away a thousand legions of demons into the *shee*-hills and the skalps at the outer borders of the land.

Demons departed forthwith, in all directions. And all about Oisin was the quiet and holy order of the church. But his heart was not in it, and he yearned for the hunt and the hounds, the feasting and wooing, the passage of arms, and the bravery and the blood of battle.

Then Oisin gave a long despairing cry:

> It is grief to me, O Patrick,
> Though God is gracious and loving,
> To speak no more of Finn –
> Most melancholy to me – and of the Fenians.
>
> Farewell to wooing and to hunting,
> Farewell to drinking and sweet music,
> Farewell to fights and to battle,
> Farewell, moreover, to sharp blades.
>
> Farewell to speed and strength,
> Farewell to slaughter and clean wounds,
> Farewell to far lands and to returning,
> Farewell to gifts and to single combat.
>
> Farewell to feasts and the full cup,
> Farewell to running and to leaping,
> Farewell to the chase on every rough hill,
> Farewell to the fights of mighty men.
>
> Alas! is not my grief a piteous tale,
> That I am fasting in the church of the poor?
> Scarce of bread and scant of food,
> My body lacks all strength and power.
>
> Farewell, O Finn, again and again,
> A hundred times, O Fenian king!
> For you indeed would conquer my thirst,
> Unlike thin porridge the holy clerics eat.

INDEX

TALES OF OLD IRELAND

Edited by Michael O'Mara

Contents

WILLIAM CARLETON

Neal Malone

William Carleton (1794–1869) was educated in the so-called 'hedge schools' – the very roughest of schooling. His stories were published under the title of Traits and Stories of the Irish Peasantry *(1830).*

THERE never was a greater-souled or doughtier tailor than little Neal Malone. Though but four feet four in height, he paced the earth with the courage and confidence of a giant; nay, one would have imagined that he walked as if he feared the world itself was about to give way under him. Let none dare to say in future that a tailor is but the ninth part of a man. That reproach had been gloriously taken away from the character of the cross-legged corporation by Neal Malone. He has wiped it off like a stain from the collar of a second-hand coat; he has pressed this wrinkle out of the lying front of antiquity; he has drawn together this rent in the respectability of his profession. No. By him who was breeches-maker to the gods – that is, except, like Highlanders, they eschewed inexpressibles – by him who cut Jupiter's frieze jocks for winter, and eke by the bottom of his thimble, we swear that Neal Malone was *more* that the ninth part of a man!

Setting aside the Patagonians, we maintain that two-thirds of mortal humanity were comprised in Neal; and perhaps we might venture to assert that two-thirds of Neal's humanity were equal to six-thirds of another man's. It is right well known that Alexander the Great was a little man, and we doubt whether, had Alexander the Great been bred to the tailoring business, he would have exhibited so much of the hero as Neal Malone. Neal was descended from a fighting family, who had signalized themselves in as many battles as ever any single hero of antiquity fought. His father, his grandfather, and his great-grandfather were all fighting men, and his ancestors in general, up, probably, to Con of the Hundred Battles himself. No wonder, therefore, that Neal's blood should cry out against the cowardice of his calling; no wonder that he should be an epitome of all that was valorous and heroic in a peaceable man, for we neglected to inform the reader that Neal, though 'bearing no base mind', never fought any man in his own person. That, however, deducted nothing from his courage. If he did not fight, it was simply because he found cowardice universal. No man would engage him; his spirit blazed in vain; his thirst for battle was doomed to remain unquenched, except by whisky, and this only increased it. In short, he could find no foe. He has often been known to challenge the first cudgel-players and pugilists of the parish; to provoke men of fourteen stone weight; and to bid mortal defiance to faction heroes of all grades – but in vain. There was that in him which told them that an encounter with Neal would strip them of their laurels. Neal saw all this with a lofty imagination; he deplored the degeneracy of the times, and thought it hard that the descendant of such a fighting family should be doomed to pass through life peaceably, whilst so many excellent rows and riots took place around him. It was a calamity to see every man's head broken but his own; a dismal thing to observe his neighbours go about with their bones in bandages, yet his untouched; and his friends beat black and blue, whilst his own cuticle remained undiscoloured.

'Blur-an'-agers!' exclaimed Neal one day, when half tipsy in the fair, 'am I never to get a bit of fightin'? Is there no cowardly *spalpeen* to stand afore Neal Malone? Be this an' be that, I'm blue-mowlded for want of a batin'! I'm disgracin' my relations by the life I'm ladin'! Will non o' ye fight me aither for love, money or whisky – frind or inimy, an' bad luck to ye? I don't care a *traneen* which, only out o' pure friendship let us have a morsel o' the rale kick-up, 'tany rate. Frind or inimy, I say agin, if you regard me – sure, that makes no differ, only let us have the fight.'

This excellent heroism was all wasted; Neal could not find a single adversary. Except he divided himself like Hotspur, and went to buffets, one hand against the other, there was no chance of a fight; no person to be found sufficiently magnanimous to encounter the tailor. On the contrary, every one of his friends – or, in other words, every man in the parish – was ready to support him. He was clapped on the back until his bones were nearly dislocated in his body, and his hand shaken until his arm lost its cunning at the needle for half-a-week afterwards. This, to be sure, was a bitter business – a state of being past endurance. Every man was his friend – no man was his enemy. A desperate position for any person to find himself in, but doubly calamitous to a martial tailor.

Many a dolorous complaint did Neal make upon the misfortune of having none to wish him ill; and what rendered this hardship doubly oppressive was the unlucky fact that no exertions of his, however offensive, could procure him a single foe. In vain did he insult, abuse, and malign all his acquaintances. In vain did he father upon them all the rascality and villainy he could think of. He lied against them with a force and originality that would have made many a modern novelist blush for want of invention – but all to no purpose. The world for once became astonishingly Christian; it paid back all his efforts to excite its resentment with the purest of charity; when Neal struck it on the one cheek, it meekly turned unto him the other. It could scarcely be expected that Neal would bear this. To have the whole world in friendship with a man is beyond doubt rather an affliction. Not to have the face of a single enemy to look upon would decidedly be considered a deprivation of many agreeable sensations by most people as well as by Neal Malone. Let who might sustain a loss, or experience a calamity, it was a matter of indifference to Neal. They were only his friends, and he troubled neither his head nor his heart about them.

Heaven help us! there is no man without his trials; and Neal, the reader perceives, was not exempt from his. What did it avail him that he carried a cudgel ready for all hostile contingencies? or knit his brows and shook his *kippeen* at the fiercest of his fighting friends? The moment he appeared, they softened into downright cordiality. His presence was the signal of peace; for, notwithstanding his unconquerable propensity to warfare, he went abroad as the genius of unanimity, though carrying in his bosom the redoubtable disposition of a warrior; just as the sun, though the source of light himself, is said to be dark enough at bottom.

It could not be expected that Neal, with whatever fortitude he might bear his other afflictions, could bear such tranquillity like a hero. To say that he bore it as one, would be to basely surrender his character; for what hero ever bore a state of tranquillity with courage? It affected his cutting out! It produced what Burton calls 'a windie melancholie', which was nothing else than an accumulation of courage that had no means of escaping, if courage can, without indignity, be ever said to escape. He sat uneasy on his lap-board. Instead of cutting out soberly, he flourished his scissors as if he were heading a faction; he wasted much chalk by scoring his cloth in wrong places, and even caught his hot goose without a holder. These symptoms alarmed his friends, who persuaded him to go to a doctor. Neal went, to satisfy them; but he knew that no prescription could drive the courage out of him – that he was too far gone in heroism to be made a coward of by apothecary stuff. Nothing in the pharmacopeia could physic him into a pacific state. His disease was simply the want of an enemy, and an unaccountable superabundance of friendship on the part of his acquaintances. How could a doctor remedy this by a prescription? Impossible. The doctor, indeed, recommended blood-letting; but to lose blood in a peaceable manner was not only cowardly, but a bad cure for courage. Neal declined it: he would lose no blood for any man until he could not help it; which was giving the character of a hero at a single touch. His blood was not to be thrown away in this manner; the only lancet ever applied to his relations was the cudgel, and Neal scorned to abandon the principles of his family.

His friends, finding that he reserved his blood for more heroic purposes than dastardly phlebotomy, knew not what to do with him.

His perpetual exclamation was, as we have already stated, 'I'm blue-mowlded for want of a batin'!' They did everything in their power to cheer him with the hope of a drubbing; told him he lived in an excellent country for a man afflicted with his malady; and promised, if it were at all possible, to create him a private enemy or two, who, they hoped to heaven, might trounce him to some purpose.

This sustained him for a while; but as day after day passed, and no appearance of action presented itself, he could not choose but increase in courage. His soul, like a sword-blade, too long in the scabbard, was beginning to get fuliginous by inactivity. He looked upon the point of his own needle, and the bright edge of his scissors, with a bitter pang when he thought of the spirit rusting within him; he meditated fresh insults, studied new plans, and hunted out cunning devices for provoking his acquaintances to battle, until by degrees he began to confound his own brain, and to commit more grievous oversights in his business than ever. Sometimes he sent home to one person a coat with the legs of a pair of trousers attached to it for sleeves, and dispatched to another the arms of the aforesaid coat tacked together as a pair of trousers. Sometimes the coat was made to button behind instead of before; and he frequently placed the pockets in the lower part of the skirts, as if he had been in league with cut-purses.

This was a melancholy situation, and his friends pitied him accordingly.

'Don't be cast down, Neal,' said they; 'your friends feel for you, poor fellow.'

'Divil carry my frinds,' replied Neal; 'sure, there's not one o' yez frindly enough to be my inimy. Tare-an'-ounze, what'll I do? I'm blue-mowlded for want of a batin'!'

Seeing that their consolation was thrown away upon him, they resolved to leave him to his fate; which they had no sooner done than Neal had thoughts of taking to the *Skiomachia* as a last remedy. In this mood he looked with considerable antipathy at his own shadow for several nights; and it is not to be questioned but that some hard battles would have taken place between them, were it not for the cunning of the shadow, which declined to fight him in any position than with its

back to the wall. This occasioned him to pause, for the wall was a
fearful antagonist, inasmuch that it knew not when it was beaten. But
there was still an alternative left. He went to the garden one clear day
about noon, and hoped to have a bout with the shade, free from
interruption. Both approached, apparently eager for the combat, and
resolved to conquer or die, when a villainous cloud, happening to
intercept the light, gave the shadow an opportunity of disappearing;
and Neal found himself once more without an opponent.

'It's aisy known,' said Neal, 'you haven't the blood in you, or you'd
come to the scratch like a man.'

He now saw that fate was against him, and that any further hostility
towards the shadow was only a tempting of Providence. He lost his
health, spirits, and everything but his courage. His countenance
became pale and peaceful-looking; the bluster departed from him; his
body shrank up like a withered parsnip. Thrice was he compelled to
take in his clothes, and thrice did he ascertain that much of his time
would be necessarily spent in pursuing his retreating person through
the solitude of his almost deserted garments.

God knows, it is difficult to form a correct opinion upon a situation
so paradoxical as Neal's was. To be reduced to skin and bone by the
downright friendship of the world, was, as the sagacious reader will
admit, next to a miracle. We appeal to the conscience of any man who
finds himself without an enemy, whether he be not a greater skeleton
than the tailor; we will give him fifty guineas provided he can show a
calf to his leg. We know he could not; for the tailor had none, and that
was because he had not an enemy. No man in friendship with the
world ever has calves to his legs. To sum up all in a paradox of our
own invention, for which we claim the full credit of originality, we
now assert that MORE MEN HAVE RISEN IN THE WORLD BY THE INJURY
OF THEIR ENEMIES THAN HAVE RISEN BY THE KINDNESS OF THEIR
FRIENDS. You may take this, reader, in any sense; apply it to hanging if
you like it is, still immutably and immovably true.

One day Neal sat cross-legged, as tailors usually sit, in the act of
pressing a pair of breeches; his hands were place, backs up, upon the
handle of his goose, and his chin rested upon the back of his hands. To

judge from his sorrowful complexion, one would suppose that he sat rather to be sketched as a picture of misery, or of heroism in distress, than for the industrious purpose of pressing the seams of a garment. There was a great deal of New Burlington Street pathos in his countenance; his face, like the times, was rather out of joint; 'the sun was just setting, and his golden beams fell, with a saddened splendour, athwart the tailor's –' – the reader may fill up the picture.

In this position sat Neal, when Mr O'Connor, the schoolmaster, whose inexpressibles he was turning for the third time, entered the workshop. Mr O'Connor himself was as finished a picture of misery as the tailor. There was a patient, subdued kind of expression in his face which indicated a very fair portion of calamity; his eye seemed charged with affliction of the first water; on each side of his nose might be traced two dry channels which, no doubt, were full enough while the tropical rains of his countenance lasted. Altogether, to conclude from appearances, it was a dead match in affliction between him and the tailor; both seemed sad, fleshless and unthriving.

'Misther O'Connor,' said the tailor, when the schoolmaster entered, 'won't you be pleased to sit down?'

Mr O'Connor sat; and after wiping his forehead. laid his hat upon the lap-board, put his half-handkerchief in his pocket, and looked upon the tailor. The tailor, in return, looked upon Mr O'Connor; but neither of them spoke for some minutes. Neal, in fact, appeared to be wrapped up in his own misery, and Mr O'Connor in his; or, as we often have much gratuitous sympathy for the distresses of our friends, we question but the tailor was wrapped up in Mr O'Connor's misery, and Mr O'Connor in the tailor's.

Mr O'Connor at length said, 'Neal, are my inexpressibles finished?'

'I am now pressin' your inexpressibles,' replied Neal; 'but, be my sowl, Mr O'Connor, it's not your inexpressibles I'm thinkin' of. I'm not the ninth part of what I was. I'd hardly make paddin' for a collar now.'

'Are you able to carry a staff still, Neal?'

'I've a light hazel one that's handy,' said the tailor; 'but where's the use of carryin' it whin I can get no one to fight wid. Sure, I'm disgracin' my relations by the life I'm ladin.' I'll go to my grave w'dout ever batin' a man, or bein' bate myself – that's the vexation. Divil the row ever I was able to kick up in my life; so that I'm fairly blue-mowlded for want of a batin'. But if you have patience –'

'Patience!' said Mr O'Connor, with a shake of the head that was perfectly disastrous even to look at – 'patience, did you say, Neal?'

'Ay,' said Neal; 'an', be my sowl, if you deny that I said patience, I'll break your head!'

'Ah, Neal,' returned the other, 'I don't deny it – for though I am teaching philosophy, knowledge, and mathematics every day in my life, yet I'm learning patience myself both night and day. No, Neal; I have forgotten to deny anything. I have not been guilty of a con-tradiction, out of my own school, for the last fourteen years. I once expressed the shadow of a doubt about twelve years ago, but ever since I have abandoned even doubting. That doubt was the last expiring effort at maintaining my domestic authority – but I suffered for it.'

'Well,' said Neal, 'if you have patience, I'll tell you what afflicts me from beginnin' to endin'.'

'I will have patience,' said Mr O'Connor, and he accordingly heard a dismal and indignant tale from the tailor.

'You have told me that fifty times over,' said Mr O'Connor, after hearing the story. 'Your spirit is too martial for a pacific life. If you follow my advice, I will teach you how to ripple the calm current of your existence to some purpose. Marry a wife. For twenty-five years I have given instructions in three branches viz., philosophy, knowledge and mathematics – I am also well versed in matrimony, and I declare that, upon my misery, and by the contents of all my afflictions, it is my solemn and melancholy opinion that if you marry a wife you will, before three months pass over your concatenated state, not have a single complaint to make touching a superabundance of peace and tranquillity, or a love of fighting.'

'Do you mane to say that any woman would make me afeard?' said the tailor, deliberately rising up and getting his cudgel. 'I'll thank you merely to go over the words agin till I thrash you widin' an inch o' your life. That's all.'

'Neal,' said the schoolmaster, meekly, 'I won't fight; I have been too often subdued ever to presume on the hope of a single victory. My spirit is long since evaporated: I am like one of your own shreds, a mere selvage. Do you not know how much my habiliments have shrunk in, even within the last five years? Hear me, Neal; and venerate my words as if they proceeded from the lips of a prophet. If you wish to taste the luxury of being subdued – if you are, as you say, blue-mowlded for want of a beating, and sick at heart of a peaceful existence – why, MARRY A WIFE. Neal, send my breeches home with all haste, for they are wanted – you understand. Farewell!'

Mr O'Connor, having thus expressed himself, departed; and Neal stood with the cudgel in his hand, looking at the door out of which he passed, with an expression of fierceness, contempt, and reflection strongly blended on the ruins of his once heroic visage.

Many a man has happiness within his reach if he but knew it. The tailor had been, hitherto, miserable because he pursued a wrong object. The schoolmaster, however, suggested a train of thought upon which Neal now fastened will all the ardour of a chivalrous temperament. Nay, he wondered that the family spirit should have so completely seized upon the fighting side of his heart as to preclude all thoughts of matrimony; for he could not but remember that his relations were as ready for marriage as for fighting. To doubt this would have been to throw a blot upon his own escutcheon. He, therefore, very prudently asked himself, to whom, if he did not marry, should he transmit his courage. He was a single man, and, dying as such, he would be the sole depository of his own valour, which, like Junius's secret, must perish with him. If he could have left it as a legacy to such of his friends as were most remarkable for cowardice, why, the case would be altered; but this was impossible, and he had now no other means of preserving it to posterity than by creating a posterity to inherit it. He saw, too, that the world was likely to become convulsed. Wars, as everybody knew, were certain to break out, and would it not be an excellent opportunity for being father to a colonel, or perhaps a

general, that might astonish the world. The change visible in Neal
after the schoolmaster's last visit absolutely thunderstruck all who
knew him. The clothes which he had rashly taken in to fit his shrivelled limbs were once more let out. The tailor expanded with a new
spirit; his joints ceased to be supple, as in the days of his valour; his eye
became less fiery, but more brilliant. From being martial, he got
desperately gallant; but somehow he could not afford to act the hero
and lover both at the same time. This, perhaps, would be too much to
expect from a tailor. His policy was better. He resolved to bring all his
available energy to bear upon the charms of whatever fair nymph he
should select for the honour of matrimony; to waste his spirit in
fighting would, therefore, be a deduction from the single purpose in
view.

The transition from war to love is by means so remarkable as we
might at first imagine. We quote Jack Falstaff in proof of this; or, if the
reader be disposed to reject our authority, then we quote Ancient
Pistol himself – both of whom we consider as the most finished
specimens of heroism that ever carried a safe skin. Acres would have
been a hero had he worn gloves to prevent the courage from oozing
out at his palms, or not felt such a unlucky antipathy to the 'snug lying
in the Abbey'; and as for Captain Bobadil, he never had an opportunity of putting his plan for vanquishing an army into practice. We
fear, indeed, that neither his character, nor Ben Jonson's knowledge of
human nature, is properly understood; for it certainly could not be
expected that a man whose spirit glowed to encounter a whole host
could, without tarnishing his dignity, if closely pressed, condescend to
fight an individual. But as these remarks on courage may be felt by the
reader as an invidious introduction of a subject disagreeable to him, we
beg to hush it for the present, and return to the tailor.

No sooner had Neal begun to feel an inclination to matrimony than
his friends knew that his principles had veered, by the change now
visible in his person and deportment. They saw he had 'ratted' from
courage, and joined love. Heretofore his life had been all winter,
darkened by storm and hurricane. The fiercer virtues had played the
devil with him; every word was thunder, every look lightning; but

now all that had passed away – before he was the *fortiter in re*, at present he was the *suaviter in modo*. His existence was perfect spring – beautifully vernal. All the amiable and softer qualities began to bud about his heart; a genial warmth was diffused over him; his soul got green within him; every day was serene; and if a cloud happened to become visible, there was a roguish rainbow astride of it, on which sat a beautiful Iris that laughed down at him, and seemed to say, 'Why the Dickens, Neal, don't you marry a wife?'

Neal could not resist the *afflatus* which descended on him; an ethereal light dwelt, he thought, upon the face of nature; the colour of the cloth which he cut out from day to day was, to his enraptured eye, like the colour of Cupid's wings – all purple; his visions were worth their weight in gold; his dreams, a credit to the bed he slept on; and his feelings, like blind puppies, young, and alive to the milk of love and kindness which they drew from his heart. Most of this delight escaped the observation of the world; for Neal, like your true lover, became shy and mysterious. It is difficult to say what he resembled. No dark lantern ever had more light shut up within itself than Neal had in his soul, although his friends were not aware of it. They knew, indeed, that he had turned his back upon valour; but beyond this their knowledge did not extend.

Neal was shrewd enough to know that what he felt must be love – nothing else could distend him with happiness, until his soul felt light and bladder-like, but love. As an oyster opens when expecting the tide, so did his soul expand at the contemplation of matrimony. Labour ceased to be a trouble to him; he sang and sewed from morning to night; his hot goose no longer burned him, for his heart was as hot as his goose; the vibrations of his head at each successive stitch were no longer sad and melancholy – there was a buoyant shake of exultation in them which showed that his soul was placid and happy within him.

Endless honour be to Neal Malone for the originality with which he managed the tender sentiment! He did not, like your common-place lovers, first discover a pretty girl, and afterwards become enamoured of her. No such thing; he had the passion prepared beforehand – cut out and made up, as it were, ready for any girl whom it might fit. This was falling in love in the abstract; and let no man condemn it without a trial, for many a long-winded argument could be urged in its defence. It is always wrong to commence business without capital, and Neal had a good stock to begin with. All we beg is, that the reader will not confound it with Platonism, which never marries; but he is at full liberty to call it Socratism, which takes unto itself a wife, and suffers accordingly.

Let no one suppose that Neal forgot the schoolmaster's kindness, or failed to be duly grateful for it. Mr O'Connor was the first person whom he consulted touching his passion. With a cheerful soul he waited on that melancholy and gentleman-like man, and in the very luxury of his heart told him that he was in love.

'In love, Neal!' said the schoolmaster. 'May I inquire with whom?'

'Wid nobody in particular yet,' replied Neal; 'but of late I'm got divilish fond o' the girls in general.'

'And do you call that being in love, Neal?' said Mr O'Connor.

'Why, what else would I call it?' returned the tailor. 'Amn't I fond of them?'

'Then it must be what is termed the Universal Passion, Neal,' observed Mr O'Connor; 'although it is the first time I have seen such an illustration of it as you present in your own person.'

'I wish you would advise me how to act,' said Neal; 'I'm as happy as a prince since I began to get fond o' them an' to think of marriage.'

The schoolmaster shook his head again, and looked rather miserable. Neal rubbed his hands with glee, and looked perfectly happy. The schoolmaster shook his head again, and looked more miserable than before. Neal's happiness also increased on the second rubbing.

Now, to tell the secret at once, Mr O'Connor would not have appeared so miserable, were it not for Neal's happiness; nor Neal so happy, were it not for Mr O'Connor's misery. It was all the result of contrast; but this you will not understand unless you be deeply read in modern novels.

Mr O'Connor, however, was a man of sense, who knew, upon this principle, that the longer he continued to shake his head the more miserable he must become and the more also would he increase Neal's happiness; but he had no intention of increasing Neal's happiness at his own expense, for, upon the same hypothesis, it would have been for Neal's interest had he remained shaking his head there and getting miserable until the day of judgment. He consequently declined giving the third shake, for he thought that plain conversation was, after all, more significant and forcible than the most eloquent nod, however badly translated.

'Neal,' said he, 'could you, by stretching your imagination, contrive to rest contented with nursing your passion in solitude, and love the sex at a distance?'

'How could I nurse and mind my business?' replied the tailor. 'I'll never nurse so as I'll have the wife; and as for 'magination, it depends upon the grain of it whether I can stretch it or not. I don't know that I ever made a coat of it in my life.'

'You don't understand me, Neal,' said the schoolmaster. 'In recommending marriage, I was only driving one evil out of you by introducing another. Do you think that if you abandoned all thoughts of a wife you would get heroic again? – that is, would you take once more to the love of fighting?'

'There is no doubt but I would,' said the tailor; 'if I miss the wife, I'll kick up such a dust as never was seen in the parish, and you're the first man that I'll kick. But now that I'm in love,' he continued, 'sure, I ought to look out for the wife.'

'Ah, Neal!' said the schoolmaster, 'you are tempting destiny. Your temerity be, with all its melancholy consequences, upon your own head.'

'Come,' said the tailor, 'it wasn't to hear you groaning to the tune of *Dhrimmindhoo*, or "The ould woman rockin' her cradle," that I came; but to know if you could help me in makin' out the wife. That's the discoorse.'

'Look at me, Neal,' said the schoolmaster, solemnly; 'I am at this moment, and have been any time for the last fifteen years, a living *caveto* against matrimony. I do not think that earth possesses such a luxury as a single, solitary life. Neal, the monks of old were happy men; they were all fat and had double chins; and, Neal, I tell you, that all fat men are in general happy. Care cannot come at them so readily as at a thin man; before it gets through the strong outworks of flesh and blood with which they are surrounded, it becomes treacherous to its original purpose, joins the cheerful spirits it meets in the system, and dances about the heart in all the madness of mirth; just like a sincere ecclesiastic who comes to lecture a good fellow against drinking, but who forgets his lecture over his cups, and is laid under the table with such success that he either never comes to finish his lecture, or comes often to be laid under the table. Look at me, Neal, how wasted, fleshless, and miserable I stand before you. You know how my garments have shrunk in, and what a solid man I was before marriage. Neal, pause, I beseech you; otherwise you stand a strong chance of becoming a nonentity like myself.'

'I don't care what I become,' said the tailor; 'I can't think that you'd be so unrasonable as to expect that any of the Malones should pass out of the world widout either bein' bate or marrid. Have reason, Mr O'Connor, an' if you can help me to the wife, I promise to take in your coat the next time for nothin'.'

'Well, then.' said Mr O'Connor, 'what would you think of the butcher's daughter, Biddy Neil? You have always had a thirst for blood, and here you may have it gratified in an innocent manner, should you ever become sanguinary again. 'Tis true, Neal, she is twice your size, and possesses three times your strength; but for that very reason, Neal, marry her if you can. Large animals are placid; and heaven preserve those bachelors whom I wish well from a small wife; 'tis such who always wield the sceptre of domestic life, and rule their husbands with a rod of iron.'

'Say no more, Mr. O'Connor,' replied the tailor; 'she's the very girl I'm in love wid, an' never fear but I'll overcome her heart if it can be done by man. Now, step over the way to my house, an' we'll have a sup on the head of it. Who's that calling?'

'Ah! Neal, I know the tones – there's a shrillness in them not to be mistaken. Farewell! I must depart – you have heard the proverb, "Those who are bound must obey." Young Jack, I presume, is squalling, and I must either nurse him, rock the cradle, or sing comic tunes for him, though heaven knows with what a disastrous heart I often sing, "Begone Dull Care," the "Rakes of Newcastle," or "Peas upon a Trencher." Neal, I say again, pause before you take this leap in the dark. Pause, Neal, I entreat you. Farewell!'

Neal, however, was gifted with the heart of an Irishman, and scorned caution as the characteristic of a coward. He had, as it appeared, abandoned all design of fighting, but the courage still adhered to him even in making love. He consequently conducted the siege of Biddy Neil's heart with a degree of skill and valour which would not have come amiss to Marshal Gerald at the siege of Antwerp. Locke or Dugald Stewart, indeed, had they been cognisant of the tailor's triumph, might have illustrated the principle on which he succeeded – as to ourselves, we can only conjecture it. Our own opinion is, that they were both animated with a congenial spirit. Biddy was the very pink of pugnacity, and could throw in a body blow, or plant a facer, with singular energy and science. Her prowess hitherto had, we confess, been displayed only within the limited range of domestic life; but, should she ever find it necessary to exercise it upon a larger scale, there was no doubt whatsoever, in the opinion of her mother, brothers and sisters, every one of whom she had successfully subdued, that she must undoubtedly distinguish herself. There was certainly one difficulty which the tailor had not to encounter in the progress of his courtship: the field was his own; he had not a rival to dispute his claim. Neither was there any opposition given by her friends; they were, on the contrary, all anxious for the match; and when the arrangements were concluded, Neal felt his hand squeezed by them in succession, with an expression more resembling condolence than joy. Neal, however, had been bred to tailoring, and not to metaphysics; he could cut out a coat very well, but we do not say that he could trace a principle – as what tailor, except Jeremy Taylor, could?

There was nothing particular in the wedding. Mr O'Connor was asked by Neal to be present at it; but he shook his head, and told him that he had not courage to attend it, or inclination to witness any man's sorrows but his own. He met the wedding-party by accident, and was heard to exclaim with a sigh, as they flaunted past him in gay exuberance of spirits – 'Ah, poor Neal! he is going like one of her father's cattle to the shambles! Woe is me for having suggested matrimony to the tailor! He will not long be under the necessity of saying that he "is blue-mowlded for want of a batin".' The butcheress will fell him like a Kerry ox, and I may have his blood to answer for, and his discomfiture to feel for, in addition to my own miseries.'

On the evening of the wedding-day, about the hour of ten o'clock, Neal – whose spirits were uncommonly exalted, for his heart lux-uriated within him – danced with his bridesmaid; after the dance he sat beside her, and got eloquent in praise of her beauty; and it is said, too, that he whispered to her, and chucked her chin with considerable gallantry. The *tête-à-tête* continued for some time without exciting particular attention, with one exception; but that exception was worth a whole chapter of general rules. Mrs Malone rose up, then sat down again, and took off a glass of the native; she got up a second time – all the wife rushed upon her heart – she approached them, and, in a fit of the most exquisite sensibility, knocked the bridesmaid down, and gave the tailor a kick of affecting pathos upon the inexpressibles. The whole scene was a touching one on both sides. The tailor was sent on all fours to the floor; but Mrs Malone took him quietly up, put him under her arm, as one would a lap-dog, and with stately step marched away to the connubial apartment, in which everything remained very quiet for the rest of the night.

The next morning Mr O'Connor presented himself to congratulate the tailor on his happiness. Neal, as his friend shook hands with him, gave the schoolmaster's fingers a slight squeeze, such as a man gives who would gently entreat your sympathy. The schoolmaster looked at him, and thought he shook his head. Of this, however, he could not be certain; for, as he shook his own during the moment of observa-tion, he concluded that it might be a mere mistake of the eye, or perhaps the result of a mind predisposed to be credulous on the subject of shaking heads.

We wish it were in our power to draw a veil, or curtain, or blind of some description over the remnant of the tailor's narrative that is to follow; but as it is the duty of every faithful historian to give the secret causes of appearances which the world in general do not understand, so we think it but honest to go on, impartially and faithfully, without shrinking from the responsibility that is frequently annexed to truth.

For the first three days after matrimony Neal felt like a man who had been translated to a new and more lively state of existence. He had expected, and flattered himself, that the moment this event should take place he would once more resume his heroism, and experience the pleasure of a drubbing. This determination he kept a profound secret – nor was it known until a future period, when he disclosed it to Mr O'Connor. He intended, therefore, that marriage should be nothing more than a mere parenthesis in his life – a kind of asterisk, pointing, in a note at the bottom, to this single exception in his general conduct – a *nota bene* to the spirit of a marital man, intimating that he had been peaceful only for a while. In truth, he was, during the influence of love over him, and up to the very day of his marriage, secretly as blue-moulded as ever for want of a beating. The heroic penchant lay snugly latent in his heart, unchecked and unmodified. He flattered himself that he was achieving a capital imposition upon the world at large – that he was actually hoaxing mankind in general – and that such an excellent piece of knavish tranquillity had never been perpetrated before his time.

On the first week after his marriage there chanced to be a fair in the next market-town. Neal, after breakfast, brought forward a bunch of *shillelaghs*, in order to select the best. The wife inquired the purpose of the selection, and Neal declared that he was resolved to have a fight that day, if it were to be had, he said, for 'love or money'. 'The thruth is,' he exclaimed, strutting with fortitude about the house – ' the thruth is, that I've done the whole of yez – I'm as blue-mowlded as ever for want of a batin'.'

'Don't go,' said the wife.

'I *will* go,' said Neal, with vehemence – 'I'll go if the whole parish was to go to prevint me.'

In about another half-hour Neal sat down quietly to his business, instead of going to the fair.

Much ingenious speculation might be indulged in upon this abrupt termination to the tailor's most formidable resolution; but, for our own part, we will prefer going on with the narrative, leaving the reader at liberty to solve the mystery as he pleases. In the meantime, we say this much – let those who cannot make it out carry it to their tailor; it is a tailor's mystery, and no one has so good a right to understand it – except, perhaps, a tailor's wife.

At the period of his matrimony Neal had become as plump and as stout as he ever was known to be in his plumpest and stoutest days. He and the schoolmaster had been very intimate about this time; but we know not how it happened that soon afterwards he felt a modest, bride-like reluctance in meeting with that afflicted gentleman. As the eve of his union approached, he was in the habit, during the schoolmaster's visits to his workshop, of alluding, in rather a sarcastic tone, considering the unthriving appearance of his friend, to the increasing lustiness of his person. Nay, he has often leaped up from his lap-board, and, in the strong spirit of exultation, thrust out his leg in attestation of his assertion, slapping it, moreover, with a loud laugh of triumph, that sounded like a knell to the happiness of his emaciated acquaintance. The schoolmaster's philosophy, however, unlike his flesh, never departed from him; his usual observation was, 'Neal, we are both receding from the same point; you increase in flesh, whilst I, heaven help me, am fast diminishing.'

The tailor received these remarks with very boisterous mirth, whilst Mr O'Connor simply shook his head, and looked sadly upon his limbs, now shrouded in a superfluity of garments, somewhat resembling a slender thread of water in a shallow summer stream, nearly wasted away, and surrounded by an unproportionate extent of channel.

The fourth month after the marriage arrived. Neal one day, near its close, began to dress himself in his best apparel. Even then, when buttoning his waistcoat, he shook his head after the manner of Mr

O'Connor, and made observations upon the great extent to which it over-folded him.

'Well,' thought he, with a sigh – 'this waistcoat certainly did fit me to a T; but it's wondherful to think how – cloth stretches.'

'Neal,' said the wife, on perceiving him dressed, 'where are you bound for?'

'Faith, for life,' replied Neal, with a mitigated swagger; 'and I'd as soon, if it had been the will of Provid–'

He paused.

'Where are you going?' asked the wife a second time.

'Why,' he answered, 'only to the dance at Jemmy Connolly's; I'll be back early.'

'Don't go,' said the wife.

'I'll go,' said Neal, 'if the whole counthry was to prevint me. Thunder an' lightnin', woman, who am I?' he exclaimed, in a loud but rather infirm voice – 'amn't I Neal Malone, that never met a man who'd fight him! – Neal Malone, that was never beat by MAN! Why, tare-an'-ounze, woman! – whoo! – I'll get enraged some time, an' play the divil! Who's afeard, I say?'

'Don't go,' added the wife a third time, giving Neal a significant look in the face.

In about another half-hour Neal sat down quietly to his business, instead of going to the dance!

Neal now turned himself, like many a sage in similar circumstances, to philosophy – that is to say, he began to shake his head upon principle, after the manner of the schoolmaster. He would, indeed, have preferred the bottle upon principle; but there was no getting at the bottle, except through the wife, and it so happened that by the time it reached him there was little consolation left in it. Neal bore all in silence; for silence, his friend had often told him, was a proof of wisdom.

Soon after this Neal one evening met Mr O'Connor by chance upon a plank which crossed a river. This plank was only a foot in breadth, so that no two individuals could pass each other upon it. We cannot find words in which to express the dismay of both on finding that they absolutely glided past one another without collision.

Both paused, and surveyed each other solemnly; but the astonishment was all on the side of Mr O'Connor.

'Neal,' said the schoolmaster, 'by all the household gods, I conjure you to speak, that I may be assured you live!'

The ghost of a blush crossed the churchyard visage of the tailor.

'Oh!' he exclaimed, 'why the devil did you tempt me to marry a wife?'

'Neal,' said his friend, 'answer me in the most solemn manner possible; throw into your countenance all the gravity you can assume; speak as if you were under the hands of the hangman, with the rope about your neck, for the question is, indeed, a trying one which I am about to put – are you still 'blue-mowlded for want of beating'?'

The tailor collected himself to make a reply; he put one leg out – the very leg which he used to show in triumph to his friend; but, alas, how dwindled! He opened his waistcoat, and lapped it round him, until he looked like a weasel on its hind legs. He then raised himself up on his tip-toes, and, in an awful whisper, replied, 'No!!! the devil a bit I'm blue-mowlded for want of a batin'.'

The schoolmaster shook his head in his own miserable manner; but, alas! he soon perceived that the tailor was as great an adept at shaking the head as himself. Nay, he saw that there was a calamitous refinement, a delicacy of shake, in the tailor's vibrations, which gave to his own nod a very commonplace character.

The next day the tailor took in his clothes, and from time to time continued to adjust them to the dimensions of his shrinking person. The schoolmaster and he, whenever they could steal a moment, met and sympathized together. Mr O'Connor, however, bore up somewhat better than Neal. The latter was subdued in heart and in spirit; thoroughly, completely, and intensely vanquished. His features became sharpened by misery, for a termagant wife is the whetstone on which all the calamities of a hen-pecked husband are painted by the devil. He no longer strutted as he was wont to do; he no longer carried a cudgel as if he wished to wage a universal battle with mankind. He was now a married man. Sneakingly and with a cowardly crawl did he creep along as if every step brought him nearer to the gallows. The schoolmaster's march of misery was far slower that Neal's: the latter distanced him. Before three years passed he had shrunk up so much that he could not walk abroad of a windy day without carrying weights in his pockets to keep him firm on the earth, which he once trod with the step of a giant. He again sought the schoolmaster, with whom, indeed, he associated as much as possible. Here he felt certain of receiving sympathy; nor was he disappointed. That worthy but miserable man and Neal often retired beyond the hearing of their respective wives, and supported each other by every argument in their power. Often have they been heard, in the dusk of evening, singing behind a remote hedge that melancholy ditty, 'Let us both be unhappy together'; which rose upon the twilight breeze with a cautious quaver of sorrow truly heartrending and lugubrious.

'Neal,' said Mr O'Connor, on one of these occasions, 'here is a book which I recommend to your perusal; it is called *The Afflicted Man's Companion*; try if you cannot glean some consolation out of it.'

'Faith,' said Neal, 'I'm for ever oblaged to you, but I don't want it. I've had *The Afflicted Man's Companion* too long, and divil an atom of consolation I can get out of it. I have one o' them, I tell you; but be me sowl, I'll not undhertake a pair o' them. The very name's enough for me.' They then separated.

The tailor's *vis vite* must have been powerful, or he would have died. In two years more his friends could not distinguish him from his own shadow – a circumstance which was of great inconvenience to him. Several grasped at the hand of the shadow instead of his; and one man was near paying it five-and-sixpence for making a pair of small-clothes. Neal, it is true, undeceived him with some trouble, but candidly admitted that he was not able to carry home the money. It was difficult, indeed, for the poor tailor to bear what he felt; it is true he bore it as long as he could; but at length he came suicidal, and often had thoughts of 'making his own quietus with his bare bodkin'. After many deliberations and afflictions he ultimately made the attempt; but, alas! he found that the blood of the Malones refused to flow upon so ignominious an occasion. So he solved the phenomenon; although the truth was, that his blood was not 'i' the vein' for 't; none was to be had. What, then, was to be done? He resolved to get rid of life by some process; and the next that occurred to him was hanging. In a solemn spirit he prepared a selvage, and suspended himself from the rafter of his workshop; but here another disappointment awaited him – he would not hang. Such was his want of gravity that his own weight proved insufficient to occasion his death by mere suspension. His third attempt was at drowning, but he was too light to sink; all the elements – all his own energies joined themselves, he thought, in a wicked conspiracy to save his life. Having thus tried every avenue to destruction, and failed in all, he felt like a man doomed to live for ever. Henceforward he shrunk and shrivelled by slow degrees, until in the course of time he became so attenuated that the grossness of human vision could no longer reach him.

This, however, could not last always. Though still alive, he was to all intents and purposes imperceptible. He could now only be heard; he was reduced to a mere essence – the very echo of human existence, *vox et praeterea nihil.* It is true the schoolmaster asserted that he occasionally caught passing glimpses of him; but that was because he had been himself nearly spiritualized by affliction, and his visual ray purged in the furnace of domestic tribulation. By and by Neal's voice lessened, got fainter and more indistinct, until at length nothing but a doubtful murmur could be heard, which ultimately could scarcely be distinguished from a ringing in his ears.

Such was the awful and mysterious fate of the tailor, who, as a hero, could not, of course, die; he merely dissolved like an icicle, wasted into immateriality, and finally melted away beyond the perception of mortal sense. Mr O'Connor is still living, and once more in the fulness of perfect health and strength. His wife, however, we may as well hint, has been dead more than two years.

WILLIAM CARLETON

Wildgoose Lodge

I HAD read the anonymous summons, but, from its general import, I
believed it to be one of those special meetings convened for some
purpose affecting the usual objects and proceedings of the body; at
least, the terms in which it was conveyed to me had nothing extraordinary or mysterious in them beyond the simple fact that it was not
to be a general but a select meeting. This mark of confidence flattered
me, and I determined to attend punctually. I was, it was true, desired
to keep the circumstance entirely to myself; but there was nothing
startling in this, for I had often received summonses of a similar nature.
I therefore resolved to attend, according to the letter of my instructions, 'on the next night, at the solemn hour of midnight, to deliberate
and act upon such matters as should then and there be submitted to
my consideration'. The morning after I received this message, I arose
and resumed my usual occupations; but from whatever cause it may
have proceeded, I felt a sense of approaching evil hang heavily upon
me. The beats of my pulse were languid, and an indefinable feeling of
anxiety pervaded my whole spirit; even my face was pale, and my eye
so heavy that my father and brothers concluded me to be ill; an
opinion which I thought at the time to be correct, for I felt exactly
that kind of depression which precedes a severe fever. I could not
understand what I experienced; nor can I yet, except by supposing
that there is in human nature some mysterious faculty by which, in

coming calamities, the dread of some fearful evil is anticipated, and that it is possible to catch a dark presentiment of the sensations which they subsequently produce. For my part, I can neither analyse nor define it; but on that day I knew it by painful experience, and so have a thousand others in similar circumstances.

It was about the middle of winter. The day was gloomy and tempestuous almost beyond any other I remember; dark clouds rolled over the hills about me, and a close, sleet-like rain fell in slanting drifts that chased each other rapidly towards the earth on the course of the blast. The outlying cattle sought the closest and calmest corners of the fields for shelter; the trees and young groves were tossed about, for the wind was so unusually high that it swept in hollow gusts through them with that hoarse murmur which deepens so powerfully on the mind the sense of dreariness and desolation.

As the shades of night fell, the storm, if possible, increased. The moon was half gone, and only a few stars were visible by glimpses, as a rush of wind left a temporary opening in the sky. I had determined, if the storm should not abate, to incur any penalty rather than attend the meeting; but the appointed hour was distant, and I resolved to be decided by the future state of the night.

Ten o'clock came, but still there was no change; eleven passed, and on opening the door to observe if there were any likelihood of its clearing up, a blast of wind, mingled with rain, nearly blew me off my feet. At length it was approaching to the hour of midnight; and on examining a third time, I found it had calmed a little, and no longer rained.

I instantly got my oak stick, muffled myself in my greatcoat, strapped my hat about my ears, and as the place of meeting was only a quarter of a mile distant, I presently set out.

The appearance of the heavens was lowering and angry, particularly in that point where the light of the moon fell against the clouds from a seeming chasm in them, through which alone she was visible. The edges of this chasm were faintly bronzed, but the dense body of the masses that hung piled on each side of her was black and impenetrable to sight. In no other point of the heavens was there any part of the sky visible – a deep veil of clouds overhung the horizon – yet was the light sufficient to give occasional glimpses of the rapid shifting which took place in this dark canopy, and of the tempestuous agitation with which the midnight storm swept to and fro beneath it.

At length I arrived at a long slated house situated in a solitary part of the neighbourhood; a little below it ran a small stream, which was now swollen above its banks, and rushing with mimic roar over the flat meadows beside it. The appearance of the bare slated building in such a night was particularly sombre; and to those, like me, who knew the purpose to which it was usually devoted, it was, or ought to have been, peculiarly so. There it stood, silent and gloomy, without any appearance of human life or enjoyment about or within it. As I approached, the moon once more had broken out of the clouds, and shone dimly upon the wet, glittering slates and windows with a death-like lustre, that gradually faded away as I left the point of observation and entered the folding-door. It was the parish chapel.

The scene which presented itself here was in keeping not only with the external appearance of the house, but with the darkness, the storm, and the hour, which was now a little after midnight. About eighty persons were sitting in dead silence upon the circular steps of the altar. They did not seem to move; and as I entered and advanced, the echo of my footsteps rang through the building with a lonely distinctness, which added to the solemnity and mystery of the circumstances about me. The windows were secured with shutters on the inside; and on the altar a candle was lighted, which burned dimly amid the sur-rounding darkness, and lengthened the shadow of the altar itself, and those of six or seven persons who stood on its upper steps, until they mingled in the obscurity which shrouded the lower end of the chapel. The faces of the men who sat on the altar-steps were not distinctly visible, yet their prominent and more characteristic features were in sufficient relief, and I observed that some of the most malignant and reckless spirits in the parish were assembled. In the eyes of those who stood at the altar, and whom I knew to be invested with authority over the others, I could perceive gleams of some latent and ferocious purpose, kindled, as I soon observed, into a fiercer expression of vengeance by the additional excitement of ardent spirits, with which they had stimulated themselves to a point of determination that mocked at the apprehension of all future responsibility, either in this world or the next.

The welcome which I received on joining them was far different from the boisterous good-humour that used to mark our greetings on other occasions: just a nod of the head from this or that person, on the part of those who sat, with a *ghud dhemur tha thu?* in a suppressed voice, even below a common whisper; but from the standing group, who were evidently the projectors of the enterprise, I received a convulsive grasp of the hand, accompanied by a fierce and desperate look, that seemed to search my eye and countenance, to try if I were a person not likely to shrink from whatever they had resolved to execute. It is surprising to think of the powerful expression which a moment of intense interest or great danger is capable of giving to the eye, the features, and the slightest actions, especially in those whose station in society does not require them to constrain nature, by the force of social courtesies, into habits that conceal their natural emotions. None of the standing group spoke; but as each of them wrung my hand in silence, his eye was fixed on mine with an expression of drunken confidence and secrecy, and an insolent determination not to be gainsaid without peril. If looks could be translated with certainty, they seemed to say, 'We are bound upon a project of vengeance, and if you do not join us, remember that we can revenge.' Along with this grasp they did not forget to remind me of the common bond by which we were united, for each man gave me the secret grip of Ribbonism[1] in a manner that made the joints of my fingers ache for some minutes afterwards.

There was one present, however – the highest in authority – whose actions and demeanour were calm and unexcited. He seemed to labour under no unusual influence whatever, but evinced a serenity so placid and philosophical that I attributed the silence of the sitting

[1] Ribbonism was a rural protest movement – a secret society, anti-Protestant and nationalist. Its many arcane rituals emphasized solidarity and loyalty to 'the cause', however vague. (Editor's note)

group, and the restraint which curbed in the outbreaking passions of those who stood, entirely to his presence. He was a schoolmaster, who taught his daily school in that chapel, and acted also, on Sunday, in the capacity of clerk to the priest – an excellent and amiable old man, who knew little of his illegal connections and atrocious conduct.

When the ceremonies of brotherly recognition and friendship were past, the captain (by which title I shall designate the last-mentioned person) stooped, and raising a jar of whiskey on the corner of the altar, held a wine-glass to its neck, which he filled, and, with a calm nod, handed it to me to drink. I shrunk back, with an instinctive horror at the profaneness of such an act, in the house, and on the altar, of God, and peremptorily refused to taste the proffered draught. He smiled mildly at what he considered my superstition, and added quietly, and in a low voice, 'You'll be wantin' it, I'm thinkin', afther the wettin' you got.'

'Wet or dry,' said I –

'Stop, man!' he replied, in the same tone; 'spake low. But why wouldn't you take the whiskey? Sure, there's as holy people to the fore as you; didn't they all take it? An' I wish we may never do worse nor dhrink a harmless glass o' whiskey to keep the cowld out, any-way.'

'Well,' said I, 'I'll jist trust to God and the consequences for the cowld, Paddy, *ma bouchal*; but a blessed dhrop of it won't be crossin' my lips, *avick*; so no more *gosther* about it – dhrink it yourself, if you like. Maybe you want it as much as I do; wherein I've the patthern of a good big coat upon me – so thick, your sowl, that if it was rainin' bullocks, a dhrop wouldn't get under the nap of it.'

He gave a calm but keen glance at me as I spoke.

'Well, Jim,' said he, 'it's a good comrade you've got for the weather that's in it; but, in the meantime, to set you a dacent patthern, I'll just take this myself;' saying which, with the jar still upon its side, and the forefinger of his left hand in its neck, he swallowed the spirits. 'It's the first I dhrank tonight,' he added; 'nor would I dhrink it now, only to show you that I've heart and spirit to do the thing that we're bound an' sworn to, when the proper time comes;' after which he laid down the glass, and turned up the jar, with much coolness, upon the altar.

During our conversation those who had been summoned to this mysterious meeting were pouring in fast; and as each person approached the altar he received from one to two or three glasses of whiskey, according as he chose to limit himself; but, to do them justice, there were not a few of those present who, in spite of their own desire, and the captain's express invitation, refused to taste it in the house of God's worship. Such, however, as were scrupulous he afterwards recommended to take it on the outside of the chapel door, which they did, as by that means the sacrilege of the act was supposed to be evaded.

About one o'clock they were all assembled except six; at least, so the captain asserted, on looking at a written paper.

'Now, boys,' said he, in the same low voice, 'we are all present except the thraitors whose names I am goin' to read to you; not that we are to count thim thraitors till we know whether or not it was in their power to come. Anyhow, the night's terrible; but, boys, you're to know that neither fire, nor wather is to prevint yees when duly summoned to attind a meeting – particularly whin the summons is widout a name, as you have been told that there is always something of consequence to be done thin.'

He then read out the names of those who were absent, in order that the real cause of their absence might be ascertained, declaring that they would be dealt with accordingly. After this, with his usual caution, he shut and bolted the door, and having put the key in his pocket, ascended the steps of the altar, and for some time traversed the little platform from which the priest usually addresses the congregation.

Until this night I have never contemplated the man's countenance with any particular interest; but as he walked the platform I had an opportunity of observing him more closely. He was slight in person, apparently not thirty, and, on a first view, appeared to have nothing remarkable in his dress or features. I, however, was not the only person whose eyes were fixed upon him at that moment; in fact, every one present observed him with equal interest, for hitherto he had kept the object of the meeting perfectly secret, and of course we all felt anxious to know it. It was while he traversed the platform that I scrutinized his features with a hope, if possible, to glean from them some evidence of what was passing within him. I could, however, mark but little, and that little was at first rather from the intelligence which seemed to subsist between him and those whom I have already mentioned as standing against the altar, than from any indication of his own. Their gleaming eyes were fixed upon him with an intensity of savage and demon-like hope which blazed out in flashes of malignant triumph, as, upon turning, he threw a cool but rapid glance at them, to intimate the progress he was making in the subject to which he devoted the undivided energies of his mind. But in the course of his meditation I could observe, on one or two occasions, a dark shade come over his countenance that contracted his brow into a deep furrow, and it was then, for the first time, that I saw the Satanic expression of which his face, by a very slight motion of its muscles, was capable. His hands, during this silence, closed and opened convulsively; his eyes shot out two or three baleful glances, first to his confederates, and afterwards vacantly into the deep gloom of the lower part of the chapel; his teeth ground against each other like those of a man whose revenge burns to reach a distant enemy; and finally, after having wound himself up to a certain determination, his features relapsed into their original calm and undisturbed expression.

At this moment a loud laugh, having something supernatural in it, rang out wildly from the darkness of the chapel: he stopped, and putting his open hand over his brows, peered down into the gloom, and said calmly, in Irish, '*Bee dhu husth; ha nihl anam inh* – Hold your tongue; it is not yet the time.'

Every eye was now directed to the same spot, but in consequence of its distance from the dim light on the altar, none could perceive the person from whom the laugh proceeded. It was by this time near two o'clock in the morning.

He now stood for a few moments on the platform, and his chest heaved with a depth of anxiety equal to the difficulty of the design he wished to accomplish.

'Brothers,' said he – 'for we are all brothers – sworn upon all that's blessed an' holy to obey whatever them that's over us, manin' among ourselves, wishes us to do – are you now ready, in the name of God, upon whose althar I stand, to fulfil yer oaths?'

The words were scarcely uttered, when those who had stood beside the altar during the night sprang from their places, and descending its steps rapidly, turned round, and raising their arms, exclaimed, 'By all that's sacred an' holy, we're willin'!'

In the meantime, those who sat upon the steps of the altar instantly rose, and following the example of those who had just spoken, exclaimed after them, 'To be sure – by all that's sacred an' holy, we're willin'!'

'Now, boys,' said the captain, 'aren't yees big fools for your pains? An' one of yees doesn't know what I mane.'

'You're our captain,' said one of those who had stood at the altar, 'an' has yer ordhers from higher quarthers; of coorse, whatever ye command upon us we're bound to obey you in.'

'Well,' said he, smiling, 'I only wanted to thry yees; an' by the oath yees tuck, there's not a captain in the country has as good a right to be proud of his min as I have. Well, yees won't rue it, maybe, when the right time comes; and for that same rason every one of yees must have a glass from the jar – thim that won't dhrink it in the chapel can dhrink it widout; an' here goes to open the door for them.'

He then distributed another glass to every man who would accept it, and brought the jar afterwards to the chapel door, to satisfy the scruples of those who would not drink within. When this was performed, and all duly excited, he proceeded:

'Now, brothers, you are solemnly sworn to obey me, and I'm sure there's no thraithur here that ud parjure himself for a thrifle; but I'm sworn to obey them that's above me, manin' still among ourselves; an' to show you that I don't scruple to do it, here goes!'

He then turned round, and taking the Missal between his hands, placed in upon the altar. Hitherto every word was uttered in a low, precautionary tone; but on grasping the book, he again turned round, and looking upon his confederates with the same Satanic expression which marked his countenance before, exclaimed, in a voice of deep determination:

'By this sacred an' holy book of God, I will perform the action which we have met this night to accomplish, be that what it may; an' this I swear upon God's book an' God's althar!'

On concluding he struck the book violently with his open hand.

At this moment the candle which burned before him went suddenly out, and the chapel was wrapped in pitchy darkness; the sound as if of rushing wings fell upon our ears; and fifty voices dwelt upon the last words of his oath with wild and supernatural tones, that seemed to echo and to mock what he had sworn. There was a pause, and an exclamation of horror from all present; but the captain was too cool and steady to be disconcerted. He immediately groped about until he got the candle, and proceeding calmly to a remote corner of the chapel, took up a half-burned turf which lay there, and after some trouble, succeeded in lighting it again. He then explained what had taken place; which indeed was easily done, as the candle happened to be extinguished by a pigeon which sat directly above it. The chapel, I should have observed, was at this time, like many country chapels, unfinished inside, and the pigeons of a neighbouring dovecote had built nests among the rafters of the unceiled roof; which circumstance also explained the rushing of the wings, for the birds had been affrighted by the sudden loudness of the noise. The mocking voices were nothing but the echoes, rendered naturally more awful by the scene, the mysterious object of the meeting, and the solemn hour of the night.

When the candle was again lighted, and these startling circumstances accounted for, the persons whose vengeance had been deepening more and more during the night rushed to the altar in a body, where each, in a voice trembling with passionate eagerness, repeated the oath; and as every word was pronounced, the same echoes heightened the wildness of the horrible ceremony by their long and unearthly tones. The countenances of these human tigers were livid with suppressed rage; their knit brows, compressed lips, and kindled eyes fell under the dim light of the taper with an expression calculated to sicken any heart not absolutely diabolical.

As soon as this dreadful rite was completed, we were again startled by several loud bursts of laughter, which proceeded from the lower darkness of the chapel; and the captain, on hearing them, turned to the place, and reflecting for a moment, said in Irish, *'Gutsho nish, avohelhee* – Come hither now, boys.'

A rush immediately took place from the corner in which they had secreted themselves all the night; and seven men appeared, whom we instantly recognized as brothers and cousins of certain persons who had been convicted some time before for breaking into the house of an honest poor man in the neighbourhood, from whom, after having treated him with barbarous violence, they took away such firearms as he kept for his own protection.

It was evidently not the captain's intention to have produced these persons until the oath should have been generally taken; but the exulting mirth with which they enjoyed the success of his scheme betrayed them, and put him to the necessity of bringing them forward somewhat before the concerted moment.

The scene which now took place was beyond all power of description; peals of wild, fiend-like yells rang through the chapel, as the party which stood on the altar, and that which had crouched in the darkness, met; wringing of hands, leaping in triumph, striking of sticks and firearms against the ground and the altar itself, dancing and cracking of fingers, marked the triumph of some hellish determination. Even the captain for a time was unable to restrain their fury; but at length he mounted the platform before the altar once more, and, with a stamp of his foot, recalled their attention to himself and the matter in hand.

'Boys,' said he, 'enough of this, and too much; an' well for us it is that the chapel is in a lonely place, or our foolish noise might do us no good. Let thim that swore so manfully jist now stand a one side, till the rest kiss the book, one by one.'

The proceedings, however, had by this time taken too fearful a shape for even the captain to compel them to a blindfold oath. The

first man he called flatly refused to answer until he should hear the
nature of the service that was required. This was echoed by the
remainder, who, taking courage from the firmness of this person,
declared generally that until they first knew the business they were to
execute none of them would take the oath. The captain's lip quivered
slightly, and his brow again became knit with the same hellish
expression which I have remarked gave him so much the appearance
of an embodied fiend; but this speedily passed away, and was succeeded by a malignant sneer, in which lurked, if there ever did in a
sneer, 'a laughing devil', calmly, determinedly atrocious.

'It wasn't worth yer whiles to refuse the oath,' said he mildly; 'for
the truth is, I had next to nothing for yees to do. Not a hand, maybe,
would have to rise; only jist to look on; an' if any resistance would be
made, to show yourselves; yer numbers would soon make them see
that resistance would be no use whatever in the present case. At all
evints, the oath of secrecy must be taken, or woe be to him that will
refuse that; he won't know the day, nor the hour, nor the minute
when he'll be made a spatchcock ov.'

He then turned round, and placing his right hand on the Missal,
swore, 'In the presence of God, and before His holy altar, that
whatever might take place that night he would keep secret from man
or mortal, except the priest, and that neither bribery, nor imprisonment, nor death would wring it from his heart.'

Having done this, he again struck the book violently, as if to
confirm the energy with which he swore, and then calmly descending
the steps, stood with a serene countenance, like a man conscious of
having performed a good action. As this oath did not pledge those
who refused to take the other to the perpetration of any specific crime,
it was readily taken by all present. Preparations were then made to
execute what was intended; the half-burned turf was placed in a little
pot; another glass of whiskey was distributed; and the door being
locked by the captain, who kept the key as parish clerk and master, the
crowd departed silently from the chapel.

The moment those who lay in the darkness during the night made
their appearance at the altar, we knew at once the persons we were to

visit; for, as I said before, they were related to the miscreants whom one of those persons had convicted, in consequence of their midnight attack upon himself and his family. The captain's object in keeping them unseen was that those present, not being aware of the duty about to be imposed on them, might have less hesitation about swearing to its fulfilment. Our conjectures were correct, for on leaving the chapel we directed our steps to the house in which this devoted man resided.

The night was still stormy, but without rain; it was rather dark, too, though not so as to prevent us from seeing the clouds careering swiftly through the air. The dense curtain which had overhung and obscured the horizon was now broken, and large sections of the sky were clear, and thinly studded with stars that looked dim and watery, as did indeed the whole firmament; for in some places black clouds were still visible, threatening a continuance of tempestuous weather. The road appeared washed and gravelly; every dyke was full of yellow water, and every little rivulet and larger stream dashed its hoarse music in our ears; every blast, too, was cold, fierce, and wintry, sometimes driving us back to a standstill, and again, when a turn in the road would bring it in our backs, whirling us along for a few steps with involuntary rapidity. At length the fated dwelling became visible, and a short consultation was held in a sheltered place between the captain and the two parties who seemed so eager for its destruction. The firearms were now loaded, and their bayonets and short pikes, the latter shod and pointed with iron, were also got ready. The live coal which was brought in the small pot had become extinguished; but to remedy this, two or three persons from a remote part of the county entered a cabin on the wayside, and under pretence of lighting their own and their comrades' pipes, procured a coal of fire – for so they called a lighted turf. From the time we left the chapel until this moment a profound silence had been maintained; a circumstance which, when I considered the number of persons present, and the mysterious and dreaded object of their journey, had a most appalling effect upon my spirits.

At length we arrived within fifty perches of the house, walking in a compact body, and with as little noise as possible; but it seemed as if the very elements had conspired to frustrate our design, for on advancing within the shade of the farm hedge, two or three persons found themselves up to the middle in water, and on stooping to ascertain more accurately the state of the place, we could see nothing but one immense sheet of it, spread like a lake over the meadows which surrounded the spot we wished to reach.

Fatal night! The very recollection of it, when associated with the fearful tempests of the elements, grows, if that were possible, yet more wild and revolting. Had we been engaged in any innocent or bene-volent enterprise, there was something in our situation just then that had a touch of interest in it to a mind imbued with a relish for the savage beauties of nature. There we stood, about a hundred and thirty in number, our dark forms bent forward, peering into the dusky expanse of water, with its dim gleams of reflected light, broken by the weltering of the mimic waves into ten thousand fragments; whilst the few stars that overhung it in the firmament appeared to shoot through it in broken lines, and to be multiplied fifty-fold in the gloomy mirror on which we gazed.

Over us was a stormy sky, and around us a darkness through which we could only distinguish, in outline, the nearest objects, whilst the wind swept strongly and dismally upon us. When it was discovered that the common pathway to the house was inundated, we were about to abandon our object and return home. The captain, however, stooped down low for a moment, and almost closing his eyes, looked along the surface of the waters, and then raising himself very calmly, said, in his usual quiet tone, 'Yees needn't go back, boys; I've found a way; jist follow me.'

He immediately took a more circuitous direction, by which we reached a causeway that had been raised for the purpose of giving a free passage to and from the house during such inundations as the present. Along this we had advanced more than half way, when we discovered a breach in it, which, as afterwards appeared, had that night been made by the strength of the flood. This, by means of our sticks and pikes, we found to be about three feet deep and eight yards broad.

Again we were at a loss how to proceed, when the fertile brain of the captain devised a method of crossing it.

'Boys,' said he, 'of coorse you've all played at leap-frog; very well, strip and go in, a dozen of you, lean one upon the back of another from this to the opposite bank, where one must stand facing the outside man, both their shoulders agin one another, that the outside man may be supported. Then we can creep over you, an' a dacent bridge you'll be, anyway.'

This was the work of only a few minutes, and in less than ten we were all safely over.

Merciful heaven! how I sicken at the recollection of what is to follow! On reaching the dry bank, we proceeded instantly, and in profound silence, to the house. The captain divided us into companies, and then assigned to each division its proper station. The two parties who had been so vindictive all the night he kept about himself; for of those who were present they only were in his confidence, and knew his nefarious purpose – their number was about fifteen. Having made these dispositions, he, at the head of about five of them, approached the house on the windy side, for the fiend possessed a coolness which enabled him to seize upon every possible advantage. That he had combustibles about him was evident, for in less than fifteen minutes nearly one-half of the house was enveloped in flames. On seeing this, the others rushed over to the spot where he and his gang were standing, and remonstrated earnestly, but in vain. The flames now burst forth with renewed violence, and as they flung their strong light upon the faces of the foremost group, I think hell itself could hardly present anything more Satanic than their countenances, now worked up into a paroxysm of infernal triumph at their own revenge. The captain's look had lost all of its calmness, every feature started out into distinct malignity; the curve in his brow was deep, and ran up to the root of the hair, dividing his face into two segments, that did not seem to have been designed for each other. His lips were half open, and the corners of his mouth a little brought back on each side, like those of a man expressing intense hatred and triumph over an enemy who is in the death-struggle under his grasp. His eyes blazed from beneath his knit eyebrows with a fire that seemed to be lighted up in the infernal pit itself. It is unnecessary and only painful to describe the rest of his gang. Demons might have been proud of such horrible visages as they exhibited; for they worked under all the power of hatred, revenge, and joy; and these passions blended into one terrible scowl, enough almost to blast any human eye that would venture to look upon it.

When the others attempted to intercede for the lives of the inmates, there were at least fifteen guns and pistols levelled at them.

'Another word,' said the captain, 'an' you're a corpse where you stand, or the first man who will dare to spake for them. No, no, it wasn't to spare them we came here. "No mercy" is the password for the night, an' by the sacred oath I swore beyant in the chapel, any one among yees that will attempt to show it will find none at my hand. Surround the house, boys, I tell ye, I hear them stirring. "No quarther – no mercy" is the ordher of the night.'

Such was his command over these misguided creatures, that in an instant there was a ring round the house to prevent the escape of the unhappy inmates, should the raging element give them time to attempt it; for none present durst withdraw themselves from the scene, not only from an apprehension of the captain's present vengeance or that of his gang, but because they knew that, even had they then escaped, an early and certain death awaited them from a quarter against which they had no means of defence. The hour now was about half past two o'clock. Scarcely had the last words escaped from the captain's lips, when one of the windows of the house was broken, and a human head, having the hair in a blaze, was descried, apparently a woman's, if one might judge by the profusion of burning tresses, and the softness of the tones, notwithstanding that it called, or rather shrieked, aloud for help and mercy. The only reply to this was the whoop from the captain and his gang of 'No mercy – no mercy!' and that instant the former and one of the latter rushed to the spot, and ere the action could be perceived, the head was transfixed with a bayonet and a pike, both having entered it together. The word mercy was divided in her mouth; a short silence ensued; the head hung down on the window, but was instantly tossed back into the flames!

This action occasioned a cry of horror from all present, except the gang and their leader, which startled and enraged the latter so much that he ran towards one of them, and had his bayonet, now reeking with the blood of its innocent victim, raised to plunge it in his body, when, dropping the point, he said in a piercing whisper that hissed in the ears of all, 'It's no use now, you know; if one's to hang, all will hang; so our safest way, you persave, is to lave none of them to tell the story. Ye may go now, if you wish; but it won't save a hair of your heads. You cowardly set! I knew if I had tould yees the sport, that none of yees, except my own boys, would come, so I jist played a thrick upon you; but remimber what you are sworn to, and stand to the oath ye tuck.'

Unhappily, notwithstanding the wetness of the preceding weather, the materials of the house were extremely combustible; the whole dwelling was now one body of glowing flame; yet the shouts and shrieks within rose awfully above its crackling, and the voice of the storm, for the wind once more blew in gusts and with great violence. The doors and windows were all torn open, and such of those within as had escaped the flames rushed towards them, for the purpose of further escape, and of claiming mercy at the hands of their destroyers; but whenever they appeared, the unearthly cry of 'No mercy' rung upon their ears for a moment, and for a moment only, for they were flung back at the points of the weapons which the demons had brought with them to make the work of vengeance more certain.

As yet there were many persons in the house whose cry for life was strong as despair, and who clung to it with all the awakened powers of reason and instinct. The ear of man could hear nothing so strongly calculated to stifle the demon of cruelty and revenge within him as the long and wailing shrieks which rose beyond the elements in tones that were carried off rapidly upon the blast, until they died away in the darkness that lay behind the surrounding hills. Had not the house been in a solitary situation, and the hour the dead of night, any person sleeping within a moderate distance must have heard them, for such a cry of sorrow rising into a yell of despair was almost sufficient to have awakened the dead. It was lost, however, upon the hearts and ears that heard it; to them – though, in justice be it said, to only comparatively a few of them – it was as delightful as the tones of soft and entrancing music.

The claims of the surviving sufferers were now modified: they supplicated merely to suffer death by the weapons of their enemies; they were willing to bear that, provided they should be allowed to escape from the flames; but no – the horrors of the conflagration were calmly and malignantly gloried in by their merciless assassins, who deliberately flung them back into all their tortures. In the course of a few minutes a man appeared upon the side-wall of the house, nearly naked; his figure, as he stood against the sky in horrible relief, was so finished a picture of woe-begone agony and supplication that it is yet as distinct in my memory as if I were again present at the scene. Every muscle, now in motion by the powerful agitation of his sufferings, stood out upon his limbs and neck, giving him an appearance of desperate strength, to which by this time he must have been wrought up; the perspiration poured from his frame, and the veins and arteries of his neck were inflated to a surprising thickness. Every moment he looked down into the flames which were rising to where he stood; and as he looked, the indescribable horror which flitted over his features might have worked upon the devil himself to relent. His words were few.

'My child,' said he, 'is still safe; she is an infant, a young crathur that never harmed you nor any one – she is still safe. Your mothers, your wives, have young innocent childher like it. Oh, spare her! – think for a moment that it's one of your own! – spare it, as you hope to meet a just God; or if you don't, in mercy shoot me first – put an end to me before I see her burned!'

The captain approached him coolly and deliberately. 'You'll prosecute no one now, you bloody informer,' said he; 'you'll convict no more boys for takin' an ould gun an' pistol from you, or for givin' you a neighbourly knock or two into the bargain.'

Just then, from a window opposite him, proceeded the shrieks of a woman, who appeared at it with the infant in her arms. She herself was almost scorched to death; but with the presence of mind and humanity of her sex, she was about to put the little babe out of the window. The captain noticed this, and with characteristic atrocity, thrust, with a sharp bayonet, the little innocent, along with the person who endeavoured to rescue it, into the red flames, where they both perished. This was the work of an instant. Again he approached the man, 'Your child is a coal now,' said he, with deliberate mockery; 'I pitched it in myself, on the point of this' – showing the weapon – 'an' now is your turn' – saying which he clambered up, by the assistance of his gang, who stood with a front of pikes and bayonets bristling to receive the wretched man, should he attempt, in his despair, to throw himself from the wall. The captain got up, and placing the point of his bayonet against his shoulder, flung him into the fiery element that raged behind him. He uttered one wild and terrific cry as he fell back, and no more. After this, nothing was heard but the crackling of the fire and the rushing of the blast; all that had possessed life within were consumed, amounting either to eleven or fifteen persons.

When this was accomplished, those who took an active part in the murder stood for some time about the conflagration; and as it threw its red light upon their fierce faces and rough persons, soiled as they now were with smoke and black streaks of ashes, the scene seemed to be changed to hell, the murderers to spirits of the damned rejoicing over the arrival and the torture of some guilty soul. The faces of those who kept aloof from the slaughter were blanched to the whiteness of death; some of them fainted, and others were in such agitation that they were compelled to lean on their comrades. They became actually powerless with horror. Yet to such a scene were they brought by the pernicious influence of Ribbonism.

It was only when the last victim went down that the conflagration shot up into the air with most unbounded fury. The house was large, deeply thatched, and well furnished; and the broad red pyramid rose up with fearful magnificence towards the sky. Abstractedly it had sublimity, but now it was associated with nothing in my mind but blood and terror. It was not, however, without a purpose that the captain and his gang stood to contemplate its effect. 'Boys,' said he, 'we had betther be sartin that all's safe; who knows but there might be some of the sarpents crouchin' under a hape o' rubbish, to come out an' gibbet us tomorrow or next day; we had betther wait awhile, anyhow, if it was only to see the blaze.'

Just then the flames rose majestically to a surprising height. Our eyes followed their direction; and we perceived, for the first time, that the dark clouds above, together with the intermediate air, appeared to reflect back, or rather to have caught, the red hue of the fire. The hills and country about us appeared with an alarming distinctness; but the most picturesque part of it was the effect or reflection of the blaze on the floods that spread over the surrounding plains. These, in fact, appeared to be one broad mass of liquid copper; for the motion of the breaking waters caught from the blaze of the high waving column, as reflected in them, a glaring light, which eddied and rose and fluctuated as if the flood itself had been a lake of molten fire.

Fire, however, destroys rapidly. In a short time the flames sank – became weak and flickering – by and by they shot out only in fits – the crackling of the timbers died away – the surrounding darkness deepened – and, ere long, the faint light was overpowered by the thick volumes of smoke that rose from the ruins of the house and its murdered inhabitants.

'Now, boys,' said the captain, 'all is safe – we may go. Remember, every man of you, what you've sworn this night on the book an' altar of God – not on a heretic Bible. If you perjure yourselves, you may hang us; but let me tell you, for your comfort, that if you do, there is them livin' that will take care the lase of your own lives will be but short.'

After this we dispersed, every man to his own home.

Reader, not many months elapsed ere I saw the bodies of this captain, whose name was Patrick Devaun, and all those who were actively concerned in the perpetration of this deed of horror, withering in the wind, where they hung gibbeted near the scene of their nefarious villainy; and while I inwardly thanked Heaven for my own narrow and almost undeserved escape, I thought in my heart how seldom, even in this world, justice fails to overtake the murderer, and to enforce the righteous judgement of God – and 'whoso sheddeth man's blood, by man shall his blood by shed.'

This tale of terror is, unfortunately, too true. The scene of hellish murder detailed in it lies at Wildgoose Lodge in the county of Louth, within about four miles of Carrickmacross, and nine of Dundalk. No such multitudinous murder has occurred, under similar circumstances, except the burning of the Sheas in the county of Tipperary. The name of the family burned in Wildgoose Lodge was Lynch. One of them had, shortly before this fatal night, prosecuted and convicted some of the neighbouring Ribbonmen, who visited him with severe marks of their displeasure in consequence of his having refused to enrol himself as a member of their body.

The language of the story is partly fictitious; but the facts are pretty closely such as were developed during the trial of the murderers. Both parties were Roman Catholics. There were, if the author mistake not, either twenty-five or twenty-eight of those who took an active part in the burning hanged and gibbeted in different parts of the county of Louth. Devaun, the ringleader, hung for some months in chains, within about a hundred yards of his own house, and about half a mile from Wildgoose Lodge. His mother could neither go into or out of her cabin without seeing his body swinging from the gibbet. Her usual exclamation on looking at him was, 'God be good to the sowl of my poor marthyr!' The peasantry, too, frequently exclaimed, on seeing him, 'Poor Paddy!' – a gloomy fact that speaks volumes.

SAMUEL LOVER

The Gridiron

Samuel Lover (1797–1868) was a novelist and painter who also composed over three hundred songs. His first book was highly successful: Legends and Stories of Ireland *(1831). He aimed at expressing Irish character in a truly Irish way.*

A CERTAIN old gentleman in the west of Ireland, whose love of the ridiculous quite equalled his taste for claret and fox-hunting, was wont, upon certain festive occasions when opportunity offered, to amuse his friends by drawing out one of his servants who was exceedingly fond of what he termed his 'thravels', and in whom a good deal of whim, some queer stories, and, perhaps more than all, long and faithful services, had established a right of loquacity.

He was one of those few trusty and privileged domestics, who, if his master unheedingly uttered a rash thing in a fit of passion, would venture to set him right.

If the squire said, 'I'll turn that rascal off,' my friend Pat would say, 'Throth you won't, sir'; and Pat was always right, for if any altercation arose upon the subject-matter in hand, he was sure to throw in some good reason, either from former service – general good conduct – or the delinquent's 'wife and childher', that always turned the scale.

But I am digressing. On such merry meetings as I have alluded to, the master, after making certain 'approaches', as a military man would say, as the preparatory steps in laying siege to some extravaganza of his servant, might, perchance, assail Pat thus:

'By the by, Sir John' (addressing a distinguished guest), 'Pat has a very curious story, which something you told me to-day reminds me of. You remember, Pat' (turning to the man, evidently pleased at the notice paid to himself) – 'you remember that queer adventure you had in France?'

'Throth I do, sir,' grins forth Pat.

'What!' exclaims Sir John, in feigned surprise. 'Was Pat ever in France?'

'Indeed he was,' cries mine host; and Pat adds, 'Ay, and farther, plase your honour.'

'I assure you, Sir John,' continues mine host, 'Pat told me a story once that surprised me very much, respecting the ignorance of the French.'

'Indeed!' rejoins the baronet. 'Really, I always supposed the French to be a most accomplished people.'

'Throth, then, they're not, sir,' interrupts Pat.

'Oh, by no means,' adds mine host, shaking his head emphatically.

'I believe, Pat, 'twas when you were crossing the Atlantic?' says the master, turning to Pat with a seductive air, and leading into the 'full and true account' – (for Pat had thought fit to visit North Amerikay, for 'a raison he had', in the autumn of the year ninety-eight).

'Yes, sir,' says Pat, 'the broad Atlantic,' a favourite phrase of his, which he gave with a brogue as broad almost as the Atlantic itself.

'It was the time I was lost in crassin' the broad Atlantic, comin' home,' began Pat, decoyed into the recital; 'whin the winds began to blow, and the sae to rowl, that you'd think the *Colleen Dhas* (that was her name) would not have a mast left.

'Well, sure enough, the masts went by the board at last, and the pumps was choaked (divil choak them for that same), and av coorse the wather gained an us, and throth, to be filled with water is neither good for man or baste; and she was sinkin' fast, settlin' down, as the sailors calls it, and faith I never was good at settlin' down in my life, and I liked it then less nor ever. Accordingly we prepared for the worst, and put out the boat, and got a sack o' bishkits, and a cashk o' pork, and a kag o' wather, and a thrifle o' rum aboard, and any other little mathers we could think iv in the mortial hurry we wor in – and, faith, there was no time to be lost, for my darlint, the *Colleen Dhas*, went down like a lump o' lead, afore we wor many strokes o' the oar away from her.

'Well, we dhrifted away all that night, and next mornin' we put up a blanket an the ind av a pole as well as we could, and thin we sailed illigant, for we dar'n't show a stitch o' canvas the night before, bekase it was blowin' like murther, savin' your presence, and sure it's the wondher of the word we worn't swallyed alive the ragin' sae.

'Well, away we wint for more nor a week, and nothin' before our two good-looking eyes but the canophy iv heaven, and the wide ocean – the broad Atlantic – not a thing was to be seen but the sae and the sky; and though the sae and the sky is mighty purty things in themselves, throth they're no great things whin you've nothin' else to look at for a week together – and the barest rock in the world, so it was land, would be more welkim.

'And then, sure enough, throth, our provisions began to run low, the bishkits, and the wather, and the rum – throth that was gone first of all – God help uz! – and oh! it was thin that starvation began to stare us in the face. ' "Oh, murther, murther, captain, darlint," says I, ' "I wish we could see land anywhere," says I.

' "More power to your elbow, Paddy, my boy," says he, ' "for sitch a good wish, and, throth, it's myself wishes the same."

' "Oh," says I, ' "that it may plaze you, sweet queen in heaven – supposing it was only a dissolute island," says I, "inhabited wid Turks, sure they wouldn't be such bad Christhans as to refuse uz a bit and a sup."

' "Whisht, whisht, Paddy,' says the captain; "don't be talkin' bad of any one," says he; "you don't know how soon you may want a good word put in for yourself, if you should be called to quarthers in th' other world all of a suddent," says he.

' "Thrue for you, captain, darlint," says I – I called him darlint, and made free wid him, you see, bekase disthress makes uz all equal – "thrue for you, captain, jewel – God betune uz and harm, I owe no man any spite" – and, throth, that was only thruth.

'Well, the last bishkit was sarved out, and, by gor, the wather itself was all gone at last, and we passed the night mighty cowld. Well, at the brake o' day the sun riz most beautiful out o' the waves, that was as bright as silver and as clear as cryshthal.

'But it was only the more crule upon uz, for we wor beginnin' to feel terrible hungry; when all at wanst I thought I spied the land – by gor, I thought I felt my heart up in my throat in a minnit, and "Thundher and turf, captain," says I, "look to leeward," says I.

' "What for?" says he.

' "I think I see the land," says I. So he ups with his bring-'um-near (that's what the sailors call a spy-glass, sir), and looks out, and, sure enough, it was.

' "Hurrah!" says he, "we're all right now; pull away, my boys," says he.

' "Take care you're not mistaken," says I; "maybe it's only a fog-bank, captain, darlint," says I.

' "Oh, no," says he, "it's the land in airnest."

' "Oh, then, whereabouts in the wide world are we, captain?" says I; "maybe it id be in Roosia or Proosia, or the Garman Oceant," says I.

' "Tut, you fool," says he, for he had that consaited way wid him – thinkin' himself cleverer nor any one else – "tut, you fool," says he; "that's France," says he.

' "Tare an ouns," says I, "do you tell me so? And how do you know it's France it is, captain, dear?" says I.

' "Bekase this is the Bay o' Bishky we're in now," says he.

' "Throth, I was thinkin' so myself," says I, "by the rowl it has; for I often heerd av it in regard o' that same"; and, throth, the likes av it I never seen before nor since, and, with the help o' God, never will.

'Well, with that my heart begun to grow light, and when I seen my life was safe, I began to grow twice hungrier nor ever – so says I, "Captain, jewel, I wish we had a gridiron."

' "Why, then," says he, "thundher and turf," says he, "what put a gridiron into your head?'

' "Bekase I'm starvin' with the hunger,' says I.

' "And sure, bad luck to you," says he, "you couldn't ate a grid-iron," says he, "barrin you wor a pelican o' the wilderness," says he.

' "Ate a gridiron!" says I. "Och, in throth, I'm not such a gommoch all out as that, anyhow. But sure if we had a gridiron we could dress a beefsteak," says I.

' "Arrah! but where's the beefsteak?" says he.

' "Sure, couldn't we cut a slice aff the pork?" says I.

' "By gor, I never thought a' that," says the captain. "You're a clever fellow, Paddy," says he, laughin'.

' "Oh, there's many a thrue word said in joke," says I.

' "Thrue for you, Paddy," says he.

' "Well, then," says I, "if you put me ashore there beyant" (for we were nearin' the land all the time), "and sure I can ask thim for to lind me the loan of a gridiron," says I.

' "Oh, by gor, the butther's comin' out o' the stirabout in airnest now," says he. "You gommoch," says he, "sure I towld you before that's France – and sure they're all furriners there," says the captain.

' "Well," says I, "and how do you know but I'm as good a furriner myself as any o' thim."

' "What do you mane?" says he.

' "I mane," says I, "what I towld you, that I'm as good as furriner myself as any o' thim."

' "Make me sinsible," says he.

' "By dad, maybe that's more nor me, or greater nor me, could do," says I; and we all began to laugh at him, for I thought I'd pay him off for his bit o' consait about the Garman Oceant.

' "Lave aff your humbuggin'," says he. "I bid you, and tell me what it is you mane at all, at all."

' "Parly-voo frongsay?" says I.

' "Oh, your humble sarvant," says he. "Why, by gor, you're a scholar, Paddy."

' "Throth, you may say that," says I.

' "Why, you're a clever fellow, Paddy," says the captain, jeerin' liike.

' "You're not the first that said that," says I. "whether you joke or no."

' "Oh, but I'm in airnest," says the captain. "And do you tell me, Paddy," says he, "that you spake Frinch?"

' "Parly-voo frongsay?" says I.

' "By gor, that bangs Banagher, and all the world knows Banagher bangs the devil. I never met the likes o' you, Paddy," says he. "Pull away, boys, and put Paddy ashore, and maybe we won't get a good bellyful before long."

'So, with that, it was no sooner said nor done – they pulled away and got close into shore in less than no time, and run the boat up in a little creek; and a beautiful creek it was, with a lovely white sthrand, an illigant place for ladies to bathe in the summer; and out I got, and it's stiff enough in my limbs I was afther bein' cramped up in the boat, and perished with the cowld and hunger; but I conthrived to scramble an, one way or the other, towards a little bit iv a wood that was close to the shore, and the smoke curlin' out of it, quite timpting like.

' "By the powdhers o' war, I'm all right," says I; "there's a house there" – and sure enough there was, and a parcel of men, women, and childher, ating their dinner round a table quite convainent. And so I wint up to the dure, and I thought I'd be very civil to thim, as I heerd the Frinch was always mighty p'lite intirely – and I thought I'd show them I knew what good manners was.

'So I took off my hat, and making a low bow, says I, "God save all here," says I.

'Well, to be sure, they all stopt ating at wanst, and begun to stare at me, and faith they almost looked me out of countenance – and I thought to myself it was not good manners at all – more be token from furriners, which they call so mighty p'lite; but I never minded that, in regard of wantin' the gridiron; and so says I, "I beg your pardon," says I, "for the liberty I take, but it's only bein' in disthress in regard of ating," says I, "that I make bowld to throuble yez, and if you could lind me the loan of a gridiron," says I, "I'd be entirely obleeged to ye."

'By gor, they all stared at me twice worse nor before, and with that, says I (knowing what was in their minds), "Indeed it's thrue for you," says I; "I'm tathered to pieces, and God knows I look quare enough, but it's by raison of the storm," says I, "which dhruv us ashore here below, and we're all starvin'," says I.

'So then they began to look at each other agin, and myself, seeing at wanst dirty thoughts was in their heads, and that they tuk me for a poor beggar comin' to crave charity – with that, says I, "Oh! not at all," says I, "by no manes; we have plenty o' mate ourselves, there below, and we'll dhress it," says I, "if you would be plased to lind us the loan of a gridiron," says I, makin' a low bow.

'Well, sir, with that, throth, they stared at me twice worse nor ever, and faith I began to think that maybe the captain was wrong, and that it was not France at all, at all; and so says I – "I beg pardon, sir," says I, to a fine ould man, with a head of hair as white as silver – "maybe I'm undher a mistake," says I, "but I thought I was in France, sir; aren't you furriners?" says I – "Parly-voo frongsay?"

' "We, munseer," says he.

' "Then would you lind me the loan of a gridiron," says I, "if you plase?"

'Oh, it was thin that they stared at me as if I had siven heads; and faith myself began to feel flusthered like, and onaisy – and so, says I, making a bow and scrape agin, "I know it's a liberty I take, sir," says I, "but it's only in the regard of bein' cast away, and if you plase, sir," says I, "Parly-voo frongsay?"

' "We, munseer," says he, mighty sharp.

' "Then would you lind me the loan of a gridiron?" says I, "and you'll obleege me."

'Well, sir, the old chap begun to munseer me, but the divil a bit of a gridiron he'd gie me; and so I began to think they were all neygars, for all their fine manners; and, throth, my blood began to rise, and says I, "By my sowl, if it was you was in disthress," says I, "and if it was to ould Ireland you kem, it's not only the gridiron they'd give you if you ax'd it, but something to put an it too, and a dhrop of dhrink into the bargain, and cead mille failte."

'Well, the word cead mille failte seemed to stchreck his heart, and the ould chap cocked his ear, and so I thought I'd give him another offer, and make him sinsible at last; and so says I, wanst more, quite slow, that he might undherstand – "Parly – voo – frongsay, munseer?"

' "We, munseer," says he.

' "Then lind me the loan of a gridiron," says I, "and bad scran to you."

'Well, bad win' to the bit of it he'd gi' me, and the ould chap begins bowin' and scrapin', and said something or other about a long tongs.

' "Phoo! – the devil sweep yourself and tongs," says I, "I don't want a tongs at all, at all; but can't you listen to raison," says I – "Parly-voo frongsay?"

' "We, munseer."

' "Then lind me the loan of a gridiron," says I, "and howld your prate."

'Well, what would you think but he shook his owld noddle, as much as to say he wouldn't; and so says I, "Bad cess to the likes o' that I ever seen – throth if you were in my country, it's not that-a-way they'd use you; the curse o' the crows on you, you ould sinner," says I; "the divil a longer I'll darken your dure."

'So he seen I was vexed, and I thought, as I was turnin' away, I seen him begin to relint, and that his conscience throubled him; and says I, turnin' back. "Well, I'll give you one chance more – you owld thief – are you a Chrishthan at all, at all? – are you a furriner," says I, "that all the world calls so p'lite? Bad luck to you; do you undherstand your own language? – Parly-voo frongsay?" says I.

' "We, munseer," says he.

' "Then, thundher and turf," says I, "will you lind me the loan of a gridiron?"

'Well, sir, the divil resave the bit of it he'd gi' me – and so with that, "The curse o' the hungry on you, you owld negardly villain," says I; "the back o' my hand and the sowl o' my foot to you; that you may want a gridiron yourself yet," says I; "and wherever I go, high and low, rich and poor shall hear o' you," says I; and with that I lift them there, sir, and kem away – and in throth it's often since that I thought that it was remarkable.'

JOHN BANIM

The Stolen Sheep

John Banim (1798–1842) was born in Kilkenny and wrote many tales of old Ireland. His most famous collection of stories was Tales of the O'Hara Family *written with his brother Michael. He was particularly successful in depicting poor Irish farmers and labourers.*

THE Irish plague, called typhus fever, raged in its terrors. In almost every third cabin there was a corpse daily. In every one, without an exception, there was what had made the corpse – hunger. It need not be added that there was poverty, too. The poor could not bury their dead. From mixed motives, of self-protection, terror, and benevolence, those in easier circumstances exerted themselves to administer relief in different ways. Money was subscribed (then came England's munificent donation – God prosper her for it!), wholesome food, or food as wholesome as a bad season permitted, was provided; and men of respectability, bracing their minds to avert the danger that threatened themselves, by boldly facing it, entered the infected house, where death reigned almost alone, and took measures to cleanse and purify the close-cribbed air and the rough, bare walls.

In the early progress of the fever, before the more affluent roused themselves to avert its career, let us cross the threshold of an individual peasant. His young wife lies dead; his second child is dying at her side; he has just sunk into a corner himself, under the first stun of disease,

long resisted. The only persons of his family who have escaped con-
tagion, and are likely to escape it, are his old father, who sits weeping
feebly upon the hob, and his first-born, a boy of three or four years
who, standing between the old man's knees, cries also for food.

We visit the young peasant's abode some time after. He has not
sunk under 'the sickness'. He is fast regaining his strength, even
without proper nourishment; he can creep out of doors and sit in the
sun. But in the expression of his sallow and emaciated face there is no
joy for his escape from the grave, as he sits there alone, silent and
brooding. His father and surviving child are still hungry – more
hungry, indeed, and more helpless than ever; for the neighbours who
had relieved the family with a potato and a mug of sour milk are now
stricken down themselves, and want assistance to a much greater
extent than they can give it.

'I wish Mr Evans was in the place,' cogitated Michaul Carroll; 'a
body could spake forn'ent him, and not spake for nothin' for all that
he's an Englishman; and I don't like the thoughts o' goin' up to the
house to the steward's face – it wouldn't turn kind to a body. May be
he'd soon come home to us, the masther himself.'

Another fortnight elapsed. Michaul's hope proved vain. Mr Evans
was still in London; though a regular resident on his small Irish estate
since it had come into his possession, business unfortunately – and he
would have said so himself – now kept him an unusually long time
absent. Thus disappointed, Michaul overcame his repugnance to
appear before the 'hard' steward. He only asked for work, however.
There was none to be had. He turned his slow and still feeble feet into
the adjacent town. It was market-day, and he took up his place among
a crowd of other claimants for agricultural employment, shouldering a
spade, as did each of his companions.

Many farmers came to the well-known 'stannin',' and hired men at
his right and at his left, but no one addressed Michaul. Once or twice,
indeed, touched perhaps by his sidelong looks of beseeching misery, a
farmer stopped a moment before him, and glanced over his figure; but
his worn and almost shaking limbs giving little promise of present
vigour in the working field, worldly prudence soon conquered the

humane feeling which started up towards him in the man's heart, and, with a choking in his throat, poor Michaul saw the arbiter of his fate pass on.

He walked homeward, without having broken his fast that day. 'Bud, *musha*, what's the harm o' that,' he said to himself; 'only here's the ould father, an' *her* pet boy, the weenock, without a pyatee either. Well, *asthore*, if they can't have the pyatees, they must have betther food – that's all; ay' – he muttered, clenching his hands at his sides, and imprecating fearfully in Irish – 'an' so they must.'

He left his house again, and walked a good way to beg a few potatoes. He did not come back quite empty-handed. His father and his child had a meal. He ate but a few himself; and when he was about to lie down in his corner for the night, he said to the old man across the room:

'Don't be a-cryin' to-night, father, you and the child there; bud sleep well, and ye'll have the good break'ast afore ye in the mornin'.'

'The good break'ast, *ma-bauchal*?[1] A-then, an' where 'ill id come from?'

'A body promised it to me, father.'

'*Avich!* Michaul, an' sure it's fun you're making of us, now, at any rate. Bud, the good night, a *chorra*,[2] an' my blessin' on your head, Michaul; an' if we keep trust in the good God, an' ax His blessin' too, mornin' and evenin', gettin' up an' lyin' down, He'll be a friend to us at last: that was always an' ever my word to you, poor boy, since you was at the years o' your own weenock, now fast asleep at my side; an' it's my word to you now; *ma-bauchal*; an' you won't forget id; and there's one sayin' the same to you, out o' heaven, this night – herself, an' her little angel-in-glory by the hand, Michaul *a-vourneen*.'

Having thus spoken in the fervent and rather exaggerated, though everyday, words of pious allusion of the Irish poor man, old Carroll soon dropped asleep, with his arms round his little grandson, both overcome by an unusually abundant meal. In the middle of the night he was awakened by a stealthy noise. Without moving, he cast his eyes

[1]. My boy.
[2] Term of endearment.

round the cabin. A small window, through which the moon broke brilliantly, was open. He called to his son, but received no answer. He called again and again: all remained silent. He arose, and crept to the corner where Michaul had lain down. It was empty. He looked out through the window into the moonlight. The figure of a man appeared at a distance, just about to enter a pasture-field belonging to Mr Evans.

The old man leaned back against the wall of the cabin, trembling with sudden and terrible misgivings. With him the language of virtue which we have heard him utter, was not cant. In early prosperity, in subsequent misfortunes, and in his late and present excess of wretchedness he had never swerved in practice from the spirit of his own exhortations to honesty before men, and love for, and depen- dence upon God, which, as he had truly said, he had constantly addressed to his son since his earliest childhood. And hitherto that son had, indeed, walked by his precepts, further assisted by a regular observance of the duties of his religion. Was he now about to turn into another path? to bring shame on his father in his old age? to put a stain on their family and their name, 'the name that a rogue or a bould woman never bore'? continued old Carroll, indulging in some of the pride and egotism for which an Irish peasant is, under his circum- stances, remarkable. And then came the thought of the personal peril incurred by Michaul; and his agitation, incurred by the feebleness of age, nearly overpowered him.

He was sitting on the floor, shivering like one in an ague fit, when he heard steps outside the house. He listened, and they ceased: but the familiar noise of an old barn door creaking on its crazy hinges came on his ear. It was now day-dawn. He dressed himself, stole out cautiously, peeped into the barn through a chink of the door, and all he had feared met full confirmation. There, indeed, sat Michaul, busily and earnestly engaged, with a frowning brow and a haggard face, in quartering the animal he had stolen from Mr Evans's field.

The sight sickened the father – the blood on his son's hands, and all. He was barely able to keep himself from falling. A fear, if not a dislike, of the unhappy culprit also came upon him. His unconscious impulse was to re-enter their cabin unperceived, without speaking a word; he succeeded in doing so; and then he fastened the door again and undressed, and resumed his place beside his innocent grandson.

About an hour afterwards, Michaul came in cautiously through the still open window, and also undressed and reclined on his straw, after glancing towards his father's bed, who pretended to be asleep. At the usual time for arising, old Carroll saw him suddenly jump up, and prepare to go abroad. He spoke to him, leaning on his elbow.

'And what *hollg*[1] is on you now, *ma-bauchal*?'

'Going for the good break'ast I promised you, father dear.'

'An' who's the good Christhthan 'ill give id to us, Michaul?'

'Oh, you'll know that soon, father: now, a good-bye' – he hurried to the door.

'A good-bye, then, Michaul; bud, tell me, what's that on your hand?'

'No-nothin',' stammered Michaul, changing colour, as he hastily examined the hand himself; 'nothin' is on id: what could there be?' (Nor was there, for he had very carefully removed all evidence of guilt from his person; and the father's question was asked upon grounds distinct from anything he then saw.)

'Well, *avich*, an' sure I didn't say anything was on it wrong; or anything to make you look so quare, an' spake so sthrange to your father, this mornin'; – only I'll ax you, Michaul, over agin, who has took such a sudd'n likin' to us, to send us the good break'ast – an' answer me sthraight, Michaul – what is id to be, that you call it so *good*?'

'The good mate, father' – he was again passing the threshold.

'Stop!' cried his father; 'stop, an' turn fornent me, Mate? – the good mate? – What 'ud bring mate into our poor house, Michaul? Tell me, I bid you again an' again, who is to give id to you?'

'Why, as I said afore, father, a body that — '

'A body that thieved id, Michaul Carroll!' added the old man, as his son hesitated, walking close up to the culprit; 'a body that thieved id, an' no other body. Don't think to blind me, Michaul. I am ould, to be

---

[1] What are you about.

sure; but sense enough is left in me to look round among the neighbours, in my own mind, an' know that none of 'em that has the will has the power to send us the mate for our break'ast in an honest way. An' I don't say, outright, that you had the same thought wid me when you consented to take it from a thief – I don't mean to say that you'd go to turn a thief's recaiver, at this hour o' your life, an' afther growin' up from a boy to a man widout bringin' a spot of shame on yourself, or on your weenock, or on one of us. No; I won't say that. Your heart was scalded, Michaul, an' your mind was darkened, for a start; an' the thought o' getting comfort for the ould father an' for the little son made you consent in a hurry, widout lookin' well afore you, or widout lookin' up to your good God.'

'Father, father, let me alone! don't spake them words to me,' interrupted Michaul, sitting on a stool, and spreading his large and hard hands over his face.

'Well, thin, an' I won't, *avich*; I won't; – nothin' to throuble you, sure: I didn't mean id; – only this, *a-vourneen*, don't bring a mouthful o' the bad, unlucky victuals into this cabin; the pyatees, the wild berries o' the bush, the wild roots o' the arth, will be sweeter to us, Michaul; the hunger itself will be sweeter; an' when we give God thanks afther our poor meal, or afther no meal at all, our hearts will be lighter, and our hopes for to-morrow sthronger, *avich-ma-chree*, than if we faisted on the fat o' the land, but couldn't ax a blessin' on our faist.'

'Well, thin, *I* won't, either, father; I won't: an' sure you have your way now. I'll only go out a little while from you – to beg; or else, as you say, to root down in the ground, with my nails, like a baste-brute, for our break'ast.'

'My *vourneen* you are, Michaul, an' my blessin' on your head; yes, to be sure, *avich*, beg, an' I'll beg wid you – sorrow a shame is in that – no, but a good deed, Michaul, when it's done to keep us honest. So come; we'll go among the Christhthans together. Only, before we go, Michaul, my own dear son, tell me – tell one thing.'

'What, father?' Michaul began to suspect.

'Never be afraid to tell me, Michaul Carroll, *ma-bauchal*? I won't – I can't be angry wid you now. You are sorry; an' your Father in heaven forgives you, and so do I. But you know, *avich*, there would be danger in quitting the place widout hiding every scrap of anything that could tell on us.'

'Tell on us! What can tell on us?' demanded Michaul; 'what's in the place to tell on us?'

'Nothin' in the cabin, I know, Michaul, but –'

'But what, father?'

'Have you left nothing in the way, out there?' whispered the old man, pointing towards the barn.

'Out there? Where? What? What do you mean at all, now, father? Sure you know it's your ownsef has kep me from as much as laying a hand on it.'

'Ay, to-day mornin'; bud you laid a hand on it last night, *avich*, an' so –'

'*Curp-an-duoul!*' imprecated Michaul – 'this is too bad, at any rate; no, I didn't – last night – let me alone, I bid you, father.'

'Come back again, Michaul,' commanded old Carroll, as the son once more hurried to the door: and his words were instantly obeyed. Michaul, after a glance abroad, and a start, which the old man did not notice, paced to the middle of the floor, hanging his head and saying in a low voice, 'Hushth now, father – it's time.'

'No, Michaul, I will not hushth; an' it's not time; come out with me to the barn.'

'Hushth!' repeated Michaul, whispering sharply: he had glanced sideways to the square patch of strong morning sunlight on the ground of the cabin, defined there by the shape of the open door, and saw it intruded upon by the shadow of a man's bust leaning forward in an earnest posture.

'Is it in your mind to go back into your sin, Michaul, an' tell me you were not in the barn, at daybreak, the mornin'?' asked his father, still unconscious of a reason for silence.

'Arrah, hushth, ould man!' Michaul made a hasty sign towards the door, but was disregarded.

'I saw you in id,' pursued old Carroll sternly 'ay, and at your work in id, too.'

'What's that you're sayin', ould Peery Carroll?' demanded a well—known voice.

'Enough to hang his son,' whispered Michaul to his father, as Mr Evans's land-steward, followed by his herdsman and two policemen, entered the cabin. In a few minutes afterwards the policemen had in charge the dismembered carcase of the sheep, dug up out of the floor in the barn, and were escorting Michaul, handcuffed, to the county gaol, in the vicinity of the next town. They could find no trace of the animal's skin, though they sought attentively for it; and this seemed to disappoint them and the steward a good deal.

From the moment that they entered the cabin, till their departure, old Carroll did not speak a word. Without knowing it, as it seemed, he sat down on his straw bed, and remained staring stupidly around him, or at one or another of his visitors. When Michaul was about to leave the wretched abode, he paced quickly towards his father, and holding out his ironed hands, and turning his cheek for a kiss, said, smiling miserably, 'God be wid you, father dear.'

Still the old man was silent, and the prisoner and all his attendants passed out on the road. But it was then the agony of old Carroll assumed a distinctness. Uttering a fearful cry, he snatched up his still sleeping grandson, ran with the boy in his arms till he overtook Michaul; and, kneeling down before him in the dust, said:

'I ax pardon o' you, *avich* – won't you tell me I have id afore you go? An' here, I've brought little Peery for you to kiss; you forgot *him*, *a-vourneen.*'

'No, father, I didn't,' answered Michaul, as he stooped to kiss the child; 'an' get up, father, get up; my hands are not my own, or I wouldn't let you do that afore your son. Get up, there's nothin' for you to throuble yourself about; that is, I mean, I have nothin' to forgive you: no, but everything to be thankful for, an' to love your for; you were always an' ever the good father to me; an' —'

The many strong and bitter feelings which till now he had almost perfectly kept in, found full vent, and poor Michaul could not go on. The parting from his father, however, so different from what it had promised to be, comforted him. The old man held him in his arms and wept on his neck. They separated with difficulty.

Peery Carroll, sitting on the roadside after he lost sight of the prisoner, and holding his screaming grandson on his knees, thought the cup of his trials were full. By his imprudence he had fixed the proof of guilt on his own child; that reflection was enough for him, and he could indulge it only generally. But he was yet to conceive distinctly in what dilemma he had involved himself as well as Michaul.

The policemen came back to compel his appearance before the magistrate; and when the little child had been disposed of in a neighbouring cabin, he understood, to his consternation and horror, that he was to be the chief witness against the sheep-stealer. Mr Evans's steward knew well the meaning of the words he had over-heard him say in the cabin, and that if compelled to swear all he was aware of, no doubt would exist of the criminality of Michaul in the eyes of a jury.

"Tis a sthrange thing to ax a father to do,' muttered Peery, more than once as he proceeded to the magistrate's; 'it's a very sthrange thing.'

The magistrate proved to be a humane man. Notwithstanding the zeal of the steward and the policemen, he committed Michaul for trial, without continuing to press the hesitating and bewildered old Peery into any detailed evidence; his nature seemed to rise against the task, and he said to the steward:

'I have enough of facts for making out a committal; if you think the father will be necessary on the trial, subpœna him.'

The steward objected that Peery would abscond, and demanded to have him bound over to prosecute, on two sureties, solvent and respectable. The magistrate assented; Peery could name no bail; and consequently he also was marched to prison, though prohibited from holding the least intercourse with Michaul.

The assizes soon came on. Michaul was arraigned; and, during his plea of 'not guilty', his father appeared, unseen by him, in the gaoler's custody, at the back of the dock, or rather in an inner dock. The trial excited a keen and painful interest in the court, the bar, the jury-box, and the crowds of spectators. It was universally known that a son had stolen a sheep, partly to feed a starving father; and that out of the mouth of that father it was now sought to condemn him.

'What will the old man do?' was the general question which ran through the assembly; and while few of the lower orders could contemplate the possibility of his swearing to the truth, many of their betters scarcely hesitated to make out for him a case of natural necessity to swear falsely.

The trial began. The first witness, the herdsman, proved the loss of the sheep and the finding of the dismembered carcass in the old barn. The policemen and the steward followed to the same effect, and the latter added the allusions which he had heard the father make to the son upon the morning of the arrest of the latter. The steward went down from the table. There was a pause, and complete silence, which the attorney for the prosecution broke by saying to the crier deliberately, 'Call Peery Carroll.'

'Here, sir,' immediately answered Peery, as the gaoler led him by a side door out of the back dock to the table. The prisoner started round; but the new witness against him had passed for an instant into the crowd.

The next instant old Peery was seen ascending the table, assisted by the gaoler and by many other commiserating hands, near him. Every glance fixed on his face. The barristers looked wistfully up from their seats round the table; the judge put a glass to his eye and seemed to study his features attentively. Among the audience there ran a low but expressive murmur of pity and interest.

Though much emaciated by confinement, anguish, and suspense, Peery's cheeks had a flush, and his weak blue eyes glittered. The half-gaping expression of his parched and haggard lips was miserable to see. And yet he did not tremble much, nor appear so confounded as upon the day of his visit to the magistrate.

The moment he stood upright on the table he turned himself fully to the judge, without a glance towards the dock.

'Sit down, sit down, poor man,' said the judge.

'Thanks to you, my lord, I will,' answered Peery, 'only, first I'd ax you to let me kneel, for a little start'; and he accordingly did kneel, and after bowing his head, and forming the sign of the cross on his fore-head, he looked up, and said, 'My Judge in heaven above, 'tis you I pray to keep me to my duty, afore my earthly judge, this day – amen' – and then, repeating the sign of the cross, he seated himself.

The examination of the witness commenced, and humanely pro-ceeded as follows – the counsel for the prosecution taking no notice of the superfluity of Peery's answers.

'Do you know Michaul, or Michael, Carroll, the prisoner at the bar?'

'Afore that night, sir, I believed I knew him well; every thought of his mind, every bit of the heart in his body: afore that night, no living creatur could throw a word at Michaul Carroll, or say he ever forgot his father's renown, or his love of his good God; an' sure the people are afther telling you by this time how it came about that night – an' you, my lord – an' ye, gintlemen – an' all good Chrishthans that hear me; – here I am to help to hang him – my own boy, and my only one – but, for all that, gintlemen, ye ought to think of it; 'twas for the weenock and the ould father that he done it; – indeed, an'deed, we hadn't a pyatee in the place; an' the sickness was among us, a start afore; it took the wife from him, and another babby; an' id had himself down, a week or so beforehand; an' all that day he was looking for work, but couldn't get a hand's turn to do; an' that's the way it was; not a mouthful for me an' little Peery; an', more betoken, he grew sorry for id, in the mornin', an' promised me not to touch a scrap of what was in the barn, – ay, long afore the steward and the peelers came on us, – but was willin' to go among the neighbours an' beg our breakfast, along wid myself, from door to door, sooner than touch it.'

'It is my painful duty,' resumed the barrister, when Peery would at length cease, 'to ask you for closer information. You saw Michael Carroll in the barn that night?'

'*Musha* – The Lord pity him and me – I did, sir,'

'Doing what?'

'The sheep between his hands,' answered Peery, dropping his head, and speaking almost inaudibly.

'I must still give you pain, I fear; stand up, take the crier's rod, and if you see Michael Carroll in court lay it on his head.'

'*Och, musha, musha*, sir, don't ax me to do that!' pleaded Peery, rising, wringing his hands, and for the first time weeping – 'och, don't, my lord, don't, and may your own judgment be favourable, the last day.'

'I am sorry to command you to do it, witness, but you must take the rod,' answered the judge, bending his head close to his notes, to hide his own tears; and, at the same time, many a veteran barrister rested his forehead on the edge of the table. In the body of the court were heard sobs.

'Michaul, *avich*! Michaul, *a corra-ma-chree*!' exclaimed Peery, when at length he took the rod, and faced round to his son, 'is id your father they make to do it, *ma-bauchal*?'

'My father does what is right,' answered Michael, in Irish.

The judge immediately asked to have his words translated; and when he learned their import, regarded the prisoner with satisfaction.

'We rest here, my lord,' said the counsel, with the air of a man freed from a painful task. The judge instantly turned to the jury-box:

'Gentlemen of the jury, that the prisoner at the bar stole the sheep in question, there can be no shade of moral doubt. But you have a very peculiar case to consider. A son steals a sheep that his own famishing father and his own famishing son may have food. His aged parent is compelled to give evidence against him here for the act. The old man virtuously tells the truth, and the whole truth, before you and me. He sacrifices his natural feelings – and we have seen that they are lively – to his honesty, and to his religious sense of the sacred obligations of an oath. Gentlemen, I will pause to observe that the old man's conduct is strikingly exemplary, and even noble. It teaches all of us a lesson. Gentlemen, it is not within the province of a judge to censure the rigour of the proceedings which have sent him before us. But I venture to anticipate your pleasure that, notwithstanding all the evidence given, you will be enabled to acquit the old man's son, the prisoner at the bar. I have said there cannot be the shade of a moral doubt that he has stolen the sheep, and I repeat the words. But, gentlemen, there is a legal doubt, to the full benefit of which he is entitled. The sheep has not been identified. The herdsman could not venture to identify it (and it would have been strange if he could) from the dismembered limbs found in the barn. To his mark on its skin, indeed, he might have positively spoken; but no skin has been discovered. Therefore, according to the evidence, and you have sworn to decide by that alone, the prisoner is entitled to your acquittal. Possibly, now that that prosecutor sees the case in its full bearing, he may be pleased with this result.'

While the jury, in evident satisfaction, prepared to return their verdict, Mr Evans, who had but a moment before returned home, entered the court, and becoming aware of the concluding words of the judge, expressed his sorrow aloud that the prosecution had ever been undertaken, that circumstances had kept him uninformed of it, though it had gone on in his name; and he begged leave to assure his lordship that it would be his future effort to keep Michaul Carroll in his former path of honesty, by finding him honest and ample employment, and, as far as in him lay, to reward the virtue of the old father.

While Peery Carroll was laughing and crying in a breath, in the arms of his delivered son, a subscription, commenced by the bar, was mounting into a considerable sum for his advantage.

THOMAS CROFTON CROKER

Daniel O'Rourke

Thomas Crofton Croker (1798–1854) was born in Cork. He was famous as a folklorist and was the author of Fairy Legends and Traditions of the South of Ireland *(1825). He also wrote* The Adventures of Barney Mahony *and* My Village versus Our Village.

PEOPLE may have heard of the renowned adventures of Daniel O'Rourke, but how few are there who know that the cause of all his perils, above and below, was neither more nor less than his having slept under the walls of the Phooka's tower! I knew the man well; he lived at the bottom of Hungry Hill, just at the right-hand side of the road as you go towards Bantry.

An old man was he at the time that he told me the story, with grey hair and a red nose: and it was on June 25, 1813, that I heard it from his own lips, as he sat smoking his pipe under the old poplar tree, on as fine an evening as ever shone from the sky. I was going to visit the caves in Dursey Island, having spent the morning at Glengariff.

'I am often *axed* to tell it, sir,' said he, 'so that this is not the first time. The master's son, you see, had come from beyond foreign parts in France and Spain, as young gentlemen used to go, before Buonaparte or any such was heard of; and sure enough there was a dinner given to all the people on the ground, gentle and simple, high and low, rich and poor. The *ould* gentlemen were the gentlemen, after all, saving your honour's presence. They'd swear at a body a little, to be sure, and maybe give one a cut of a whip now and then, but we were no losers by it in the end; and they were so easy and civil, and kept such rattling houses, and thousands of welcomes; and there was no grinding for rent, and few agents; and there was hardly a tenant on the estate that did not taste of his landlord's bounty often and often in the year; – but now it's another thing: no matter for that, sir, for I'd better be telling you my story.

'Well, we had everything of the best, and plenty of it; and we ate, and we drank, and we danced, and the young master by the same token danced with Peggy Barry, from the Bohereen – a lovely young couple they were, though they are both low enough now. To make a long story short, I got, as a body may say, the same thing as tipsy almost, for I can't remember ever at all, no ways, how it was I left the place: only I did leave it, that's certain. Well, I thought, for all that, in myself, I'd just step to Molly Cronohan's, the fairy-woman, to speak a word about the bracket heifer that was bewitched; and so as I was crossing the stepping-stones of the ford of Ballyasheenough, and was looking up at the stars and blessing myself – for why? it was Lady-day – I missed my foot, and souse I fell into the water. "Death alive!" thought I, "I'll be drowned now!"

'However, I began swimming, swimming, swimming away for the dear life, till at last I got ashore, somehow or other, but never the one of me can tell how, upon a *dissolute* island.

'I wandered and wandered about there, without knowing where I wandered, until at last I got into a big bog. The moon was shining as bright as day, or your fair lady's eyes, sir (with your pardon for mentioning her), and l looked east and west, and north and south, and every way, and nothing did I see but bog, bog, bog; – I could never find out how I got into it; and my heart grew cold with fear, for sure and certain I was that it would be my *berrin* place. So I sat down upon a stone, which, as good luck would have it, was close by me, and I began to scratch my head and sing the *Ullagone* – when all of a sudden the moon grew black, and I looked up, and saw something for all the world as if it was moving down between me and it, and I could not tell what it was. Down it came with a pounce, and looked at me full in the face; and what was it but an eagle? as fine a one as ever flew from the kingdom of Kerry.

'So he looked at me in the face, and says he to me, "Daniel O'Rourke," says he. "how do you do?"

'"Very well, I thank you, sir," says I; "I hope you're well"; wondering out of my senses all the time how an eagle came to speak like a Christian.

'"What brings you here, Dan?" says he.

'"Nothing at all, sir," says I; "only I wish I was safe home again."

'"Is it out of the island you want to go, Dan?" says he.

'"'Tis, sir," says I; so I up and told him how I had taken a drop too much; and fell into the water; how I swam to the island; and how I got into the bog and did not know my way out of it.

'"Dan," says he after a minute's thought, "though it is very improper for you to get drunk on Lady-day, yet as you are a decent sober man, who 'tends mass well, and never flings stones at me nor mine, nor cries out after us in the fields – my life for yours," says he; "so get up on my back, and grip me well for fear you'd fall off, and I'll fly you out of the bog."

'"I am afraid," says I, "your honour's making game of me; for who ever heard of riding a-horseback on an eagle before?"

'"'Pon the honour of a gentleman," says he, putting his right foot on his breast, "I am quite in earnest; and so now either take my offer or starve in the bog; besides, I see that your weight is sinking the stone."

'It was true enough as he said, for I found the stone every minute going from under me. I had no choice; so thinks I to myself, faint heart never won fair lady, and this is fair persuadance: – "I thank your honour," says I, "for the loan of your civility, and I'll take your kind offer."

'I therefore mounted upon the back of the eagle, and held him tight enough by the throat, and up he flew in the air like a lark. Little I knew the trick he was going to serve me. Up, up, up – God knows how far up he flew.

'"Why, then," said I to him – thinking he did not know the right

road home – very civilly, because why? – I was in his power entirely; –
"sir," says I, "please your honour's glory, and with humble submission
to your better judgment, if you'd fly down a bit, you're now just over
my cabin, and I could be put down there, and many thanks to your
worship."

'"*Arrah*, Dan," said he, "do you think me a fool? Look down in the
next field, and don't you see two men and a gun? By my word it
would be no joke to be shot this way, to oblige a drunken blackguard
that I picked up off of a *could* stone in a bog."

'"Bother you," said I to myself, but I did not speak out, for where
was the use? Well, sir, up he kept flying, flying, and I asking him every
minute to fly down, and all to no use.

'"Where in the world are you going, sir?" says I to him.

'"Hold your tongue, Dan," says he; "mind your own business, and
don't be interfering with the business of other people."

'"Faith, this is my business, I think," says I.

'"Be quiet, Dan," says he; so I said no more.

'At last where should we come to but to the moon itself. Now you
can't see it from this, but there is, or there was in my time, a reaping-
hook sticking out of the side of the moon, this way' (drawing the
figure thus on the ground with the end of his stick).

'"Dan," said the eagle, "I'm tired with this long fly; I had no notion
'twas so far."

'"And my lord, sir," said I, "who in the world *axed* you to fly so far
– was it I? Did not I beg, and pray, and beseech you to stop half an
hour ago?'

'"There's no use talking, Dan," said he, "I'm tired bad enough, so
you must get off and sit down on the moon until I rest myself."

'"Is it sit down on the moon?" said I; "is it upon that little round
thing, then? why then, sure, I'd fall off in a minute, and be *kilt* and
split, and smashed all to bits: you are a vile deceiver – so you are."

'"Not at all, Dan," said he; "you can catch fast hold of the reaping-
hook that's sticking out of the side of the moon, and 'twill keep you
up."

'"I won't then," said I.

' "Maybe not," said he quite quiet. "If you don't, my man, I shall just give you a shake, and one slap of my wing, and send you down to the ground, where every bone in your body will be smashed as small as a drop of dew on a cabbage-leaf in the morning."

' "Why, then, I'm in a fine way," said I to myself, "ever to have come along with the likes of you"; and so giving him a hearty curse in Irish, for fear he'd know what I said, I got off his back with a heavy heart, took a hold of the reaping-hook, and sat down upon the moon; and a mighty cold seat it was, I can tell you that.

'When he had me there fairly landed, he turned about on me, and said, "Good-morning to you, Daniel O'Rourke," said he, "I think I've nicked you fairly now. You robbed my nest last year" ('twas true enough for him, but how he found it out is hard to say), "and in return you are freely welcome to cool your heels dangling upon the moon like a cockthrow."

' "Is that all, and is this the way you leave me, your brute you?" says I. "You ugly unnatural *baste*, and is this the way you serve me at last? Bad luck to yourself, with your hook'd nose, and to all your breed, you blackguard."

' "'Twas all to no manner of use; he spread out his great big wings, burst out a-laughing, and flew away like lightening. I bawled after him to stop; but I might have called and bawled for ever without his minding me. Away he went, and I never saw him from that day to this – sorrow fly away with him! You may be sure I was in a disconsolate condition, and kept roaring out for the bare grief, when all at once a door opened right in the middle of the moon, creaking on its hinges as if it had not been opened for a month before – I suppose they never thought of greasing 'em – and out there walks – who do you think but the man in the moon himself? I knew him by his bush.

' "Good-morrow to you, Daniel O'Rourke," said he: "how do you do?"

' "Very well, thank your honour," said I. "I hope your honour's well."

' "What brought you here, Dan?" said he. So I told him how I was a little overtaken in liquor at the master's, and how I was cast on a *dissolute* island, and how I lost my way in the bog, and how the thief of an eagle promised to fly me out of it, and how instead of that he had fled me up to the moon.

' "Dan," said the man in the moon, taking a pinch of snuff, when I was done, "you must not stay here."

' "Indeed, sir," says I, "'tis much against my will I'm here at all; but how am I to go back?"

' "That's your business," said he, "Dan: mine is to tell you that here you must not stay, so be off in less than no time."

' "I'm doing no harm," says I, "only holding on hard by the reaping-hook lest I fall off."

' "That's what you must not do, Dan," says he.

' "Pray, sir," says I, "may I ask how many you are in family that you would not give a poor traveller lodging: I'm sure 'tis not so often you're troubled with strangers coming to see you, for 'tis a long way."

' "I'm by myself, Dan," says he; "but you'd better let go the reaping-hook."

' "Faith, and with your leave," says I, "I'll not let go the grip, and the more you bids me, the more I won't let go – so I will."

' "You had better, Dan," says he again.

' "Why, then, my little fellow," says I, taking the whole weight of him with my eye from head to foot, "there are two words to that bargain; and I'll not budge, but you may if you like."

' "We'll see how that is to be," says he; and back he went, giving the door such a great bang after him (for it was plain he was huffed) and I thought the moon and all would fall down with it.

'Well, I was preparing myself to try strength with him, when back again he comes with the kitchen cleaver in his hand, and without saying a word, he gives two bangs to the handle of the reaping-hook that was keeping me up, and *whap!* it came in two.

' "Good-morning to you, Dan," says the spiteful little old black-guard when he saw me cleanly falling down with a bit of the handle in my hand: "I thank you for your visit, and fair weather after you, Daniel."

'I had not time to make any answer to him, for I was tumbling over and over, and rolling and rolling at the rate of a fox-hunt. "God help me," says I, "but this is a pretty pickle for a decent man to be seen in at this time of night; I am now sold fairly."

'The word was not out of my mouth, when whiz! what should fly by close to my ear but a flock of wild geese, all the way from my own bog of Ballyasheenough, else how should they know *me*? The *ould* gander, who was their general, turning about his head, cried out to me, "Is that you, Dan?"

' "The same," said I, not a bit daunted now at what he said, for I was by this time used to all kinds of *bedevilment*, and, besides, I knew him of *ould*.

' "Good-morrow to you," says he, "Daniel O'Rourke; how are you in health this morning?"

' "Very well, sir," says I, "I thank you kindly," drawing my breath, for I was mightily in want of some. "I hope your honour's the same."

' "I think 'tis falling you are, Daniel," says he.

' "You may say that, sir," says I.

' "And where are you going all the way so fast?" said the gander.

'So I told him how I had taken the drop, and how I came on the island, and how I lost my way in the bog, and how the thief of an eagle flew me up to the moon, and how the man in the moon turned me out.

' "Dan," said he, "I'll save you; put out your hand and catch me by the leg, and I'll fly you home."

' "Sweet is your hand in a pitcher of honey, my jewel," says I, though all the time I thought in myself that I don't much trust you; but there was no help, so I caught the gander by the leg, and away I and the other geese flew after him as fast as hops.

'We flew, and we flew, and we flew, until we came right over the wide ocean. I knew it well, for I saw Cape Clear to my right hand sticking up out of the water.

' "Ah! my lord," said I to the goose, for I thought it best to keep a civil tongue in my head anyway, "fly to land, if you please."

' "It is impossible, you see, Dan," said he, "for a while, because you see we are going to Arabia."

' "To Arabia?" said I; "that's surely some place in foreign parts, far away. Oh, Mr Goose! why then, to be sure, I'm a man to be pitied among you."

' "Whist, whist, you fool," said he, "hold your tongue; I tell you Arabia is a very decent sort of place, as like West Carbery as one egg is like another, only there is a little more sand there."

'Just as we were talking a ship hove in sight, scudding so beautiful before the wind: "Ah! then, sir," said I, "will you drop me on the ship, if you please?"

' "We are not fair over it," said he.

' "We are," said I.

' "We are not," said he, "If I dropped you now, you would go splash into the sea."

' "I would not," says I: "I know better than that, for it's just clean under us, so let me drop now at once."

' "If you must, you must," said he. "There, take your own way"; and he opened his claw, and faith he was right – sure enough I came down plump into the very bottom of the salt sea! Down to the very bottom I went, and I gave myself up then for ever, when a whale walked up to me, scratching himself after his night's sleep, and looked me full in the face, and never the word did he say, but lifting up his tail he splashed me all over again with the cold salt water, till there wasn't a dry stitch upon my whole carcass; and I heard somebody saying – 'twas a voice I knew too – "Get up, you drunken brute, off of that"; and with that I woke up, and there was Judy with a tub full of water, which she was splashing all over me, – for, rest her soul! though she was a good wife, she never could bear to see in drink, and had a bitter hand of her own!

' "Get up," said she again; "and of all places in the parish would no place *save* your turn to lie down upon but under the *ould* walls of Carrigaphooka? an uneasy resting I am sure you had of it."

'And sure enough I had; for I was fairly bothered out of my senses with eagles, and men of the moon, and flying ganders, and whales, driving me through bogs, and up to the moon, and down to the bottom of the green ocean. If I was in drink ten times over, long would it be before I'd lie down in the same spot again, I know that."

GERALD GRIFFIN

The Dilemma of Phadrig

Gerald Griffin (1803–1840) was born at Limerick. He was a writer of great promise who died young. 'The Dilemma of Phadrig' with its delight in old Irish superstitions is one of his most characteristic offerings. He wrote many stories and novels but in 1838 he burned all his manuscripts and entered the Christian Brothers and devoted himself to teaching in the North Monastery, Cork.

'There's no use in talken about it, Phadrig. I know an' I feel that all's over wit me. My pains are all gone, to be sure – but in place o' that, there's a weight like a quern stone down upon my heart, an I feel it blackenen within me. All I have to say is – think o' your own Mauria when she's gone, an be kind to poor Patcy.'

'Ah, darlen, don't talk that way – there's hopes yet – what'll I do, what'll the child do witout you?'

'Phadrig, there's noan. I'm goen fast, an if you have any regard for me, you won't say anythin that'll bring the thoughts o' you an him between me an the thoughts o' heaven, for that's what I must think of now. An if you marry again –'

'Oh, Mauria, honey, will you kill me entirely? Is it *I'll* marry again?'

'– If it be a thing you should marry again,' Mauria resumed, without taking any notice of her husband's interruption, 'you'll bear in mind that the best mother that ever walked the ground will love her own above another's. It stands with raisin an natur. The gander abroad will pull a strange goslen out of his own flock; and you know yourself, we could never get the bracket hen to sit upon Nelly O'Leary's chickens, do what we could. Everything loves its own. Then, Phadrig, if you see the floury potaties – an the top o' the milk – an the warm seat be the hob – an the biggest bit o' meat on a Sunday goen away from Patcy – you'll think o' your poor Mauria, an do her part by him; just quietly, and softly, an without blamen the woman – for it is only what's nait'rel, an what many a stepmother does without thinking o' themselves. An above all things, Phadrig, take care to make him mind his books and his religion, to keep out o' bad company, an study his readin-made-aisy, and that's the way he'll be a blessing an a comfort to you in your old days, as I once thought he would be to me in mine.'

Here her husband renewed his promises in a tone of deep affliction.

'An now for yourself, Phadrig. Remember the charge that's upon you, and don't be goen out venturen your life in a little canvas canoe, on the bad autumn days, at Ballybunion; nor wit foolish boys at the Glin and Tarbert fairs' – an don't be so wake-minded as to be trusten to card-drawers, an fairy doctors, an the like; for it's the last word the priest said to me was, that you were too superstitious, and that's a great shame an a heavy sin. But tee you! Phadrig, dear, there's that rogue of a pig at the potaties over –'

Phadrig turned out the grunting intruder, bolted the hurdle-door, and returned to the bedside of his expiring helpmate. That tidy housekeeper, however, exhausted by the exertion which she had made to preserve, from the mastication of the swinish tusk, the fair produce of her husband's conacre of white-eyes, had fallen back on the pillow and breathed her last.

Great was the grief of the widowed Phadrig for her loss – great were the lamentations of her female friends at the evening wake – and great was the jug of whisky-punch which the mourners imbibed at the mouth, in order to supply the loss of fluid which was expended from the eyes. According to the usual cottage etiquette, the mother of the deceased, who acted as mistress of the ceremonies, occupied a capacious hay-bottomed chair near the fireplace – from which she only rose when courtesy called on her to join each of her female acquaintances as they arrived, in the death-wail which (as in politeness bound) they poured forth over the pale piece of earth that lay coffined in the centre of the room. This mark of attention, however, the old lady was observed to omit with regard to one of the fair guests – a round-faced, middle-aged woman, called Milly Rue – or Red Milly, probably because her head might have furnished a solution of the popular conundrum, 'Why is a red-haired lady like a sentinel on his post?'

The fair Milly, however, did not appear to resent this slight, which was occasioned (so the whisper went among the guests) by the fact that she had been an old and neglected love of the new widower. All the fiery ingredients in Milly's constitution appeared to be comprehended in her glowing ringlets – and those, report says, were as ardent in hue as their owner was calm and regulated in her temper. It would be a cold morning, indeed, that a sight of Milly's head would not warm you – and a hot fit of anger which a few tones of her kind and wrath-disarming voice would not cool. She dropped, after she had concluded her 'cry', a conciliating curtsey to the sullen old lady, took an unobtrusive seat at the foot of the bed, talked of the 'notable' qualities of the deceased, and was particularly attentive to the flaxen-headed little Patcy, whom she held in her lap during the whole night, cross-examining him in his reading and multiplication, and presenting him, at parting, in token of her satisfaction at his proficiency, with a copy of *The Seven Champions of Christendom*, with a fine marble cover and pictures. Milly acted in this instance under the advice of a prudent mother, who exhorted her, 'whenever she thought o' maken presents, that way, not to be layen her money out in cakes or gingerbread, or things that would be ett off at wanst, an no more about them or the giver – but to give a strong toy, or a book, or somethen that would last, and bring her to mind now and then, so as that when a person 'ud ask where they got that, or who gev it, they'd say, "from Milly Rue," or "Milly gev it, we're obleest to her," an' be talken an thinken of her when she'd be away.'

To curb in my tale, which may otherwise become restive and unmanageable – Milly's deep affliction and generous sympathy made a serious impression on the mind of the widower, who more than all was touched by that singularly accidental attachment which she seemed to have conceived for little Patcy. Nothing could be farther from his own wishes than any design of a second time changing his condition; but he felt that it would be going a grievous wrong to the memory of his first wife if he neglected this opportunity of providing her favourite Patcy with a protector, so well calculated to supply her place. He demurred a little on the score of true love, and the violence which he was about to do his own constant heart – but like the bluff King Henry, his conscience – 'aye – his conscience,' – touched him, and the issue was that a roaring wedding shook the walls which had echoed to the wail of death within the few preceding months.

Milly Rue not only supplied the place of a mother to young Patcy, but presented him in the course of a few years with two merry play-fellows, a brother and a sister. To do her handsome justice, too, poor Mauria's anticipations were completely disproved by her conduct, and it would have been impossible for a stranger to have detected the stepson of the house from any shade of undue partiality in the mother. The harmony in which they dwelt was unbroken by any accident for many years.

The first shock which burst in with a sudden violence upon their happiness was one of a direful nature. Disease, that pale and hungry fiend who haunts alike the abodes of wealth and of penury; who brushes away with his baleful wing the bloom from beauty's cheek, and the balm of slumber from the pillow of age; who troubles the hope of the young mother with dreams of ghastliness and gloom, and fears that come suddenly, she knows not why nor whence; who sheds his poisonous dews alike on the heart that is buoyant and the heart that is broken; this stern and conquering demon scorned not to knock, one summer morning, at the door of Phadrig's cow-house, and to lay his iron fingers upon a fine milch-cow, a sheeted-stripper which con-stituted (to use his own emphatic phrase) the poor farmer's 'substance', and to which he might have applied the well-known lines which run nearly as follows:

She's straight in her back, and thin in her tail;

> She's fine in her horn, and good at the pail;
> She's calm in her eyes, and soft in her skin;
> She's a grazier's without, and a butcher's within.

All the 'cures' in the pharmacopoeia of the village apothecary were expended on the poor animal, without any beneficial effect; and Phadrig, after many conscientious qualms about the dying words of his first wife, resolved to have recourse to that infallible refuge in such cases – a fairy doctor.

He said nothing to the afflicted Milly about his intention, but slipped out of the cottage in the afternoon, hurried to the Shannon side near Money Point, unmoored his light canvas-built canoe, seated himself in the frail vessel, and fixing his paddles on the *towl-pin*, sped away over the calm face of the waters towards the isle of Scattery, where the renowned Crohoore-na-Oona, or Connor-of-the-Sheep, the Mohammed of the cottages, at this time took up his residence. This mysterious personage, whose prophecies are still commented on among the cottage circles with looks of deep awe and wonder, was much revered by his contemporaries as a man 'who had seen a dale'; of what nature those sights or visions were was intimated by a mysterious look, and a solemn nod of the head.

In a little time Phadrig ran his little canoe aground on the sandy beach of Scattery, and, drawing her above high-water mark, proceeded to the humble dwelling of the gifted Sheep-shearer with feelings of profound fear and anxiety. He passed the lofty round tower – the ruined grave of St Senanus, in the centre of the little isle – the mouldering church, on which the eye of the poring antiquary may still discern the sculptured image of the two-headed monster, with which cottage tradition says the saint sustained so fierce a conflict on landing in the islet – and which the translator of Odranus has vividly described as 'a dragon, with his fore-part covered with huge bristles, standing on end like those of a boar; his mouth gaping wide open with a double row of crooked, sharp tusks, and with such openings that his entrails might be seen; his back like a round island, full of scales and shells; his legs short and hairy, with such steely talons, that the pebble-stones, as he ran along them, sparkled – parching the way wherever he went, and making the sea boil about him where he dived – such was his excessive fiery heat.' Phadrig's knees shook beneath him when he remembered this awful description – and thought of the legends of Lough Dhoola, on the summit of Mount Callon, to which the hideous animal was banished by the saint, to fast on a trout and a half per diem to the end of time; and where, to this day, the neighbouring fishermen declare that, in dragging the lake with their nets, they find the half trout as regularly divided in the centre as if it were done with a knife and scale.

While Phadrig remained with mouth and eyes almost as wide open as those of the sculptured image of the monster which had fascinated him to the spot, a sudden crash among the stones and dock-weed in an opposite corner of the ruin made him start and yell as if the original were about to quit Lough Dhoola on parole of honour, and use him as a relish after the trout and a half. The noise was occasioned by a little rotund personage, who had sprung from the mouldering wall, and now stood gazing fixedly on the terrified Phadrig, who continued returning that steady glance with a half-frightened, half-crying face – one hand fast clenched upon his breast, and the other extended, with an action of avoidance and deprecation. The person of the stranger was stout and short, rendered still more so by a stoop, which might almost have been taken for a hump – his arms hung forward from his shoulders, like those of a long-armed ape – his hair was grey and bushy, like that of a wanderoo – and his sullen grey eye seemed to be inflamed with ill-humour – his feet were bare and as broad as a camel's – and a leathern girdle buckling round his waist secured a tattered grey frieze riding-coat, and held an enormous pair of shears, which might have clipped off a man's head as readily, perhaps, as a lock of wool. This last article of costume afforded a sufficient indication to Phadrig that he stood in the presence of the awful object of his search.

'Well! an who are *you*?' growled the Sheep-shearer, after surveying Phadrig attentively for some moments.

The first gruff sound of his voice made the latter renew his start and roar for fright; after which, composing his terrors as well as he might, he replied, in the words of Autolycus, 'I am only a poor fellow, sir.'

'Well! an what's your business with me?'

'A cure, sir, I wanted for her. A cow o' mine that's very bad inwardly, an we can do nothen for her; an I thought may be you'd know what is it ail'ded her – an prevail on *them*' (this word was pronounced with an emphasis of deep meaning) 'to leave her to uz.'

'Huth!' the Sheep-shearer thundered out, in a tone that made poor Phadrig jump six feet backwards with a fresh yell, 'do you daare to spake of *them* before me. Go along! you villyan o' the airth, an wait for me outside the church, an I'll tell you all about it there; but, first – do you think I can get the *gentlemen* to do anything for me *gratish* – without offeren 'em a trate or a haip'-orth?'

'If their honours wouldn't think two tin-pennies and a fi'penny bit too little – It's all I'm worth in the wide world.'

'Well! we'll see what they'll say to it. Give it here to me. Go now – be off with yourself – if you don't want to have 'em all a-top o' you in a minnit.'

This last hint made our hero scamper over the stones like a startled fawn; nor did he think himself safe until he reached the spot where he had left his canoe, and where he expected the coming of the Sheep-shearer; conscience-struck by the breach of his promise to his dying Mauria, and in a state of agonizing anxiety with respect to the lowing patient in the cow-house.

He was soon after rejoined by Connor-of-the-Sheep.

'There is one way,' said he, 'of saving your cow – but you must lose one of your childer if you wish to save it.'

'O Heaven presarve uz, sir, how is that, if you plase?'

'You must go home,' said the Sheep-shearer, 'and say nothen to anybody, but fix in your mind which o' your three childer you'll give for the cow; an when you do that, look in his eyes, an he'll sneeze, an don't you bless him, for the world. Then look in his eyes again, an he'll sneeze again, an still don't think o' blessen him, be any mains. The third time you'll look in his eyes he'll sneeze a third time – an if you don't bless him the third time, he'll die – but your cow will live.'

'An this is the only cure you have to gi' me?' exclaimed Phadrig, his indignation at the moment overcoming his natural timidity.

'The only cure. It was by a dale to do I could prevail on them to let you make the choice itself.'

Phadrig declared stoutly against this decree, and even threw out some hints that he would try whether or no Shaun Lauther, or Strong John, a young rival of the sheep-shearing fairy doctor, might be able to make a better bargain for him with the 'gentlemen'.

'Shaun Lauther!' exclaimed Connor-of-the-Sheep, in high anger – 'Do you compare me to a man that never seen any more than yourself? – that never saw so much as the skirt of a dead man's shroud in the moonlight – or heard as much as the moanen of a sowlth[1] in an old graveyard? Do you know me? Ask them that do – an they'll tell you how often I'm called up in the night, and kep posten over bog an mountain, till I'm ready to drop down with the sleep – while few voices are heard, I'll be bail, at Shaun Lauther's windey – a little knollidge given him in his drames. It is then that I get mine. Didn't I say before the King o' France was beheaded that a blow would be struck wit an axe in that place, that the sound of it would be heard all over Europe? An wasn't it true? Didn't I hear the shots that were fired at Gibaralthur, an tell it over in Dooly's forge, that the place was relieved that day? – an didn't the news come afterwards in a month's time that I toult nothen but the truth?'

Phadrig had nothing to say in answer to this overwhelming list of interrogatories – but to apologize for his want of credulity, and to express himself perfectly satisfied.

With a heavy heart he put forth in his canoe upon the water and prepared to return. It was already twilight, and as he glided along the peaceful shores he ruminated mournfully within his mind on the course which he should pursue. The loss of the cow would be, he considered, almost equivalent to total ruin – and the loss of any one of his lovely children was a probability which he could hardly bear to dwell on for a moment. Still it behoved him to weigh the matter well.

[1] Bodiless spirit.

Which of them now – supposing it possible that he could think of sacrificing any – which of them would he select for the purpose? The choice was a hard one. There was little Mauria, a fair-haired, blue-eyed little girl – but he could not, for an instant, think of losing her, as she happened to be named after his first wife; her brother, little Shamus, was the least useful of the three, but he was the youngest – 'the child of his old age – a little one!' His heart bled at the idea; he would lose the cow, the pig along with it, before he would harm a hair of the darling infant's head. He thought of Patcy – and he shuddered and leaned heavier on his oars, as if to flee away from the horrible doubt which stole into his heart with that name. It must be one of the three, or the cow was lost for ever. The two first-mentioned he certainly would not lose – and Patcy; Again he bade the fiend begone, and trembling in every limb, made the canoe speed rapidly over the tide in the direction of his home.

He drew the little vessel ashore and proceeded towards his cabin. They had been waiting supper for him, and he learned with renewed anxiety that the object of his solicitude, the milch-cow, had rather fallen away than improved in her condition during his absence. He sat down in sorrowful silence with his wife and children to their humble supper of potatoes and thick milk.

He gazed intently on the features of each of the young innocents as they took their places on the suggan chairs that flanked the board. Little Mauria and her brother Shamus looked fresh, mirthful, and blooming from their noisy play in the adjoining paddock, while their elder brother, who had spent the day at school, wore – or seemed, to the distempered mind of his father, to wear a look of sullenness and chagrin. He was thinner, too, than most boys of his age – a circumstance which Phadrig had never remarked before. It might be the first indications of his poor mother's disease, consumption, that were beginning to declare themselves in his constitution; and if so, his doom was already sealed – and whether the cow died or not, Patcy was certain to be lost. Still the father could not bring his mind to resolve on any settled course, and their meal proceeded in silence.

Suddenly the latch of the door was lifted by some person outside,

and a neighbour entered to inform Phadrig that the agent to his
landlord had arrived in the adjacent village for the purpose of driving
matters to extremity against all those tenants who remained in arrear.
At the same moment, too, a low moan of anguish from the cow
outside announced the access of a fresh paroxysm of her distemper,
which it was very evident the poor animal could never come through
in safety.

In an agony of distress and horror the distracted father laid his
clenched fingers on the table, and looked fixedly in the eyes of the
unsuspecting Patcy. The child sneezed, and Phadrig closed his lips
hard, for fear a blessing might escape him. The child at the same time,
he observed, looked paler than before.

Fearful lest the remorse which began to awake within his heart
might oversway his resolution, and prevent the accomplishment of his
unnatural design, he looked hurriedly a second time into the eyes of
the little victim. Again the latter sneezed, and again the father, using a
violent effort, restrained the blessing which was struggling at his heart.
The poor child drooped his head upon his bosom, and letting the
untasted food fall from his hand, looked so pale and mournful as to
remind his murderer of the look which his mother wore in dying.

It was long – very long – before the heart-struck parent could
prevail on himself to complete the sacrifice. The visitor departed; and
the first beams of a full moon began to supplant the faint and lingering
twilight which was fast fading in the west. The dead of the night drew
on before the family rose from their silent and comfortless meal. The
agonies of the devoted animal now drew rapidly to a close, and
Phadrig still remained tortured by remorse on the one hand, and by
selfish anxiety on the other.

A sudden sound of anguish from the cow-house made him start
from his seat. A third time he fixed his eyes on those of his child – a
third time the boy sneezed – but here the charm was broken.

Milly Rue, looking with surprise and tenderness on the fainting
boy, said, 'Why, then, Heaven bless you, child! – It must be a cold you
caught, you're sneezen so often.'

Immediately the cow sent forth a bellow of deep agony, and

expired; and at the same moment a low and plaintive voice outside the door was heard, exclaiming, 'And Heaven bless you, Milly! and the Almighty bless you, and spare you a long time over your children!'

Phadrig staggered back against the wall – his blood froze in his veins – his face grew white as death – his teeth chattered – his eyes stared – his hair moved upon his brow, and the chilling damp of terror exuded over all his frame. He recognized the voice of his first wife; and her pale, cold eye met his at that moment, as her shade flitted by the window in the thin moonlight, and darted on him a glance of mournful reproach. He covered his eyes with his hands, and sunk, senseless, into a chair, while the affrighted Milly and Patcy, who at once assumed his glowing health and vigour, hastened to his assistance. They had all heard the voice, but no one saw the shade nor recognized the tone excepting the conscience-smitten Phadrig.

GEORGE MOORE

Home Sickness

George Moore (1852–1933) was from County Mayo. He was Anglo-Irish and one of the co-founders of Dublin's Abbey Theatre. He followed the realistic approach of Zola and Balzac and his best-known collection of short stories is The Untilled Field. *Among his many novels,* Esther Waters *(1894) is his most famous but he also wrote* A Modern Lover *(1833) and his autobiography:* Hail and Farewell *(1911–14).*

HE told the doctor he was due in the bar-room at eight o'clock in the morning; the bar-room was in a slum in the Bowery; and he had only been able to keep himself in health by getting up at five o'clock and going for long walks in the Central Park.

'A sea-voyage is what you want,' said the doctor. 'Why not go to Ireland for two or three months? You will come back a new man.'

'I'd like to see Ireland again.'

And he began to wonder how the people at home were getting on. The doctor was right. He thanked him, and three weeks after he landed in Cork.

As he sat in the railway-carriage he recalled his native village, built among the rocks of the large headland stretching out into the winding lake. He could see the houses and the streets, and the fields of the tenants, and the Georgian mansion and the owners of it; he and they had been boys together before he went to America. He remembered the villagers going every morning to the big house to work in the stables, in the garden, in the fields – mowing, reaping, digging, and

Michael Malia building a wall; it was all as clear as if it were yesterday, yet he had been thirteen years in America; and when the train stopped at the station, the first thing he did was to look round for any changes that might have come into it. It was the same blue limestone station as it was thirteen years ago, with the same five long miles between it and Duncannon. He had once walked these miles gaily, in little over an hour, carrying a heavy bundle on a stick, but he did not feel strong enough for the walk today, though the evening tempted him to try it. A car was waiting at the station, and the boy, discerning from his accent and his dress that Bryden had come from America, plied him with questions, which Bryden answered rapidly, for he wanted to hear who were still living in the village, and if there was a house in which he could get a clean lodging. The best house in the village, he was told, was Mike Scully's, who had been away in a situation for many years, as a coachman in the King's County, but had come back and built a fine house with a concrete floor. The boy could recommend the loft, he had slept in it himself, and Mike would be glad to take in a lodger, he had no doubt. Bryden remembered that Mike had been in a situation at the big house. He had intended to be a jockey, but had suddenly shot up into a fine tall man, and had become a coachman instead; and Bryden tried to recall his face, but could only remember a straight nose and a somewhat dusky complexion.

So Mike had come back from King's County, and had built himself a house, had married – there were children for sure running about; while he, Bryden, had gone to America, but he had come back; perhaps he, too, would build a house in Duncannon, and – his reverie was suddenly interrupted by the carman.

'There's Mike Scully,' he said, pointing with his whip, and Bryden saw a tall, finely built, middle-aged man coming through the gates, who looked astonished when he was accosted, for he had forgotten Bryden even more completely than Bryden had forgotten him; and many aunts and uncles were mentioned before he began to understand.

'You've grown into a fine man, James,' he said, looking at Bryden's great width of chest. 'But you're thin in the cheeks, and you're very sallow in the cheeks too.'

'I haven't been very well lately – that is one of the reasons I've come back; but I want to see you all again.'

'And thousand welcome you are.'

Bryden paid the carman, and wished him 'God-speed'. They divided the luggage, Mike carrying the bag and Bryden the bundle, and they walked round the lake, for the townland was at the back of the domain; and while walking he remembered the woods thick and well forested; now they were wind-worn, the drains were choked, and the bridge leading across the lake inlet was falling away. Their way led between long fields where herds of cattle were grazing, the road was broken – Bryden wondered how the villagers drove their carts over it, and Mike told him that the landlord could not keep it in repair, and he would not allow it to be kept in repair out of the rates, for then it would be a public road, and he did not think there should be a public road through his property.

At the end of many fields they came to the village, and it looked a desolate place, even on this fine evening, and Bryden remarked that the county did not seem to be as much lived in as it used to be. It was at once strange and familiar to see the chickens in the kitchen; and, wishing to re-knit himself to the old customs, he begged of Mrs Scully not to drive them out, saying they reminded him of old times.

'And why wouldn't they?' Mike answered, 'he being one of ourselves bred and born in Duncannon, and his father before him.'

'Now, is it truth ye are telling me?' and she gave him her hand, after wiping it on her apron, saying he was heartily welcome, only she was afraid he wouldn't care to sleep in a loft.

'Why shouldn't I sleep in a loft, a dry loft! You're thinking a good deal of America over here,' he said, 'but I reckon it isn't all you think it. Here you work when you like and you sit down when you like; but when you've had a touch of blood-poisoning as I had, and when you have seen young people walking with a stick, you think that there is something to be said for old Ireland.'

'You'll take a sup of milk, won't you? You must be dry,' said Mrs
Scully.

And when he had drunk the milk, Mike asked him if he would like
to go inside or if he would like to go for a walk.

'Maybe resting you'd like to be.'

And they went into the cabin and started to talk about the wages a
man could get in America, and the long hours of work.

And after Bryden had told Mike everything about America that he
thought of interest, he asked Mike about Ireland. But Mike did not
seem to be able to tell him much. They were all very poor – poorer,
perhaps, then when he left them.

'I don't think anyone except myself has a five-pound note to his
name.'

Bryden hoped he felt sufficiently sorry for Mike. But after all,
Mike's life and prospects mattered little to him. He had come back in
search of health, and he felt better already; the milk had done him
good, and the bacon and the cabbage in the pot sent forth a savoury
odour. The Scullys were very kind, they pressed him to make a good
meal; a few weeks of country air and food, they said, would give him
back the health he had lost in the Bowery; and when Bryden said he
was longing for a smoke, Mike said there was no better sign than that.
During his long illness he had never wanted to smoke, and he was a
confirmed smoker.

It was comfortable to sit by the mild peat fire watching the smoke of
their pipes drifting up the chimney, and all Bryden wanted was to be
left alone; he did not want to hear of anyone's misfortunes, but about
nine o'clock a number of villagers came in, and Bryden remembered
one or two of them – he used to know them very well when he was a
boy; their talk was as depressing as their appearance, and he could feel
no interest whatever in them. He was not moved when he heard that
Higgins the stonemason was dead; he was not affected when he heard
that Mary Kelly, who used to go to do the laundry at the Big House,
had married; he was only interested when he heard she had gone to
America. No, he had not met her there; America is a big place. Then
one of the peasants asked him if he remembered Patsy Carabine, who

used to do the gardening at the Big House. Yes, he remembered Patsy well. He had not been able to do any work on account of his arm; his house had fallen in; he had given up his holding and gone into the poorhouse. All this was very sad, and to avoid hearing any further unpleasantness, Bryden began to tell them about America. And they sat round listening to him; but all the talking was on his side; he wearied of it; and looking round the group he recognized a ragged hunchback with grey hair; twenty years ago he was a young hunchback and, turning to him, Bryden asked him if he were doing well with his five acres.

'Ah, not much. This has been a poor season. The potatoes failed; they were watery – there is no diet in them.'

These peasants were all agreed that they could make nothing out of their farms. Their regret was that they had not gone to America when they were young; and after striving to take an interest in the fact that O'Connor had lost a mare and a foal worth forty pounds, Bryden began to wish himself back in the slum. And when they left the house he wondered if every evening would be like the present one. Mike piled fresh sods on the fire, and he hoped it would show enough light in the loft for Bryden to undress himself by.

The cackling of some geese in the street kept him awake, and he seemed to realize suddenly how lonely the country was, and he foresaw mile after mile of scanty fields stretching all round the lake with one little town in the far corner. A dog howled in the distance, and the fields and the boreens between him and the dog appeared as in a crystal. He could hear Michael breathing by his wife's side in the kitchen, and he could barely resist the impulse to run out of the house, and he might have yielded to it, but he wasn't sure that he mightn't awaken Mike as he came down the ladder. His terror increased, and he drew the blanket over his head. He fell asleep and awoke and fell asleep again, and lying on his back he dreamed of the men he had seen sitting round the fireside that evening, like spectres they seemed to him in his dream. He seemed to have been asleep only a few minutes when he heard Mike calling him. He had come half-way up the ladder, and was telling him that breakfast was ready.

'What kind of a breakfast will he give me?' Bryden asked himself as he pulled on his clothes. There were tea and hot griddle cakes for breakfast, and there were fresh eggs; there was sunlight in the kitchen, and he liked to hear Mike tell of the work he was going to be at in the farm – one of about fifteen acres, at least ten of it was grass; he grew an acre of potatoes, and some corn, and some turnips for his sheep. He had a nice bit of meadow, and he took down his scythe, and as he put the whetstone in his belt Bryden noticed a second scythe, and he asked Mike if he should go down with him and help him to finish the field.

'It's a long time since you've done any mowing, and it's heavier work than you think for. You'd better go for a walk by the lake.' Seeing that Bryden looked a little disappointed he added, 'If you like you can come up in the afternoon and help me to turn the grass over.' Bryden said he would, and the morning passed pleasantly by the lake shore – a delicious breeze rustled in the trees, and the reeds were talking together, and the ducks were talking in the reeds; a cloud blotted out the sunlight, and the cloud passed and the sun shone, and the reed cast its shadow again in the still water; there was a lapping always about the shingle; the magic of returning health was sufficient distraction for the convalescent; he lay with his eyes fixed upon the castles, dreaming of the men that had manned the battlements; whenever a peasant driving a cart or an ass or an old woman with a bundle of sticks on her back went by, Bryden kept them in chat, and he soon knew the village by heart. One day the landlord from the Georgian mansion set on the pleasant green hill came along, his retriever at his heels, and stopped, surprised at finding somebody whom he didn't know on his property. 'What, James Bryden!' he said. And the story was told again how ill health had overtaken him at last, and he had come home to Duncannon to recover. The two walked as far as the pine-wood, talking of the county, what it had been, the ruin it was slipping into, and as they parted Bryden asked for the loan of a boat.

'Of course, of course!' the landlord answered, and Bryden rowed about the islands every morning; and resting upon his oars looked at the old castles, remembering the prehistoric raiders that the landlord had told him about. He came across the stones to which the lake-dwellers had tied their boats, and these signs of ancient Ireland were pleasing to Bryden in his present mood.

As well as the great lake there was a smaller lake in the bog where the villagers cut their turf. This lake was famous for its pike, and the landlord allowed Bryden to fish there, and one evening when he was looking for a frog with which to bait his line he met Margaret Dirken driving home the cows for the milking. Margaret was the herdsman's daughter, and lived in a cottage near the Big House; but she came up to the village whenever there was a dance, and Bryden had found himself opposite to her in the reels. But until this evening he had had little opportunity of speaking to her, and he was glad to speak to someone, for the evening was lonely, and they stood talking together.

'You're getting your health again,' she said, 'and will be leaving us soon.'

'I'm in no hurry.'

'You're grand people over there; I hear a man is paid four dollars a day for his work.'

'And how much,' said James, 'has he to pay for his food and for his clothes?'

Her cheeks were bright and her teeth small, white and beautifully even; and a woman's soul looked at Bryden out of her soft Irish eyes. He was troubled and turned aside, and catching sight of a frog looking at him out of a tuft of grass, he said:

'I have been looking for a frog to put upon my pike line.'

The frog jumped right and left, and nearly escaped in some bushes, but he caught it and returned with it in his hand.

'It is just the kind of frog a pike will like,' he said. 'Look at its great white belly and its bright yellow back.'

And without more ado he pushed the wire to which the hook was fastened through the frog's fresh body, and dragging it through the mouth he passed the hooks through the hind-legs and tied the line to the end of the wire.

'I think,' said Margaret, 'I must be looking after my cows; it's time I got them home.'

'Won't you come down to the lake while I set my line?'

She thought for a moment and said:

'No, I'll see you from here.'

He went down to the reedy tarn, and at his approach several snipe got up, and they flew above his head uttering sharp cries. His fishing-rod was a long hazel-stick, and he threw the frog as far as he could in the lake. In doing this he roused some wild ducks; a mallard and two ducks got up, and they flew towards the larger lake in a line with an old castle; and they had not disappeared from view when Bryden came towards her, and he and she drove the cows home together that evening.

They had not met very often when she said: 'James, you had better not come here so often calling to me.'

'Don't you wish me to come?'

'Yes, I wish you to come well enough, but keeping company isn't the custom of the country, and I don't want to be talked about.'

'Are you afraid the priest would speak against us from the altar?'

'He has spoken against keeping company, but it is not so much what the priest says, for there is no harm in talking.'

'But if you're going to be married, there is no harm in walking out together.'

'Well, not so much, but marriages are made differently in these parts; there isn't much courting here.'

And next day it was known in the village that James was going to marry Margaret Dirken.

His desire to excel the boys in dancing had caused a stir of gaiety in the parish, and for some time past there had been dancing in every house where there was a floor fit to dance upon; and if the cottager had no money to pay for a barrel of beer, James Bryden, who had money, sent him a barrel, so that Margaret might get her dance. She told him that they sometimes crossed over into another parish where the priest was not so averse to dancing, and James wondered. And next morning at Mass he wondered at their simple fervour. Some of them held their hands above their head as they prayed, and all this was very new and very old to James Bryden. But the obedience of these people to their priest surprised him. When he was a lad they had not been so obedient, or he had forgotten their obedience; and he listened in mixed anger and wonderment to the priest, who was scolding his parishioners, speaking to them by name, saying that he had heard there was dancing going on in their homes. Worse than that, he said he had seen boys and girls loitering about the road, and the talk that went on was of one kind – love. He said that newspapers containing love stories were finding their way into the people's houses, stories about love, in which there was nothing elevating or ennobling. The people listened, accepting the priest's opinion without question. And their pathetic submission was the submission of a primitive people clinging to religious authority, and Bryden contrasted the weakness and incompetence of the people about him with the modern rest-lessness and cold energy of the people he left behind him.

One evening, as they were dancing, a knock came to the door, and the piper stopped playing, and the dancers whispered:

'Someone has told on us: it is the priest.'

And the awe-stricken villagers crowded round the cottage fire, afraid to open the door. But the priest said that if they didn't open the door he would put his shoulder to it and force it open. Bryden went towards the door, saying he would allow no one to threaten him, priest or no priest, but Margaret caught his arm and told him that if he said anything to the priest, the priest would speak against them from the altar, and they would be shunned by the neighbours.

'I've heard of your goings-on,' he said, 'of your beer-drinking and dancing. I'll not have it in my parish. If you want that sort of thing you'd had better go to America.'

'If that is intended for me, sir, I'll go back tomorrow. Margaret can follow.'

'It isn't the dancing, it's the drinking I'm opposed to,' said the priest, turning to Bryden.

'Well, no one has drunk too much, sir,' said Bryden.

'But you'll sit here drinking all night,' and the priest's eyes went to the corner where the women had gathered, and Bryden felt that the priest looked on the women as more dangerous than the porter. 'It's after midnight,' he said, taking out his watch.

By Bryden's watch it was only half past eleven, and while they were arguing about the time, Mrs Scully offered Bryden's umbrella to the priest, for in his hurry to stop the dancing the priest had gone out without his; and, as if to show Bryden that he bore him no ill will, the priest accepted the loan of the umbrella, for he was thinking of the big marriage fee that Bryden would pay him.

'I shall be badly off for the umbrella tomorrow,' Bryden said, as soon as the priest was out of the house. He was going with his father-in-law to a fair. His father-in-law was learning him how to buy and sell cattle. The country was mending, and a man might become rich in Ireland if he only had a little capital. Margaret had an uncle on the other side of the lake who would give twenty pounds, and her father would give another twenty pounds. Bryden had saved two hundred pounds. Never in the village of Duncannon had a young couple begun life with so much prospect of success, and some time after Christmas was spoken of as the best time for the marriage; James Bryden said that he would not be able to get his money out of America before the spring. The delay seemed to vex him, and he seemed anxious to be married, until one day he received a letter from America, from a man who had served in the bar with him. This friend wrote to ask Bryden if he were coming back. The letter was no more than a passing wish to see Bryden again. Yet Bryden stood looking at it, and everyone wondered what could be in the letter. It seemed momentous, and they hardly believed him when he said it was from a friend who wanted to know if his health were better. He tried to forget the letter, and he looked at the worn fields, divided by walls of loose stones, and a great longing came upon him.

The smell of the Bowery slum had come across the Atlantic, and had found him out in his western headland; and one night he awoke from a dream in which he was hurling some drunken customer through the open doors into the darkness. He had seen his friend in his white duck jacket throwing drink from glass into glass amid the din of voices and strange accents; he had heard the clang of money as it was swept into the till, and his sense sickened for the bar-room. But how should he tell Margaret Dirken that he could not marry her? She had built her life upon this marriage. He could not tell her that he would not marry her ... yet he must go. He felt as if he were being hunted; the thought that he must tell Margaret that he could not marry her hunted him day after day as a weasel hunts a rabbit. Again and again he went to meet her with the intention of telling her that he did not love her, that their lives were not for one another, that it had all been a mistake, and that happily he had found out it was a mistake soon enough. But Margaret, as if she guessed what he was about to speak of, threw her arms about him and begged him to say he loved her, and that they would be married at once. He agreed that he loved her, and that they would be married at once. But he had not left her many minutes before the feeling came upon him that he could not marry her – that he must go away. The smell of the bar-room hunted him down. Was it for the sake of the money that he might make there that he wished to go back? No, it was not the money. What then? His eyes fell on the bleak country, on the little fields divided by bleak walls; he remembered the pathetic ignorance of the people, and it was these things that he could not endure. It was the priest who came to forbid the dancing. Yes, it was the priest. As he stood looking at the line of the hills, the bar-room seemed by him. He heard the politicians, and the excitement of politics was in his blood again. He must go away from this place – he must get back to the bar-room. Looking up, he saw the scanty orchard, and he hated the spare road that led to the village, and he hated the little hill at the top of which the village began, and he hated more than all other places the house where he was to live with Margaret Dirken – if he married her. He could see it from where he stood – by the edge of the lake, with twenty acres of pasture land about it, for the landlord had given up part of his demesne land to them.

He caught sight of Margaret, and he called her to come through the stile.

'I have just had a letter from America.'

'About the money?'

'Yes, about the money. But I shall have to go over there.'

He stood looking at her, wondering what to say; and she guessed that he would tell her that he must go to America before they were married.

'Do you mean, James, you will have to go at once?'

'Yes,' he said 'at once. But I shall come back in time to be married in August. It will only mean delaying our marriage a month.'

They walked on a little way talking, and every step he took James felt that he was a step nearer the Bowery slum. And when they came to the gate Bryden said:

'I must walk on or I shall miss the train.'

'But,' she said, 'you are not going now – you are not going today?'

'Yes, this morning. It is seven miles. I shall have to hurry not to miss the train.'

And then she asked him if he would ever come back.

'Yes,' he said, 'I am coming back.'

'If you are coming back, James, why don't you let me go with you?'

'You couldn't walk fast enough. We should miss the train.'

'One moment, James. Don't make me suffer; tell me the truth. You are not coming back. Your clothes – where shall I send them?'

He hurried away, hoping he would come back. He tried to think that he liked the country he was leaving, that it would be better to have a farmhouse and live there with Margaret Dirken than to serve drinks behind a counter in the Bowery. He did not think he was telling her a lie when he said he was coming back. Her offer to forward his clothes touched his heart, and at the end of the road he stood and asked himself if he should go back to her. He would miss the train if he waited another minute, and he ran on. And he would have missed the train if he had not met a car. Once he was on the car he felt himself safe – the country was already behind him. The train and the boat at Cork were mere formulae; he was already in America.

And when the tall skyscraper stuck up beyond the harbour, he felt the thrill of home that he had not found in his native village and wondered how it was that the smell of the bar seemed more natural than the smell of fields, and the roar of crowds more welcome than the

silence of the lake's edge. He entered into negotiations for the purchase of the bar-room. He took a wife, she bore him sons and
daughters, the bar-room prospered, property came and went; he grew
old, his wife died, he retired from business, and reached the age when
a man begins to feel there are not many years in front of him, and that
all he has had to do in life has been done. His children married,
lonesomeness began to creep about him in the evening, and when he
looked into the firelight, a vague tender reverie floated up, and
Margaret's soft eyes and name vivified the dusk. His wife and children
passed out of mind, and it seemed to him that a memory was the only
real thing he possessed, and the desire to see Margaret again grew
intense. But she was an old woman, she had married, maybe she was
dead. Well, he would like to be buried in the village where he was
born.

There is an unchanging, silent life within every man that none
knows but himself, and his unchanging silent life was his memory of
Margaret Dirken. The bar-room was forgotten and all that concerned
it, and the things he saw most clearly were the green hillside, and the
bog lake and the rushes about it, and the greater lake in the distance,
and behind it the blue line of wandering hills.

GEORGE MOORE

Some Parishioners

I

THE way before Father Maguire was plain enough, yet his uncle's apathy and constitutional infirmity of purpose seemed at times to thwart him. Only two or three days ago, he had come running down from Kilmore with the news that a baby had been born out of wedlock, and what do you think? Father Stafford had shown no desire that his curate should denounce the girl from the altar.

'The greatest saints,' he said, 'have been kind, and have found excuses for the sins of others.'

And a few days later, when he told his uncle that the Salvationists had come to Kilmore, and that he had walked up the village street and slit their drum with a carving-knife, his uncle had not approved of his conduct, and what had especially annoyed Father Tom was that his uncle seemed to deplore the slitting of the drum in the same way as he deplored that the Kavanaghs had a barrel of porter in every Saturday, as one of those regrettable excesses to which human nature is liable. On being pressed, he agreed with his nephew that dancing and drinking were no preparation for the Sabbath, but he would not agree that evil could be suppressed by force. He even hinted that too strict a rule brought about a revolt against the rule, and when Father Tom expressed his disbelief at any revolt against the authority of the priest, Father Stafford said:

'They may just leave you, they may just go to America.'

'Then you think that it is our condemnation of sin that is driving the people to America?'

'My dear Tom, you told me the other day that you met a boy and girl walking along the roadside, and drove them home. You told me you were sure they were talking about things they shouldn't talk about; you have no right to assume these things. You're asking of the people an abstinence you don't practise yourself. Sometimes your friends are women.'

'Yes. But –'

Father Tom's anger prevented him from finding an adequate argument, and Father Stafford pushed the tobacco-bowl towards his nephew.

'You're not smoking, Tom.'

'Your point is that a certain amount of vice is inherent in human nature, and that if we raise the standard of virtuous living our people will escape from us to New York or London.'

'The sexes mix freely everywhere in Western Europe; only in Ireland and Turkey is there any attempt made to separate them.'

Later in the evening Father Tom insisted that the measure of responsibility was always the same.

'I should be sorry,' said his uncle, 'to say that those who inherit drunkenness bear the same burden of responsibility as those who come of parents who are quite sane –'

'You cannot deny, uncle John, that free will and predestination –'

'My dear Tom, I really must go to bed. It is after midnight.'

And as he walked home, Father Maguire thought of the great change he perceived in his uncle. He liked an hour's small-talk after dinner, his pipe, his glass of grog, his bed at eleven o'clock, and Father Maguire thought with sorrow of their great disputations, sometimes prolonged till after three o'clock. The passionate scholiast of Maynooth seemed to him unrecognizable in the esurient Vicar-General, only occasionally interested in theology, at certain hours and when he felt particularly well. The first seemed incompatible with the second, his mind not being sufficiently acute to see that after all no one can discuss theology for more than five and twenty years without wearying of the subject.

The moon was shining among the hills and the mystery of the landscape seemed to aggravate his sensibility, and he asked himself if the guardians of the people should not fling themselves into the forefront of the battle. If men came to preach heresy in his parish was he not justified in slitting their drum?

He had recourse to prayer, and he prayed for strength and for guidance. He had accepted the Church, and in the Church he saw only apathy, neglect and bad administration on the part of his superiors ... He had read that great virtues are, like large sums of money, deposited in the bank, whereas humility is like the pence, always at hand, always current. Obedience to our superiors is the sure path. He could not persuade himself that it was right for him to allow the Kavanaghs to continue a dissolute life of drinking and dancing. They were the talk of the parish; and he would have spoken against them from the altar, but his uncle had advised him not to do so. Perhaps his uncle was right; he might be right regarding the Kavanaghs. In the main he disagreed with his uncle, but in this particular instance it might be well to wait and pray that matters might improve.

Father Tom believed Ned Kavanagh to be a good boy. Ned was going to marry Mary Byrne, and Father Tom had made up this marriage. The Byrnes did not care for the marriage – they were prejudiced against Ned on account of his family. But he was not going to allow them to break off the marriage. He was sure of Ned, but in order to make quite sure he would get him to take the pledge. Next morning, when the priest had done his breakfast, the servant opened the door, and told him that Ned Kavanagh was outside, and wanted to see him.

It was a pleasure to look at this nice clean boy, with his winning smile, and the priest thought that Mary could not wish for a better husband. The priest had done his breakfast, and was about to open his newspaper, but he wanted to see Ned Kavanagh, and he told his servant to let him in. Ned's smile seemed a little fainter than usual, and his face was paler; the priest wondered, and presently Ned told the priest that he had come to confession, and, going down on his knees, he told the priest that he had been drunk last Saturday night, and that he had come to take the pledge. He would never do any good while he was at home, and one of the reasons he gave for wishing to marry Mary Byrne was his desire to leave home. The priest asked him if matters were mending, and if his sister showed any signs of wishing to be married.

'Sorra sign,' said Ned.

'That's bad news you're bringing me,' said the priest, and he walked up and down the room, and they talked over Kate's wilful character.

'From the beginning she didn't like living at home,' said the priest.

'I wouldn't be caring about living at home,' said Ned.

'But for a different reason,' said the priest. 'You want to leave home to get married, and have a wife and children, if God is pleased to give you children.'

He sat thinking of the stories he had heard. He had heard that Kate had come back from her last situation in a cab, wrapped up in blankets, saying she was ill. On inquiry it was found that she had only been three or four days in her situation; three weeks had to be accounted for. He had questioned her himself regarding this interval, but had not been able to get any clear and definite answer from her.

'She and mother do be always quarrelling about Pat Connex.'

'It appears,' said the priest, 'that your mother went out with a jug of porter under her apron, and offered a sup of it to Pat, who was talking with Peter M'Shane, and now he is up at your cabin every Saturday.'

'That's so,' said Ned.

'Mrs Connex was here the other day, and I tell you that if Pat marries your sister he will find himself cut off with a shilling.'

'She's been agin us all the while,' said Ned. 'Her money has made her proud, but I wouldn't be blaming her. If I had the fine house she has, maybe I would be as proud as she.'

'Maybe you would,' said the priest. 'But what I'm thinking of is your sister Kate. She'll never get Pat Connex. Pat won't ever go against his mother.'

'Well, you see he comes up and plays the melodeon on Saturday night,' said Ned, 'and she can't stop him from doing that.'

'Then you think,' said the priest, 'that Pat will marry your sister?'

'I don't think she is thinking about him.'

'If she doesn't want to marry him, what's all this talk about?'

'She does like to be meeting Pat in the evenings and to be walking out with him, and him putting his arm round her waist and kiss her, saving your reverence's presence.'

'It is strange that you should be so unlike. You come here and ask me to speak to Mary Byrne's parents for you, and that I'll do, Ned, and it will be all right. You will make a good husband, and though you were drunk last night, you have taken the pledge to-day. And I will make a good marriage for Kate, too, if she'll listen to me.'

'And who may your reverence be thinking of?'

'I'm thinking of Peter M'Shane. He gets as much as six shillings a week and his keep on Murphy's farm, and his mother has got a bit of money, and they have a nice, clean cabin. Now listen to me. There is a poultry lecture at the schoolhouse to- night. Do you think you could bring your sister with you?'

'We did use to keep a great many hins at home, and Kate had the feeding of them, and now she's turned agin them, and she wants to live in town, and she even tells Pat Connex she would not marry a farmer, however much he was worth.'

'But if you tell her that Pat Connex will be at the lecture, will she come?'

'Yes, your reverence, if she believes me.'

'Then do as I bid you,' said the priest; 'you can tell her that Pat Connex will be there.'

II

After leaving the priest Ned crossed over the road to avoid the public-house, and went for a walk on the hills. It was about five when he turned towards the village. On his way there he met his father, and Ned told him that he had been to see the priest, and that he was going to take Mary to the lecture.

'They're quarrelling at home.'

Michael was very tired, and he thought it was pretty hard to come home after a long day's work to find his wife and daughter quarrelling.

'I am sorry your dinner isn't ready, father,' said Kate, 'but it won't be long now. I'll cut the bacon.'

'I met Ned on the road,' her father answered. 'It's sorry I am that he has gone to fetch Mary. He's going to take her to the lecture on poultry-keeping at the schoolhouse.'

'Ah, he has been to the priest, has he?' said Kate, and her mother asked why she said that, and the wrangle began again.

Ned was the peacemaker; there was generally quiet in the cabin when he was there. And he dropped in as Michael was finishing his dinner, bringing with him Mary, a small, fair girl, who everybody said would keep his cabin tidy. His mother and sister were broad-shouldered women with blue-black hair and red cheeks, and it was said that he had said he would like to bring a little fair hair in the family.

'We've just looked in for a minute,' said Mary. 'Ned said that perhaps you'd be coming with us.'

'All the boys in the village will be there to-night,' said Ned. 'You had better come with us.' And pretending he wanted to get a coal of fire to light his pipe, Ned whispered to Kate as he passed her, 'Pat Connex will be there.'

She looked at the striped sunshade she had brought back from the dressmaker's – she had once been apprenticed to a dressmaker – but Ned said that a storm was blowing and she had better leave the sunshade behind.

The rain beat in their faces and the wind came sweeping down the mountain and made them stagger. Sometimes the road went straight on, sometimes it turned suddenly and went uphill. After walking for a mile they came to the schoolhouse. A number of men were waiting outside, and one of the boys told them that the priest had said they were to keep a look-out for the lecturer, and Ned said that he had better stay with them, that his lantern would be useful to show her the way. The women had collected into one corner, and the priest was walking up and down a long, smoky room, his hand thrust into the pockets of his overcoat. Now he stopped in his walk to scold two children who were trying to light a peat fire in a tumble-down grate.

'Don't be tired, go on blowing,' he said. 'You are the laziest child I have seen this long while.'

Ned came in and blew out his lantern, but the lady he had mistaken for the lecturer was a lady who had come to live in the neighbourhood lately, and the priest said:

'You must be very much interested in poultry, ma'am, to come out on such a night as this.'

The lady stood shaking her waterproof.

'Now, then, Lizzie, run to your mother and get the lady a chair.'

And when the child came back with the chair, and the lady was seated by the fire, he said:

'I'm thinking there will be no lecturer here tonight, and that it would be kind of you if you were to give the lecture yourself. You have read some books about poultry, I am sure?'

'Well, a little – but –'

'Oh, that doesn't matter,' said the priest. 'I'm sure the book you have read is full of instruction.'

He walked up the room towards a group of men and told them they must cease talking, and coming back to the young woman he said:

'We shall be much obliged if you will say a few words about poultry. Just say what you have in your mind about the different breeds.'

The young woman again protested, but the priest said:

'You will do it very nicely.' And he spoke like one who is not accustomed to being disobeyed. 'We will give the lecturer five minutes more.'

'Is there no farmer's wife who could speak?' the young lady asked in a fluttering voice. 'She'd know much more than I. I see Biddy M'Hale there. She has done very well with her poultry.'

'I dare say she has,' said the priest. 'but the people would pay no attention to her. She is one of themselves. It would be no amusement to them to hear her.'

The young lady asked if she might have five minutes to scribble a few notes. The priest said he would wait a few minutes, but it did not matter much what she said.

'But couldn't someone dance or sing?' said the young lady.

'Dancing and singing!' said the priest. 'No!'

And the young lady hurriedly scribbled a few notes about fowls for laying, fowls for fattening, regular feeding, warm houses, and something about a percentage of mineral matter. She had not half finished when the priest said:

'Now will you stand over there near the harmonium. Whom shall I announce?'

The young woman told him her name, and he led her to the harmonium and left her talking, addressing most of her instruction to Biddy M'Hale, a long, thin, pale-faced woman, with wistful eyes.

'This won't do,' said the priest, interrupting the lecturer – 'I'm not speaking to you, miss, but to my people. I don't see one of you taking notes, not even you, Biddy M'Hale, though you have made a fortune out of your hins. Didn't I tell you from the pulpit that you were to bring pencil and paper and write down all you heard? If you had known years ago all this young lady is going to tell you, you would be rolling in your carriages to-day.'

Then the priest asked the lecturer to go on, and the lady explained that to get hens to lay about Christmas time, when eggs fetched the best price, you must bring on your pullets early.

'You must,' she said, 'set your eggs in January.'

'You hear that,' said the priest. 'Is there anyone who has got anything to say about that? Why is it that you don't set your eggs in January?'

No one answered, and the lecturer went on to tell of the advantages that would come to the poultry-keeper whose eggs were hatched in December.

As she said this, the priest's eyes fell upon Biddy M'Hale, and, seeing that she was smiling, he asked her if there was any reason why eggs could not be hatched in the beginning of January.

'Now, Biddy, you must know all about this, and I insist on your telling us. We are here to learn.'

Biddy did not answer.

'Then what were you smiling at?'

'I wasn't smiling, your reverence.'

'Yes; I saw you smiling. Is it because you think there isn't a brooding hin in January?'

It had not occurred to the lecturer that hens might not be brooding so early in the year, and she waited anxiously. At last Biddy said:

'Well, your reverence, it isn't because there are no hins brooding. You'll get brooding hins at every time in the year; but, you see, you couldn't be rearing chickens earlier than March. The end of February is the earliest ever I saw. But, sure, if you could be rearing them in January, all that the young lady said would be quite right. I have nothing to say agin it. I have no fault to find with anything she says, your reverence.'

'Only that it can't be done,' said the priest. 'Well, you ought to know, Biddy.'

The villagers were laughing.

'That will do,' said the priest. 'I don't mind your having a bit of amusement, but you're here to learn.'

And as he looked round the room, quieting the villagers into silence, his eyes fell on Kate. He looked for the others, and spied Pat Connex and Peter M'Shane near the door. 'They're here, too,' he thought. 'When the lecture is over I will see them and bring them all together. Kate Kavanagh won't go home until she promises to marry Peter. I have had enough of her goings on in my parish.'

But Kate had caught sight of Peter. She would get no walk home with Pat that night, and she suspected her brother of having done this for a purpose and got up to go.

'I don't want anyone to leave this room,' said the priest. 'Kate Kavanagh, why are you going? Sit down till the lecture is over.'

And as Kate had not the strength to defy the priest, she sat down, and the lecturer continued for a little while longer. The priest could see that the lecturer had said nearly all she had to say, and he had begun to wonder how the evening's amusement was to be prolonged. It would not do to let the people go home until Michael Dunne had closed his public-house, and the priest looked round the audience thinking which one he might call upon to say a few words on the subject of poultry-keeping.

From one of the back rows a voice was heard: 'What about the pump, your reverence?'

'Well, indeed, you may ask,' said the priest.

And immediately he began to speak of the wrong they had suffered by not having a pump in the village. The fact that Almighty God had endowed Kilmore with a hundred mountain streams did not release the authorities from the obligation of supplying the village with a pump. Had not the authorities put up one in the neighbouring village?

'You should come out,' he said, 'and fight for your rights. You should take off your coats like men, and if you do I'll see that you get your rights,' and he looked round for someone to speak.

There was a landlord among the audience, and as he was a Catholic the priest called upon him to speak. He said that he agreed with the priest in the main. They should have their pump, if they wanted a pump; if they didn't, he would suggest that they asked for something else. Farmer Byrne said he did not want a pump, and then everyone spoke his mind, and things got mixed. The Catholic landlord regretted that Father Maguire was against allowing a poultry-yard to the patients in the lunatic asylum. If, instead of supplying a pump, the Government would sell them eggs for hatching at a low price, something might be gained. If the Government would not do this, the Government might be induced to supply books on poultry free of charge. It took the Catholic landlord half an hour to express his ideas regarding the asylum, the pump, and the duties of the Government, and in this way the priest succeeded in delaying the departure of the audience till after closing time. 'However fast they walk,' he said to himself, 'they won't get to Michael Dunne's public-house in ten minutes, and he will be shut by then.' It devolved upon him to bring the evening's amusement to a close with a few remarks, and he said:

'Now, the last words I have to say to you I'll address to the women.

Now listen to me. If you pay more attention to your poultry you'll never be short of half a sovereign to lend your husbands, your sons, or your brothers.'

These last words produced an approving shuffling of feet in one corner of the room, and seeing that nothing more was going to happen the villagers got up and they went out very slowly, the women curtseying and the men lifting their caps to the priest as they passed him.

He had signed to Ned and Mary that he wished to speak to them, and after he had spoken to Ned he called Kate and reminded her that he had not seen her at confession lately.

'Pat Connex and Peter M'Shane, now don't you be going. I will have a word with you presently.'

And while Kate tried to find an excuse to account for her absence from confession, the priest called to Ned and Mary, who were talking at a little distance. He told them he would be waiting for them in church to-morrow, and he said he had never made a marriage that gave him more pleasure. He alluded to the fact that they had come to him. He was responsible for this match, and he accepted the responsibility gladly. His uncle, the Vicar-General, had delegated all the work of the parish to him.

'Father Stafford,' he said abruptly, 'will be very glad to hear of your marriage, Kate Kavanagh.'

'My marriage,' said Kate . . . . 'I don't think I shall ever be married.'

'Now, why do you say that?' said the priest.

Kate did not know why she had said that she would never be married. However, she had to give some reason, and she said:

'I don't think, your reverence, anyone would have me.'

'You are not speaking your mind,' said the priest, a little sternly. 'It is said that you don't want to be married, that you like courting better.'

'I'd like to be married well enough.'

'Those who wish to make safe, reliable marriages consult their parents and they consult the priest. I have made your brother's marriage for him. Why don't you come to me and ask me to make up a marriage for you?'

'I think a girl should make her own marriage, your reverence.'

'And what way do you go about making up a marriage? Walking about the roads in the evening, and turning into public-houses, and leaving your situations. It seems to me, Kate Kavanagh, you have been a long time making up this marriage.'

'Now, Pat Connex, I've got a word with you. You're a good boy, and I know you don't mean any harm by it; but I have been hearing tales about you. You've been up to Dublin with Kate Kavanagh. Your mother came up to speak to me about this matter yesterday, and she said: "Not a penny of my money will he ever get if he marries her," meaning the girl before you. Your mother said: "I've got nothing to say against her, but I've got a right to choose my own daughter-in-law." Those are your mother's very words, Pat, so you had better listen to reason. Do you hear me, Kate?'

'I hear your reverence.'

'And if you hear me, what have you got to say to that?'

'He's free to go after the girl he chooses, your reverence,' said Kate.

'There's been courting enough,' the priest said. 'If you aren't going to be married you must give up keeping company. I see Paddy Boyle outside the door. Go home with him. Do you hear what I'm saying, Pat? Go straight home, and no stopping about the roads. Just do as I bid you; go straight home to your mother.'

Pat did not move at the bidding of the priest. He stood watching Kate as if he were waiting for a sign from her, but Kate did not look at him.

'Do you hear what I'm saying to you?' said the priest.

'Yes, I hear,' said Pat.

'And aren't you going?' said the priest.

Everyone was afraid Pat would raise his hand against the priest, and they looked such strong men, both of them, that everyone wondered which would get the better of the other.

'You won't go home when I tell you to do so. We will see if I can't put you out of the door then.'

'If you weren't a priest,' said Pat, 'the divil a bit of you would put me out of the door.'

'If I weren't a priest I would break every bone in your body for talking to me like that. Now out you go,' he said, taking him by the collar, and he put him out.

'And now, Kate Kavanagh,' said the priest, coming back from the door, 'you said you didn't marry because no man would have you. Peter has been waiting for you ever since you were a girl of sixteen years old, and I may say it for him, since he doesn't say much himself, that you have nearly broken his heart.'

'I'm sure I never meant it. I like Pether.'

'You acted out of recklessness without knowing what you were doing.'

A continual smile floated round Peter's moustache, and he looked like a man to whom rebuffs made no difference. His eyes were patient and docile; and whether it was the presence of this great and true love by her side, or whether it was the presence of the priest, Kate did not know, but a great change came over her, and she said:

'I know that Pether has been very good, that he has a liking for me .... If he wishes to put the ring on me –'

When Kate gave him her hand there was a mist in his eyes, and he stood trembling before her.

CANON SHEEHAN

A Spoiled Priest[1]

Canon Patrick, Augustine, Sheehan (1852–1913) was highly prized as a short story writer in Catholic Ireland and, though sometimes religiose, is perspicacious about the moral problems facing the priesthood. He was born in Cork where he was ordained in 1875. His first novel, Geoffrey Austin, Student *(1895) and its sequel,* The Triumph of Failure *(1898) dealt with the problems of Catholic youth. Among his other books are* Glenanaar *(1905),* Luke Delmege *(1905) and* Lisheen *(1907).*

HE kept his school in a large town in county Waterford. His range of attainments was limited; but what he knew he knew well, and could impart it to his pupils. He did his duty conscientiously by constant, unremitting care, and he emphasized his teachings by frequent appeals to the ferule.

However, on one day in midsummer it would be clearly seen that all hostilities were suspended and a truce proclaimed. This one day in each year was eagerly looked forward to by the boys. The master would come in, dressed in his Sunday suit, with a white rose in his button-hole, and on his lips a smile – a deep, broad, benevolent smile – which, to preserve his dignity, he would vainly try to conceal. No

[1] This is the term used in some parts of the country to express the failure of a student who has just put his foot within the precincts of the sanctuary, and been rejected. Up to quite a recent period such an ill-fated youth was regarded by the peasantry with a certain amount of scorn, not unmingled with superstition. Happily, larger ideas are being developed even on this subject; and not many now believe that no good fortune can ever be the lot of him who has made the gravest initial mistake of his life. (Author's footnote)

implement of torture was visible on that day; and the lessons were repeated, not with the usual rigid formalism but in a perfunctory manner, *ad tempus terendum*. Twelve o'clock would strike, the master would smite the desk and cry:

'Donovan, take the wheelbarrow and bring down Master Kevin's portmanteau from the station.'

Then there was anarchy. Forms were upset, desks overturned, caps flung high as the rafters, and a yell, such as might be given by Comanches around the stake, broke from three hundred boys as they rushed pell-mell from the school. The master would make a feeble effort at restoring order, but his pride in his boy, coming home from Maynooth, stifled the habitual tyranny which brooked no dis-obedience or disorder. In two long lines the boys, under the com-mand of some natural leader, would be drawn up in front of the school. In half-an-hour the wheelbarrow and trunk would be rolled up the gravelled walk; then the expected hero would appear. One tremendous salvo of cheers, and then a glorious holiday!

There was, however, amongst these young lads, one to whom the home-coming of the Maynooth student was of special interest. He was a fair-haired, delicate boy, with large, wistful blue eyes, that looked at you as if they saw something behind and beyond you. He was a bit of a dreamer, too; and when the other lads were shouting at play, he went alone to some copse of thicket, and with a book, or more often without one, would sit and think, and look dreamily at floating clouds or running stream, and then, with a sigh, go back to the weary desk again. Now, he had one idol enshrined in the most sacred recesses of his heart, and that was Kevin O'Donnell. It is quite probable his worship commenced when he heard his sisters at home discussing the merits of this young student in that shy, half-affec-tionate, half-reverential manner in which Irish girls are wont to speak of candidates for the priesthood. And when he heard, around the winter fireside, stories of the intellectual prowess of his hero, in that exaggerated fashion which the imagination of the Irish people so much affects, he worshipped in secret this 'Star of the South', and made desperate vows on sleepless nights to emulate and imitate him. What, then, was his delight when, on one of these glorious summer holidays, the tall, pale-faced student, 'lean' like Dante, 'from much thought', came and invited all his friends to the tea and music that were dispensed at the school-house on Sunday evenings; and when he turned round and, placing his hand on the flaxen curls of the boy, said:

'And this little man must come too; I insist on it.'

Oh! those glorious summer evenings, when the long yellow streamers of the sun lit up the dingy school-house, and the master, no longer the Rhadamanthus of the ruler and rattan, but the magician and conjurer, drew the sweetest sounds from the old violin, and the girls, in their Sunday dresses, swept round in dizzy circles; when the tea and lemonade, and such fairy cakes went round; and the hero, in his long black coat, came over and asked the child how he enjoyed himself, and the boy thought it was heaven, or at least the vestibule and atrium thereof. But even this fairy-land was nothing to the home-coming, when the great tall student lifted the sleepy boy on his shoulders, and wrapped him round against the night air with the folds of his great Maynooth cloak, that was clasped with brass chains that ran through lions' heads, and took him out under the stars, and the warm summer air played around them; and in a delicious half-dream they went home, and the child dreamt of fairy princesses and celestial music, and all was incense and adulation before his idol and prodigy. Ah! the dreams of childhood. What a heaven they would make this world, if only children could speak, and if only their elders would listen!

So two or three years sped by, and then came a rude shock. For one day in the early summer, the day on which the students were expected home, and the boys were on the tiptoe of expectation for their glorious holiday, a quiet, almost inaudible whisper went round that there was something wrong. The master came into school in his ordinary dress; there was no rose in his button-hole; he was quiet, painfully, pitifully quiet; he looked aged, and there were a few wrinkles round his mouth never seen before. A feeling of awe crept over the faces of the boys. They feared to speak. The sight of the old

man going around listlessly, without a trace of the old fury, touched
them deeply. They would have preferred one of his furious explosions
of passion. Once in the morning he lifted the rattan to a turbulent
young ruffian, but, after swishing it in the air, he let it fall, like one
paralysed, to the ground, and then he broke the stick across his knees,
and flung the fragments from the window. The boys could have cried
for him. He dismissed them at twelve o'clock, and they dispersed
without a cheer.

'What was it all? Was Kevin dead?

By-and-by, in whispers around the hearth, he heard that Kevin was
coming home no more. Some one whispered: 'He was expelled;' but
this supposition was rejected angrily. 'He would never be priested,'
said another.

'Why?'

'No one knows. The professors won't tell.'

And some said they expected it all along. 'These great stars fall
sometimes; he was too proud and stuck-up, he wouldn't spake to the
common people – the ould neighbours.' But in most hearts there was
genuine regret, and the truest sympathy for the poor father and
mother, to whom this calamity meant the deepest disgrace. They
would never lift their heads again. Often, for hours together, Kevin's
mother would linger around the fireside, receiving such sympathy as
only Irish hearts can give. Her moans sank deep into the soul of the
listening child.

'Sure I thought that next Sunday I would see my poor boy in
vestments at the altar of God, and then I could die happy. Oh, wirra,
wirra! O Kevin! Kevin! what did you do? what did you do at all, at all?
When he was a little weeshy fellow he used to be playing at saying
Mass – "Dominus vobiscum," and his little sisters used to be serving.
Once his father beat him because he thought it wasn't right. And I
said: "Let the boy alone, James; sure you don't know what God has in
store for him. Who knows what God has in store for him. Who knows
but one day we'll be getting his blessing." Oh, my God, Thy will be
done!'

'How do you know yet?' the friends would say; 'perhaps he's only gone to Dublin, and may be home to-morrow.'

'Thank you kindly, ma'am, but no. Sure his father read the letter for me. "Good-bye, father," it said; "good-bye, mother; you'll never see me again. But I've done nothing to disgrace ye. Would father let me see his face once more? I'll be passing by on the mail to-morrow on my way to America."'

'And did he go to see him?'

'Oh no! he wouldn't. His heart was that black against his son he swore he should never see his face again.'

'Wisha, then,' the women would say, 'how proud he is! What did the poor boy do? I suppose he never made a mistake himself, indeed!'

But the young girls kept silent. They had mutely taken down the idol from their shrine, or rather drawn the dark veil of pitying forgetfulness over it. A student refused Orders was something too terrible. The star had fallen in the sea.

His little friend, however, was loyal to the heart's core. He knew that his hero had done no wrong. He was content to wait and see him justified. He would have given anything to have been able to say a parting word. If he had known Kevin was passing by, shrouded in shame, he would have made his way to the station and braved even the hissing engine, that was always such a terror to him, to touch the hand of his friend once more and assure him of his loyalty. He thought with tears in his eyes of the lonely figure crossing the dread Atlantic; and his nurse was sure he was in for a fit of illness, for the boy moaned in his sleep, and there were tears on his cheeks at midnight.

But from that day his son's name never passed the father's lips. He had uttered in his own mind the cold, iron sentence: 'Non ragioniam di lor.'

The years sped on relentlessly. Never a word came from the exiled student. In a few months the heart-broken mother died. The great school passed into the hands of monks; and the master, in his old age, had to open a little school in the suburbs of the town. Families had been broken up and dispersed, and event after event had obliterated every vestige of the little tragedy, even to the names of the chief actors or sufferers. But in the heart of the little boy, Kevin O'Donnell's name was written in letters of fire and gold. His grateful memory held fast its hero. Then he, too, had to go to college – and for the priesthood. On his very entrance into his Diocesan Seminary he was asked his name and birthplace. When he mentioned the latter, a professor exclaimed:

'Why, Kevin O'Donnell was from there!'

The boy nearly choked. A few weeks after, his heart in his mouth, he timidly approached the Professor, and asked:

'Did you know Kevin O'Donnell?'

'Why, of course,' said the priest, 'he was a class-fellow of mine.'

'What was – was – thought of him in Maynooth?'

'Why, that he was the cleverest, ablest, jolliest, dearest fellow that ever lived. You couldn't help loving him. He swept the two soluses in his logic year, led his class up to the second year's divinity, then fell away, but again came to the front easily in his fourth. We used to say that he "thought in Greek".'

'And why did he leave? Why wasn't he ordained?'

'Ah! there's the mystery, and it's a clever man that could answer it. No one knows.'

They became great friends by reason of this common love for the disgraced student, and one evening in the early summer the Professor told the boy all he knew. He had an attentive listener. The conversation came around in this way. Something in the air, or the glance of the sun, or some faint perfume of hyacinth or early rose, awoke remembrances in the mind of the boy, and he said, as they sat under some dwarfed elms:

'This reminds me of Kevin and his holidays at home. The same summer evening, the same sunlight – only a little faded to me – the old school-room lighted up by the sunset, the little musical parties, the young ladies in their white dresses, my head swimming round as they danced by in polka and schottische –'

'Ha!' said the professor. But, recovering himself, he said hastily:

'Well, go on!'

'Oh, nothing more!' said the boy, 'but my homeward rides on

Kevin's shoulders, and the long folds of his cloak wrapped around me, and – and – how I worshipped him!'

There was a pause, the Professor looking very solemn and thoughtful.

'But, father,' said the boy, 'you never told me. How did it all happen?'

'This way,' said the Professor, shaking himself from his reverie. 'You must know, at least you will know some time, that there is in Maynooth one day – a day of general judgment, a 'Dies iræ, dies illa' – before which the terrors of Jehoshaphat, far away as they are, pale into utter insignificance. It is the day of the 'Order list' – or, in plainer language, it is the dread morning when those who are deemed worthy are called to Orders, and those who are deemed unworthy are rejected. It is a serious ordeal to all. Even the young logician, who is going to be called to tonsure only, looks with fearful uncertainty to his chances. It is always a stinging disgrace to be set aside – or, in college slang, 'to be clipped'. But for the fourth year's divine who is finishing his course, it is the last chance, and woe to him if he fails! He goes out into the world with the brand of shame upon him, and men augur no good of his future. Now, our friend Kevin had been unmercifully 'clipped' up to the last day. Why, we could not ascertain. He was clever; too clever. He had no great faults of character; he was a little careful, perhaps foppish, in his dress; he affected a good deal of culture and politeness; but, so far as we could see, and students are the best judges, there was nothing in his conduct or character to unfit him for the sacred office. But we don't know. There are no mistakes made in that matter. Students who are unfit sometimes steal into the sanctuary, but really fit and worthy students are never rejected. There may be mistakes in selection; there are none in rejection. Well, the fateful morning came. We were all praying for poor Kevin. The most impenetrable silence is kept by the Professors on this matter. Neither by word nor sign could we guess what chances he had; and this added to our dread interest in him. In fact, nothing else was talked of but Kevin's chances; and I remember how many and how diverse were the opinions entertained about them. The bell rang, and we all trooped into the Senior Prayer Hall. We faced the altar, three hundred and fifty anxious students, if I except the deacons and subdeacons, who, with their books – that is, their breviaries – under their arms, looked jaunty enough. I was one of them, for I was ordained Deacon the previous year, and I was certain of my call to Priesthood; but my heart was like lead. Kevin walked in with me.

‘ “Cheer up, old man,” I said; “I tell you it will be all right. Come, sit near me.” His face was ashen, his hands cold and trembling. He picked up the end of his soutane, and began to open and close the buttons nervously. The superiors – four Deans, the Vice-President, and President – came in and took their places in the gallery behind us, and at the end of the hall. An awful silence filled the place. Then the President began, after a brief formula, to call out rapidly in Latin the names of those who were selected “ad primam tonsuram”. He passed on to the Porters, the Lectors, the Acolytes, the Exorcists. Then came the higher Orders, and hearts beat anxiously. But this was rapidly over. Then came the solemn words, “Ad Presbyteratum”. Poor Kevin dropped his soutane, and closed his hands tightly. My name was read out first in alphabetical order. Kevin’s name should come in between the names O’Connor and Quinn. The President read rapidly down the list, called:

> Gulielmus O’Connor, Dunensis;
> Matthæus Quinn, Midensis;

and thus sentence was passed.

Kevin was rejected. I heard him start, and draw in his breath rapidly two or three times. I was afraid to look at him. The list was closed. The Superiors departed, apparently heedless of the dread desolation they had caused; for nothing is so remarkable in our colleges as the apparent utter indifference of Professor and Superiors to the feelings or interests of the students. I said “apparent” because, as a matter of fact, the keenest interest is felt in every student from his entrance to his departure. His is not only constantly under surveillance, but he is spoken of, canvassed, his character, talents, habits passed under survey by those grave, solemn men, who preserve, in their intercourse with the students, a sphinx-like silence and indifference, which to many is painful and inexplicable.

'Well, the ordeal was over; and we rose to depart. Then Kevin turned round and looked at me. He smiled in a ghastly way, and said: "This little tragedy is over."

'I said nothing. Words would have been mockery under such a stunning blow. Nothing else was talked of in the house for the remaining days. There was infinite sympathy for poor Kevin, and even the Superiors dropped the veil of reserve, and spoke kindly to him. It is customary to ask some one of the Superiors the cause of rejection. To keep away from them savours of pride. Kevin went to the Vice-President, a kindly old man, and asked why he was deemed unfit for Orders. The old priest placed his hands on Kevin's shoulders and said, through his tears:

' "Nothing in particular, my dear; but some general want of the ecclesiastical manner and spirit."

' "I haven't been a hypocrite," replied Kevin, "I wore my heart on my sleeve. Perhaps if –' he said no more.

'The examinations were over. The day for the distribution of prizes came on. The Bishops assembled in the Prayer Hall. The list of prizemen was called. Kevin was first in Theology, first in Scripture, second in Ecclesiastical History, first in Hebrew. It was a ghastly farce. Kevin, of course, was not there. Later in the day a deputation of the students of the diocese waited on their Bishop. It was a most unusual proceeding. They asked the Bishop to ordain Kevin, in spite of the adverse decision of the College authorities. They met under the President's apartments. The Bishop, grave and dignified, listened with sympathy, and when their representations had been made, he said he would consult the President.

'It was a faint gleam of hope. They waited, Kevin in their midst, for three-quarters of an hour, hoping, despairing, anxious. The Bishop came down. With infinite pity he looked at Kevin, and said: "I am sorry, Mr O'Donnell, I can do nothing for you. I cannot contravene the will of the Superiors." Then the last hope fled. Next day Kevin

was on his way to America. That is all. You'll understand it better
when you go to Maynooth.'

He did go in due time, and he understood the story better. Like a
careful dramatist, he went over scene after scene in the College life of
Kevin. He found his desk, his cell; he sought out every tradition in the
College concerning him; and that College, completely sequestered
from the outer world as it is, is very rich in traditions, and tenacious of
them. He stood in the wide porch under the President's apartments
and pictured the scene of Kevin's final dismissal from the sacred
ministry. And the first time he sat in the Prayer Hall, at the calling of
the Order list, although he himself was concerned, he forgot everything but the picture of his hero, unnerved, despairing, and saw his
ghastly smile, and heard: 'This little tragedy is over.'

Once or twice he ventured to ask one of the deans whether he had
ever heard of Kevin O'Donnell, and what was the secret of his
rejection.

'Ah! yes, he knew him well. Clever, ambitious, rather worldly-
minded. Why was he finally thought unfit for Orders? Well, there
were various opinions. But no one knew.'

It happened that one of the old men-servants knew Kevin well.

'Mr O'Donnell, of C—? A real gintleman. Wouldn't ask you to
clane his boots without giving you half-a-crown. Heard he was a
doctor, doing well; was married, and had a large family.'

'You heard a lie,' said the student, the strongest expression he had
ever used. But the thing rankled in his heart. Was his hero dethroned?
or was the drapery of the veil drawn across the shrine? No; but he had
seen the feet of clay under the beautiful statue. The Irish instinct
cannot understand a married hero – at least in the sense in which this
youth worshipped Kevin O'Donnell as a hero.

The years rolled by. Ah, those years, leaden-footed to the hot wishes
of youth, how swiftly, with all their clouds and shadows, and all their
misty, nimble radiances, they roll by and break and dissolve into airy
nothings against the azure of eternity!

Our little hero-worshipper was a priest, and, after some years, was

appointed temporarily to a curacy in his native parish. I am afraid he
was sentimental, for he loved every stone and tree and bush in the
neighbourhood. He lived in the past. Here was the wall against which
he had played ball – the identical smooth stone, which he had to be so
careful to pick out; here was the rough crease, where they had played
cricket; here the little valleys where they had rolled their marbles; here
the tiny trout-stream, where they had fished. How small it seems now!
What a broad, terrible river it was to the child of thirty years ago! But
he loved to linger most of all around the old school-house, to sit
amongst the trees again, and to call up all the radiant dreams that float
through the 'moonlight of memory'. Alas! all, or nearly all, the
companions of his childhood had fallen or fled. The few that remained
he interrogated often about the past. This, too, with them, was fading
into a soft dream. Their children were around their knees, and life was
terribly real to them.

One night, again in the soft summer, he was suddenly called to the
sick-bed of a dying woman. He hastily dressed and went. The doctor
was before him, but reverently made way.

'It will be slow, sir,' he said, 'and I must wait.'

The young priest performed his sacred duties to the dying woman,
and then, out of sheer sympathy, he remained sitting by the fire,
chatting with the husband of the patient.

It appeared that the dispensary doctor was away on another call, and
they had taken the liberty to call in this strange doctor, who had been
only a few months in the country, and had taken Rock Cottage for a
few years. He was a tall, angular man, his face almost concealed under
a long, black beard, streaked with white. He was a silent man, it
appeared, but very clever. The 'head doctors' in Cork couldn't hold a
candle to him. He would take no money. He was very good to the
poor. His name was Dr Everard.

The young priest had seen him from time to time, but had never
spoken to him. Perhaps his curiosity was piqued to know a little more
of him. Perhaps he liked him for his kindness to the poor. At any rate
he would remain and walk home with him. Late in the summer night,
or rather, early in the summer dawn, the doctor came out from the

sick-room and asked for water to wash his hands. He started at the young priest waiting; and the latter passed in to the sick woman, who, now relieved, looked pleased and thankful. He said a few kind words and came out quickly. The doctor was just swinging on his broad shoulders a heavy military cloak; and the priest, lifting his eyes, saw the same old lions' heads and the brass chain-clasps that he remembered so well in Kevin's cloak so many years ago.

'Our roads lead in the same direction,' said the priest. 'May I accompany you?'

'Certainly,' said the doctor.

It was a lovely summer morning, dawn just breaking roseate and clear, preluding a warm day. The birds were up and alert, trying to get out all the day's programme of song and anthem before the dread heat should drive them to shelter and silence. The river rolled sluggishly along, thin and slow and underfed, for the mountains were dry and barren, and the fruitful clouds were afar. No men were stirring. The shops were closely shuttered; but here and there a lamp, left lighted, looked sickly in the clear dawnlight. Their footsteps rang hollow with echoes along the street, and one or two dogs barked in muffled anger as the steps smote on their ears. They had been talking about many things, and the young priest had mentioned casually that this was his native place.

'And there's the very house I was born in.' The doctor stopped, and looked curiously at the shuttered house, as if recalling some memories. But he said nothing.

At last they left the town; and the priest, rambling on about his reminiscences, and the other listening attentively, they came at last opposite the old school-house, and by some spontaneous impulse they rested their arms on a rude gate and gazed towards it. Then the young priest broke out into his old rhapsody about the summer twilights, and the violin, and the merry dances of the girls, and all those things round which, commonplace though they may be, memory flings a nimbus of light that spiritualizes and beautifies them. And then his own secret hero-worship for the great Kevin, and the ride on his shoulders home from the dance and the supper, and the great cloak that enveloped him –

'Just like yours, with the same brass clasps and chains, that jingled, oh! such music in my memory.'

The doctor listened gravely and attentively. Then he asked:

'And what became of this wonderful Kevin?'

And he was told his history. And how the heart of one faithful friend yearned after him in his shame, and believed in him, and knew, by a secret but infallible instinct, that he was true and good and faithful, although thrust from the Sanctuary in shame.

'We may meet yet,' continued the young priest. 'Of course he could not remember me. But it was all sad, pitifully sad; and I am sure he had grave trials and difficulties to overcome. You know it is in moments of depression, rather than of exultation, that the great temptations come.'

'Good night, or rather good morning,' said the doctor. 'What did you say your hero's name was? Kevin – I think –'

'Yes, Kevin O'Donnell,' said the priest.

A few weeks after the doctor disappeared, and Rock Cottage was closed again. Twelve months later the young priest was dining with his Bishop, and the latter asked him:

'Did you ever hear of a Kevin O'Donnell, from your town?'

'Yes, of course, my Lord. He was a Maynooth student many years ago.'

'Well, here is a letter from him, from Florence, demanding his *exeat*, in order that he may be ordained priest.'

A rush of tumultuous delight flushed the cheeks of the young priest, but he only said: 'I knew 'twould come all right in the end.'

He went home. There was a letter on his desk. Florence was the post-mark. With trembling fingers he read: –

'CERTOSA, FIRENZE,

July 12, 187–.

'FRIEND AND CHILD, – You have saved a soul! And it is the soul of your early friend, Kevin. Embittered and disappointed, I left Ireland many years ago. Not one kindly word nor friendly grasp was with me in my farewell. I came back to Ireland, successful as to worldly affairs, but bitter and angry towards God and man. I had but one faith left – to do good in a world where I had received naught but evil. Your faith in me has revived my faith in God. I see now that we are in His hands. If a little child could retain the memory of small kindnesses for thirty years, can we think that the great All-Father has forgotten? You are puzzled; you do not know me. Well, I am the doctor with the great cloak, who accompanied you from a sick-call some months ago. I did not know you. I had forgotten your name. But while you spoke, and showed me how great was your fidelity and love, my heart thawed out towards God and man. I left hurriedly and hastened here. I am, thank God, a professed Carthusian, and the Orders denied me in Maynooth Prayer Hall thirty years ago I shall receive in a few days.

'Farewell, and thank God for a gentle heart. You never know where its dews may fall, and bring to life the withered grass or the faded flower – Yours in Christ,

'KEVIN O'DONNELL (late Dr Everard.)'

SOMERVILLE AND ROSS

The Holy Island

E. Œ Somerville (1858–1949) and 'Martin Ross' (1862–1950), the pen name of her cousin Violet Florence Martin, wrote humorous novels of the Irish gentry which include The Real Charlotte, In Mr Knox's Country *and* Some Experiences of an Irish R M *from which this story is taken (An R M is a Resident Magistrate.)*

FOR three days of November a white fog stood motionless over the country. All day and all night smothered booms and bangs away to the south-west told that the Fastnet gun was hard at work, and the sirens of the American liners uplifted their monstrous female voices as they felt their way along the coast of Cork. On the third afternoon the wind began to whine about the windows of Shreelane, and the barometer fell like a stone. At 11 p.m. the storm rushed upon us with the roar and the suddenness of a train; the chimneys bellowed, the tall old house quivered, and the yelling wind drove against it, as a man puts his shoulder against a door to burst it in.

We none of us got much sleep, and if Mrs Cadogan is to be believed – which experience assured me she is not – she spent the night in devotional exercises, and in ministering to the panic-stricken kitchenmaid by the light of a Blessed candle. All that day the storm screamed on, dry-eyed; at nightfall the rain began, and next morning, which happened to be Sunday, every servant in the house was a messenger of Job, laden with tales of leakages, floods, and fallen trees, and inflated with the ill-concealed glory of their kind in evil tidings. To Peter

Cadogan, who had been to early Mass, was reserved the crowning satisfaction of reporting that a big vessel had gone on the rocks at Yokahn Point the evening before, and was breaking up fast; it was rumoured that the crew had got ashore, but this feature, being favourable and uninteresting, was kept as much as possible in the background. Mrs Cadogan, who had been to America in an ocean liner, became at once the latest authority on shipwrecks, and was of opinion that 'whoever would be dhrownded, it wouldn't be thim lads o' sailors. Sure wasn't there the greatest storm ever was in it the time meself was on the say, and what'd thim fellows do but to put us below entirely in the ship, and close down the doors on us, the way their-selves'd leg it when we'd be dhrownding!'

This view of the position was so startlingly novel that Philippa withdrew suddenly from the task of ordering dinner, and fell up the kitchen stairs in unsuitable laughter. Philippa has not the most rudimentary capacity for keeping her countenance.

That afternoon I was wrapped in the slumber, balmiest and most profound, that follows on a wet Sunday luncheon, when Murray, our DI of police, drove up in uniform, and came into the house on the top of a gust that set every door banging and every picture dancing on the walls. He looked as if his eyes had been blown out of his head, and he wanted something to eat very badly.

'I've been down at the wreck since ten o'clock this morning,' he said, 'waiting for her to break up, and once she does there'll be trouble. She's an American ship, and she's full up with rum, and bacon, and butter, and all sorts. Bosanquet is there with all his coastguards, and there are five hundred country people on the strand at this moment, waiting for the fun to begin. I've got ten of my fellows there, and I wish I had as many more. You'd better come back with me, Yeates, we may want the Riot Act before all's done!'

The heavy rain had ceased, but it seemed as if it had fed the wind instead of calming it, and when Murray and I drove out of Shreelane, the whole dirty sky was moving, full sailed, in from the south-west, and the telegraph wires were hanging in a loop from the post outside the gate. Nothing except a Skebawn car-horse would have faced the whooping charges of the wind that came at us across Corran Lake; stimulated mysteriously by whistles from the driver, Murray's yellow hireling pounded woodenly along against the blast, till the smell of the torn sea-weed was borne upon it, and we saw the Atlantic waves come towering into the bay of Tralagough.

The ship was, or had been, a three-masted barque; two of her masts were gone, and her bows stood high out of water on the reef that forms one of the shark-like jaws of the bay. The long strand was crowded with black groups of people, from the bank of heavy shingle that had been hurled over on to the road, down to the slope where the waves pitched themselves and climbed and fought and tore the gravel back with them, as though they had dug their fingers in. The people were nearly all men, dressed solemnly and hideously in their Sunday clothes; most of them had come straight from Mass without any dinner, true to that Irish instinct that places its fun before its food. That the wreck was regarded as a spree of the largest kind was sufficiently obvious. Our car pulled up at a public-house that stood askew between the road and the shingle; it was humming with those whom Irish publicans are pleased to call 'Bonâ feeds', and sundry of the same class were clustered round the door. Under the wall on the leeside was seated a bagpiper, droning out 'The Irish Washerwoman' with nodding head and tapping heel, and a young man was cutting a few steps of a jig for the delectation of a group of girls.

So far Murray's constabulary had done nothing but exhibit their imposing chest measurements and spotless uniforms to the Atlantic, and Bosanquet's coastguards had only salvaged some spars, the debris of a boat, and a dead sheep, but their time was coming. As we stumbled down over the shingle, battered by the wind and pelted by clots of foam, some one beside me shouted, 'She's gone!' A hill of water had smothered the wreck, and when it fell from her again nothing was left but the bows, with the bowsprit hanging from them in a tangle of rigging. The clouds, bronzed by an unseen sunset, hung low over her; in that greedy pack of waves, with the remorseless rocks above and below her, she seemed the most lonely and tormented of creatures.

About half-an-hour afterwards the cargo began to come ashore on the top of the rising tide. Barrels were plunging and diving in the trough of the waves, like a school of porpoises; they were pitched up the beach in waist-deep rushes of foam; they rolled down again, and were swung up and shouldered by the next wave, playing a kind of Tom Tiddler's ground with the coastguards. Some of the barrels were big and dangerous, some were small and nimble like young pigs, and the bluejackets were up to their middles as their prey dodged and ducked, and the police lined out along the beach to keep back the people. Ten men of the RIC can do a great deal, but they cannot be in more than twenty or thirty places at the same instant; therefore they could hardly cope with a scattered and extremely active mob of four or five hundred, many of whom had taken advantage of their privileges as 'bona-fide travellers', and all of whom were determined on getting at the rum.

As the dusk fell the thing got more and more out of hand; the people had found out that the big puncheons held the rum, and had succeeded in capturing one. In the twinkling of an eye it was broached, and fifty backs were shoving round it like a football scrummage. I have heard many rows in my time: I have seen two Irish regiments – one of them Militia – at each other's throats in Fermoy barracks; I have heard Philippa's water spaniel and two fox-terriers hunting a strange cat round the dairy; but never have I known such untrammelled bedlam as that which yelled round the rum-casks on Tralagough strand. For it was soon not a question of one broached cask, or even of two. The barrels were coming in fast, so fast that it was impossible for the representatives of law and order to keep on any sort of terms with them. The people, shouting with laughter, stove in the casks, and drank rum at 34° above proof, out of their hands, out of their hats, out of their boots. Women came fluttering over the hillsides through the twilight, carrying jugs, milk-pails, anything that would hold the liquor; I saw one of them, roaring with laughter, tilt a filthy zinc bucket to an old man's lips.

With the darkness came anarchy. The rising tide brought more and yet more booty: great spars came lunging in on the lap of the waves, mixed up with cabin furniture, seamen's chests, and the black and slippery barrels, and the country people continued to flock in, and the drinking became more and more unbridled. Murray sent for more men and a doctor, and we slaved on hopelessly in the dark; collaring half-drunken men, shoving pig-headed casks up hills of shingle, hustling in among groups of roaring drinkers – we rescued perhaps one barrel in half-a-dozen. I began to know that there were men there who were not drunk and were not idle; I was also aware, as the strenuous hours of darkness passed, of an occasional rumble of cart wheels on the road. It was evident that the casks which were broached were the least part of the looting, but even they were beyond our control. The most that Bosanquet, Murray, and I could do was to concentrate our forces on the casks that had been secured, and to organize charges upon the swilling crowds in order to upset the casks that they had broached. Already men and boys were lying about, limp as leeches, motionless as the dead.

'They'll kill themselves before morning, at this rate!' shouted Murray to me. 'They're drinking it by the quart! Here's another barrel; come on!'

We rallied our small forces, and after a brief but furious struggle succeeded in capsizing it. It poured away in a flood over the stones, over the prostrate figures that sprawled on them, and a howl of reproach followed.

'If ye pour away any more o' that, Major,' said an unctuous voice in my ear, 'ye'll intoxicate the stones and they'll be getting up and knocking us down!'

I had been aware of a fat shoulder next to mine in the throng as we heaved the puncheon over, and I now recognized the ponderous wit and Falstaffian figure of Mr James Canty, a noted member of the Skebawn Board of Guardians, and the owner of a large farm near at hand.

'I never saw worse work on this strand,' he went on. 'I considher these debaucheries a disgrace to the counthry.'

Mr Canty was famous as an orator, and I presume that it was from long practice among his fellow PLG's that he was able, without apparent exertion, to out-shout the storm.

At this juncture the long-awaited reinforcements arrived, and along with them came Dr Jerome Hickey, armed with a black bag. Having mentioned that the bag contained a pump – not one of the common or garden variety – and that no pump on board a foundering ship had more arduous labours to perform, I prefer to pass to other themes. The wreck, which had at first appeared to be as inexhaustible and as variously stocked as that in the *Swiss Family Robinson*, was beginning to fail in its supply. The crowd were by this time for the most part incapable from drink, and the fresh contingent of police tackled their work with some prospect of success by the light of a tar barrel, contributed by the owner of the public-house. At about the same time I began to be aware that I was aching with fatigue, that my clothes hung heavy and soaked upon me, that my face was stiff with the salt spray and the bitter wind, and that it was two hours past dinner-time. The possibility of fried salt herrings and hot whisky and water at the public-house rose dazzlingly before my mind, when Mr Canty again crossed my path.

'In my opinion ye have the whole cargo under conthrol now, Major,' he said, 'and the police and the sailors should be able to account for it all now by the help of the light. Wasn't I the finished fool that I didn't think to send up to my house for a tar barrel before now! Well – we're all foolish sometimes! But indeed it's time for us to give over, and that's what I'm after saying to the Captain and Mr Murray. You're exhausted now the three of ye, and if I might make so bold, I'd suggest that ye'd come up to my little place and have what'd warm ye before ye'd go home. It's only a few perches up the road.'

The tide had turned, the rain had begun again, and the tar barrel illumined the fact that Dr Hickey's dreadful duties alone were pressing. We held a council and finally followed Mr Canty, picking our way through wreckage of all kinds, including the human variety. Near the public-house I stumbled over something that was soft and had a squeak in it; it was the piper, with his head and shoulders in an overturned rum-barrel, and the bagpipes still under his arm.

I knew the outward appearance of Mr Canty's house very well. It was a typical southern farmhouse, with dirty whitewashed walls, a slated roof, and small, hermetically-sealed windows staring at the morass of manure which constituted the yard. We followed Mr Canty up the filthy lane that led to it, picked our way round vague and squelching spurs of the manure heap, and were finally led through the kitchen into a stifling best parlour. Mrs Canty, a vast and slatternly matron, had evidently made preparations for us; there was a newly-lighted fire pouring flame up the chimney from layers of bogwood, there were whisky and brandy on the table, and a plateful of biscuits sugared in white and pink. Upon our hostess was a black silk dress which indifferently concealed the fact that she was short of boot-laces, and that the boots themselves had made many excursions to the yard and none to the blacking-bottle. Her manners, however, were admirable, and while I live I shall not forget her potato cakes. They came in hot and hot from a pot-oven, they were speckled with car-away seeds, they swam in salt butter, and we ate them shamelessly and greasily, and washed them down with hot whisky and water; I knew to a nicety how ill I should be next day, and heeded not.

'Well, gentlemen,' remarked Mr Canty later on, in his best Board of Guardians' manner, 'I've seen many wrecks between this and the Mizen Head, but I never witnessed a scene of more disgraceful excess than what was in it tonight.'

'Hear, hear!' murmured Bosanquet with unseemly levity.

'I should say,' went on Mr Canty, 'there was at one time to-night upwards of one hundhred men dead dhrunk on the strand, or anyway so dhrunk that if they'd attempt to spake they'd foam at the mouth.'

'The craytures!' interjected Mrs Canty sympathetically.

'But if they're dhrunk to-day,' continued our host, 'it's nothing at all to what they'll be to-morrow and afther to-morrow, and it won't be on the strand they'll be dhrinkin' it.'

'Why, where will it be?' said Bosanquet, with his disconcerting English way of asking a point-blank question.

Mr Canty passed his hand over his red cheeks.

'There'll be plenty asking that before all's said and done, Captain,' he said, with a compassionate smile, 'and there'll be plenty that could give the answer if they'll like, but by dam I don't think ye'll be apt to get much out of the Yokahn boys!'

'The Lord save us, 'twould be better to keep out from the likes o' thim!' put in Mrs Canty, sliding a fresh avalanche of potato cakes on to the dish; 'didn't they pull the clothes off the gauger and pour potheen down his throath till he ran screeching through the streets o' Ske-bawn!'

James Canty chuckled.

'I remember there was a wreck here one time, and the undher-writers put me in charge of the cargo. Brandy it was – cases of the best Frinch brandy. The people had a song about it, what's this the first verse was –

> One night to the rocks of Yokahn
> Came the barque *Isabella* so dandy,
> To pieces she went before dawn,
> Herself and her cargo of brandy.
> And all met a wathery grave
> Excepting the vessel's car*pen*ther,
> Poor fellow, so far from his home.

Mr Canty chanted these touching lines in a tuneful if wheezy tenor. 'Well, gentlemen, we'll all friends here,' he continued, 'and it's no harm to mention that this man below at the public-house came askin' me would I let him have some of it for a consideration. "Sullivan," says I to him, "if ye ran down gold in a cup in place of the brandy, I wouldn't give it to you. Of coorse," says I, "I'm not sayin' but that if a bottle was to get a crack of a stick, and it to be broken, and a man to drink a glass out of it, that would be no more than an accident." "That's no good to me," says he, "but if I had twelve gallons of that brandy in Cork," says he, "by the Holy German!" says he, saying an awful curse, "I'd sell twenty-five out of it!" Well, indeed, it was true for him; it was grand stuff. As the saying is, it would make a horse out of a cow!'

'It appears to be a handy sort of place for keeping a pub,' said Bosanquet.

'Shut to the door, Margaret,' said Mr Canty with elaborate caution. 'It'd be a queer place that wouldn't be handy for Sullivan!'

A further tale of great length was in progress when Dr Hickey's Mephistophelian nose was poked into the best parlour.

'Hullo, Hickey! Pumped out? eh?' said Murray.

'If I am, there's plenty more like me,' replied the Doctor enigmatically, 'and some of them three times over! James, did these gentlemen leave you a drop of anything that you'd offer me?'

'Maybe ye'd like a glass of rum, Doctor?' said Mr Canty with a wink at his other guests.

Dr Hickey shuddered.

I had next morning precisely the kind of mouth that I had anticipated, and it being my duty to spend the better part of the day administering justice in Skebawn, I received from Mr Flurry Knox and other of my brother magistrates precisely the class of condolences on my 'Monday head' that I found least amusing. It was unavailing to point out the resemblance between hot potato cakes and molten lead, or to dilate on their equal power of solidifying; the collective wisdom of the Bench decided that I was suffering from contraband rum, and rejoiced over me accordingly.

During the next three weeks Murray and Bosanquet put in a time only to be equalled by that of the heroes in detective romances. They began by acting on the hint offered by Mr Canty, and were rewarded by finding eight barrels of bacon and three casks of rum in the heart of Mr Sullivan's turf rick, placed there, so Mr Sullivan explained with much detail, by enemies, with the object of getting his licence taken away. They stabbed potato gardens with crowbars to find the buried barrels, they explored the chimneys, they raided the cow-houses; and in every possible and impossible place they found some of the cargo of the late barque *John D. Williams*, and, as the sympathetic Mr Canty said, 'For as much as they found, they left five times as much afther them!'

It was a wet, lingering autumn, but towards the end of November the rain dried up, the weather stiffened, and a week of light frosts and blue skies was offered as a tardy apology. Philippa possesses, in common with many of her sex, an inappeasable passion for picnics, and her ingenuity for devising occasions for them is only equalled by her gift for enduring their rigours. I have seen her tackle a moist chicken pie with a splinter of slate and my stylograph pen. I have known her to take the tea-basket to an auction, and make tea in a four-wheeled inside car, regardless of the fact that it was coming under the hammer in ten minutes, and that the kettle took twenty minutes to boil. It will therefore be readily understood that the rare occasions when I was free to go out with a gun were not allowed to pass uncelebrated by the tea-basket.

'You'd much better shoot Corran Lake tomorrow,' my wife said to me one brilliant afternoon. 'We could send the punt over, and I could meet you on Holy Island with —'

The rest of the sentence was concerned with ways, means, and the tea-basket, and need not be recorded.

I had taken the shooting of a long snipe bog that trailed from Corran Lake almost to the sea at Tralagough, and it was my custom to begin to shoot from the seaward end of it, and finally to work round the lake after duck.

Tomorrow proved a heavenly morning, touched with frost, gilt with sun. I started early, and the mists were still smoking up from the calm, all-reflecting lake, as the Quaker stepped out along the level road, smashing the thin ice on the puddles with his big feet. Behind the calves of my legs sat Maria, Philippa's brown Irish water-spaniel, assiduously licking the barrels of my gun, as was her custom when the ecstasy of going out shooting was hers. Maria had been given to Philippa as a wedding-present, and since then it had been my wife's ambition that she should conform to the Beth Gelert standard of being 'a lamb at home, a lion in the chase'. Maria did pretty well as a lion: she hunted all dogs unmistakably smaller than herself, and whenever it was reasonably possible to do so she devoured the spoils of the chase, notably jack snipe. It was as a lamb that she failed; objectionable as I have no doubt a lamb would be as a domestic pet, it at least would not snatch the cold beef from the luncheon-table, nor yet, if banished for its crimes, would it spend the night in scratching the paint off the hall door. Maria bit beggars (who valued their disgusting limbs at five shillings the square inch), she bullied the servants, she concealed ducks' claws and fishes' backbones behind the sofa cushions, and yet, when she laid her brown snoud upon my knee, and rolled her blackguard amber eyes upon me, and smote me with her feathered paw, it was impossible to remember her iniquities against her. On shooting mornings Maria ceased to be a buccaneer, a glutton, and a hypocrite. From the moment when I put my gun together her breakfast stood untouched until it suffered the final degradation of being eaten by the cats, and now in the trap she was shivering with excitement, and agonizing in her soul lest she should even yet be left behind.

Slipper met me at the cross roads from which I had sent back the trap; Slipper, redder in the nose than anything I had ever seen off the stage, very husky as to the voice, and going rather tender on both feet. He informed me that I should have a grand day's shooting, the head-poacher of the locality having, in a most gentlemanlike manner, refrained from exercising his sporting rights the day before, on hearing that I was coming. I understood that this was to be considered as a mark of high personal esteem, and I set to work at the bog with suitable gratitude.

In spite of Mr O'Driscoll's magnanimity, I had not a very good morning. The snipe was there, but in the perfect stillness of the weather it was impossible to get near them, and five times out of six they were up, flickering and dodging, before I was within shot. Maria became possessed of seven devils and broke away from heel the first time I let off my gun, ranging far and wide in search of the bird I had missed, and putting up every live thing for half a mile round, as she went splashing and steeple-chasing through the bog. Slipper expressed his opinion of her behaviour in language more appallingly picturesque and resourceful than any I have heard, even in the Skebawn Court-house; I admit that at the time I thought he spoke every suitably. Before she was recaptured every remaining snipe within earshot was lifted out of it by Slipper's steam-engine whistles and my own infuriated bellows; it was fortunate that the bog was spacious and that there was still a long tract of it ahead, where beyond these voices there was peace.

I worked my way on, jumping treacle-dark drains, floundering through the rustling yellow rushes, circumnavigating the bog-holes, and taking every possible and impossible chance of a shot; by the time I had reached Corran Lake I had got two-and-a-half brace, retrieved by Maria with a perfection that showed what her powers were when the sinuous adroitness of Slipper's woodbine stick was fresh in her mind. But with Maria it was always the unexpected that happened. My last snipe, a jack, fell in the lake, and Maria, bursting through the reeds with kangaroo bounds, and cleaving the water like a torpedo-boat, was a model of all the virtues of her kind. She picked up the bird with a snake-like dart of her head, clambered with it on to a tussock, and there, well out of reach of the arm of the law, before our indignant eyes crunched it twice and bolted it.

'Well,' said Slipper complacently, some ten minutes afterwards, 'divil such a bating ever I gave a dog since the day Prince kill owld Mrs Knox's paycock! Prince was a lump of a brown tarrier I had one time, and faith I kicked the toes out o' me owld boots on him before I had the owld lady composed!'

However composing Slipper's methods may have been to Mrs Knox, they had quite the contrary effect upon a family party of duck that had been lying in the reeds. With horrified outcries they broke into flight, and now were far away on the ethereal mirror of the lake, among strings of their fellows that were floating and quacking in preoccupied indifference to my presence.

A promenade along the lake-shore demonstrated the fact that without a boat there was no more shooting for me; I looked across to the island where, some time ago, I had seen Philippa and her punt arrive. The boat was tied to an overhanging tree, but my wife was nowhere to be seen. I was opening my mouth to give a hail, when I saw her emerge precipitately from among the trees and jump into the boat; Philippa had not in vain spent many summers on the Thames, she was under way in a twinkling, sculled a score of strokes at the rate of a finish, then stopped and stared at the peaceful island. I called to her, and in a minute or two the punt had crackled through the reeds, and shoved its blunt nose ashore at the spot where I was standing.

'Sinclair,' said Philippa in awe-struck tones, 'there's something on the island!'

'I hope there's something to eat there,' said I.

'I tell you there *is* something there, alive,' said my wife with her eyes as large as saucers; 'it's making an awful sound like snoring.'

'That's the fairies, ma'am,' said Slipper with complete certainty; 'sure I know them that seen fairies in that island as thick as the grass, and every one o' them with little caps on them.'

Philippa's wide gaze wandered to Slipper's hideous pug face and back to me.

'It was not a human being, Sinclair!' she said combatively, though I had not uttered a word.

Maria had already, after the manner of dogs, leaped, dripping, into the boat: I prepared to follow her example.

'Major,' said Slipper, in a tragic whisper, 'there was a man was a night on that island one time, watching duck, and Thim People cot him, and dhragged him through Hell and through Death, and threw him in the tide—'

'Shove off the boat,' I said, too hungry for argument.

Slipper obeyed, throwing his knee over the gunwale as he did so, and tumbling into the bow; we could have done without him very comfortably, but his devotion was touching.

Holy Island was perhaps a hundred yards long, and about half as many broad; it was covered with trees and a dense growth of rhododendrons; somewhere in the jungle was a ruined fragment of a chapel, smothered in ivy and briars, and in a little glade in the heart of the island there was a holy well. We landed, and it was obviously a sore humiliation to Philippa that not a sound was to be heard in the spellbound silence of the island, save the cough of a heron on a tree-top.

'It *was* there,' she said, with an unconvinced glance at the surrounding thickets.

'Sure, I'll give a thrawl through the island, ma'am,' volunteered Slipper with unexpected gallantry, 'an' if it's the divil himself is in it, I'll rattle him into the lake!'

He went swaggering on his search, shouting, 'Hi, cock!' and whacking the rhododendrons with his stick, and after an interval returned and assured us that the island was uninhabited. Being provided with refreshments he again withdrew, and Philippa and Maria and I fed variously and at great length, and washed the plates with water from the holy well. I was smoking a cigarette when we heard Slipper addressing the solitudes at the farther end of the island, and ending with one of his whisky-throated crows of laughter.

He presently came lurching towards us through the bushes, and a glance sufficed to show even Philippa – who was as incompetent a judge of such matters as many of her sex – that he was undeniably screwed.

'Major Yeates!' he began, 'and Mrs Major Yeates, with respex to ye, I'm bastely dhrunk! Me head is light since the 'fluenzy, and the doctor told me I should carry a little bottle-een o' sperrits–'

'Look here,' I said to Philippa, 'I'll take him across, and bring the boat back for you.'

'Sinclair,' responded my wife with concentrated emotion, 'I would rather die than stay on this island alone!'

Slipper was getting drunker every moment, but I managed to stow him on his back in the bows of the punt, in which position he at once began to uplift husky and wandering strains of melody. To this accompaniment we, as Tennyson says,

> moved from the brink like some full-breasted swan,
> That, fluting a wild carol ere her death,
> Ruffles her pure cold plume, and takes the flood
> With swarthy web.

Slipper would certainly have been none the worse for taking the flood, and, as the burden of 'Lannigan's Ball' strengthened and spread along the tranquil lake, and the duck once more fled in justifiable consternation, I felt much inclined to make him do so.

We made for the end of the lake that was nearest Shreelane, and, as we rounded the point of the island, another boat presented itself to our view. It contained my late entertainer, Mrs Canty, seated bulkily in the stern, while a small boy bowed himself between the two heavy oars.

'It's a lovely evening, Major Yeates,' she called out. 'I'm just going to the island to get some water from the holy well for me daughter that has an impression on her chest. Indeed, I thought 'twas yourself was singing a song for Mrs Yeates when I heard you coming, but sure Slipper is a great warrant himself for singing.'

'May the divil crack the two legs undher ye!' bawled Slipper in acknowledgment of the compliment.

Mrs Canty laughed genially, and her boat lumbered away.

I shoved Slipper ashore at the nearest point. Philippa and I paddled to the end of the lake, and abandoning the duck as a bad business, walked home.

A few days afterwards it happened that it was incumbent upon me to attend the funeral of the Roman Catholic Bishop of the diocese. It was what is called in France *um bel enterrement*, with inky flocks of tall-hatted priests, and countless yards of white scarves, and a repast of monumental solidity at the Bishop's residence. The actual interment was to take place in Cork, and we moved in long and imposing procession to the railway station, where a special train awaited the cortège. My friend Mr James Canty was among the mourners: an important and active personage, exchanging condolences with the priests, giving directions to porters, and blowing his nose with a trumpeting mournfulness that penetrated all the other noises of the platform. He was condescending enough to notice my presence, and found time to tell me that he had given Mr Murray 'a sure word' with regard to some of '*the wreckage*' – this with deep significance, and a wink of an inflamed and tearful eye. I saw him depart in a first-class carriage, and the odour of sanctity; seeing that he was accompanied by seven priests, and that both windows were shut, the latter must have been considerable.

Afterwards, in the town, I met Murray, looking more pleased with himself than I had seen him since he had taken up the unprofitable task of smuggler-hunting.

'Come along and have some lunch,' he said, 'I've got a real good thing on this time! That chap Canty came to me late last night, and told me he knew for a fact that the island on Corran Lake was just stiff with barrels of bacon and rum, and that I'd better send every man I could spare today to get them into the town. I sent the men out at eight o'clock this morning; I think I've gone one better than Bosanquet this time!'

I began to realize that Philippa was going to score heavily on the subject of the fairies that she had heard snoring on the island, and I imparted to Murray the leading features of our picnic there.

'Oh, Slipper's been up to his chin in that rum from the first,' said Murray. 'I'd like to know who is sleeping partner was!'

It was beginning to get dark before the loaded carts of the salvage party came lumbering past Murray's windows and into the yard of the police-barrack. We followed them, and in so doing picked up Flurry Knox, who was sauntering in the same direction. It was a good haul, five big casks of rum, and at least a dozen smaller barrels of bacon and butter, and Murray and his Chief Constable smiled seraphically on one another as the spoil was unloaded and stowed in a shed.

'Wouldn't it be as well to see how the butter is keeping?' remarked Flurry, who had been looking on silently, with, as I had noticed, a still and amused eye. 'The rim of that small keg there looks as if it had been shifted lately.'

The sergeant looked hard at Flurry; he knew as well as most people that a hint from Mr Knox was usually worth taking. He turned to Murray.

'Will I open it, sir?'

'Oh! open it if Mr Knox wishes,' said Murray, who was not famous for appreciating other people's suggestions.

The keg was opened.

'Funny butter,' said Flurry.

The sergeant said nothing. The keg was full of black bog-mould. Another was opened, and another, all with the same result.

'Damnation!' said Murray, suddenly losing his temper. 'What's the use of going on with those? Try one of the rum casks.'

A few moments passed in total silence while a tap and a spigot were sent for and applied to the barrel. The sergeant drew off a mugful and put his nose to it with the deliberation of a connoisseur.

'Water, sir,' he pronounced, 'dirty water, with a small indication of sperrits.'

A junior constable tittered explosively, met the light blue glare of Murray's eye, and withered away.

'Perhaps it's holy water!' said I, with a wavering voice.

Murray's glance pinned me like an assegaii, and I also faded into the background.

'Well,' said Flurry in dulcet tones, 'if you want to know where the stuff is that was in those barrels, I can tell you, for I was told it myself half-an-hour ago. It's gone to Cork with the Bishop by special train!'

Mr Canty was undoubtedly a man of resource. Mrs Canty had mistakenly credited me with an intelligence equal to her own, and on receiving from Slipper a highly colourful account of how audibly Mr Canty had slept off his potations, had regarded the secret of Holy Island as having been given away. That night and the two succeeding ones were spent in the transfer of the rum to bottles, and the bottles and the butter to fish boxes; these were, by means of a slight lubrication of the railway underlings loaded into a truck as 'Fresh Fish, Urgent', and attached to the Bishop's funeral train, while the police, decoyed far from the scene of action, were breaking their backs over barrels of bog-water. 'I suppose,' continued Flurry pleasantly, 'you don't know the pub that Canty's brother has in Cork. Well, I do. I'm going to buy some rum there next week, cheap.'

'I shall proceed against Canty!' said Murray, with fateful calm.

'You won't proceed far,' said Flurry; 'you'll not get as much evidence out of the whole country as'd hang a cat.'

'Who was your informant?' demanded Murray.

Flurry laughed. 'Well, by the time the train was in Cork, yourself and the Major were the only two men in the town that weren't talking about it.'

W. B. YEATS

The Twisting of the Rope

William Butler Yeats (1865–1939), in addition to his poetry and plays, also wrote one novel and three volumes of short stories. 'The Twisting of the Rope' is from Tales of Red Hanrahan.

HANRAHAN was walking the roads one time near Kinvara at the fall of day, and he heard the sound of a fiddle from a house a little way off the roadside. He turned up the path to it, for he never had the habit of passing by any place where there was music or dancing or good company, without going in. The man of the house was standing at the door, and when Hanrahan came near he knew him and he said: 'A welcome before you, Hanrahan, you have been lost to us this long time.' But the woman of the house came to the door and she said to her husband: 'I would be as well pleased for Hanrahan not to come in to-night, for he has no good name now among the priests, or with women that mind themselves, and I wouldn't wonder from his walk if he has a drop of drink taken.' But the man said, 'I will never turn away Hanrahan of the poets from my door,' and with that he bade him enter.

There were a good many neighbours gathered in the house, and some of them remembered Hanrahan; but some of the little lads that were in the corners had only heard of him, and they stood up to have a view of him, and one of them said: 'Is not that Hanrahan that had the school, and that was brought away by Them?' But his mother put her hand over his mouth and bade him be quiet, and not be saying things like that. 'For Hanrahan is apt to grow wicked,' she said, 'if he hears talk of that story, or if any one goes questioning him.' One or another called out then, asking him for a song, before he had rested himself; and he gave him whiskey in a glass, and Hanrahan thanked him and wished him good health and drank it off.

The fiddler was tuning his fiddle for another dance, and the man of the house said to the young men, they would all know what dancing was like when they saw Hanrahan dance, for the like of it had never been seen since he was there before. Hanrahan said he would not dance, he had better use for his feet now, travelling as he was through the five provinces of Ireland. Just as he said that, there came in at the half-door Oona, the daughter of the house, having a few bits of bog deal from Connemara in her arms for the fire. She threw them on the hearth and the flame rose up, and showed her to be very comely and smiling, and two or three of the young men rose up and asked for a dance. But Hanrahan crossed the floor and brushed the others away, and said it was with him she must dance, after the long road he had travelled before he came to her. And it is likely he said some soft word in her ear, for she said nothing against it, and stood out with him, and there were little blushes in her cheeks. Then other couples stood up, but when the dance was going to begin, Hanrahan chanced to look down, and he took notice of his boots that were worn and broken, and the ragged grey socks showing through them; and he said angrily it was a bad floor, and the music no great things, and he sat down in the dark place beside the hearth. But if he did, the girl sat down there with him.

The dancing went on, and when that dance was over another was called for, and no one took much notice of Oona and Red Hanrahan for a while, in the corner where they were. But the mother grew to be uneasy, and she called to Oona to come and help her to set the table in the inner room. But Oona, that had never refused her before, said she would come soon, but not yet, for she was listening to whatever he was saying in her ear. The mother grew yet more uneasy then, and she would come nearer them, and let on to be stirring the fire or sweeping the hearth, and she would listen for a minute to hear what the poet was saying to her child. And one time she heard him telling about white-handed Deirdre, and how she brought the sons of Usnach to their death; and how the blush in her cheeks was not so red as the blood of kings' sons that was shed for her, and her sorrows had never gone out of mind; and he said it was maybe the memory of her that made the cry of the plover on the bog as sorrowful in the ear of the poets as the keening of young men for a comrade. And there would never have been that memory of her, he said, if it was not for the poets that had put her beauty in their songs. And the next time she did not well understand what he was saying, but as far as she could hear it had the sound of poetry though it was not rhymed, and this is what she heard him say: 'The sun and the moon are the man and the girl, they are my life and your life, they are travelling and ever travelling through the skies as if under the one hood. It was God made them for one another. He made your life and my life before the beginning of the world, he made them that they might go through the world, up and down, like the two best dancers that go on with the dance up and down the long floor of the barn, fresh and laughing, when all the rest are tired out and leaning against the wall.'

The old woman went then to where her husband was playing cards, but he would take no notice of her, and then she went to a woman of the neighbours and said: 'Is there no way we can get them from one another?' and without waiting for an answer she said to some young men that were talking together: 'What good are you when you cannot make the best girl in the house come out and dance with you? And go now the whole of you,' she said, 'and see can you bring her away from the poet's talk.' But Oona would not listen to any of them, but only moved her hand as if to send them away. Then they called to Hanrahan and said he had best dance with the girl himself or let her dance with one of them. When Hanrahan heard what they were saying he said: 'That is so, I will dance with her; there is no man in the house must dance with her but myself.'

He stood up with her then, and led her out by the hand, and some of the young men were vexed, and some began mocking at his ragged coat and his broken boots. But he took no notice, and Oona took no notice, but they looked at one another as if all the world belonged to themselves alone. But another couple that had been sitting together like lovers stood out on the floor at the same time, holding one another's hands and moving their feet to keep time with the music. But Hanrahan turned his back on them as if angry, and in place of dancing he began to sing, and as he sang he held her hand, and his voice grew louder, and the mocking of the young men stopped, and the fiddle stopped, and there was nothing heard but his voice that had in it the sound of the wind. And what he sang was a song he had heard or had made one time in his wanderings on Slieve Echtge, and the words of it as they can be put into English were like this:

> O Death's old bony finger
> Will never find us there
> In the high hollow townland
> Where's love to give and to spare;
> Where boughs have fruit and blossom
> At all times of the year;
> Where rivers are running over
> With red beer and brown beer.
> An old man plays the bagpipes
> In a gold and silver wood;
> Queens, their eyes blue like the ice,
> Are dancing in a crowd.

And while he was singing it Oona moved nearer to him, and the colour had gone from her cheek, and her eyes were not blue now, but grey with the tears that were in them, and any one that saw her would have thought she was ready to follow him there and then from the west to the east of the world.

But one of the young men called out: 'Where is that country he is singing about? Mind yourself, Oona, it is a long way off, you might be a long time on the road before you would reach to it.' And another said: 'It is not the Country of the Young you will be going if you go with him, but to Mayo of the bogs.' Oona looked at him then as if she would question him, but he raised her head in his hand, and called out between singing and shouting: 'It is very near us that country is, it is on every side; it may be on the bare hill behind it is, or it may be in the heart of the wood.' And he said out very loud and clear: 'In the heart of the wood; oh, death will never find us in the heart of the wood. And will you come with me there, Oona?' he said.

But while he was saying this the two old women had gone outside the door, and Oona's mother was crying, and she said: 'He has put an enchantment on Oona. Can we not get the men to put him out of the house?'

'That is a thing you cannot do,' said the other woman, 'for he is a poet of the Gael, and you know well if you would put a poet of the Gael out of the house, he would put a curse on you that would wither the corn in the fields and dry up the milk of the cows, if it had to hang in the air seven years.'

'God help us,' said the mother, 'and why did I ever let him into the house at all, and the wild name he has!'

'It would have been no harm at all to have kept him outside, but there would great harm come upon you if you put him out by force. But listen to the plan I have to get him out of the house by his own doing, without any one putting him from it at all.'

It was not long after that the two women came in again, each of them having a bundle of hay in her apron. Hanrahan was not singing now, but he was talking to Oona very fast and soft, and he was saying: 'The house is narrow but the world is wide, and there is no true lover that need be afraid of night or morning or sun or stars or shadows of evening, or any earthly thing.' 'Hanrahan,' said the mother then, striking him on the shoulder, 'will you give me a hand here for a minute?' 'Do that, Hanrahan,' said the woman of her neighbours, 'and help us to make this hay into a rope, for you are ready with your hands, and a blast of wind has loosened the thatch on the haystick.'

'I will do that for you,' said he, and he took the little stick in his hands, and the mother began giving out the hay, and he twisting it, but he was hurrying to have done with it, and to be free again. The women went on talking and giving out the hay, and encouraging him, and saying what a good twister of a rope he was, better than their own neighbours or than any one they had ever seen. And Hanrahan saw that Oona was watching him, and he began to twist very quick and with his head high, and to boast of the readiness of his hands, and the learning he had in his head, and the strength in his arms. And as he was boasting, he went backward, twisting the rope always till he came to the door that was open behind him, and without thinking he passed the threshold and was out on the road. And no sooner was he there than the mother made a sudden rush, and threw out the rope after him, and she shut the door and the half-door and put a bolt upon them.

She was well pleased when she had done that, and laughed out loud, and the neighbours laughed and praised her. But they heard him beating at the door, and saying words of cursing outside it, and the mother had but time to stop Oona that had her hand upon the bolt to open it. She made a sign to the fiddler then, and he began a reel, and one of the young men asked no leave but caught hold of Oona and brought her into the thick of the dance. And when it was over and the fiddle had stopped, there was no sound at all of anything outside, but the road was as quiet as before.

As to Hanrahan, when he knew he was shut out and that there was neither shelter nor drink nor a girl's ear for him that night, the anger and the courage went out of him, and he went on to where the waves were beating on the strand.

He sat down on a big stone, and he began swinging his right arm and singing slowly to himself, the way he did always to hearten himself when every other thing failed him. And whether it was that time or another time he made the song that is called to this day 'The Twisting of the Rope', and that begins, 'What was the dead cat that put me in this place,' is not known.

But after he had been singing a while, mist and shadows seemed to gather about him, sometimes coming out of the sea, and sometimes moving upon it. It seemed to him that one of the shadows was the queen-woman he had seen in her sleep at Slieve Echtge; not in her sleep now, but mocking, and calling out to them that were behind her: 'He was weak, he was weak, he had no courage.' And he felt the strands of the rope in his hand yet, and went on twisting it, but it seemed to him as he twisted that it had all the sorrows of the world in it. And then it seemed to him as if the rope had changed in his dream into a great water-worm that came out of the sea, and that twisted itself about him, and held him closer and closer, and grew from big to bigger till the whole of the earth and skies were wound up in it, and the stars themselves were but the shining of the ridges of its skin. And then he got free of it, and went on, shaking and unsteady, along the edge of the strand, and the grey shapes were flying here and there around him. And this is what they were saying, 'It is a pity for him that refuses the call of the daughters of the Sidhe, for he will find no comfort in the love of the women of the earth to the end of life and time, and the cold of the grave is in his heart for ever. It is death he has chosen; let him die, let him die, let him die.'

FRANK MATHEW

The Reverend Peter Flannery

Frank Mathew (1865–1924) evoked Irish life in many stories. This one is from his best book At the Rising of the Moon.

MY friend the Reverend Peter Flannery is the sternest-looking and the gentlest of men. To look at him you would fancy he had spent a fierce life; but the truth is that he has lived in a wilderness and that in his broad parish of Moher there is not a mouse afraid of him.

 I first met him in an hotel at Lisdoonvarna. One night there was singing, and a big, truculent old priest sang in his turn:

> When we went a-gipsying,
> A long time ago

He was very serious and hoarse. With his grim face and white hair he looked the last man in the world to 'go a-gipsying'. Afterwards I came to know Peter, and spent many evenings with him in the little house where he lives with an old housekeeper of singular ugliness and a turbulent small boy known as Patrick Flannery. I found him absurdly simple, a man knowing nothing of the world and troubling himself little about anything beyond the borders of Moher; but though he is so unpretending he has deep respect for his dignity as a parish priest. On one of those evenings in his naked little parlour he told me the story of the only adventure of his life.

A small island with a ruined house on it lies near the shore of the most desolate part of the parish; at high tide it is ringed with white jumping waves, but at ebb it is set in a black rim of rocks. A miser was strangled there for his money by his daughter, seventy years ago, so the house is known for miles around as the 'House of the Murder'. Then it was a headland, but afterwards the encroaching sea cut it off from the coast. The Moher folk say the island is haunted by the ghost of an old man with a choked face and with purple foam on his lips, and is given up to the Evil Spirits.

One stormy winter's night, nearly twelve years ago now, Peter Flannery was riding back from visiting a dying woman near Liscannor. It was raining, the wind was dead against him; he had seldom been out on such a night though his life-work took him on many a wild lonely ride. As he reached the Liscannor Cross-roads his horse stopped, and a heart-broken voice came from under the trees.

'Remember the Dark Man! For God's sake remember the Dark Man!' He knew that it was Andy Lonergan, the 'Dark Man' – that is, the blind man – who haunted that place day and night.

'Is that yourself, Andy?' said he.

''Tis so, your reverence, but 'tis the black night to be abroad, sure the Banshee is keenin' on th' island.'

'The Banshee, is it? I know, I know, and manny's the time I've heard that same, Andy. There's never a rough night without her.'

'Is it the wind ye mane, father? I know the wind's cry if annyone, but 'twasn't only that on th' island to-night; 'twas a woman's voice, sometimes 'twas like a child's. There'll be sore hearts in Moher the morn.'

'Ah well, Andy! manny's the queer thing ye've heard in your time,' said Peter, and he rode homewards, but Andy's words kept in his head. Now, the blind man was half crazed, yet dared not lie about the Banshee; perhaps there was some poor soul out on the island. At last he turned his horse; as he rode back past the Cross-roads he called out, 'Are ye there, Andy?' but no answer came. The horse seemed to have strong objections to going seaward, and Peter himself had misgivings; he is a Clare man, the son of a Ballyvaughan fisherman, and though of course he does not believe in the Banshee, yet would rather not have gone where there was any chance of meeting her. Then he thought – suppose Andy was fooling him! He could fancy the blind man sitting hidden and grinning at him as he rode back pass the Cross-roads. It would be a fine joke in Moher; he flushed at such irreverence.

Then he reached the shore, and dismounting fastened his horse to a wall, and walked down across the slipping shingle, crunching it under foot; he was tripped by tangles of seaweed, and stumbled over a fishing coracle, could see scarcely a yard in front of him. ''Tis a blind man's holiday,' he thought. 'Faith, Dark Andy could see as much as I can, and why couldn't McCaura leave his coracle in a sensible place?' He went to the water's edge, the foam splashed over him, he could see nothing but the white flashes of breakers and was deafened by the noise. A few minutes of this was enough; he turned back with a smile at the absurdity of his going out there at that time of night. 'There's no fool like an old one,' he said; then stopped to listen again, and in a pause (when the wind seemed to be taking breath for a howl) heard a child's cry from the island. How could a baby be on the island in a hurricane, when there was not a soul for miles around would go there for love or money at any time? His misgivings rushed back with uncanny legends of lost souls bound on the winds or imprisoned in the waves that always keep racing towards the land yet always break before reaching it. This might be some Devil's trap. True, he could exorcise the Devil, but would rather not.

He waited during the new howl of the wind – it seemed endless – then in the next pause heard the child's voice again; it was an unmistakably human squall. ''Tis a child, sure enough,' he said, 'an' a strong one at that.' The question for him was not how did the baby get on the island, but how was he to get it off? McCaura's cabin was a mile away across the bog, and on such a night no one would be out except Dark Andy, who would be worse than useless. The only thing was to go out to the island himself, so he groped his way to the coracle.

Now a coracle is a sort of punt, a shallow frame covered with tarpaulin, a ticklish craft, but it can live in the wildest sea, though as

Peter said — "'Tis always on the look-out for a chance to drown ye.' He
shouldered it as one to the manner born. Many a day and night had he
spent afloat in the time when he was a fisher-boy; he thought how
often since then he had longed to put out to sea, only his mighty
dignity as a parish priest forbade it. His old bones were stiff, but he was
as strong as ever.

Well, to cut a long story short, he launched that coracle and reached
the island, not without risky and hard work. Dragging the coracle
ashore, he made his way to the ruined house; the roof had fallen in,
the windows were gone, only the walls were left. He could see
nothing, but the child's cry guided him, and then in a corner he found
a woman lying huddled on a heap of fallen plaster and laths; her face
was to the wall, her left arm clutched a tiny baby. He knelt down by
her and touched her forehead — she was dead. By her dress he knew
she came from the Arran Islands. Perhaps she had been brought to the
'House of the Murder' to keep the birth secret; or perhaps the fishers
bringing her to the mainland had been caught by the gale, and could
place her in no better shelter in the time of her trouble. Now the
Arran folk were familiar to him, many were of his kindred; he must
have known this woman from her babyhood, and as a slip of a girl
running barefoot on the hills. He turned her face to him, but could
only see it dimly; it was much changed too, and half hidden by wet
hair. Then the thought came that he had no right to pry into her
secret; he laid her head back reverently. She lay there with her face to
the wall as if she had died in shame.

He took the baby and chafed it, wrapping his woollen comforter
round it; he thought it was dying — his knowledge of babies was small
— so he decided to baptize it at once. There was no lack of water, for
the rain was still falling in torrents, so he filled a cup that was lying with
some untasted food by the mother, and baptized that whining infant as
reverently and solemnly as if he had been in a great cathedral.

It must have been a strange scene in the 'House of the Murder' —
the gaunt old man dripping from the rain and the sea, holding the
baby tenderly and awkwardly, with the body of the mother lying
beside them. He gave the baby the name Patrick, the first that came to

him, '*Pathricius, ego te baptizo,*' and so forth in his queer Latin brogue, and the small new Christian howled dismally, and the gale answering howled outside. Then he unbuttoned the breast of his greatcoat and fastened the baby inside – so that only its ridiculous red face could be seen – and started for home. Crossing more easily this time, he found his old horse huddled in dumb resignation under the lee of the wall, and rode home through the storm at a good pace with a light heart. Every now and then the child cried to show that the life was in it, and then he tried to quiet it tenderly with 'Be hushed now, *vick machree*, son of my heart! Ah! Be sthill, Pathrick. Be aisy, ye cantakerous little cur!'

There was great work that night in the little house, when the old priest and his housekeeper welcomed their guest. And when the baby was cosily asleep, Peter got into his big arm-chair and mixed himself a steaming tumbler of punch – for no man values punch more, though of course in strict moderation – and he felt he deserved it to-night. 'An' would ye believe it?' and at this point of his story his voice shook with pathos – 'would ye believe it, and th' instant when I was putting it to me lips the clock sthruck twelve, and so I couldn't taste a dhrop, not a single dhrop!' For if he had tasted it after midnight he could not have said Mass. This was a lame ending to his one adventurous night. The baby was kept in the priest's house, and, when the gale went down, the mother's body was brought from the island and buried; I think Father Peter found afterwards who she was, though her name never passed his lips.

For nearly twelve years 'Pathrick' has ruled the priest's house, thriving under the rough tenderness of Peter Flannery. Meanwhile Peter has led always the same life, rising in the early morning to say Mass in the cold chapel before a scanty congregation of women; many of them pray aloud with shut eyes and entire disregard of their neighbours, and Patrick now serves him as clerk, looking very serious in his little white surplice, like a Cupid in a monk's cowl.

Then he rides on his sick-calls, miles and miles away through the bogs and over the hills, for he goes at any hour of the day or night to any one who chooses to summon him; or he walks down to the school – where he usually finds Patrick standing in the corner with his face to the wall, in disgrace – or he goes his rounds through the Village of Moher. Many a time have I seen him striding down the Village 'like an executioner' and the dirty little ragged children running to meet him and snuggling their smeared faces against his long coat. The first time babies see him they yell as if he was the Devil; but the next time they would yell louder still if he forgot to fondle them. Many a time have I seen him standing in the street, beleaguered by a cluster of women, scowling nervously over them and looking to see if there is any chance of rescue; while they all talk at once, quarrelling among themselves:

'Ah! Peggy Lonergan, dacint woman, be whisht, can't ye?'

'Mary Ronan, I take shame o' ye to be throublin' the holy priest so. Won't ye be lettin' me have a single word wid him?'

And now in the evenings he has something to dream about, and when he sits alone by the fire in his naked parlour, smoking his old pipe – with his tumbler of punch smoking too, to keep him company – he dreams of the great future of Patrick Flannery. He sees that urchin grow up as a model, go to Maynooth and win prizes there, rise rapidly in the Church, and even become a Bishop. It is true Pat will have to change greatly before them, for it is a queer Bishop he would make now; but time works wonders and Pat has a good heart.

Peter hears him preaching the great sermons himself has never preached to the great congregations he has never seen. And he thinks that 'His Lordship Docthor Flannery' has a pleasing sound, that Bishop Flannery will be loved by all, that blessings will go with him; it is he that will have an eye for true worth and never let a plain man spend his life in a wilderness while smoother-tongued men have all they want. But at this point, the dream breaks, for he knows in his heart that he would be sorry to leave his wilderness; so when the clock strikes nine he slowly finishes his punch, knocks out the ashes from his pipe and goes up the steep stairs to his bedroom, quavering in his hoarse voice,

When we went a-gipsying,
A long time ago.

AGNES CASTLE

Rosanna

Mrs Agnes Castle was the author, with her husband Egerton Castle, of 'costume'
romances of old England in the manner of Sir Walter Scott. She was also capable of
writing excellent short stories set in Ireland, of which this is an example.

SITTING by the fire we were, smoking our bits of pipes, just him and
me together, when, of a sudden, he turns on me an' he says: 'Da,' he
says, 'it's about time I was thinking of taking a wife,' says he.

'An' is that way wid ye?' I says. 'Troth, an' I'm thinking as much
meself this long time. Sure it's scandalizing discomfirture we're living
in.' I says, 'ever since poor auld Maria went and died on us, – the Lord
be merciful to her soul! Your poor mother, – the Lord be merciful to
her! – she'd like to tear the eyes out of them sluts of girls this minute, –
the blessed saint in Heaven, that she is! Thrue for ye, me boy, it's a
wife we want, and who'd be the wan to look out but yourself, since
it's the auld fellow I'm getting, entirely. And who'll it be?' says I, that
innicent, niver suspecting he'd be so undutiful as to be making his
choice unbeknownst to me – let alone that same grand choice!
'Who'll be it?' I axes him. 'What would ye say to Miss Condren at the
Cross Roads? It's thrue she's a long nose of her own; but what's that?
She's the rale auld family.'

'What 'ud I say to Miss Condren?' cries he. 'It's making game o' me
ye are, I think. What 'ud I say to Judy Condren?' says he, grinning at

me wid all his white teeth an' thim clinched over his pipe. 'Sure, if I saw that long nose of hers poking about here – "Take your snipe's beak out of this house," that's what I'd say to her.'

'Then it's one of them thriftless Roches ye've got in your mind,' says I; 'not but what auld Roche is a dacent feller, an' the girls has fine figures of their own, I'm not denying. But it's not much fortune they'd be bringing a boy.'

'Is it I,' he cried, "d take up wid one of them? Bedad, I'm surprised at ye for mintioning them at all! What would I be doing with such flithereens, streeling about wid their ribbins an' their feathers an' the impident airs of them?'

'Then it'll be Mary Cassidy, I'll be bound,' says I.

'No such thing,' says he; 'she's been walking wid Jim Nolan this month past.'

'Will it be Miss O'Donnell?' says I.

'It will not,' says he; 'I'd rather go single all me days.'

'Well, in the name of God,' says I, 'who is it to be, thin? May be it's a town-girl ye're set on after all. There's Miss Hinnegan at the hotel, – it's not the family connection I'd choose for ye, Johnny, the O'Moores have never wedded wid trade yet – but they do be sayin' it's rolling in gold she'll be when auld Hinnegan dies. She'll not say no to ye, Johnny. Troth, and I was noticing them were quare looks she was giving ye last Saturday after the pig-fair.'

'An' what sort of looks would ye have her give anny wan wid them crass eyes of hers,' says me young man, an' he takes his pipe out of his mouth an' bursts out laughing. 'Sure, God help her, she can't look one way widout lookin' the other. She'd be the right sort to put things straight for us.'

At that I bid him lave off his moidering thricks, for I knew it was humbugging me, he was, an' not a bit of marrying on him. An' he never answered me back a word, but was spacheless, playing a chune on the stem of his pipe wid his fingers, an' puffing at it, an' it black out. An' thin he says: 'It's not money we want wid a wife; ye're a warm man, father – an' its not beholden to a slip of a girl we'd be – you an' me.'

'It's aisy talking that-a-way,' says I, 'but it 'ud be no use at all, at all, for a fine young feller like yourself to go taking up wid a body that hadn't enough to keep herself. It 'ud not be respectable,' says I, 'not what your father's son was rared up to.'

'An' as for family,' says he, kind of dreamy, as if he had not heard me, 'isn't it the rale auld stock we are ourselves? O'Moores of Moorestown, discindints of Rory O'Moore, – king's blood,' says he, 'an' what's Roches, an' Condrens, an' O'Donnells to that? It's no sort of use to try and ally ourselves wid thim as'll match us,' says he; 'an' why? Because they're not to be found – that's why. We'll mate to plaze ourselves,' he says, as bould as brass; 'an' what we want is a little young crathur wid a heart full of love; a little weeshy, dawshy, coaxing bit of a thing wid eyes the colour of violets, that would swally ye'r heart alive and niver let it out again; an' a head full of curls that would drive a boy wild just to look at!'

'What sort of blasphemious talk is that out of ye?' cries I, interrupting him. 'It's meself ye'll have wild in a minute or two,' for I didn't fancy the looks of him, wid his head on one side an' a kind of silly smile on him. 'What in the whole wide worrld's upon ye?' says I. 'Spake out, man, or I'll drag the tongue out of ye jaws an' make you tell the thrut that-a-way.'

He turns upon me wid his hands on his knees, an' his face the colour of the peeonies in the garden beyant. 'Da,' he says, an' rasps his throat; 'Father,' he says an' thin out he bursts. 'You've no right,' he says, 'to be casting up at her thim rogues and vagabonds of parints of hers! Shure her mother isn't her mother at all, on'y her stepmother; an' as for her father – bad scran to him – he's the greatest bla'guard between this and Dublin. However, it's not fair,' says he, 'to be goin' on this way, for sure it's niver themselves they are, at all, but blind drunk every day of the week, an' Sundays into the bargain. But as for herself, it's the purty little crathur she is, like an angel from heaven, her that's niver seen nothing but hell's wickedness since the day she was born. She doesn't rightly know how to set about anything yit, an' if she is a Protestant it's on'y because she know no betther. She learnt no wickedness off anny of thim, an' troth it's a Catholic she'll be the minute she's told how.'

'Tare an' ages,' says I. 'ye murthering villain, hold yer tongue! Hold yer tongue, you spawn of hell, an' tell me the name of her widout another word!'

He was white now from red he was before, but his impidence was beyond everything. 'It's Rosanna Moriarty,' he says.

'Well, I let out a screech – I have a quick kind of temper, not a bad one, mind ye, but hasty-like. My poor mother – God be merciful to her! – manny's the time she'd tell us of the day I nearly murthered her wid the pitaty knife, an' I but seven years of age; an' the day I had me little sisther – God be merciful to her, that's poor auld Maria, I mean – strangled wid her apron-strings for letting me little pet rabbits run away. Blue in the face she was, an' I pulling at the strings as hard as I could! We used to be kilt wid the laughing, talking of it. But I was always the rale good Catholic, an' sure me blood was up entirely. I was like to kill him dead that minute, break his head open on him, an' small blame to me. But I controlled meself. Wid a moighty effort I kep' calm. 'Johnny O'Moore,' I says, 'ye black, onfilial, heathen scrawn of a bla'guard scamp, mintion that name in my hearing again an' I'll have your life, as sure as you stand there.'

Wid that he says no more, an' I says no more, nor was the subject as much as remarked upon between us till the next time he had impidence enough to dare, an' that was the very week after.

What did that owdacious rogue of a Moriarty go for to do, but die on us all of a suddent in the Delirious Trimmings, as the Docthur called it – a real roaring fit of drunkenness – an' his limb of a wife, she takes to her heels an' off wid her out of the place, sorra a one knew where, an' the little schemer of a Rosanna left behind on our hands together wid the corpse an' a power of debts.

It was auld Jim Roche first gave us the news; an' says he: 'It's rale bad Rosanna is, the crathur! Sure they can't get her away from the poor fella' at all, an' neither bite nor sup has crossed her lips this blessed day. It 'ud break your heart to see her, with them purty red curls of hers hanging every way, and them big black eyes of hers swollen up wid the crying. An' him the bitther bad father!'

An' then I see me fine young man start up from his corner an' off wid him widout a word.

Sure I knew the way it 'ud be. Some one would be offering to take in the girl out of charity, an' me fella' would have to be keeping up them sperrits of hers and' consoling of her an' wiping away all them tears – him as cute as a pet fox from the day he was weaned! But there's two of us can be cute, thinks I, an' out of the place she goes, or my name's not Larry O'Moore. There's the workhouse for her, an' the likes of her, beyant in the town. She'll be fed, an' warmed, an' clothed dacenter there than ever she's been in her life, an' my money helping to do it into the bargain. But I'll not have her left here to be bringing disgrace into my family. So I just says a word to Jim Roche, an' then I took a bit of a stroll, an' wint here and there, an' dropt into this wan an' that, an' be jabers I gave them all the hint. There isn't wan but 'ud be afeard to fall out wid me for they, most of them, owes me a bit an' I've been a good friend to them in the bad times. An', to tell the thrut, I'm plisanter as a friend than as an enemy.

Av course not a boy of them let on he understood what I was dhriving at: they wouldn't be that onpolite, an' I wouldn't have misdemeaned meself by speaking too plain. But, lonnies, it's aisy to say a good deal when you're saying nothin' at all, and when I came home, sure, I knew I had settled the young gintleman's nonsense for him, for as grand as he thought himself.

The auld cuckoo-clock had gone twelve (an' it's twenty minutes late regular) before Johnny came back that night. A rale warm spring night it was, black and moist, an' all his curls were plastered down his cheeks wid the way he'd been stravaguing round.

I was sitting waiting for him, smoking me pipe wid a peaceful soul, for it was a good stroke of work I had done the day, an' so I kep' telling meself, when in he burst like a wild fella.

'Father,' says he, 'I've tauld ye I wanted to marry Rosanna Moriarty; an' I mean to marry her,' he says.

'Och, listen to him,' says I, scornful; 'sure it's wandering in his speech, he is!'

'Father,' he says, rale earnest and eager, 'I've always been a good son to you. I've never been drunk nor contradictious, an' when other young men would have gone off an' seen the world, I've kep' at home an' worked an' helped you. In the name of God,' says he, pitiful-like, 'do not drive me to be undutiful now! Oh, father, it is a poor little innocent thing she is, an' it's alone and desolate she is, an' by Heaven,' he cries, 'this is a hard cruel worrld! There's not one of them'll give her a shelter or a crust this blessed night; an' on'y for auld Kitty who's sittin' and wakin' the corpse, the poor crathur 'ud be alone wid the dead this minute -- enough to drive her distracted entirely! But give your consent to our wedding,' he cries, 'an' then it's who'll have her, I'll be bound. The cauld-hearted scoundrels as could shut their doors on her that way – why, it's fighting for her they'll be then! But I'll be even wid them yet, the whole lot of them, whatever black curse of cruelty has come over them, at all, at all.'

I was puffing away at my pipe, an' for the life of me I could not but give an agreeable smile to meself, thinking it was the rale proper kind of respect I was held in all over the place; not but that I knew there was not one of them as 'ud dare to go agin me.

When he sees me smile, he stops suddent and gives me a quare look. 'Father,' says he, 'I see what you have been after. God forgive you,' he says, 'but it's a wicked man you are.'

'Whisht, now, don't be goin' on,' says I; 'you will live to thank me yet.'

'An' what is to become of that poor young crathur?' says he, quite quiet; 'have ye thought of that? She cannot live alone in that auld tumble-down place, an' her that purty an' little, an' black Mac (divel take him!) wid his eye on her this many a day. What is to become of her, father?'

'Let her go to the workhouse,' says I; 'she need not fear black Mac there, for they keep them away from each other fast enough, the young boys an' the young girls too. They will be coming, no doubt, to bury the father from the Union to-morrow; let them take the daughter too; it's the right place for her.'

Wid that, he lets the awfullest oath ever ye heard. 'She'll not go there,' he says, 'so long as I'm alive.'

'May I ax what you intend to do, then?' says I, very polite.

'I have tauld you already,' says he; 'I intend to marry her.'

'An' may I inquire what yez are going to live on then? For I warn ye fair,' says I, in a white rage – for I seen by the obstinate look of him that he was set on his wickedness – 'I warn ye,' says I, 'that across this thrashle ye will niver step once ye take up wid that Protestant slut of Moriarty's; nor a penny of me money ye will never see, neither now nor when I am gone.'

'Is that your last word?' says he, an' stands up.

'It's me last word,' says I. 'as I'm a living man.'

'Then, good-bye, father,' says he.

'Good-bye,' says I, 'an' me curse upon you,' says I. 'My father's curse on the two of yez!'

Well, out he stamps widout as much as another word, an' I sits by the fire thinking it's home again he'll be before I can turn round. Sure an' I never thought he'd have thrown me over that-a-way, an' him an' me always together from the time he was a babby. But the turf itself burnt white under my eyes, an' the dawn broke that cauld an' desolate into the room, but sorra a bit of him come back to me. An' for three days I heard no news of him, an' sure I was that dark an' down in meself not wan dared to speak to me. The fellers was afraid to tell me the thrut, an' to be plain wid ye, I was not, so to say, encouraging to conversation. Bedad, I would not let them think I cared a halfpenny what that scoundrel of a boy was up to, when he chose to go against his father that rate.

He niver came home to me, an' I axed no questions of nobody. But on the Thursday it was, Mrs Malony (his Rivirence's housekeeper, a contrary fidget of an auld woman she is) stops me just as I was passing the door. 'Oh, Mr O'Moore,' she cries, in that mincing way of hers, 'what is this I hear about Johnny?' she says. 'Father O'Hara will be fit to be tied,' she says, 'when he comes back from visiting His Holiness at Rome.'

'What may ye have heard, ma'am?' says I. 'For it's little I know or want to know about him.'

'Oh,' she says, throwing up her eyes like an auld hen in a fit, 'oh, Mr O'Moore, sir, do not ax me; I couldn't defile my tongue by speaking of it.'

'Well, an' that happens to come right,' says I, 'for I don't want to hear. Though if you can reconcile it to your conscience to be keeping the thrut from his own father, it is surprised at ye I am, Mrs Malony, an' that's all I have got to say.'

Sure, it was just itching the auld girl was to tell me the bad news. 'Is it possible you don't know, Mr O'Moore?' she says. 'Oh dear, how can I bring meself to discourse of such a scandal! It is the real saint we all thought Mr Johnny, an' him so good in the choir, an' so regular at the Stations. Och, the shame of it!' she says. 'Father O'Hara will be leppin' mad, he will! But there's little shame about either of them,' she says, 'going about that brazen, an' buying things together – set up house they have as bold as man an' wife – the like was niver seen hereabouts before. Set up house in that ruinacious auld cabin of Moriarty's, an' him not a week dead yet. And she, the dirthy Protestant. Now if she'd been a Catholic itself – Och, it's a terrible visitation to the place, an' the remarks of the folks, an' the illusions, an' the jokes, – it's shocking altogether! Could not ye speak to your son, now?'

'Mrs Malony,' says I, an' I niver turned a hair, 'he is no longer anny son of mine, an' I will thank ye to remember it. I have cast him off,' I says; 'he is no O'Moore, at all, at all, to be bringing disgrace upon the name of them that has been kings in the land. An' as for that other,' says I, 'I'm wondering how ye have the face to mintion her to me!' Wid that I made her an iligant bow an' left her.

Well, that was the cruel, hard time for me. And, as if they'd given each other the word, sure every one in the place had something to say to me about them, wonst it was out that I knew their goings on. This boy told me wan thing, an' that boy would tell another, till it is distracted I was. An' sure did not one up to me an' says he: 'Ye'd better let them be married off at wonst,' says he, 'an' save the shame of it.' I struck him prostrate for that same, for as auld as I am. 'I will let them go to hell together,' says I.

If only Father O'Hara had been back home, but it's visiting His Holiness in Rome he was, an' not expected for another week.

Sunday was the rale disgraceful day. On my entry into the chapel, before I could as much as kneel down, I hears a kind of stir in the place behind me, an' I sees all them rows of Roche girls nudging each other and tossing their heads. An' there was a kind of titter among the boys, an' auld Biddy Flannagan, the crathur, who always kneels in the middle just before the rails, where she can have a good view of his Rivirence an' plenty of room to be rocking herself about, looks over her shoulder, an' snorts like an auld say-pig, an' rolls her eyes that wild-like I thought she was struck wid an apple-complex. An' then what should I see but my young gentleman marching up the chapel, an' Miss Moriarty, if ye plaze, alongside of him in a bran new black gown, an' a white sun-bonnet – he looking neither to right nor left, an' she watching him with them saucer eyes, that had done all the mischief. An' when he salutes the altar, she gives a little dip beside him, the heathen! He kneels down at the end of the bench an' she inside. An' in a minute or two out comes little Father Jo, the curate from town beyant, who says Mass of a Sunday when Father O'Hara is away; an' glad I was to see him, for the cheeks was burning off of me. When he done the Gospel, an' he had off wid his vestment, an' come to the altar-steps to read out the notices an' everyone was quiet listening to what he was going to say, if the first things he lets out is not the banns of marriage between John O'Connell O'Moore of Moorestown in this parish an' Rosanna Moriarty of Mount Pleasant in the same! Begorrah, the whole place was swimming round wid me. Spacheless I was, an' all I could do was just to look at them, thinking it 'ud be a wonder if the auld flags would not open and swalley them up.

Himself was sitting like a lamb, niver stirring hand nor foot, his eyes fixed rale pious on the alther, as if butther would not melt in his mouth. An' she, wid her sun-bonnet tumbled off them red curls of

hers, as rosy over the impident face of her as ye plaze, wid a kind of
dimple coming an' going on one side of her cheek that was just
bursting wid smiles as anny one could see. At the sight of them I don't
know what came over me, bit I gives a kind of bawl, and ups on me
feet. 'Your Rivirence,' says I, 'I forbid them banns.'

An' Father Jo, who was rambling on quite aisy, stops as if he had
been shot. 'What's that?' says he, very sharp – you could have heard a
pin drop. But my blood was up, an' the whole place looking at me. 'I
forbid them banns,' I says; 'an' if your Rivirence wants to know about
the impidiment, sure there she is, an' sorra a bit of spiritual relation
either, but a real orange heretic, an' not a bit of shame on her, the
dirthy streel, shamming prayer beside the poor boy she had deluded
entirely – an' her breaking all the Commandments this minute. She'll
not wed him, I'll have her know it.'

'This is very onseemly,' says Father Jo, as pink as a babby to the
roots of his hair; 'I cannot have this disturbance in the chapel,' he says.

'But your Rivirence,' says I, 'didn't ye give it out this minute? "If
any one is aware," says you, and sure –'

'Whisht!' says he; 'this is scandalizing behaviour.'

'An' it is that same, yer Rivirence,' says I, 'but that's no fault of
mine.'

'Sit down,' says he; 'I'll see ye after Mass in the vestry.'

An' Johnny niver a word out of him, but sitting there like a statue. I
sees her crudle up to him like a child, an' now an' agin she shoots a
look at me out of her eyes that was swalleying up her face – too big
was they entirely. And what wid one thing an' another, I felt that mad,
that it's not a prayer I said that day.

Well, I gives Father Jo a bit o' me mind in the vestry; but not a ha'-
porth of good could I get out of him. 'Ye must speak to Father
O'Hara,' says he, 'for I cannot interfere.'

An' when I got out of the chapel, och, to hear them all talking!
'What's the meaning of her coming to chapel wid him, and her a
Protestant?' says one. 'Why it's converting her he is,' says another, and
wid that they were all fit to die wid laughing. An' didn't that scrawn of
hell, black Mac, catch up the pair of them on the road, an' out with

some of his impidence, an' did not Johnny an' he have the grandest set-to that ever was seen in these parts, an' did not Johnny give him such a pair of black eyes that the folks do be talking about it still? The finest shindy ever they saw, they tell me: but sure, I could not be taking pleasure out of anything wid the shame of the world upon me.

Well, on Tuesday evening, as I was sitting down to me bit of a supper, on the stroke of ten o'clock, who should come tearing in upon me but Father O'Hara himself. It is the holy show he was with grime an' the smuts of the railway on the pale face of him, an' his long white hair hanging wild-like over his eyes. 'What is this I hear,' he says, widout as much as reaching me his hand, 'what is this I hear about Johnny?' I was right glad to tell him the story, but when I had finished I thought he was going to murther me entirely. Rale wicked, he was, an' I as innicent as the babe unborn.

'You onnatural man,' says he, 'an' can ye sit there and tell me in cold blood that you have drove these unfort'nit children into sin? Och, God help us all,' he cries, 'that I should have to come home to this! I have been among yez forty years come Christmas an' I have had the grief of the world over yez all, God knows,' he says. 'An' manny an' manny a time I have seen yez break our Divine Master's holy commandments; manny a time, my poor flock, I have had to weep over yez and for yez. I have seen yez fighting, an' injuring, an' cheating each other, an' seen yez in jail an' in throuble, an' known in me sorrowful soul that the sentence of the law was just. When we had that terrible murther here,' he went on, ''tis fifteen year ago now, on'y for the grace of God an' His powerful consolation an' the sight of the poor sinner's beautiful penitence, sure I must have died of the agony in me heart, for it is the heart of a father I have to yez all. But niver,' he says, 'niver before in all the days I have been among yez have anny of my children fell into such sin as this. An' to think it should be the child of me predelection, little Johnny,' he cries, his voice breaking with sorrow, 'him that was my pride an' my joy, him that your sainted wife, Laurence O'Moore, laid in me arms wid her last dying effort! Oh, man,' he goes on, turning on me again, 'I hold you responsible before the throne of God for all the guilt that lies on the souls of that poor boy an' girl to-night.'

An' not bit of reason wud he hear from me. Priests an' women is that-a-way where the young folks is concerned: they do be forgetting the Fourth Commandment altogether. I could not pacify him at all, at all. 'Come wid me,' he says, 'come this minute, an' let us seek these childer. Not another night will I consent to let them stray without the Fold. Come, Laurence,' he says, 'in the name of your God, I command you; come and repair in so far as His mercy will permit the cruel wrong you have done!'

Nothing would serve him but I must set out wid him into the night beyant that very instant. An' on'y that I was afeared for his sake, on account of the state he was in, an' him such an auld man an' so frail, sure I had niver have demeaned meself by going a step.

But out he runs me, an' down the lane, an' across the village — thanks to goodness there was none about — an' up the bit of bog to the shanty, where Johnny had set up wid his light-of-love. The moon burst out of the clouds; there was a soft wind blowing round us, an' his Rivirence's face shone as pale as death wid all the white locks round it, an' him skimming along like a hare, so that I was hard set to keep up wid him. Well, we soon come in sight of Mount Pleasant. There it stood in the moonlight, wid the thatch falling off the roof, an' the mud of the walls crumbling away, the miserablest, most God-forsake hole of a place I ever see. An' as I thought of my on'y son disgracing himself by coming down to such a residence, I could not help it, but I let a curse on the pair of them.

His Rivirence whisks round an' lifts his hand, an' then he clutches me with one hand by the arm, an' points wid the other. 'See yonder!' he says, wid a kind of strangled whisper. 'See yonder, you sinful man!' An' he pointed to a black heap lying in the shade of the hovel across the door; an' then he motioned me back, so stern I durst not disobey him, an' himself went forward up to it.

'Johnny, my poor child,' he says — his voice was like a cooing dove's — 'Johnny, my poor child, what are ye lying out there for?'

An' Johnny, for Johnny it was, sleeping like a tramp on the bare turf, he up like a shot, an' rubbed his eyes, an' stared at Father O'Hara like wan daft. 'Oh, your Rivirence,' says he, reproachful like, 'sure you not have me lying widin wid the poor little girl, an' the holy words not spoken over us yet!' An' his Rivirence he beat his hands together, and fell upon the fella's neck and sobbed aloud. 'I thank God,' he cries, 'I thank God!'

'Father O'Hara, is it you?' cries Johnny, that surprised and as if he had just waked out of a dream. 'Oh, father, we have wanted ye sore, an' it's the cruel time we have had! An' it's the cruel things that people have said of us, an' she as innicent as the flowers of the field. Sure she does not know what they do be meaning. My heart's been fit to break,' he says.

An' then his Rivirence let a shout for me. 'Come here,' he says, 'Laurence O'Moore, an' bless your good son, an' give praise to the Father above that kep' him and his bride from sin, when his earthly father would have driven them into it. Come here an' tell him that ye have seen the hardness of your heart, an' repented. Tell him that he an' the good little girl he has chosen for his wife will be welcome to your hearth. An' in the meantime,' he says, 'Rosanna shall come to my house; an' Johnny, me boy, it's meself will give the wedding-feast.' An' after that what could I do?

SHAN F. BULLOCK

They That Mourn

Shan Bullock (1865–1935) was born in County Fermanagh and is best known for his collection of short stories, Ring O'Rushes *(1896), from which this story is taken. He published other short stories,* The Awkward Squad *(1893) and* By Thrasna River *(1895),* The Squireen *(1903) and* Dan the Dollar *(1905), a series of novels about Fermanagh life.*

BUNN market was over, its hurry and haggle. In corners and quiet spots of the big market-yard, you saw men and women carefully counting their little stores of silver, testing the coins with their teeth, knotting them firmly in red pocket-handkerchiefs, finally stowing them away in their long wide pockets as cautiously as though every sixpence were a diamond. In the streets, people were leisurely moving towards the shops, where tills were rattling, and counters teeming, and trade, for a few hours, mightily flourishing after its whole six days of blissful stagnation.

A cart laden with butter, chiefly in firkins, issued from the market-yard gate, a man between the shafts, one at either wheel, two pulling behind, all noisily endeavouring to keep the cart from running amuck downhill into the river. Close behind, like chief mourners after a hearse, one might fancy, came Tim Kerin and Nan his wife; a battered, slow-footed couple, heavily burdened with the big load of their years, white haired both of them, and lean as greyhounds. Heavily they shuffled along in their clumsy boots; the man with one arm across

his back, the other swinging limply; the woman holding up her skirt
with one hand, and gripping with the other the handle of an empty
basket; both looking fixedly over the tail-board of the cart at the few
pounds of butter for which they had slaved hard for weeks, and for
which, after hours of haggling, they had just received a few most
precious shillings. Fixedly they watched it, and mournfully almost, as
though they were bidding it a last farewell.

They passed through the gate, straggled across the footpath, and
silently watched the cart zigzag down the street, run presently against
the kerb, and, amid great shouting, discharge its contents into the
packing-house.

'Faith,' said Tim, across his shoulder, "twas cliverly done. I wonder,
some day, they don't break their necks.' He wagged his head
dubiously; Nan tucked up her skirt; the two turned their faces uphill,
and set out to share their profits with the shops. The butter was gone,
and sorrow go with it: 'twas a heartbreak.

Tim Kerin's share of the profits was a shining sixpence, reluctantly
tendered to him by Nan his wife, who now walked a couple of steps
behind him, with eighteenpence shut tight in her hand, and the
remainder of the butter-money (only a shilling or two) tied fast in a
cotton bag and safely stowed away in the neck of her linsey-woolsey
dress. Threepence of Tim's sixpence was to buy tobacco, a penny
might go in the purchase of a weekly newspaper, a penny would buy a
pair of whangs (leather laces) for his boots; the penny remaining, when
all those luxuries had been honestly paid for, would buy a whole
tumblerful of frothing porter. A whole tumblerful! At sight of it, with
his mind's eye, Tim's lips dried and his feet went quicker over the
cobble stones.

Nan's lips were tight, her brow wrinkled. She was figuring. It
would take her to be powerful 'cute to fill her basket with the value of
eighteenpence. Och, the lot o' things she wanted: tea, sugar, bacon, a
herring for the Sunday's dinner, a bit o' white bread – and – and
supposing there were a penny or two left over (with knowing bar-
gaining there might be), was it likely, now, that Mr Murphy, the
draper, would let her have cheap a yard of narrow soiled lace to go

round the border of her nightcaps? Twopence might do, threepence would be sure to – Aw, glory be to goodness, did anybody ever hear of such romancin', such extravagance? Sure it was runnin' wild her wits were! Threepence for lace indeed!

A friend stepped from behind a cart and caught Nan by the arm. What! was it pass a neighbour like that Mrs Kerin would do? Pass her ouldest friend, Mrs Brady, as if she were a milestone, and never pass the time of day, or tell how she sold her butter, or how the world was using herself? 'Och, och, Mrs Kerin,' moaned Mrs Brady, 'what have I done to ye at all, at all?'

Nan stopped and put out her hand; then volubly began explaining: sure, sorrow the sight of Mrs Brady she had seen; sure, she never passed a neighbour without speaking; sure, 'twas walking along romancin' she was, figuring in her head, seeing how far she could make the few shillings go. 'An' how are you, ma'am?' asked Nan, when full pardon for her oversight had been generously given and gratefully received. 'How are you an' all your care?'

Swiftly the two old heads bobbed together; ceaselessly the tongues began to wag; freely the full tide of their softly drawling speech flowed gurgling round the little nothings of their little world.

Meanwhile, Tim, his sixpence hot in his palm, had taken a turn through the throng of the streets; had questioned his neighbours about sales and prices (just as though his pockets bulged with bank-notes); had spelt out the time on the big market-house clock as he stood by the town pump listening to the hoarse drone of a ballad singer; and now, on the sidewalk of Main Street, stood dreamily looking through a shop window at a pile of newspapers which stood precariously among an array of tobacco pipes and sweet bottles. If he brought a paper, Tim was thinking, he would have a whole week's diversion o' nights; if he didn't buy it, he would save the price of another tumblerful o' – A heavy hand fell on his shoulder.

'Hello, Tim,' said his neighbour, Shan Grogan; 'havin' a wee squint at the sugar-sticks is it, ye are?'

'Aw ay,' answered Tim, turning; 'aw ay! I was just lookin' at the papers there, an' wonderin' what an ojus lot o' news they give us nowadays for a penny. Enough to keep one goin' for a week. Powerful it is.'

'Yis,' said Shan; 'it's a wonderful world. But aisy, Tim; ha' ye been to the Post lately?'

'Naw,' said Tim.

'Well, look in there if you're passin', me son. The lassie that sells the stamps asked me to tell ye. Away quick; mebbe she'll give ye news for nothin'.'

'Now, now,' answered Tim. 'I'm obliged to ye, Shan; I'm obliged to ye. Now, now,' he repeated to himself, as he shuffled off along the pavement; 'now, now. Is Shan havin' a wee joke, I wonder?' he said; and coming to the post-office doubtfully sidled in.

'Me name is Kerin, Miss,' he said to the clerk, very humbly as to one of the representatives of mighty Government itself, 'Tim for Christian; an' they tell me ye'd mebbe be havin' somethin' for me?'

The girl handed him a letter bearing the Chicago postmark, stamped in one of the bottom corners, and carrying its address thence right up to the top of the envelope. Tim bore it tenderly to the door and carefully inspected it; then took it back to the counter.

'Whose countersign might that be, Miss, if ye please?' he asked, and placed his thumb over the postmark. Humbly he asked; curtly he was answered.

'Chicago?' said Tim. 'Ay, ay! I'm obliged to ye, Miss; I'm obliged to ye. May the Lord be good to ye, an' send ye a duke for a husband. Good-day to ye, Miss,' said he; then, with his hand deep in his pocket and the letter in his hand, stepped out into the street and went off in search of Nan.

It's from Padeen, he kept thinking to himself, as he walked joyfully along, his feet clattering loosely on the pavement, his old face turning here and there, watching for his wife; it's from Padeen, sure as ever was. Aw! but he was glad. Aw! but Nan would be glad. So long it was, ages and ages ago, since they heard from him. 'Twasn't Padeen's handwrite – naw! but sure it might have altered; everything altered in the Big Country. Ay! 'twas only poor ould Ireland that kept the same – never any worse, never any better. But where was Nan? Sure she ought to be in the shops. He was dying to find her. Up and down he went; at last found her still bobbing heads at the top of Bridge Street· with her friend Mrs Brady.

'Aw, it's here ye are, Nan?' said he, coming up. 'An' me huntin' the town for ye. It's yourself is well, Mrs Brady, I'm hopin'? That's right, that's right.'

His voice came strangely broken and shrill; his eyes danced like a child's; still his hand gripped the letter in his pocket.

'What's the matter, Tim?' whispered Nan. 'Is it news ye have?'

'Ay, ay,' he answered. 'Come away till I tell ye; come away.'

He turned and, with Nan at his heels, set off almost at a run downhill towards the river. Aw! but his heart was thumpin'.

'Aisy, Tim,' cried Nan behind him; 'aisy, man, or me breath – me breath –'

Without answering, or slackening his pace, Tim went on, turned through the butter-market gate, crossed the empty yard, came to the furthermost corner of one of the long low sheds, and there halted, with his face to the wall. Aw! but his heart was thumpin'. Presently, Nan came to him, panting and flurried.

'What is it, Tim?' she asked; 'what is it?'

Slowly Tim brought out his letter, and, holding it by both hands, let his wife look at it.

'It's – it's from Padeen!' cried she; 'it's from Padeen!'

'Yis,' said Tim; 'yis. It's not his hand-write; but – but it must be from him.'

'Aw, glory be to God!' cried Nan. 'Glory be to God! Sure it's ages since we heard from the boy, ages!'

She put down her basket, and, with her head between Tim's shoulder and the wall, looked fixedly at the envelope. Aw! but she was glad to see it. Such a time it was since they had heard from Padeen! A whole two years it was, come Christmas, since the last letter came, with that money order in it, an' the beautiful picture of Padeen himself, dressed out in his grand clothes, with a gold chain across his waistcoat, and a big gold ring on his finger. A whole two years almost. And now maybe –

'Aw, Tim, open it quick,' she panted; 'open it quick!'

'Mebbe,' said Tim, 'we'd better wait till we get home. The light's bad, an' —'

'No — no, Tim! No — no; it'd kill me to wait.'

'Ay?' said Tim; then slowly drew his knife from his pocket and tenderly cut open the top of the envelope. His fingers trembled greatly as he fumbled with the enclosure. Nan's hand went quick to her heart.

'Aw, quick, Tim!' she cried. 'Quick, quick!'

'Don't — don't flooster me, woman,' said Tim; 'I can't — can't —' The next moment his shaking old fingers held a sheet of notepaper, and a black-edged card on which, in large letters, beneath a long silvern cross, were the words: PATRICK KERIN.

Nan fell back with a step; her fingers clutched at her dress over her heart. Tim's knife clattered upon the stones, and the envelope fluttered down. For a while they stood there silent, dread-stricken. At last Nan spoke. 'Read, Tim,' she said. 'Read!'

'I — I can't.'

'Ye must, Tim; it's better, Let us know the worst, for God's sake! Read, Tim.'

'I — I —' Tim began; then quickly opened the sheet. 'It's — it's too dark here,' he mumbled; 'I — I want me specs.'

'Read what ye can, Tim — an' quick, for God's sake!'

So Tim, still with his face to the wall, raised the letter to catch the light, and began to read:

CHICAGO CITY, U.S.A.

DEAR – DEAR MISTER KERIN, — *It is my — my sad duty to in-form you that your son Patrick died* ('Aw, Padeen, Padeen!') *of ty — typhus here on the 2nd of this month at twelve o'clock a.m.* ('God's mercy!' cried Nan). *As his oldest friend, I was with him at the end. He died in peace. He was buried at his request in — Cemetery. I — I send you something to – to keep . . . .*

'Aw, I can read no more,' said Tim, with a groan; 'it's too dark. I can read no more. Me poor auld Padeen!'

Nan turned and looked vacantly across at the busy street, dry-eyed and grey-faced. Ah! her poor Padeen, dead and buried away among the strangers, dead and buried, and never, never would she see him again, never hear his voice, never grip his hand! Dead, dead! her big, handsome, noble son ....

She turned to Tim and caught him by the sleeve.

'Come away home, Tim,' she said. 'Come away wi' me.' Tim looked at her.

'Ah! Nan, Nan,' he said, as the big tears sprang to his eyes. 'Nan, me girl, but's it's hard!'

'Ah yis,' said she, and lifted her basket; 'but come away, Tim, come away. Home's the best place for us.'

'Yis,' said Tim, wiping his eyes with his hand. 'Yis, Nan.' Then, Nan leading the way and Tim shuffling after, the two old people (mourners now in real earnest) crossed the yard; and at the gate Nan halted.

'I think,' said she, as Tim came up, 'I think we can manage this week wi'out the bits o' groceries. Sure they're only luxuries anyway. I'll go an' see if Mr Murphy can find me a bit o' crape for me bonnet. Yis.'

'Do,' said Tim. 'Do, Nan; an' when you're about it,' he said, taking his sixpence from his pocket and handing it to her, 'ye may as well get me a bit for me hat. Ay! sure I can do wi'out me tabaccy for one week. Aw yis! Away quick, Nan; an' hurry back, me girl, hurry back.'

So Nan turned up towards the market-house; but Tim went downhill towards the bridge; and when, presently, Nan came to him, carrying her little packet of crape in her big basket, Tim's head was bowed over the parapet and he was mumbling tearfully:

'Aw, me poor Padeen, me poor Padeen!'

Nan plucked at his sleeve.

'Come away home, Tim,' she said; 'come away.' And at the word Tim raised his head, dried his eyes, and set off slowly after Nan up the long, dusty road that wearily led towards home.

SEAMAS MACMANUS

The Bewitched Fiddle

Seamas MacManus (1869–1960) was born in County Donegal. He wrote many tales of old Ireland and the Irish peasantry in particular. 'The Bewitched Fiddle' is based on a story told him in his boyhood and is full of humour. In his time, he was a writer highly popular in the United States where he lived for some time, dying in New York.

FAIX, it's a good long wheen of years since it happened now. It was ould Jimmy Higgerty, that was uncle to Mickey acrass there, reharsed the passage to me. An' it was ould Jimmy himself, more betoken, that was the cause of the whole affair – for Jimmy, ye know, was what we call a canny man, very knowin' intirely, an' up to all sorts of saicrets that you nor me nor one belonging to us, thanks be to Providence, knows nothin' at all, at all about. Jimmy was right-han' man with the fairies; an' if ye'd believe all the stories ye hear goin' he come through some quare things, too, in his day – used to be out, they say, as reg'lar as the sunset, an' away ridin' aist an' waist with the good people, an' gettin' insight into their ways of workin'; an' sure it's meself that rec'le'ts if there was only a bit of a year-oul' calve sick from one end of the barony to the other, it was nothin' but post haste for Jimmy Higgerty to cure it – an', sure enough, when Jimmy put the charm on it, it either lived or died afther; there was no middle coorse.

Well, howsomiver, in Jimmy's day there was in Doorin a one Solomon Casshidy; an' the same Solomon in his young days was a thrifle wild – the fact is (to kill the hare at a blow), Solomon was the completest rascal ivir run on two feet, an' was a parable for the counthry. Christenin', weddin', wake, funeral, patthern, fair, or market nivir wint off complete without Solomon Casshidy; dance, raffle, or spree of any sort, shape, or patthern nivir missed Solomon Casshidy, who, by the way, was the very life an' sowl of the gatherin's; an' people would as soon think of doin' without the fiddler at one of these merry-makin's as without Solomon Casshidy. An' that just put me in mind that Solomon was the dandy hand at the fiddle; the bate of him wasn't to be got between cock-crow an' candlelight the longest day in June. He would charm the heart of a whin-bush; arrah, good luck to your wit, man, he'd actially make the fiddle spake! They say it was as good as a sarcus to hear how he'd handle it.

But poor Solomon, good luck to him, soon came to the end of his tether, an', afther takin' all the fun he could out of the worl', he, as himself said, turned over a new laif an' begun to look at the other side of the picther. An' I'm thinkin' whatsomiver he seen on the other side of it must have been deuced onpleasant, for the rollickin', singin', laughin', fiddlin', reckless, ne'er-do-well Solomon pulled a face on him the length of a tailyer's lapboord, an' if any of his ould comrades attimpted to make him convarsible on the fun that was goin' in any quarther of the counthry, Solomon would dhrop his jaws, an' fetch a groan would frighten a corp'; an' 'My fren',' he would say, 'this is all vanity, vanity! Life is hollow, an' these frivolities are only snares spread in our paths by the divil.'

Anyhow, Solomon was an althered man, an' where he would go formerly to honour the Sabbath by a rousin' game of *caman* with the good boys, he was now seen makin' his way to the meetin'-house with a Bible anondher his arm the size of a salt-box, an' as many hime-books as would set up a hawker in a daicent way of thradin', an' he obsarvin' naither to the right nor to the left, but away a thousand miles ahead of him, as if he was always thryin' to make out the way to heaven somewhere in the skies foreninst him; an' where he would of another time be makin' his way across the counthry, maybe to the shouldher of Srual mountain for a spree, with the fiddle anondher his coat, ye might now meet him in the dusk of the evenin', still with the fiddle ondher the coat, but on a far betther errand – goin' to some prayer-meetin' at Inver, or Killymard, or Ballywell, or the divil only knows where; he wouldn't go within an ass's roar of a raffle-house; an' if you tould him there was to be a dance or any other wee divarshin in sich and sich a place he'd strive to put the breadth of a townlan' betwixt him an' it, for he said the divil was chained to the back-stone of any house that there was a hornpipe played in.

Well, one evenin', it was in October, an' jist about night-fallin', Solomon was makin' his way for Billy Knox's of the head of the Glibe, where a great and very pious man, one Bartholomew Binjamir Rankin, was to hold a prayer-meetin' for the benefit of all the well-disposed sinners in that stretch of counthry; an' throth, it seems to me that, onless the Glibe's changed mortially within the last jinnyration, there must have been a daicent quantity of sinners in them same parts. But, as I was sayin', Solomon was this evenin' on the good arrand, with his fiddle peepin' out from ondher his coat – for ye see, Solomon's ould practice whin he was a sinner come in handy now that he was a saint, an' no prayer-meetin' could be held without Solomon's fiddle to steady the voices, when they joined to sing the himes. She was a splendid piece of a fiddle, an' Solomon, when he turned over the new laif, was goin' out to brak her neck across the nixt ditch, when he remembered how she might come in handy this way, so he said to himself (as he tould afther), that 'he'd make the occasion of his sins a steppin'-stone to new vartues, an' cause her that was hairtofore jiggin' him down to the place below, now fiddle him into heaven'.

He thought to himself this evenin' that he'd jist light the pipe to keep him company as he jogged on, so where do ye think he'd dhrop into, on purpose to light it, but ould Jimmy Higgerty's, the fairyman's, that I reharsed to yet about before. On layin' 'Pagganinny', as he called the fiddle, down on a stool, whilst he was puttin' a screed of coal to the pipe, Jimmy Higgerty lifted her, an' dhrawin' the bow acrass her, he took a bar of a lively tune out of her, when Solomon jumped up as if he was sthruck.

'Higgerty, me good man,' he says, 'you have shocked me. Thim vain airs,' siz he, 'has been long unknown to that fiddle, an' I trusted that she would nivir more be an insthrument that the divil would gamble for sowls on. Paice, paice, and dhraw not the bow in idle vanity again!'

'Arrah, good morra to ye,' siz Jimmy, that way back to him, 'but it's delicate yer narves must have got intirely, lately. Throth, Misther Casshidy, I seen the time this wouldn't frighted ye one bit'; an' all at oncet he sthruck up, 'Go to the divil an' shake yerself,' while poor Solomon stood thrimblin' in the middle of the flure like a man with the aguey. While Jimmy finished up with a flourish that would have delighted Solomon the days he was at himself (for, be the same token, Solomon was no miss at handlin' the bow naither), he cut some quare figures with his left han' three times over the fiddle, an' handin' it to Solomon, he says, 'May ye nivir have more raison to be frightened than by a jig from the same fiddle – *that's all I say!'*

Poor Solomon didn't know the hidden mainin' of them words, or it would have made him look crooked; nor he didn't know naither that Jimmy had put *pisherogues* on the fiddle; but all the same he took it from him with a glum look enough, and afther praichin' an edifyin' sarmon on frivolities, an' death an' jedgment, to Jimmy Higgerty, he betook him on the road again.

There was a wonderful congregation of the sinners an' saints of the Glibe – but the sinners had the best of it anyhow, in regards to numbers – in Bill Knox's that night. An' Bartholomew Binjamin Rankin was there, an' it was as good as a sarmin in itself just to get one glance at his face. There was as much holiness an' piety in it, ye'd a'most think, as would save the sowls of a whole barony., Solomon, who now got all sorts an' sizes of respect, as bein' a reformed sinner, an' was looked up to with ten times as much honour and rivirence as was paid to them that was saints all their life, got a salt, as was usual, beside the praicher. An' it's himself that was proud, an' he'd look down on the common crowd below with a most pityin' look on his face. An' the well-disposed ones in the congregation would look up at Solomon an' then give a groan that ye might hear at Srual; an' Solomon would look down on the sinners an' give another groan that ye might hear him at Barnesmore; an' then both Solomon an' the sinners would look up at the rafthers, an' give a groan that ye might hear at Muckish. Afther some time, when they had got faistin' their sowls fairly well on Solomon, a hime was called out, a very solemn one. 'An',' says the praicher, lookin' at Solomon, 'our saintly brother here, of whom aich and ivery heart in this gatherin' feels proud, an' whose pious ways are the glorification, admiration, an' edifycation of every true Christian since he gave up his ungodly life, an' turned onto the path of righteousness – brother Solomon will give us the keynote, an' lend us the aid of his unmusical box, throughout.'

Brother Solomon, be me socks, dhrew a face on him the length of his own fiddle, as if he was thinkin' of his own unworthiness, poor man, an' says:

'If affords me a pious pleasure to dhraw my bow ondher the circumstances – that bow which so often snared me into the divil's sarvice; but I thank God with my heart that I have long since departed from my wicked, wicked, unspaikably vile an' sinful ways; an' this han' has long since forgotten them vain and ungodly airs that at one time occupied every spare moment of my then onChristian life – long since, I say, have I buried deep in obliveen every remimbrance of thim wicked tunes, an' the cunnin' of my han' is now only used for a far loftier an' betther purpose. Bretherin, I shall begin.'

And Solomon dhraws the bow across the fiddle, an' of all the himes tunes which was prented, what do ye think does he sthrike up? 'Go to the divil an' shake yerself!' Och, it's as thrue as I'm telling it to ye. But, *ochón*, if there wasn't consternation in that house, I'm a gintleman! Solomon himself stopped suddent, for all the world lookin' like a stuck pig; an' he looked at the praicher, an' the praicher looked at him, and the congregation looked at both of them, and then Solomon prayed from his heart as he nivir prayed afore, that the Lord in His marcy might make the flure open and swallow him. The flure, though, as I suppose ye have guessed, did not open, but Bartholomew Binjamin's mouth did, an' he sayed, siz he:

'Bretherin! bretherin! this is a sad fallin' away! Alas ! alas! Who should have thought that Brother Solomon, the deformed sinner, would have returned to his ould godless coorses! The rulin' passion, my dear bretherin, is so sthrong in him – waxin' sthrong with new strength – that he has onvoluntarily bethrayed the divil that has again got hould on him. Bretherin, let us pray for him!'

An' in a jiffey the thunderstruck congregation were on their knees prayin' like Trojans for the delivery of poor Solomon from the divil. Solomon, of course, for appairance' sake, had to take to his knees, too, but between you an' me, it's meself's afeard that all the prayers he said would not fetch him very far on the way to the first milestone that leads to heaven. I'll wager whoivir heerd him, that his prayers were sweet ones, that the divil might saize ould Jimmy Higgerty an' carry him off body an' bones, an' give him a toastin' on a special griddle down below. When they thought they had prayed long enough, an' that the divil was gone out of Solomon, they got up to their feet again, and they turned up the whites of their eyes till Bartholomew Binjamin announced that they would oncest more put Brother Solomon's faith to the test, to see if he had profited by the few minutes' sperritial recreation that they had indulged in. Solomon lifted the bow, an' afore he started he turned up the whites of his eyes in the usual fashion, as if he was lookin' for guidance, but in his heart he was only callin' down another black curse on Jimmy Higgerty.

'Bretherin!' siz he, as solemn as a judge – 'Bretherin! The temper' (by which he meant the divil of coorse) 'possessed the fiddle, and not my humble self; in witness whereof just attind to the solemn an' addyfyin' air I will now produce for ye.' An' down comes the bow on the fiddle, an' up starts that beautiful jig tune, 'The Siege of Carrick'!

Och, tarnation to me waistcoat, but there was sich a scene in two minnits as would charm a dancin' masther! When Solomon played the first bar of it, he could as soon comb his head with his toes as he could stop it. But that wasn't the best of it. Bartholomew Binjamin, instead of goin' into a cowld dead faint, as one would expect, begun to shuffle his feet in a suspicious way, an' afore ye'd say 'thrapsticks' he was weltin' the flure like the broth of a boy, tearin' away at the jig like the ould Nick! An' in the squintin' of yer eye there wasn't a sowl anondher the roof, man, woman, or child, saint or sinner, that wasn't whackin' away at it like the forties, iviry man of them leatherin' the flure like a thrasher, jumpin' up till their heads would a'most sthrike the rafters, an' yellin' like red Injins, whilst me brave Solomon played like a black, put new life into the fiddle at ivery squeak, an' gave the jiggers whativer wee encouragement that he could spare time from the fiddle for:

'Come, boys, yez haven't fair play to foot it properly here. Yez is the finest set at a jig that I have faisted me eyes on since I give up me ungodly ways, an' it would be a pity for not to give yez ivery privilege – it's a fine clear moonlight, an' we'll go outside where we'll have room an' fair play at it. Come along, me mirry, mirry lads!' An' Solomon fiddled away out of the dure, an' the whole congregation leapt an' flung an' jigged it out in all possible an' onpossible shapes afther him. Och, they say it was a sight for sore eyes to see the capers that the party cut; ivery man jack of them tryin' to see who could be crazier than his naybour; an' out they got that way on the road, like a lunatic asylum turned loose for a holiday; an' Solomon headed down the road in the direction of Donegal, while the whole countryside turned out when they heard the yellin' an' fiddlin' an' prancin', an' seein' Solomon headin' them with the fiddle, an' Bartholomew Binjamin fillin' the front rank in company with his two feet, an' he jiggin' it away at the rate of a christenin'! The people were first inclined to laugh, but be the powdhers the nixt thing they done was join in themselves, an' foot it way afther the fiddle ninety-nine times crazier than the congregation. An' hot foot they kept it goin', up hill an' down dale, over height an' hollow, with fresh batches joinin' in at ivery lane an' turn, an' Solomon, the boy, layin' into the fiddle at a rate as if he was gettin' a salary for it; an', be the boots, by the time they raiched the foot of the road, you niver seen in all your born days a harvest fair or a Repale meetin' as big as it was!

Here Solomon turned to the left, with the purcession still jiggin' it afther him, an' he nixt got onto the lane that leads up to the Killymard ould graveyard, an' over the stile, in among the graves with the mirry company brakin' their necks over, afther him; an' when they got in here, Solomon made thracks for a nate dandy bit of a tombstone in the centre of the yard, an' upon it he h'isted himself, with Bartholomew Binjamin up beside him, whilst the remainder of the party reshumed their attitudes all roun' about, an' they fightin' like wild cats to see who would get pursession of the tombstones, for they say they were as good as barn-doors for dancin' on. An' throgs, there might be purty good dancers there, but divil resave the one of them that Solomon and Bartholomew Binjamin couldn't take the shine out of. They had a bran' new tombstone, the pick an' choice of all in the yard, an' if they didn't do it in royal style, an' cut a copy to the crowd, call me a cuckoo!

But what would ye have of it, but the nixt man lands on the scene was Sandy Montgomery, the Recthor. He was passin' the road, an' seein' the fun in the graveyard, he come up in a t'undherin' passion to horsewhip iviry mother's sowl of them. But, sweet good luck to ye, if he didn't jump up on the fiddler's tombstone, an' catchin' Bartholomew Binjamin by the han', foot it away, likewise.

An' it would have gone on to daylight in the mornin', if ould Jimmy Higgerty, the rascal, who followed the fun the whole way from the Glibe, for the purpose of tastifyin' to it – if he hadn't come behin' Solomon an' tould him to kick up his right heel, dhraw his left thumb three times over the sthrings of the fiddle, an' look over his left shouldher at the moon, an' then see what music he'd take out of it. No sooner sayed nor done; an' all at once the tune changed to a hime tune, all mournful, an' iviry heel in the graveyard was paralyzed. Ivery sowl of them looked at one another like they wor wakenin' out of a dhraim.

Solomon himself dhrew up, an' he gave a bewildhered look all roun' him, an' then looked at Sandy Montgomery, who was standin' forenenst him on the stone, an' he as pale as a sheet. Ivery man of the three on the tombstone gave themselves up as lost men, ruinated intirely, out an' out, afther making' such spectacles of themselves for the counthry. The Recthor lost conthrol of himself completely, an' puttin' his fist anondher Solomon's nose, he says:

'Ye common scoundhril, ye; ye've made me disgrace my cloth, ye cut-throat villain –'

But afore he could get another word, Solomon, who had some of the spunk of his early days in him still, and was a thrifle hasty, besides that his dandher was riz in regards to the purty pickle he was in – Solomon ups with the fiddle, an' dhrawin' it roun' his head with a swing, he takes the Recthor across the noddle an' knocked him a'most into kingdom come, away off the tombstone. But, my hearty, in swingin' the fiddle, doesn't he catch Bartholomew Binjamin, who was standin' behind him, a nate little bit of a knock on the skull. So, now turnin' round to apologize to him, Bartholomew Binjamin ups with his fist an' plants it undher Solomon's nose, too, for he was just commencin' a norration.

'Ye mane, onprincipled, ungodly bla'guard!'

But Solomon couldn't stand this neither. He says to himself he might as well be hung for a sheep as a lamb, and that when he knocked down a Recthor, he might with an asier conscience knock down a praicher. So he took the praicher a wallop with the fiddle that left him sprawlin' in the Recthor's lap with his heels uppermost, and Solomon leapt from the tombstone, an' off through the crowd for the bare life, wallopin' them right an' left. They all slunk home afther a while with their tails between their legs, but poor Solomon was the worst of all. He made 'Pagganinny' into smithereens – what remained of her. An' he didn't lift his head for twelve months afther.

DANIEL CORKERY

The Breath of Life

Daniel Corkery (1878–1964) was Professor of English at University College, Cork from 1931–47. His best-known books are A Munster Twilight *(1916) and* The Threshold of Quiet *(1917). He also wrote many plays. Professor Corkery opened many readers' eyes to the forgotten riches of eighteenth-century Gaelic poetry and the ancient Irish cultural heritage.*

THE opera company which I had accompanied as first violinist on so many tours suddenly collapsing, I found myself rather unexpectedly out of an engagement. I communicated with my society, and after a day's delay I was ordered to go at once to Clonmoyle.

I was in the worst of humours. Clonmoyle was one of those places in Ireland which, instead of increasing in size and importance as places ought, seem to have become accustomed to doing the very opposite. Once a city, it was now but a straggling town. What had brought an opera company to try its fortunes there I could make no guess at, yet there it was, and with difficulties accumulating about it. Here was I myself, for instance, in Clonmoyle because the manager had found it impossible to supplement his scanty travelling orchestra with local players; and several others as well as I had had to travel day and night to be in time for the opening performance. Only one local musician had been dug up; and of him this story.

In everything he stood apart from us. He was old, well over sixty, however young in appearance. He was large and heavy in build, easy-going, ruminative. We, the others in the band, were rather meagre, high-strung, irritable, worried – as is the way of our tribe; on this trip particularly so (consider my own case: a first-class violinist in such surroundings!). He, on the other hand, smiled the whole day long, and his voice whispered rather than spoke. It did not seem to trouble him that the old ramshackle theatre was mouldy, damp, foul-smelling. He did not seem to notice the cruel draughts that swept us while we played, and benumbed our fingers. It made no difference to him if the manager was in a vile temper over the receipts, and our conductor still worse, his rheumatism playing old Harry with him.

At our first rehearsal I discovered he could not play in tune. 'I'm in for it!' I said, for a week of such fellowship I knew only too well would leave me a wreck. And even as I said this I saw the conductor staring hard at where the two of us were sitting side by side; was it possible he thought it was I who was playing like that! He might well have thought so, for my companion's face was not a guilty face; how any one could play so consistently flat and still smile was a problem beyond me. Yes, Ignatius O'Byrne, such was his name, still smiled and still flattened. The fact is, he was the happiest alive; it was as if he had come into an inheritance. Here he was fiddling away in his beloved operas, and it was thirty years since he had last done so. These long thirty years, he explained to me in an interval, he had been rehearsing them in his untidy lodgings in a back street, and more than that, he had been thinking them out, phrase by phrase, 'walking in the mists upon these rain-soaked hills' – I give his very words. As he spoke he swept his hand in a half-circle as if even there in the theatre he could still behold them, the dreary hills that surround Clonmoyle on every side and overlay it, as it were, with a sort of perpetual gloom. And then he added: 'Behind music is the breath of life.' A curious man, surely; I watched his face. It was glowing, glowing, as long as the music held. And once when in some happy passage the whole band was singing like one, 'Bravo, Bravo!' I heard him whisper, and later on 'Bra-vissimo!' and he ceased playing, ceased, until I thought of nudging him with my elbow. And so, little by little, I came to forgive him his flat playing and his awkward bowing.

Our conductor, a brute of a man, his body twisted into a knot by rheumatism, was now constantly looking in our direction; but whenever I saw him doing so I would make my violin sing for all it was worth; were we not brothers in the same craft, this old man and I? At rehearsal the second day my efforts to cover his wretched playing failed; the conductor left his place, tied up and all as he was in that knot of pain, shuffled over to where we sat, and stood between us! That settled for him which of us was playing flat. He scowled at the old resurrected musician, hissed out a fierce, wicked word under his breath, and hobbled back to his place. That night, just to make matters worse, I suppose, old Byrne played altogether vilely! He had a scarce a phrase in tune. When the curtain fell he had to face a little tragic opera of his own – the tragedy of old age and failing powers. He took it all without a word. 'The breath of life is behind music,' he whispered to me as he came from the interview; then he bent down, carefully wrapped his fiddle in a piece of braize cloth, put it in his case and made off.

The final explosion came at the rehearsal next day. He and I were the first to arrive. The score of last night's opera, it was the *Marriage of Figaro*, still lay on the conductor's stand. He turned the pages. They were pencilled all over with directions as to the tempos of the various movements. Along these pencillings old Bryne ran his finger. I could see he was having his revenge. I could see him lift his brows – just a little – as if he were amused, partly astonished. But no word escaped him. Soon the conductor came in and we began. We had not got far when we heard 'Get out!' roared in a terrible voice, the voice of one who had not slept for several nights. The old man rose up, wrapped his baize cloth around his instrument, and moved between the chairs. As he went how still the house was, only a chair moving, and his own almost silent feet! And how we watched him! But when he got as far as the conductor's chair he paused, glanced once more at the open score, once again ran his finger along the pencillings, and laughed a tiny little laugh!

I felt his going more than I should care to tell. Will you believe me? I had told that old musician, that stranger, the whole story of the sorrows of my life. Yes, I told him things I had hardly ever made clear even to myself! And he replied: 'Is it not behind music, the breath of life?' as if sorrow was there for the one purpose of being transmuted into sweet sound! I recalled his words as I went to my task that night.

And that night the extraordinary thing happened; our conductor failed to make an appearance: his rheumatism had conquered. There was then a call for our leader. He was found. Alas, he was not in a condition to conduct anything. He could scarcely stand. And he became quite cross about it; we had to leave him there in his corner, resining his bow like anything and scowling like mad. What between principals, chorus, and band, all thinking they stood a chance of losing a night's pay, and the manager flustering about like a whirlwind, our little den beneath the stage was deafening; I slipped quietly out into the house. There outside the rail was old Byrne! 'What's the matter?' he whispered. As I told him, up came the manager.

'Mr Melton,' he said to me, 'will you please take the baton to-night?'

A very flattering compliment, indeed, and I should have taken that baton, if our band did not happen to be the scraggiest ever scraped together from the ends of the earth; our leader was in the condition I have mentioned. As we spoke I saw the players getting into their places, a tempting sight, yet still I hesitated, foreseeing collapse and ignominy.

'It is not possible,' I began, but over the rail old Byrne was climbing like a boy. He had clutched the baton from the manager's hand. He had leaped into the conductor's chair. He gave but one glance to the right, to the left. 'Now, boys,' he said, and at the words we swam, sank, buried ourselves in the rich, broad, gentle strains of the overture to *Faust*. Some wide gesture he had used, some thrill in his tone had bidden us to do so – to lose ourselves in the soul of the music. At the first chord we had got within the skin of it, as the saying is. And never was the mood broken; every progression told, and not a colour tone was faulty or blurred. That memorable waltz, which use has almost spoiled, he made a new thing of it – we were all spirits in thin air, so lightly it went. But our triumph was the tremendous trio at the close.

The old man stood up to it, hiding the stage from a large sector of the house. What did he care! We felt his huge shabby figure above us as a darkness, a vastness of great potency. It commanded stage, orchestra, house, with a strong yet benign power. The voices, tenor, soprano, bass – all the instruments, strings, brass, wood, drums, the very shell of the old house itself, became as one instrument and sang the great strain with such strength and perfection that some of us trembled lest we should fall down with excitement and spoil everything.

'Oh!' we all sighed when it was over. For such moments does the artist live. I was so glad I had told him the story of my sorrows!

Now, sir, around Clonmoyle, as I have said, is a rampart of dark hills, bleak and rain-sodden, treeless and desolate. Why do I again mention them? 'Wherever did you learn to conduct?' I asked him, as we made for our lodgings.

'There!' he answered, and his outstretched hand gestured around the deserted hills, 'behind music we must get at the breath of life.' Bare, wind-swept hills! – curious place to find out the secrets of life! Or what he did he mean by 'Life'? It cannot be that the breath of life that is behind all great music is the sigh of loneliness?

'And you took him with the company?'

'No, sir; an opera company, like any other company, must pay its way.'

SEAMUS O'KELLY

The Rector

Seamus O'Kelly (1875–1918) was born in County Galway. He was a playwright as well as a short story writer. His novel, The Lady in the Deerpark, *was published in 1917. He was the editor of the Sinn Fein newspaper,* Nationality, *in Dublin. He died of a heart attack when British troops raided the offices in 1918.*

THE Rector came round the gable of the church. He walked down the sanded path that curved to the road. Half-way down he paused, meditated, then turning, gazed at the building. It was square and solid, bulky against the background of the hills. The Rector hitched up his cuffs as he gazed at the structure. Critical puckers gathered in little lines across the preserved, peach-like cheeks. He put his small, nicely-shaped head to one side. There was a proprietorial, concerned air in his attitude. One knew that he was thinking of the repairs to the church, anxious about the gutters, the downpipe, the missing slates on the roof, the painting of the doors and windows. He struck an attitude as he pondered the problem of the cracks on the pebble-dashed walls. His umbrella grounded on the sand with decision. He leaned out a little on it with deliberation, his lips unconsciously shaping the words of the ultimatum he should deliver to the Select Vestry. His figure was slight, he looked old-world, almost funereal, something that had become detached, that was an outpost, half-forgotten, lonely; a man who had sunk into a parish where there was nothing to do. He

mumbled a little to himself as he came down to the gate in the high
wall that enclosed the church grounds.

A group of peasants was coming along the yellow, lonely road,
talking and laughing. The bare-footed women stepped with great
active strides, bearing themselves with energy. They carried heavy
baskets from the market town, but were not conscious of their weight.
The carded-wool petticoats, dyed a robust red, brought a patch of
vividness to the landscape. The white 'bauneens' and soft black hats of
the men afforded a contrast. The Rector's eyes gazed upon the group
with a schooled detachment. It was the look of a man who stood
outside of their lives, who did not expect to be recognized, and who
did not feel called upon to seem conscious of these peasant folk. The
eyes of the peasants were unmoved, uninterested, as they were lifted
to the dark figure that stood at the rusty iron gate leading into the
enclosed church grounds. He gave them no salutation. Their conversation, voluble, noisy, dropped for a moment, half through
embarrassment, half through a feeling that something alive stood by
the wayside. A vagueness in expression on both sides was the outward
signal that two conservative forces had met for a moment and refused
to compromise.

One young girl, whose figure and movements would have kindled
the eye of an artist, looked up and appeared as if she would smile. The
Rector was conscious of her vivid face, framed in a fringe of black hair,
of a mischievousness in her beauty, some careless abandon in the
swing of her limbs. But something in the level dark brows of the
Rector, something that was dour, forbade her smile. It died in a little
flush of confusion. The peasants passed and the Rector gave them
time to make some headway before he resumed his walk to the
Rectory.

He looked up at the range of hills, great in their extent, mighty in
their rhythm, beautiful in the play of light and mist upon them. But to
the mind of the Rector they expressed something foreign, they were
part of a place that was condemned and lost. He began to think of the
young girl who, in her innocence, had half-smiled at him. Why did
she not smile? Was she afraid? Of what was she afraid? What evil thing

had come between her and that impulse of youth? Some consciousness – of what? The Rector sighed. He had, he was afraid, knowledge
of what it was. And that knowledge set his thoughts racing over their
accustomed course. He ran over the long tradition of his grievances –
grievances that had submerged him in a life that had not even a place
in this wayside countryside. His mind worked its way down through
all the stages of complaint until it arrived at the *Ne Temere* decree. The
lips of the Rector no longer formed half-spoken words; they became
two straight, tight little thin lines across the teeth. They would remain
that way all the afternoon, held in position while he read the letters in
the *Irish Times*. He would give himself up to thoughts of politics, of
the deeds of wicked men, of the transactions that go on within and
without governments, doping his mind with the drug of class opiates
until it was time to go to bed.

Meantime he had to pass a man who was breaking stones in a ditch
by the roadside. The hard cracks of the hammer were resounding on
the still air. The man looked up from his work as the Rector came
along; the grey face of the stone-breaker had a melancholy familiarity
for him. The Rector had an impulse – it was seldom he had one. He
stood in the centre of the road. The *Ne Temere* decree went from his
mind.

'Good-day, my man,' he said, feeling that he had made another
concession, and that it would be futile as all the others.

'Good-day, sir,' the stone-breaker made answer, hitching himself
upon the sack he had put under his haunches, like one very ready for a
conversation.

There was a pause. The Rector did not know very well how to
continue. He should, he knew, speak with some sense of colloquial-
ism as if he was to get on with this stone-breaker, a person for whom
he had a certain removed sympathy. The manner of these people's
speech was really a part of the grievances of the Rector. Their conversation, he often secretly assured himself, was peppered with
Romish propaganda. But the Rector made another concession.

'It's a fine day, thank God,' he said. He spoke like one who was
delivering a message in an unfamiliar language. 'Thank God' was local,

and might lend itself to an interpretation that could not be approved. But the Rector imported something into the words that was a protection, something that was of the pulpit, that held a solemnity in its pessimism.

'A fine day, indeed, glory be to God!' the stone-breaker made answer. There was a freshness in his expression, a cheerfulness in the prayer, that made of it an optimism.

The Rector was so conscious of the contrast that it gave him pause again. The peach-like colourings on the cheeks brightened, for a suspicion occurred to him. Could the fellow have meant anything? Had he deliberately set up an optimistic Deity in opposition to the pessimistic Deity of the Rector? The Rector hitched up the white cuffs under his dark sleeves, swung his umbrella, and resumed his way, his lips puckered, a little feverish agitation seizing him.

'A strange, down-hearted kind of a man,' the stone-breaker said to himself, as he reached out for a lump of limestone and raised his hammer. A redbreast, perched on an old thorn bush, looking out on the scene with curious eyes, stretched his wing and his leg, as much as to say, 'Ah, well,' sharpened his beak on a twig, and dropped into the ditch to pick up such gifts as the good earth yielded.

The Rector walked along the road pensive, but steadfast, his eyes upon the alien hills, his mind travelling over ridges of problems that never afforded the gleam of solution. He heard a shout of a laugh. Above the local accents that held a cadence of the Gaelic speech he heard the sharp clipped Northern accent of his own gardener and general factotum. He had brought the man with him when he first came to Connacht, half as a mild form of colonization, half through a suspicion of local honesty. He now saw the man's shaggy head over the Rectory garden wall, and outside it were the peasants.

How was it that the gardener got on with the local people? How was it that they stood on the road to speak with him, shouting their extravagant laughter at his keen, dry Northern humour?

When he first came the gardener had been more grimly hostile to the place than the Rector himself. There had been an ugly row on the road, and blows had been struck. But that was some years ago. The gardener now appeared very much merged in the life of the place; the gathering outside the Rectory garden was friendly, almost a family party. How was it to be accounted for? Once or twice the Rector found himself suspecting that at the bottom of the phenomenon there might be all unconscious among these people a spirit of common country, of a common democracy, a common humanity, that forced itself to the surface in course of time. The Rector stood, his lips working, his nicely-shaped little head quivering with a sudden agitation. For he found himself thinking along unusual lines, and for that very reason dangerous lines – frightfully dangerous lines, he told himself, as an ugly enlightenment broke across his mind, warming it up for a few moments and no more. As he turned in the gate at the Rectory it was a relief to him – for his own thoughts were frightening him – to see the peasants moving away and the head of the gardener disappear behind the wall. He walked up the path to the Rectory, the lawn dotted over with sombre yew trees all clipped into the shape of torpedoes, all trained directly upon the forts of Heaven! The house was large and comfortable, the walls a faded yellow. Like the church, it was thrown up against the background of the hills. It had all the sombre exclusiveness that made appeal to the Rector. The sight of it comforted him at the moment, and his mental agitation died down. He became normal enough to resume his accustomed outlook, and before he had reached the end of the path his mind had become obsessed again by the thought of the *Ne Temere* decree. Something should, he felt convinced, be done, and done at once.

He ground his umbrella on the step in front of the Rectory door and pondered. At last he came to a conclusion, inspiration lighting up his faded eyes. He tossed his head upwards.

'I must write a letter to the papers,' he said. 'Ireland is lost.'

JAMES JOYCE

The Dead

James Joyce (1882–1941). Dubliners *published in 1914 was Joyce's first published work except for* Chamber Music *(1907), a volume of verse. 'The Dead' is an unquestioned masterpiece – a matchless evocation of an evening party in Dublin before the First World War.*

LILY, the caretaker's daughter, was literally run off her feet. Hardly had she brought one gentleman into the little pantry behind the office on the ground floor and helped him off with his overcoat, than the wheezy hall-door bell clanged again and she had to scamper along the bare hallway to let in another guest. It was well for her she had not to attend to the ladies also. But Miss Kate and Miss Julia had thought of that and had converted the bathroom upstairs into a ladies' dressing-room. Miss Kate and Miss Julia were there, gossiping and laughing and fussing, walking after each other to the head of the stairs, peering down over the banisters and calling down to Lily to ask her who had come.

It was always a great affair, the Misses Morkan's annual dance. Everybody who knew them came to it, members of the family, old friends of the family, the members of Julia's choir, any of Kate's pupils that were grown up enough, and even some of Mary Jane's pupils too. Never once had it fallen flat. For years and years it had gone off in splendid style, as long as anyone could remember: ever since Kate and Julia, after the death of their brother Pat, had left the house in Stoney

Batter and taken Mary Jane, their only niece, to live with them in the dark, gaunt house on Usher's Island, the upper part of which they had rented from Mr Fulham, the corn-factor on the ground floor. That was a good thirty years ago if it was a day. Mary Jane, who was then a little girl in short clothes, was now the main prop of the household, for she had the organ in Haddington Road. She had been through the Academy and gave a pupils' concert every year in the upper room of the Antient Concert Rooms. Many of her pupils belonged to the better-class families on the Kingstown and Dalkey line. Old as they were, her aunts also did their share. Julia, though she was quite grey, was still the leading soprano in Adam and Eve's, and Kate, being too feeble to go about much, gave music lessons to beginners on the old square piano in the back room. Lily, the caretaker's daughter, did housemaid's work for them. Though their life was modest, they believed in eating well; the best of everything: diamond-bone sirloins, three-shilling tea and the best bottled stout. But Lily seldom made a mistake in the orders, so that she got on well with her three mistresses. They were fussy, that was all. But the only thing they would not stand was back answers.

Of course, they had good reason to be fussy on such a night. And then it was long after ten o'clock and yet there was no sign of Gabriel and his wife. Besides they were dreadfully afraid that Freddy Malins might turn up screwed. They would not wish for worlds that any of Mary Jane's pupils should see him under the influence; and when he was like that it was sometimes very hard to manage him. Freddy Malins always came late, but they wondered what could be keeping Gabriel: and that was what brought them every two minutes to the banisters to ask Lily had Gabriel or Freddy come.

'O, Mr Conroy,' said Lily to Gabriel when she opened the door for him, 'Miss Kate and Miss Julia thought you were never coming. Good night, Mrs Conroy.'

'I'll engage they did,' said Gabriel, 'but they forget that my wife here takes three mortal hours to dress herself.'

He stood on the mat, scraping the snow from his goloshes, while Lily led his wife to the foot of the stairs and called out:

'Miss Kate, here's Mrs Conroy.'

Kate and Julia came toddling down the dark stairs at once. Both of them kissed Gabriel's wife, said she must be perished alive, and asked was Gabriel with her.

'Here I am as right as the mail, Aunt Kate! Go on up, I'll follow,' called out Gabriel from the dark.

He continued scraping his feet vigorously while the three women went upstairs, laughing, to the ladies' dressing-room. A light fringe of snow lay like a cape on the shoulders of his overcoat and like toecaps on the toes of his goloshes; and, as the buttons of his overcoat slipped with a squeaking noise through the snow-stiffened frieze, a cold, fragrant air from out-of-doors escaped from crevices and folds.

'Is it snowing again, Mr Conroy?' asked Lily.

She had preceded him into the pantry to help him off with his overcoat. Gabriel smiled at the three syllables she had given his surname and glanced at her. She was a slim, growing girl, pale in complexion and with hay-coloured hair. The gas in the pantry made her look still paler. Gabriel had known her when she was a child and used to sit on the lowest step nursing a rag doll.

'Yes, Lily,' he answered, 'and I think we're in for a night of it.'

He looked up at the pantry ceiling, which was shaking with the stamping and shuffling of feet on the floor above, listened for a moment to the piano and then glanced at the girl, who was folding his overcoat carefully at the end of a shelf.

'Tell me, Lily,' he said in a friendly tone, 'do you still go to school?'

'O no, sir,' she answered. 'I'm done schooling this year and more.'

'O, then,' said Gabriel gaily, 'I suppose we'll be going to your wedding one of these fine days with your young man, eh?'

The girl glanced back at him over her shoulder and said with great bitterness:

'The men that is now is only all palaver and what they can get out of you.'

Gabriel coloured, as if he felt he had made a mistake, and, without looking at her, kicked off his goloshes and flicked actively with his muffler at his patent-leather shoes.

He was a stout, tallish young man. The high colour of his cheeks
pushed upwards even to his forehead, where it scattered itself in a few
formless patches of pale red; and on his hairless face there scintillated
restlessly the polished lenses and the bright gilt rims of the glasses
which screened his delicate and restless eyes. His glossy black hair was
parted in the middle and brushed in a long curve behind his ears where
it curled slightly beneath the groove left by his hat.

When he had flicked lustre into his shoes he stood up and pulled his
waistcoat down more tightly on his plump body. Then he took a coin
rapidly from his pocket.

'O Lily,' he said, thrusting it into her hands, 'it's Christmas-time,
isn't it? Just ... here's a little ...'

He walked rapidly to the door.

'O no, sir!' cried the girl, following him. 'Really, sir, I wouldn't
take it.'

'Christmas-time! Christmas-time!' said Gabriel, almost trotting to
the stairs and waving his hand to her in deprecation.

The girl, seeing that he had gained the stairs, called out after him:
'Well, thank you, sir.'

He waited outside the drawing-room door until the waltz should
finish, listening to the skirts that swept against it and to the shuffling of
feet. He was still discomposed by the girl's bitter and sudden retort. It
had cast a gloom over him which he tried to dispel by arranging his
cuffs and the bows of his tie. He then took from his waistcoat pocket a
little paper and glanced at the headings he had made for his speech. He
was undecided about the lines from Robert Browning, for he feared
they would be above the heads of his hearers. Some quotation that
they would recognize from Shakespeare or from the Melodies would
be better. The indelicate clacking of the men's heels and the shuffling
of their soles reminded him that their grade of culture differed from
his. He would only make himself ridiculous by quoting poetry to
them which they could not understand. They would think that he was
airing his superior education. He would fail with them just as he had
failed with the girl in the pantry. He had taken up a wrong tone. His
whole speech was a mistake from first to last, an utter failure.

Just then his aunts and his wife came out of the ladies' dressing-room. His aunts were two small, plainly dressed old women. Aunt Julia was an inch or so the taller. Her hair, drawn low over the tops of her ears, was grey; and grey also, with darker shadows, was her large flaccid face. Though she was stout in build and stood erect, her slow eyes and parted lips gave her the appearance of a woman who did not know where she was or where she was going. Aunt Kate was more vivacious. Her face, healthier than her sister's, was all puckers and creases, like a shrivelled red apple, and her hair, braided in the same old-fashioned way, had not lost its ripe nut colour.

They both kissed Gabriel frankly. He was their favourite nephew, the son of their dead sister, Ellen, who had married T.J. Conroy of the Port and Docks.

'Gretta tells me you're not going to take a cab back to Monkstown tonight, Gabriel,' said Aunt Kate.

'No,' said Gabriel, turning to his wife, 'we had quite enough of that last year, hadn't we? Don't you remember, Aunt Kate, what a cold Gretta got out of it? Cab windows rattling all the way, and the east wind blowing in after we passed Merrion. Very jolly it was. Gretta caught a dreadful cold.'

Aunt Kate frowned severely and nodded her head at every word.

'Quite right, Gabriel, quite right,' she said. 'You can't be too careful.'

'But as for Gretta there,' said Gabriel, 'she'd walk home in the snow if she were let.'

Mrs Conroy laughed.

'Don't mind him, Aunt Kate,' she said. 'He's really an awful bother, what with green shades for Tom's eyes at night and making him do the dumb-bells, and forcing Eva to eat the stirabout. The poor child! And she simply hates the sight of it! ... O, but you'll never guess what he makes me wear now!'

She broke out into a peal of laughter and glanced at her husband, whose admiring and happy eyes had been wandering from her dress to her face and hair. The two aunts laughed heartily, too, for Gabriel's solicitude was a standing joke with them.

'Goloshes!' said Mrs Conroy. 'That's the latest. Whenever it's wet underfoot I must put on my goloshes. Tonight even, he wanted me to put them on, but I wouldn't. The next thing he'll buy me will be a diving suit.'

Gabriel laughed nervously and patted his tie reassuringly, while Aunt Kate nearly doubled herself, so heartily did she enjoy the joke. The smile soon faded from Aunt Julia's face and her mirthless eyes were directed towards her nephew's face. After a pause she asked:

'And what are goloshes, Gabriel?'

'Goloshes, Julia!' exclaimed her sister. 'Goodness me, don't you know what goloshes are? You wear them over your . . . boots, Gretta, isn't it?'

'Yes,' said Mrs Conroy. 'Gutta-percha things. We both have a pair now. Gabriel says everyone wears them on the Continent.'

'O, on the Continent,' murmured Aunt Julia, nodding her head slowly.

Gabriel knitted his brows and said, as if he were slightly angered:

'It's nothing very wonderful, but Gretta thinks it very funny, because she says the word reminds her of Christy Minstrels.'

'But tell me, Gabriel,' said Aunt Kate, with brisk tact. 'Of course, you've seen about the room. Gretta was saying . . . '

'O, the room is all right,' replied Gabriel. 'I've taken one in the Gresham.'

'To be sure,' said Aunt Kate, 'by far the best thing to do. And the children, Gretta, you're not anxious about them?'

'O, for one night,' said Mrs Conroy. 'Besides, Bessie will look after them.'

'To be sure,' said Aunt Kate again. 'What a comfort it is to have a girl like that, one you can depend on! There's that Lily, I'm sure I don't know what has come over her lately. She's not the girl she was at all.'

Gabriel was about to ask his aunt some questions on this point, but she broke off suddenly to gaze after her sister, who had wandered down the stairs and was craning her neck over the banisters.

'Now, I ask you,' she said almost testily, 'where is Julia going? Julia! Julia! Where are you going?'

Julia, who had gone half-way down one flight, came back and announced blandly:

'Here's Freddy.'

At the same moment a clapping of hands and a final flourish of the pianist told that the waltz had ended. The drawing-room door was opened from within and some couples came out. Aunt Kate drew Gabriel aside hurriedly and whispered into his ear:

'Slip down, Gabriel, like a good fellow and see if he's all right, and don't let him up if he's screwed. I'm sure he's screwed. I'm sure he is.'

Gabriel went to the stairs and listened over the banisters. He could hear two persons talking in the pantry. Then he recognized Freddy Malins' laugh. He went down the stairs noisily.

'It's such a relief,' said Aunt Kate to Mrs Conroy, 'that Gabriel is here. I always feel easier in my mind when he's here ... Julia, there's Miss Daly and Miss Power will take some refreshment. Thanks for your beautiful waltz, Miss Daly. It made lovely time.'

A tall wizen-faced man, with a stiff grizzled moustache and swarthy skin, who was passing out with his partner, said:

'And may we have some refreshment, too, Miss Morkan?'

'Julia,' said Aunt Kate summarily, 'and here's Mr Browne and Miss Furlong. Take them in, Julia, with Miss Daly and Miss Power.'

'I'm the man for the ladies,' said Mr Browne, pursing his lips until his moustache bristled, and smiling in all his wrinkles. 'You know, Miss Morkan, the reason they are so fond of me is –'

He did not finish the sentence, but, seeing that Aunt Kate was out of earshot, at once led the three young ladies into the back room. The middle of the room was occupied by two square tables placed end to end, and on these Aunt Julia and the caretaker were straightening and smoothing a large cloth. On the sideboard were arrayed dishes and plates, and glasses and bundles of knives and forks and spoons. The top of the closed square piano served as a sideboard for viands and sweets. At a smaller sideboard in one corner two young men were standing, drinking hop-bitters.

Mr Browne led his charges thither and invited them all, in jest, to some ladies' punch, hot, strong, and sweet. As they said they never took anything strong, he opened three bottles of lemonade for them. Then he asked one of the young men to move aside, and, taking hold of the decanter, filled out for himself a goodly measure of whisky. The young men eyed him respectfully while he took a trial sip.

'God help me,' he said, smiling, 'it's the doctor's orders.'

His wizened face broke into a broader smile, and the three young ladies laughed in musical echo to his pleasantry, swaying their bodies to and fro, with nervous jerks of their shoulders. The boldest said:

'O, now, Mr Browne, I'm sure the doctor never ordered anything of the kind.'

Mr Browne took another sip of his whisky and said, with sidling mimicry:

'Well, you see, I'm the famous Mrs Cassidy, who is reported to have said: "Now, Mary Grimes, if I don't take it, make me take it, for I feel I want it."'

His hot face had leaned forward a little too confidentially and he had assumed a very low Dublin accent, so that the young ladies, with one instinct, received his speech in silence. Miss Furlong, who was one of Mary Jane's pupils, asked Miss Daly what was the name of the pretty waltz she had played; and Mr Browne, seeing that he was ignored, turned promptly to the two young men, who were more appreciative.

A red-faced young woman, dressed in pansy, came into the room, excitedly clapping her hands and crying:

'Quadrilles! Quadrilles!'

Close on her heels came Aunt Kate, crying:

'Two gentlemen and three ladies, Mary Jane!'

'O, here's Mr Bergin and Mr Kerrigan,' said Mary Jane. 'Mr Kerrigan, will you take Miss Power? Miss Furlong, may I get you a partner, Mr Bergin. O, that'll just do now.'

'Three ladies, Mary Jane,' said Aunt Kate.

The two young gentlemen asked the ladies if they might have the pleasure, and Mary Jane turned to Miss Daly.

'O, Miss Daly, you're really awfully good, after playing for the last two dances, but really we're so short of ladies tonight.'

'I don't mind in the least, Miss Morkan.'

'But I've a nice partner for you, Mr Bartell D'Arcy, the tenor. I'll get him to sing later on. All Dublin is raving about him.'

'Lovely voice, lovely voice!' said Aunt Kate.

As the piano had twice begun the prelude to the first figure Mary Jane led her recruits quickly from the room. They had hardly gone when Aunt Julia wandered slowly into the room, looking behind her at something.

'What is the matter, Julia?' asked Aunt Kate anxiously. 'Who is it?'

Julia, who was carrying in a column of table-napkins, turned to her sister and said, simply, as if the question had surprised her:

'It's only Freddy, Kate, and Gabriel with him.'

In fact, right behind her Gabriel could be seen piloting Freddy Malins across the landing. The latter, a young man of about forty, was of Gabriel's size and build, with very round shoulders. His face was fleshy and pallid, touched with colour only at the thick hanging lobes of his ears and at the wide wings of his nose. He had coarse features, a blunt nose, a convex and receding brow, tumid and protruded lips. His heavy-lidded eyes and the disorder of his scanty hair made him look sleepy. He was laughing heartily in a high key at a story which he had been telling Gabriel on the stairs and at the same time rubbing the knuckles of his left fist backwards and forwards into his left eye.

'Good evening, Freddy,' said Aunt Julia.

Freddy Malins bade the Misses Morkan a good evening in what seemed an off-hand fashion by reason of the habitual catch in his voice and then, seeing that Mr Browne was grinning at him from the sideboard, crossed the room on rather shaky legs and began to repeat in an undertone the story he had just told to Gabriel.

'He's not so bad, is he?' said Aunt Kate to Gabriel.

Gabriel's brows were dark, but he raised them quickly and answered:

'O, no, hardly noticeable.'

'Now, isn't he a terrible fellow!' she said, 'And his poor mother made him take the pledge on New Year's Eve. But come on, Gabriel, into the drawing-room.'

Before leaving the room with Gabriel she signalled to Mr Browne by frowning and shaking her forefinger in warning to and fro. Mr Browne nodded in answer and, when she had gone, said to Freddy Malins:

'Now, then, Teddy, I'm going to fill you out a good glass of lemonade just to buck you up.'

Freddy Malins, who was nearing the climax of his story, waved the offer aside impatiently, but Mr Browne, having first called Freddy Malins' attention to a disarray in his dress, filled out and handed him a full glass of lemonade. Freddy Malins' left hand accepted the glass mechanically, his right hand being engaged in the mechanical readjustment of his dress. Mr Browne, whose face was once more wrinkling with mirth, poured out for himself a glass of whisky while Freddy Malins exploded, before he had well reached the climax of his story, in a kink of high-pitched bronchitic laughter and, setting down his untasted and overflowing glass, began to run the knuckles of his left fist backwards and forwards into his left eye, repeating words of his last phrase as well as his fit of laughter would allow him.

Gabriel could not listen while Mary Jane was playing her Academy piece, full of runs and difficult passages, to the hushed drawing-room. He liked music, but the piece she was playing had no melody for him and he doubted whether it had any melody for the other listeners, though they had begged Mary Jane to play something. Four young men, who had come from the refreshment-room to stand in the doorway at the sound of the piano, had gone away quietly in couples after a few minutes. They only persons who seemed to follow the music were Mary Jane herself, her hands racing along the keyboard or lifted from it at the pauses like those of a priestess in momentary imprecation, and Aunt Kate standing at her elbow to turn the page.

Gabriel's eyes, irritated by the floor, which glittered with beeswax under the heavy chandelier, wandered to the wall above the piano. A picture of the balcony scene in *Romeo and Juliet* hung there and beside it was a picture of the two murdered princes in the Tower which Aunt Julia had worked in red, blue, and brown wools when she was a girl. Probably in the school they had gone to as girls that kind of work had been taught for one year. His mother had worked for him as a birthday present a waistcoat of purple tabinet, with little foxes' heads upon it, lined with brown satin and having round mulberry buttons. It was strange that his mother had had no musical talent, though Aunt Kate used to call her the brains carrier of the Morkan family. Both she and Julia had always seemed a little proud of their serious and matronly sister. Her photograph stood before the pier-glass. She had an open book on her knees and was pointing out something in it to Constantine who, dressed in a man-o'-war suit, lay at her feet. It was she who had chosen the names of her sons, for she was very sensible of the dignity of family life. Thanks to her, Constantine was now senior curate in Balbriggan and, thanks to her, Gabriel himself had taken his degree in the Royal University. A shadow passed over his face as he remembered her sullen opposition to his marriage. Some slighting phrases she had used still rankled in his memory; once she had spoken of Gretta as being country cute and that was not true of Gretta at all. It was Gretta who had nursed her during all her last long illness in their house at Monkstown.

He knew that Mary Jane must be near the end of her piece, for she was playing again the opening melody with runs of scales after every bar, and while he waited for the end the resentment died down in his heart. The piece ended with a trill of octaves in the treble and a final deep octave in the bass. Great applause greeted Mary Jane as, blushing and rolling up her music nervously, she escaped from the room. The most vigorous clapping came from the four young men in the doorway who had gone away to the refreshment-room at the beginning of the piece but had come back when the piano had stopped.

Lancers were arranged. Gabriel found himself partnered with Miss Ivors. She was a frank-mannered, talkative young lady, with a freckled face and prominent brown eyes. She did not wear a low-cut bodice,

and the large brooch which was fixed in the front of her collar bore on
it an Irish device and motto.

When they had taken their places she said abruptly:

'I have a crow to pluck with you.'

'With me?' said Gabriel.

She nodded her head gravely.

'What is it?' asked Gabriel, smiling at her solemn manner.

'Who is G.C.?' answered Miss Ivors, turning her eyes upon him.

Gabriel coloured and was about to knit his brows, as if he did not
understand, when she said bluntly:

'O, innocent Amy! I have found out that you write for *The Daily
Express*. Now aren't you ashamed of yourself?'

'Why should I be ashamed of myself?' asked Gabriel, blinking his
eyes and trying to smile.

'Well, I'm ashamed of you,' said Miss Ivors frankly. 'To say you'd
write for a paper like that. I didn't think you were a West Briton.'

A look of perplexity appeared on Gabriel's face. It was true that he
wrote a literary column every Wednesday in *The Daily Express*, for
which he was paid fifteen shillings. But that did not make him a West
Briton surely. The books he received for review were almost more
welcome than the paltry cheque. He loved to feel the covers and turn
over the pages of newly printed books. Nearly every day when his
teaching in the college had ended he used to wander down the quays
to the second-hand booksellers, to Hickey's on Bachelor's Walk, to
Webb's or Massey's on Aston's Quay, or to O'Clohissey's in the by-
street. He did not know how to meet her charge. He wanted to say
that literature was above politics. But they were friends of many years'
standing and their careers had been parallel, first at the University and
then as teachers: he could not risk a gradiose phrase with her. He
continued blinking his eyes and trying to smile and murmured lamely
that he saw nothing political in writing reviews of books.

When their turn to cross had come he was still perplexed and
inattentive. Miss Ivors promptly took his hand in a warm grasp and
said in a soft friendly tone:

'Of course, I was only joking. Come, we cross now.'

When they were together again she spoke of the University question and Gabriel felt more at ease. A friend of hers had shown her his review of Browning's poems. That was how she had found out the secret: but she liked the review immensely. Then she said suddenly:

'O, Mr Conroy, will you come for an excursion to the Aran Isles this summer? We're going to stay there a whole month. It will be splendid out in the Atlantic. You ought to come. Mr Clancy is coming, and Mr Kilkelly and Kathleen Kearney. It would be splendid for Gretta too if she'd come. She's from Connacht, isn't she?'

'Her people are,' said Gabriel shortly.

'But you will come, won't you?' said Miss Ivors, laying her warm hand eagerly on his arm.

'The fact is,' said Gabriel, 'I have just arranged to go –'

'Go where?' asked Miss Ivors.

'Well, you know, every year I go for a cycling tour with some fellows and so –'

'But where?' asked Miss Ivors.

'Well, we usually go to France or Belgium or perhaps Germany,' said Gabriel awkwardly.

'And why do you go to France and Belgium,' said Miss Ivors, 'instead of visiting your own land?'

'Well,' said Gabriel, 'it's partly to keep in touch with the languages and partly for a change.'

'And haven't you your own language to keep in touch with – Irish?' asked Miss Ivors.

'Well,' said Gabriel, 'if it comes to that, you know, Irish is not my language.'

Their neighbours had turned to listen to the cross-examination. Gabriel glanced right and left nervously and tried to keep his good humour under the ordeal, which was making a blush invade his forehead.

'And haven't you your own land to visit,' continued Miss Ivors, 'that you know nothing of, your own people, and your own country?'

'O, to tell you the truth,' retorted Gabriel suddenly, 'I'm sick of my own country, sick of it!'

'Why?' asked Miss Ivors.

Gabriel did not answer, for his retort had heated him.

'Why?' repeated Miss Ivors.

They had to go visiting together and, as he had not answered her, Miss Ivors said warmly:

'Of course, you've no answer.'

Gabriel tried to cover his agitation by taking part in the dance with great energy. He avoided her eyes, for he had seen a sour expression on her face. But when they met in the long chain he was surprised to feel his hand firmly pressed. She looked at him from under her brows for a moment quizzically until he smiled. Then, just as the chain was about to start again, she stood on tiptoe and whispered into his ear:

'West Briton!'

When the lancers were over Gabriel went away to a remote corner of the room where Freddy Malins' mother was sitting. She was a stout, feeble old woman with white hair. Her voice had a catch in it like her son's and she stuttered slightly. She had been told that Freddy had come and that he was nearly all right. Gabriel asked her whether she had had a good crossing. She lived with her married daughter in Glasgow and came to Dublin on a visit once a year. She answered placidly that she had had a beautiful crossing and that the captain had been most attentive to her. She spoke also of the beautiful house her daughter kept in Glasgow, and of all the friends they had there. While her tongue rambled on Gabriel tried to banish from his mind all memory of the unpleasant incident with Miss Ivors. Of course the girl, or woman, or whatever she was, was an enthusiast, but there was a time for all things. Perhaps he ought not to have answered her like that. But she had no right to call him a West Briton before people, even in joke. She had tried to make him ridiculous before people, heckling him and staring at him with her rabbit's eyes.

He saw his wife making her way towards him through the waltzing couples. When she reached him she said into his ear:

'Gabriel, Aunt Kate wants to know won't you carve the goose as usual. Miss Daly will carve the ham and I'll do the pudding.'

'All right,' said Gabriel.

'She's sending in the younger ones first as soon as this waltz is over so that we'll have the table to ourselves.'

'Were you dancing?' asked Gabriel.

'Of course I was. Didn't you see me? What row had you with Molly Ivors?'

'No row. Why? Did she say so?'

'Something like that. I'm trying to get that Mr D'Arcy to sing. He's full of conceit, I think.'

'There was no row,' said Gabriel moodily, 'only she wanted me to go for a trip to the west of Ireland and I said I wouldn't.'

His wife clasped her hands excitedly and gave a little jump.

'O, do go, Gabriel,' she cried.'I'd love to see Galway again.'

'You can go if you like,' said Gabriel coldly.

She looked at him for a moment, then turned to Mrs Malins and said:

'There's a nice husband for you, Mrs Malins.'

While she was threading her way back across the room Mrs Malins, without adverting to the interruption, went on to tell Gabriel what beautiful places there were in Scotland and beautiful scenery. Her son-in-law brought them every year to the lakes and they used to go fishing. Her son-in-law was a splendid fisher. One day he caught a beautiful big fish and the man in the hotel cooked it for their dinner.

Gabriel hardly heard what she said. Now that supper was coming near he began to think again about his speech and about the quotation. When he saw Freddy Malins coming across the room to visit his mother Gabriel left the chair free for him and retired into the embrasure of the window. The room had already cleared and from the back room came the clatter of plates and knives. Those who still remained in the drawing-room seemed tired of dancing and were conversing quietly in little groups. Gabriel's warm, trembling fingers tapped the cold pane of the window. How cool it must be outside! How pleasant it would be walk out alone, first along by the river and then through the park! The snow would be lying on the branches of the trees and formimg a bright cap on the top of the Wellington

Monument. How much more pleasant it would be there than at the supper-table!

He ran over the headings of his speech: Irish hospitality, sad memories, the Three Graces, Paris, the quotation from Browning. He repeated to himself a phrase he had written in his review: 'One feels that one is listening to a thought-tormented music.' Miss Ivors had praised the review. Was she sincere? Had she really any life of her own behind all her propagandism? There had never been any ill-feeling between them until that night. It unnerved him to think that she would be at the supper-table, looking up at him, while he spoke, with her critical quizzing eyes. Perhaps she would not be sorry to see him fail in his speech. An idea came into his mind and gave him courage. He would say, alluding to Aunt Kate and Aunt Julia: 'Ladies and Gentlemen, the generation which is now on the wane among us may have had its faults, but for my part I think it had certain qualities of hospitality, of humour, of humanity, which the new and very serious and hyper-educated generation that is growing up around us seems to me to lack.' Very good: that was one for Miss Ivors. What did he care that his aunts were only two ignorant old women?

A murmur in the room attracted his attention. Mr Browne was advancing from the door, gallantly escorting Aunt Julia, who leaned upon his arm, smiling and hanging her head. An irregular musketry of applause escorted her also as far as the piano and then, as Mary Jane seated herself on the stool, and Aunt Julia, no longer smiling, half turned so as to pitch her voice fairly into the room, gradually ceased. Gabriel recognized the prelude. It was that of an old song of Aunt Julia's – 'Arrayed for the Bridal'. Her voice, strong and clear in tone, attacked with great spirit the runs which embellish the air, and though she sang very rapidly she did not miss even the smallest of the grace notes. To follow the voice, without looking at the singer's face, was to feel and share the excitement of swift and secure flight. Gabriel applauded loudly with all the others at the close of the song, and loud applause was borne in from the invisible supper-table. It sounded so genuine that a little colour struggled into Aunt Julia's face as she bent to replace in the music-stand the old leather-bound song-book that had her initials on the cover. Freddy Malins, who had listened with his head perched sideways to hear her better, was still applauding when everyone else had ceased and talking animatedly to his mother, who nodded her head gravely and slowly in acquiescence. At last, when he could clap no more, he stood up suddenly and hurried across the room to Aunt Julia whose hand he seized and held in both his hands, shaking it when words failed him or the catch in his voice proved too much for him.

'I was just telling my mother,' he said, 'I never heard you sing so well, never. No, I never heard your voice so good as it is tonight. Now! Would you believe that now? That's the truth. Upon my word and honour that's the truth. I never heard your voice sound so fresh and so ... so clear and fresh, never.'

Aunt Julia smiled broadly and murmured something about compliments as she released her hand from his grasp. Mr Browne extended his open hand towards her and said to those who were near him in the manner of a showman introducing a prodigy to an audience:

'Miss Julia Morkan, my latest discovery!'

He was laughing very heartily at this himself when Freddy Malins turned to him and said:

'Well, Browne, if you're serious you might make a worse discovery. All I can say is I never heard her sing half so well as long as I am coming here. And that's the honest truth.'

'Neither did I,' said Mr Browne. 'I think her voice has greatly improved.'

Aunt Julia shrugged her shoulders and said with meek pride:

'Thirty years ago I hadn't a bad voice as voices go.'

'I often told Julia,' said Aunt Kate emphatically, 'that she was simply thrown away in that choir. But she never would be said by me.'

She turned as if to appeal to a good sense of the others against a refractory child, while Aunt Julia gazed in front of her, a vague smile of reminiscence playing on her face.

'No,' continued Aunt Kate, 'she wouldn't be said or led by anyone, slaving there in that choir night and day, night and day. Six o'clock on Christmas morning! And all for what?'

'Well, isn't it for the honour of God, Aunt Kate?' asked Mary Jane, twisting round on the piano-stool and smiling.

Aunt Kate turned fiercely on her niece and said:

'I know all about the honour of God, Mary Jane, but I think it's not at all honourable for the Pope to turn out the women out of the choirs that have slaved there all their lives and put little whipper-snappers of boys over their heads. I suppose it is for the good of the Church, if the Pope does it. But it's not just, Mary Jane, and it's not right.'

She had worked herself into a passion and would have continued in defence of her sister, for it was a sore subject with her, but Mary Jane, seeing that all the dancers had come back, intervened pacifically.

'Now, Aunt Kate, you've giving scandal to Mr Browne, who is of the other persuasion.'

Aunt Kate turned to Mr Browne, who was grinning at this allusion to his religion, and said hastily:

'O, I don't question the Pope's being right. I'm only a stupid old woman and I wouldn't presume to do such a thing. But there's such a thing as common everyday politeness and gratitude. And if I were in Julia's place I'd tell that Father Healey straight up to his face . . .'

'And besides, Aunt Kate,' said Mary Jane, 'we really are all hungry and when we are hungry we are all very quarrelsome.'

'And when we are thirsty we are also quarrelsome,' added Mr Browne.

'So that we had better go to supper,' said Mary Jane, 'and finish the discussion afterwards.'

On the landing outside the drawing-room Gabriel found his wife and Mary Jane trying to persuade Miss Ivors to stay for supper. But Miss Ivors, who had put on her hat and was buttoning her cloak, would not stay. She did not feel in the least hungry and she had already overstayed her time.

'But only for ten minutes, Molly,' said Mrs Conroy. 'That won't delay you.'

'To take a pick itself,' said Mary Jane, 'after all your dancing.'

'I really couldn't,' said Miss Ivors.

'I am afraid you didn't enjoy yourself at all,' said Mary Jane hopelessly.

'Ever so much, I assure you,' said Miss Ivors, 'but you really must let me run off now.'

'But how can you get home?' asked Mrs Conroy.

'O, it's only two steps up the quay.'

Gabriel hesitated a moment and said:

'If you will allow me, Miss Ivors, I'll see you home if you are really obliged to go.'

But Miss Ivors broke away from them.

'I won't hear of it,' she cried. 'For goodness' sake go in to your suppers and don't mind me. I'm quite well able to take care of myself.'

'Well, you're the comical girl, Molly,' said Mrs Conroy frankly.

'*Beannacht libh,*' cried Miss Ivors, with a laugh, as she ran down the staircase.

Mary Jane gazed after her, a moody puzzled expression on her face, while Mrs Conroy leaned over the banisters to listen for the hall-door. Gabriel asked himself was he the cause of her abrupt departure? But she did not seem to be in ill humour – she had gone away laughing. He stared blankly down the staircase.

At the moment Aunt Kate came toddling out of the supper-room, almost wringing her hands in despair.

'Where is Gabriel?' she cried. 'Where on earth is Gabriel? There's everyone waiting in there, stage to let, and nobody to carve the goose!'

'Here I am, Aunt Kate!' cried Gabriel, with sudden animation, 'ready to carve a flock of geese, if necessary.'

A fat brown goose lay at one end of the table, and at the other end, on a bed of creased paper strewn with sprigs of parsley, lay a great ham, stripped of its outer skin and peppered over with crust crumbs, a neat paper frill round its shin, and beside this was a round of spiced beef. Between these rival ends ran parallel lines of side-dishes: two little minsters of jelly, red and yellow; a shallow dish full of blocks of blancmange and red jam, a large green leaf-shaped dish with a stalk-shaped handle, on which lay bunches of purple raisins and peeled almonds, a companion dish on which lay a solid rectangle of Smyrna figs, a dish of custard topped with grated nutmeg, a small bowl full of chocolates and sweets wrapped in gold and silver papers and a glass vase in which stood some tall celery stalks. In the centre of the table there stood, as sentries to a fruit-stand which upheld a pyramid of oranges and American apples, two squat old-fashioned decanters of cut glass, one containing port and the other dark sherry. On the closed square piano a pudding in a huge yellow dish lay in waiting, and behind it were three squads of bottles of stout and ale and minerals drawn up according to the colours of their uniforms, the first two black, with brown and red labels, the third and smallest squad white, with transverse green sashes.

Gabriel took his seat boldly at the head of the table and, having looked to the edge of the carver, plunged his fork firmly into the goose. He felt quite at ease now, for he was an expert carver and liked nothing better than to find himself at the head of a well-laden table.

'Miss Furlong, what shall I send you?' he asked. 'A wing or a slice of the breast?'

'Just a small slice of the breast.'

'Miss Higgins, what for you?'

'O, anything at all, Mr Conroy.'

While Gabriel and Miss Daly exchanged plates of goose and plates of ham and spiced beef, Lily went from guest to guest with a dish of hot floury potatoes wrapped in a white napkin. This was Mary Jane's idea and she had also suggested apple sauce for the goose, but Aunt Kate had said that plain roast goose without apple sauce had always been good enough for her and she hoped she might never eat worse. Mary Jane waited on her pupils and saw that they got the best slices, and Aunt Kate and Aunt Julia opened and carried across from the piano bottles of stout and ale for the gentlemen and bottles of minerals for the ladies. There was a great deal of confusion and laughter and noise, the noise of orders and counter-orders, of knives and forks, of corks and glass-stoppers. Gabriel began to carve second helpings as soon as he had finished the first round without serving himself. Everyone protested loudly, so that he compromised by taking a long draught of stout, for he had found the carving hot work. Mary Jane settled down quietly to her supper, but Aunt Kate and Aunt Julia were still toddling round the table, walking on each other's heels, getting in each other's way and giving each other unheeded orders. Mr Browne begged of them to sit down and eat their suppers and so did Gabriel, but they said there was time enough, so that, at last, Freddy Malins stood up and, capturing Aunt Kate, plumped her down on her chair amid general laughter.

When everyone had been well served Gabriel said, smiling:

'Now, if anyone wants a little more of what vulgar people call stuffing let him or her speak.'

A chorus of voices invited him to begin his own supper, and Lily came forward with three potatoes which she had reserved for him.

'Very well,' said Gabriel amiably, as he took another preparatory draught, 'kindly forget my existence, ladies and gentlemen, for a few minutes.'

He set to his supper and took no part in the conversation with which the table covered Lily's removal of the plates. The subject of talk was the opera company which was then at the Theatre Royal. Mr Bartell D'Arcy, the tenor, a dark-complexioned young man with a smart moustache, praised very highly the leading contralto of the company, but Miss Furlong thought she had a rather vulgar style of production. Freddy Malins said there was a Negro chieftain singing in the second part of the Gaiety pantomine who had one of the finest tenor voices he had ever heard.

'Have you heard him?' he asked Mr Bartell D'Arcy across the table.

'No,' answered Mr Bartell D'Arcy carelessly.

'Because,' Freddy Malins explained, 'now I'd be curious to hear your opinion of him. I think he has a grand voice.'

'It takes Teddy to find out the really good things,' said Mr Browne familiarly to the table.

'And why couldn't he have a voice too?' asked Freddy Malins sharply. 'Is it because he's only a black?'

Nobody answered this question and Mary Jane led the table back to the legitimate opera. One of her pupils had given her a pass for

Mignon. Of course it was very fine, she said, but it made her think of poor Georgina Burns. Mr Browne could go back farther still, to the old Italian companies that used to come to Dublin – Tietjens, Ilma de Murzka, Campanini, the great Trebelli, Giuglini, Ravelli, Aramburo. Those were the days, he said, when there was something like singing to be heard in Dublin. He told too of how the top gallery of the old Royal used to be packed night after night, of how one night an Italian tenor had sung five encores to 'Let me like a Soldier fall', introducing a high C every time, and of how the gallery boys would sometimes in their enthusiasm unyoke the horses from the carriage of some great *prima donna* and pull her themselves through the streets to her hotel. Why did they never play the grand old operas now, he asked, *Dinorah, Lucrezia Borgia*? Because they could not get the voices to sing them: that was why.

'O, well,' said Mr Bartell D'Arcy, 'I presume there are as good singers today as there were then.'

'Where are they?' asked Mr Browne defiantly.

'In London, Paris, Milan,' said Mr Bartell D'Arcy warmly. 'I suppose Caruso, for example, is quite as good, if not better than any of the men you have mentioned.'

'Maybe so,' said Mr Brown. 'But I may tell you I doubt it strongly.'

'O, I'd give anything to hear Caruso sing,' said Mary Jane.

'For me,' said Aunt Kate, who had been picking a bone, 'there was only one tenor. To please me, I mean. But I suppose none of you ever heard of him.'

'Who was he, Miss Morkan?' asked Mr Bartell D'Arcy politely.

'His name,' said Aunt Kate, 'was Parkinson. I heard him when he was in his prime and I think he had then the purest tenor voice that was ever put into a man's throat.'

'Strange,' said Mr Bartell D'Arcy. 'I never even heard of him.'

'Yes, yes, Miss Morkan is right,' said Mr Browne. 'I remember hearing old Parkinson, but he's too far back for me.'

'A beautiful, pure, sweet, mellow English tenor,' said Aunt Kate with enthusiasm.

Gabriel having finished, the huge pudding was transferred to the table. The clatter of forks and spoons began again. Gabriel's wife served out spoonfuls of the pudding and passed the plates down the table. Midway down they were held up by Mary Jane, who replenished them with raspberry or orange jelly or with blancmange and jam. The pudding was of Aunt Julia's making, and she received praises for it from all quarters. She herself said that it was not quite brown enough.

'Well, I hope, Miss Morkan,' said Mr Browne, 'that I'm brown enough for you because, you know, I'm all Brown.'

All the gentlemen, except Gabriel, ate some of the pudding out of compliment to Aunt Julia. As Gabriel never ate sweets the celery had been left for him. Freddy Malins also took a stalk of celery and ate it with his pudding. He had been told that celery was a capital thing for the blood and he was just then under doctor's care. Mrs Malins, who had been silent all through the supper, said that her son was going down to Mount Melleray in a week or so. The table then spoke of Mount Melleray, how bracing the air was down there, how hospitable the monks were and how they never asked for a penny-piece from their guests.

'And do you mean to say,' asked Mr Browne incredulously, 'that a chap can go down there and put up there as if it were a hotel and live on the fat of the land and then come away without paying anything?'

'O, most people give some donation to the monastery when they leave,' said Mary Jane.

'I wish we had an institution like that in our Church,' said Mr Browne candidly.

He was astonished to hear that the monks never spoke, got up at two in the morning and slept in their coffins. He asked what they did it for.

'That's the rule of the order,' said Aunt Kate firmly.

'Yes, but why?' asked Mr Browne.

Aunt Kate repeated that it was the rule, that was all. Mr Browne still seemed not to understand. Freddy Malins explained to him, as best he could, that the monks were trying to make up for the sins committed by all the sinners in the outside world. The explanation was not very clear, for Mr Browne grinned and said:

'I like that idea very much, but wouldn't a comfortable spring bed do them as well as a coffin?'

'The coffin,' said Mary Jane, 'is to remind them of their last end.'

As the subject had grown lugubrious it was buried in a silence of the table, during which Mrs Malins could be heard saying to her neighbour in an indistinct undertone:

'They are very good men, the monks, very pious men.'

The raisins and almonds and figs and apples and oranges and chocolates and sweets were now passed about the table, and Aunt Julia invited all the guests to have either port or sherry. At first Mr Bartell D'Arcy refused to take either, but one of his neighbours nudged him and whispered something to him, upon which he allowed his glass to be filled. Gradually as the last glasses were being filled the conversation ceased. A pause followed, broken only by the noise of the wine and by unsettling of chairs. The Misses Morkan, all three, looked down at the tablecloth. Someone coughed once or twice, and then a few gentlemen patted the table gently as a signal for silence. The silence came and Gabriel pushed back his chair and stood up.

The patting at once grew louder in encouragement and then ceased altogether. Gabriel leaned his ten trembling fingers on the tablecloth and smiled nervously at the company. Meeting a row of upturned faces he raised his eyes to the chandelier. The piano was playing a waltz tune and he could hear the skirts sweeping against the drawing-room door. People, perhaps, were standing in the snow on the quay outside, gazing up at the lighted windows and listening to the waltz music. The air was pure there. In the distance lay the park, where the trees were weighted with snow. The Wellington Monument wore a gleaming cap of snow that flashed westwards over the white field of Fifteen Acres.

He began:

'Ladies and Gentlemen,

'It has fallen to my lot this evening, as in years past, to perform a very pleasing task, but a task for which I am afraid my poor powers as a speaker are all too inadequate.'

'No, no!' said Mr Browne.

'But, however that may be, I can only ask you tonight to take the will for the deed, and to lend me your attention for a few moments while I endeavour to express to you in words what my feelings are on this occasion.

'Ladies and Gentlemen, it is not the first time that we have gathered together under this hospitable roof, around this hospitable board. It is not the first time that we have been the recipients – or perhaps, I had better say, the victims – of the hospitality of certain good ladies.'

He made a circle in the air with his arm and paused. Everyone laughed or smiled at Aunt Kate and Aunt Julia and Mary Jane, who all turned crimson with pleasure. Gabriel went on more boldly:

'I feel more strongly with every recurring year that our country has no tradition which does it so much honour and which it should guard so jealously as that of its hospitality. It is a tradition that is unique as far as my experience goes (and I have visited not a few places abroad) among the modern nations. Some would say, perhaps, that with us it is rather a failing than anything to be boasted of. But granted even that, it is, to my mind, a princely failing, and one that I trust will long be cultivated among us. Of one thing, at least, I am sure. As long as this one roof shelters the good ladies aforesaid – and I wish from my heart it may do so for many and many a long year to come – the tradition of genuine warm-hearted courteous Irish hospitality, which our fore-fathers have handed down to us and which we must hand down to our descendants, is still alive among us.'

A hearty murmur of assent ran round the table. It shot through Gabriel's mind that Miss Ivors was not there and that she had gone away discourteously: and he said with confidence in himself:

'Ladies and Gentlemen,

'A new generation is growing up in our midst, a generation actu-ated by new ideas and new principles. It is serious and enthusiastic for these new ideas and its enthusiasm, even when it is misdirected, is, I believe, in the main sincere. But we are living in a sceptical and, if I

may use the phrase, a thought-tormented age: and sometimes I fear
that this new generation, educated or hyper-educated as it is, will lack
those qualities of humanity, of hospitality, of kindly humour which
belonged to an older day. Listening tonight to the names of all those
great singers of the past it seemed to me, I must confess, that we were
living in a less spacious age. Those days might, without exaggeration,
be called spacious days: and if they are gone beyond recall, let us hope,
at least, that in gatherings such as this we shall still speak of them with
pride and affection, still cherish in our hearts the memory of those
dead and gone great ones whose fame the world will not willingly let
die.'

'Hear, hear!' said Mr Browne loudly.

'But yet,' continued Gabriel, his voice falling into a softer inflec-
tion, 'there are always in gatherings such as this sadder thoughts that
will recur to our minds: thoughts of the past, of youth, of changes, of
absent faces that we miss here tonight. Our path through life is strewn
with many such sad memories: and were we to brood upon them
always we could not find the heart to go on bravely with our work
among the living. We have all of us living duties and living affections
which claim, and rightly claim, our strenuous endeavours.

'Therefore, I will not linger on the past. I will not let any gloomy
moralizing intrude upon us here tonight. Here we are gathered
together for a brief moment from the bustle and rush of our everyday
routine. We are met here as friends, in the spirit of good-fellowship, as
colleagues, also, to a certain extent, in the true spirit of *camaraderie*, and
as the guests of – what shall I call them? – the Three Graces of the
Dublin musical world.'

The table burst into applause and laughter at this allusion. Aunt Julia
vainly asked each of her neighbours in turn to tell her what Gabriel
had said.

'He says we are the Three Graces, Aunt Julia,' said Mary Jane.

Aunt Julia did not understand, but she looked up, smiling, at
Gabriel, who continued in the same vein:

'Ladies and Gentlemen,

'I will not attempt to play tonight the part that Paris played on another occasion. I will not attempt to choose between them. The task would be an invidious one and one beyond my poor powers. For when I view them in turn, whether it be our chief hostess herself, whose good heart, whose too good heart, has become a byword with all who know her; or her sister, who seems to be gifted with perennial youth and whose singing must have been a surprise and a revelation to us all tonight; or, last but not least, when I consider our youngest hostess, talented, cheerful, hard-working and the best of nieces, I confess, Ladies and Gentlemen, that I do not know to which of them I should award the prize.'

Gabriel glanced down at his aunts and, seeing the large smile on Aunt Julia's face and the tears which had risen to Aunt Kate's eyes, hastened to his close. He raised his glass of port gallantly, while every member of the company fingered a glass expectantly, and said loudly:

'Let us toast them all three together. Let us drink to their health, wealth, long life, happiness, and prosperity and may they long continue to hold the proud and self-won position which they hold in their profession and the position of honour and affection which they hold in our hearts.'

All the guests stood up, glass in hand, and turning towards the three seated ladies, sang in unison, with Mr Browne as leader:

> *For they are jolly gay fellows,*
> *For they are jolly gay fellows,*
> *For they are jolly gay fellows,*
> *Which nobody can deny.*

Aunt Kate was making frank use of her handkerchief and even Aunt Julia seemed moved. Freddy Malins beat time with his pudding-fork and the singers turned towards one another, as if in melodious conference, while they sang with emphasis:

> *Unless he tells a lie,*
> *Unless he tells a lie.*

Then, turning once more towards their hostesses, they sang:

> *For they are jolly gay fellows,*
> *For they are jolly gay fellows,*
> *For they are jolly gay fellows,*
> *Which nobody can deny.*

The acclamation which followed was taken up beyond the door of the supper room by many of the other guests and renewed time after time, Freddy Malins acting as officer with his fork on high.

The piercing morning air came into the hall where they were standing so that Aunt Kate said:

'Close the door, somebody. Mrs Malins will get her death of cold.'

'Browne is out there, Aunt Kate,' said Mary Jane.

'Browne is everywhere,' said Aunt Kate, lowering her voice.

Mary Jane laughed at her tone.

'Really,' she said archly, 'he is very attentive.'

'He has been laid on here like the gas,' said Aunt Kate in the same tone, 'all during the Christmas.'

She laughed herself this time good-humouredly and then added quickly:

'But tell him to come in, Mary Jane, and close the door. I hope to goodness he didn't hear me.'

At that moment the hall-door was opened and Mr Browne came in from the doorstep, laughing as if his heart would break. He was dressed in a long green overcoat with mock astrakhan cuffs and collar and wore on his head an oval fur cap. He pointed down the snow-covered quay from where the sound of shrill prolonged whistling was borne in.

'Teddy will have all the cabs in Dublin out,' he said.

Gabriel advanced from the little pantry behind the office, struggling into his overcoat and, looking round the hall, said.

'Gretta not down yet?'

'She's getting on her things, Gabriel,' said Aunt Kate.

'Who's playing up there?' asked Gabriel.

'Nobody. They're all gone.'

'O no, Aunt Kate,' said Mary Jane. 'Bartell D'Arcy and Miss O'Callaghan aren't gone yet.'

'Someone is fooling at the piano anyhow,' said Gabriel.

Mary Jane glanced at Gabriel and Mr Browne and said with a shiver:

'It makes me feel cold to look at you two gentlemen muffled up like that. I wouldn't like to face your journey home at this hour.'

'I'd like nothing better this minute,' said Mr Browne stoutly, 'than a rattling fine walk in the country or a fast drive with a good spanking goer between the shafts.'

'We used to have a very good horse and trap at home,' said Aunt Julia, sadly.

'The never-to-be-forgotten Johnny,' said Mary Jane, laughing.

Aunt Kate and Gabriel laughed too.

'Why, what was wonderful about Johnny?' asked Mr Browne.

'The late lamented Patrick Morkan, our grandfather, that is,' explained Gabriel, 'commonly known in his later years as the old gentleman, was a glue-boiler.'

'O, now, Gabriel,' said Aunt Kate, laughing, 'he had a starch mill.'

'Well, glue or starch,' said Gabriel, 'the old gentleman had a horse by the name of Johnny. And Johnny used to work in the old gentleman's mill, walking round and round in order to drive the mill. That was all very well; but now comes the tragic part about Johnny. One fine day the old gentleman thought he'd like to drive out with the quality to a military review in the park.'

'The Lord have mercy on his soul,' said Aunt Kate, compassionately.

'Amen,' said Gabriel. 'So the old gentleman, as I said, harnessed Johnny and put on his very best tall hat and his very best stock collar and drove out in grand style from his ancestral mansion near Back Lane, I think.'

Everyone laughed, even Mrs Malins, at Gabriel's manner, and Aunt Kate said:

'O, now, Gabriel, he didn't live in Back Lane, really. Only the mill was there.'

'Out from the mansion of his forefathers,' continued Gabriel, 'he drove with Johnny. And everything went on beautifully until Johnny came in sight of King Billy's statue: and whether he fell in love with the horse King Billy sits on or whether he thought he was back again in the mill, anyway he began to walk round the statue.'

Gabriel paced in a circle round the hall in his goloshes amid the laughter of the others.

'Round and round he went,' said Gabriel, 'and the old gentleman, who was a very pompous old gentleman, was highly indignant. "Go on, sir! What do you mean, sir? Johnny! Johnny! Most extraordinary conduct! Can't understand the horse!"'

The peals of laughter which followed Gabriel's imitation of the incident were interrupted by a resounding knock at the hall door. Mary Jane ran to open it and let in Freddy Malins. Freddy Malins, with his hat well back on his head and his shoulders humped with cold, was puffing and steaming after his exertions.

'I could only get one cab,' he said.

'O, we'll find another along the quay,' said Gabriel.

'Yes,' said Aunt Kate. 'Better not keep Mrs Malins standing in the draught.'

Mrs Malins was helped down the front steps by her son and Mr Browne and, after many manoeuvres, hoisted into the cab. Freddy Malins clambered in after her and spent a long time settling her on the seat, Mr Browne helping him with advice. At last she was settled comfortably and Freddy Malins invited Mr Browne into the cab. There was a good deal of confused talk, and then Mr Browne got into the cab. The cabman settled his rug over his knees, and bent down for the address. The confusion grew greater and the cabman was directed differently by Freddy Malins and Mr Browne, each of whom had his head out through a window of the cab. The difficulty was to know where to drop Mr Browne along the route, and Aunt Kate, Aunt Julia, and Mary Jane helped the discussion from the doorstep with cross-directions and contradictions and abundance of laughter. As for Freddy Malins he was speechless with laughter. He popped his head in and out of the window every moment to the great danger of his hat, and told his mother how the discussion was progressing, till at last Mr Browne shouted to the bewildered cabman above the din of everybody's laughter:

'Do you know Trinity College?'

'Yes, sir,' said the cabman.

'Well, drive bang up against Trinity College gates,' said Mr Browne, 'and then we'll tell you where to go. You understand now?'

'Yes, sir,' said the cabman.

'Make like a bird for Trinity College.'

'Right, sir,' said the cabman.

The horse was whipped up and the cab rattled off along the quay amid a chorus of laughter and adieux.

Gabriel had not gone to the door with the others. He was in a dark part of the hall gazing up the staircase. A woman was standing near the top of the first flight, in the shadow also. He could not see her face but he could see the terrcotta and salmon-pink panels of her skirt which the shadow made appear black and white. It was his wife. She was leaning on the banisters, listening to something. Gabriel was surprised at her stillness and strained his ear to listen also. But he could hear little save the noise of laughter and dispute on the front steps, a few chords struck on the piano and a few notes of a man's voice singing.

He stood still in the gloom of the hall, trying to catch the air that the voice was singing and gazing up at his wife. There was grace and mystery in her attitude as if she were a symbol of something. He asked himself what is a woman standing on the stairs in the shadow, listening to distant music, a symbol of? If he were a painter he would paint her in that attitude. Her blue felt hat would show off the bronze of her hair against the darkness and the dark panels of her skirt would show off the light ones. *Distant Music* he would call the picture if he were a painter.

The hall-door was closed, and Aunt Kate, Aunt Julia, and Mary Jane came down the hall, still laughing.

'Well, isn't Freddy Malins terrible?' said Mary Jane. 'He's really terrible.'

Gabriel said nothing, but pointed up the stairs towards where his wife was standing. Now that the hall-door was closed the voice and the piano could be heard more clearly. Gabriel held up his hand for them to be silent. The song seemed to be in the old Irish tonality and the singer seemed uncertain both of his words and of his voice. The voice, made plaintive by distance and by the singer's hoarseness, faintly illuminated the cadence of the air with words expressing grief:

> *O, the rain falls on my heavy locks*
> *And the dew wets my skin,*
> *My babe lies cold . . .*

'O,' exclaimed Mary Jane. 'It's Bartell D'Arcy singing, and he wouldn't sing all the night. O, I'll get him to sing a song before he goes.'

'O, do, Mary Jane,' said Aunt Kate.

Mary Jane brushed past the others and ran to the staircase, but before she reached it the singing stopped and the piano was closed abruptly.

'O, what a pity!' she cried. 'Is he coming down, Gretta?'

Gabriel heard his answer yes and saw her come down towards them. A few steps behind her were Mr Bartell D'Arcy and Miss O'Callaghan.

'O, Mr D'Arcy,' cried Mary Jane, 'it's downright mean of you to break off like that when we were all in raptures listening to you.'

'I have been at him all the evening,' said Miss O'Callaghan, 'and Mrs Conroy, too, and he told us he had a dreadful cold and couldn't sing.'

'O, Mr D'Arcy,' said Aunt Kate, 'now that was a great fib to tell.'

'Can't you see that I'm as hoarse as a crow?' said Mr D'Arcy roughly.

He went into the pantry hastily and put on his overcoat. The others, taken back by his rude speech, could find nothing to say. Aunt Kate wrinkled her brows and made signs to the others to drop the subject. Mr D'Arcy stood swathing his neck carefully and frowning.

'It's the weather,' said Aunt Julia, after a pause.

'Yes, everybody has colds,' said Aunt Kate readily, 'everybody.'

'They say,' said Mary Jane, 'we haven't had snow like it for thirty years, and I read this morning in the newspapers that the snow is general all over Ireland.'

'I love the look of snow,' said Aunt Julia sadly.

'So do I,' said Miss O'Callaghan. 'I think Christmas is never really Christmas unless we have the snow on the ground.'

'But poor Mr D'Arcy doesn't like the snow,' said Aunt Kate, smiling.

Mr D'Arcy came from the pantry, fully swathed and buttoned, and in a repentant tone told them the history of his cold. Everyone gave him advice and said it was a great pity and urged him to be very careful of his throat in the night air. Gabriel watched his wife, who did not join in the conversation. She was standing right under the dusty fanlight and the flame of the gas lit up the rich bronze of her hair, which he had seen her drying at the fire a few days before. She was in the same attitude and seemed unaware of the talk about her. At last she turned towards them and Gabriel saw that there was colour on her cheeks and that her eyes were shining. A sudden tide of joy went leaping out of his heart.

'Mr D'Arcy,' she said, 'what is the name of that song you were singing?'

'It's called "The Lass of Aughrim",' said Mr D'Arcy, 'but I couldn't remember it properly. Why? Do you know it?'

' "The Lass of Aughrim",' she repeated. 'I couldn't think of the name.'

'It's a very nice air,' said Mary Jane. 'I'm sorry you were not in voice tonight.'

'Now, Mary Jane,' said Aunt Kate, 'don't annoy Mr D'Arcy. I won't have him annoyed.'

Seeing that all were ready to start she shepherded them to the door, where good night was said:

'Well, good night, Aunt Kate, and thanks for the pleasant evening.'

'Good night, Gabriel. Good night, Gretta!'

'Good night, Aunt Kate, and thanks ever so much. Good night, Aunt Julia.'

'O, good night, Gretta, I didn't see you.'

'Good night, Mr D'Arcy. Good night, Miss O'Callaghan.'

'Good night, Miss Morkan.'

'Good night, again.'

'Good night, all. Safe home.'

'Good night. Good night.'

The morning was still dark. A dull, yellow light brooded over the houses and the river; and the sky seemed to be descending. It was slushy underfoot, and only streaks and patches of snow lay on the roofs, on the parapets of the quay and on the area railings. The lamps were still burning redly in the murky air and, across the river, the palace of the Four Courts stood out menacingly against the heavy sky.

She was walking on before him with Mr Bartell D'Arcy, her shoes in a brown parcel tucked under one arm and her hands holding her skirt up from the slush. She had no longer any grace of attitude, but Gabriel's eyes were still bright with happiness. The blood went bounding along his veins and the thoughts went rioting through his brain, proud, joyful, tender, valorous.

She was walking on before him so lightly and so erect that he longed to run after her noiselessly, catch her by the shoulders and say something foolish and affectionate into her ear. She seemed to him so frail that he longed to defend her against something and then to be alone with her. Moments of their secret life together burst like stars upon his memory. A heliotrope envelope was lying beside his breakfast-cup and he was caressing it with his hand. Birds were twittering in the ivy and the sunny web of the curtain was shimmering along the floor: he could not eat for happiness. They were standing on the crowded platform and he was placing a ticket inside the warm palm of her glove. He was standing with her in the cold. Her face, fragrant in the cold air, was quite close to his, and suddenly he called out to the man at the furnace:

'Is the fire hot, sir?'

But the man could not hear with the noise of the furnace. It was just as well. He might have answered rudely.

A wave of yet more tender joy escaped from his heart and went coursing in warm flood along his arteries. Like the tender fire of stars moments of their life together, that no one knew of or would ever know of, broke upon and illumined his memory. He longed to recall to her those moments, to make her forget the years of their dull existence together and remember only their moments of ecstasy. For the years, he felt, had not quenched his soul or hers. Their children, his writing, her household cares had not quenched all their souls' tender fire. In one letter that he had written to her then he had said: 'Why is it that words like these seem to me so dull and cold? Is it because there is no word tender enough to be your name?'

Like distant music these words that he had written years before were borne towards him from the past. He longed to be alone with her. When the others had gone away, when he and she were in the room in their hotel, then they would be alone together. He would call her softly:

'Gretta!'

Perhaps she would not hear at once: she would be undressing. Then something in his voice would strike her. She would turn and look at him ...

At the corner of Winetavern Street they met a cab. He was glad of its rattling noise as it saved him from conversation. She was looking out of the window and seemed tired. The others spoke only a few words, pointing out some building or street. The horse galloped along wearily under the murky morning sky, dragging his old rattling box after his heels, and Gabriel was again in a cab with her, galloping to catch the boat, galloping to their honeymoon.

As the cab drove across O'Connell Bridge Miss O'Callaghan said:

'They say you never cross O'Connell Bridge without seeing a white horse.'

'I see a white man this time,' said Gabriel.

'Where?' asked Mr Bartell D'Arcy.

Gabriel pointed to the statue, on which lay patches of snow. Then he nodded familiarly to it and waved his hand.

'Good night, Dan,' he said gaily.

When the cab drew up before the hotel, Gabriel jumped out and, in spite of Mr Bartell D'Arcy's protest, paid the driver. He gave the man a shilling over his fare. The man saluted and said:

'A prosperous New Year to you, sir.'

'The same to you,' said Gabriel cordially.

She leaned for a moment on his arm in getting out of the cab and while standing at the kerb-stone, bidding the others good night. She leaned lightly on his arm, as lightly as when she had danced with him a few hours before. He had felt proud and happy then, happy that she was his, proud of her grace and wifely carriage. But now, after the kindling again of so many memories, the first touch of her body, musical and strange and perfumed, sent through him a keen pang of lust. Under cover of her silence he pressed her arm closely to his side, and, as they stood at the hotel door, he felt that they had escaped from their lives and duties, escaped from home and friends and run away together with wild and radiant hearts to a new adventure.

An old man was dozing in a great hooded chair in the hall. He lit a candle in the office and went before them to the stairs. They followed him in silence, their feet falling in soft thuds on the thickly carpeted stairs. She mounted the stairs behind the porter, her head bowed in the ascent, her frail shoulders curved as with a burden, her skirt girt tightly about her. He could have flung his arms about her hips and held her still, for his arms were trembling with desire to seize her and only the stress of his nails against the palms of his hands held the wild impulse of his body in check. The porter halted on the stairs to settle his guttering candle. They halted, too, on the steps below him. In the silence Gabriel could hear the falling of molten wax into the tray and the thumping of his own heart against his ribs.

The porter led them along a corridor and opened a door. Then he set his unstable candle down on a toilet-table and asked at what hour they were to be called in the morning.

'Eight,' said Gabriel.

The porter pointed to the tap of the electric-light and began a muttered apology, but Gabriel cut him short.

'We don't want any light. We have light enough from the street.

And I say,' he added, pointing to the candle, 'you might remove that handsome article, like a good man.'

The porter took up his candle again, but slowly, for he was surprised by such a novel idea. Then he mumbled good night and went out. Gabriel shot the lock to.

A ghastly light from the street lamp lay in a long shaft from one window to the door. Gabriel threw his overcoat and hat on a couch and crossed the room towards the window. He looked down into the street in order that his emotion might calm a little. Then he turned and leaned against a chest of drawers with his back to the light. She had taken off her hat and cloak and was standing before a large swinging mirror, unhooking her waist. Gabriel paused for a few moments, watching her, and then said:

'Gretta!'

She turned away from the mirror slowly and walked along the shaft of light towards him. Her face looked so serious and weary that the words would not pass Gabriel's lips. No, it was not the moment yet.

'You looked tired,' he said.

'I am a little,' she answered.

'You don't feel ill or weak?'

'No, tired: that's all.'

She went on to the window and stood there, looking out. Gabriel waited again and then, fearing that diffidence was about to conquer him, he said abruptly:

'By the way, Gretta!'

'What is it?'

'You know that poor fellow Malins?' he said quickly.

'Yes. What about him?'

'Well, poor fellow, he's a decent sort of chap, after all,' continued Gabriel in a false voice. 'He gave me back that sovereign I lent him, and I didn't expect it, really. It's a pity he wouldn't keep away from that Browne, because he's not a bad fellow, really.'

He was trembling now with annoyance. Why did she seem so abstracted? He did not know how he could begin. Was she annoyed, too, about something? If she would only turn to him or come to him of her own accord! To take her as she was would be brutal. No, he must see some ardour in her eyes first. He longed to be master of her strange mood.

'When did you lend him the pound?' she asked, after a pause.

Gabriel strove to restrain himself from breaking out into brutal language about the sottish Malins and his pound. He longed to cry to her from his soul, to crush her body against his, to overmaster her. But he said:

'O, at Christmas, when he opened that little Christmas-card shop, in Henry Street.'

He was in such a fever of rage and desire that he did not hear her come from the window. She stood before him for an instant, looking at him strangely. Then, suddenly raising herself on tiptoe and resting her hands lightly on his shoulders, she kissed him.

'You are a very generous person, Gabriel,' she said.

Gabriel, trembling with delight at her sudden kiss and at the quaintness of her phrase, put his hands on her hair and began smoothing it back, scarcely touching it with his fingers. The washing had made it fine and brilliant. His heart was brimming over with happiness. Just when he was wishing for it she had come to him of her own accord. Perhaps her thoughts had been running with his. Perhaps she had felt the impetuous desire that was in him, and then the yielding mood had come upon her. Now that she had fallen to him so easily, he wondered why he had been so diffident.

He stood, holding her head between his hands. Then, slipping one arm swiftly about her body and drawing her towards him, he said softly:

'Gretta, dear, what are you thinking about?'

She did not answer nor yield wholly to his arm. He said again, softly:

'Tell me what it is, Gretta. I think I know what is the matter. Do I know?'

She did not answer at once. Then she said in an outburst of tears: 'O, I am thinking about that song, "The Lass of Aughrim".'

She broke loose from him and ran to the bed and, throwing her arms across the bed-rail, hid her face. Gabriel stood stock-still for a moment in astonishment and then followed her. As he passed in the way of the cheval-glass he caught sight of himself in full length, his broad, well-filled shirt-front, the face whose expression always puzzled him when he saw it in a mirror, and his glimmering gilt-rimmed eye-glasses. He halted a few paces from her and said:

'What about the song? Why does that make you cry?'

She raise her head from her arms and dried her eyes with the back of her hand like a child. A kinder note than he had intended went into his voice.

'Why, Gretta?' he asked.

'I am thinking about a person long ago who used to sing that song.'

'And who was the person long ago?' asked Gabriel, smiling.

'It was a person I used to know in Galway when I was living with my grandmother,' she said.

The smile passed away from Gabriel's face. A dull anger began to gather again at the back of his mind and the dull fires of his lust began to glow angrily in his veins.

'Someone you were in love with?' he asked ironically.

'It was a young boy I used to know,' she answered, 'named Michael Furey. He used to sing that song, "The Lass of Aughrim". He was very delicate.'

Gabriel was silent. He did not wish her to think that he was interested in this delicate boy.

'I can see him so plainly,' she said, after a moment. 'Such eyes as he had: big, dark eyes! And such an expression in them – an expression!'

'O, then, you were in love with him?' said Gabriel.

'I used to go out walking with him,' she said, 'when I was in Galway.'

A thought flew across Gabriel's mind.

'Perhaps that was why you wanted to go to Galway with that Ivors girl?' he said coldly.

She looked at him and asked in surprise:

'What for?'

Her eyes made Gabriel feel awkward. He shrugged his shoulders and said:

'How do I know? To see him, perhaps.'

She looked away from him along the shaft of light towards the window in silence.

'He is dead,' she said at length. 'He died when he was only seventeen. Isn't it a terrible thing to die so young as that?'

'What was he?' asked Gabriel, still ironically.

'He was in the gasworks,' she said.

Gabriel felt humiliated by the failure of his irony and by the evocation of this figure from the dead, a boy in the gasworks. While he had been full of memories of their secret life together, full of tenderness and joy and desire, she had been comparing him in her mind with another. A shameful consciousness of his own person assailed him. He saw himself as a ludicrous figure, acting as a penny-boy for his aunts, a nervous, well-meaning sentimentalist, orating to vulgarians and idealizing his own clownish lusts, the pitiable fatuous fellow he had caught a glimpse of in the mirror. Instinctively he turned his back more to the light lest she might see the shame that burned upon his forehead.

He tried to keep up his tone of cold interrogation, but his voice when he spoke was humble and indifferent.

'I suppose you were in love with this Michael Furey, Gretta,' he said.

'I was great with him at that time,' she said.

Her voice was veiled and sad. Gabriel, feeling now how vain it would be to try to lead her whither he had purposed caressed one of her hands and said, also sadly:

'And what did he die of so young, Gretta? Consumption was it?'

'I think he died for me,' she answered.

A vague terror seized Gabriel at this answer, as if, at that hour when he had hoped to triumph, some impalpable and vindictive being was coming against him, gathering force against him in its vague world. But he shook himself free of it with an effort of reason and continued to caress her hand. He did not question her again, for he felt that she would tell him of herself. Her hand was warm and moist: it did not respond to his touch, but he continued to caress it just as he had caressed her first letter to him that spring morning.

'It was in the winter,' she said, 'about the beginning of the winter when I was going to leave my grandmother's and come up here to the convent. And he was ill at the time in his lodgings in Galway and wouldn't be let out and his people in Oughterard were written to. He was in decline, they said, or something like that. I never knew rightly.'

She paused for a moment and sighed.

'Poor fellow,' she said. 'He was very fond of me and he was such a gentle boy. We used to go out together, walking you know, Gabriel, like the way they do in the country. He was going to study singing only for his health. He had a very good voice, poor Michael Furey.'

'Well; and then?' asked Gabriel.

'And then when it came to the time for me to leave Galway and come up to the convent he was much worse and I wouldn't be let see him, so I wrote him a letter saying I was going up to Dublin and would be back in the summer, and hoping he would be better then.'

She paused for a moment to get her voice under control, and then went on:

'Then the night before I left, I was in my grandmother's house in Nuns' Island, packing up, and I heard gravel thrown up against the window. The window was so wet I couldn't see, so I ran downstairs as I was and slipped out the back into the garden and there was the poor fellow at the end of the garden, shivering.'

'And did you not tell him to go back?' asked Gabriel.

'I implored of him to go home at once and told him he would get his death in the rain. But he said he did not want to live. I can see his eyes as well as well! He was standing at the end of the wall where there was a tree.'

'And did he go home?' asked Gabriel.

'Yes, he went home. And when I was only a week in the convent he died and was buried in Oughterard, where his people came from. O, the day I heard that, that he was dead!'

She stopped, choking with sobs, and, overcome by emotion, flung herself face downward on the bed, sobbing in the quilt. Gabriel held her hand for a moment longer, irresolutely, and then, shy of intruding on her grief, let it fall gently and walked quietly to the window.

She was fast asleep.

Gabriel, leaning on his elbow, looked for a few moments unresentfully on her tangled hair and half-open mouth, listening to her deep-drawn breath. So she had had that romance in her life: a man had died for her sake. It hardly pained him now to think how poor a part he, her husband, had played in her life. He watched her while she slept, as though he and she had never lived together as man and wife. His curious eyes rested long upon her face and on her hair: and, as he thought of what she must have been then, in that time of her girlish beauty, a strange, friendly pity for her entered his soul. He did not like to say even to himself that her face was no longer beautiful, but he knew that it was no longer the face for which Michael Furey had braved death.

Perhaps she had not told him all the story. His eyes moved to the chair over which she had thrown some of her clothes. A petticoat string dangled to the floor. One boot stood upright, its limp upper fallen down; the fellow of it lay upon its side. He wondered at his riot of emotions of an hour before. From what had it proceeded? From his aunt's supper, from his own foolish speech, from the wine and dancing, the merry-making when saying good night in the hall, the pleasure of the walk along the river in the snow. Poor Aunt Julia! She, too, would soon be a shade with the shade of Patrick Morkan and his horse. He had caught that haggard look upon her face for a moment when she was singing 'Arrayed for the Bridal'. Soon, perhaps, he would be sitting in that same drawing-room, dressed in black, his silk hat on his knees. The blinds would be drawn down and Aunt Kate would be sitting beside him, crying and blowing her nose and telling him how Julia had died. He would cast about in his mind for some words that might console her, and would find only lame and useless ones. Yes, yes: that would happen very soon.

The air of the room chilled his shoulders. He stretched himself cautiously along under the sheets and lay down beside his wife. One by one, they were all becoming shades. Better pass boldly into that other world, in the full glory of some passion, than fade and wither dismally with age. He thought of how she who lay beside him had locked in her heart for so many years that image of her lover's eyes when he had told her that he did not wish to live.

Generous tears filled Gabriel's eyes. He had never felt like that himself towards any woman, but he knew that such a feeling must be love. The tears gathered more thickly in his eyes and in the partial darkness he imagined he saw the form of a young man standing under a dripping tree. Other forms were near. His soul had approached that region where dwell the vast hosts of the dead. He was conscious of, but could not apprehend, their wayward and flickering existence. His own identity was fading out into a grey impalpable world: the solid world itself, which these dead had one time reared and lived in, was dissolving and dwindling.

A few light taps upon the pane made him turn to the window. It had begun to snow again. He watched sleepily the flakes, silver and dark, falling obliquely against the lamp-light. The time had come for him to set out on his journey westward. Yes, the newspapers were right: snow was general all over Ireland. It was falling on every part of the dark central plain, on the treeless hills, falling softly upon the Bog of Allen and, further westward, softly falling into the dark mutinous Shannon waves. It was falling, too, upon every part of the lonely churchyard on the hill where Michael Furey lay buried. It lay thickly drifted on the crooked crosses and headstones, on the spears of the little gate, on the barren thorns. His soul swooned slowly as he heard the snow falling faintly through the universe and faintly falling, like the descent of their last end, upon all the living and the dead.